Uncertain Times

Never let a small lie stand in the way of a good story

George S. Smith

PublishAmerica
Baltimore

© 2008 by George S. Smith.
All rights reserved. No part of this book may be reproduced, stored in a retrieval system or transmitted in any form or by any means without the prior written permission of the publishers, except by a reviewer who may quote brief passages in a review to be printed in a newspaper, magazine or journal.

First printing

All characters in this book are fictitious, and any resemblance to real persons, living or dead, is coincidental.

PublishAmerica has allowed this work to remain exactly as the author intended, verbatim, without editorial input.

Cover design by Ralph Strabala.

ISBN: 1-60672-020-1
PUBLISHED BY PUBLISHAMERICA, LLLP
www.publishamerica.com
Baltimore

Printed in the United States of America

I dislike authors who compare writing a book to giving birth, but at least now I understand them.

Dr. C. Jason Smith
"Alien Woman"

There was a time when I believed book dedications were dumb. That was before I started—and completed—an honest-to-God-it-has-a-beginning-and-an-ending novel.

Dedications are not dumb. If you think they are dumb, chances are you have not written a novel. Dedications are necessary. This page is dedicated to those who helped me through the grueling process. Thank you.

To Uncle France, for telling his great-nieces and great-nephews stories meshed liberally with lies and always making us wonder which was which.

To Bridget Farris, for taking time from a well-earned vacation to read a rough draft. Her notes, suggestions, and wildly sarcastic comments were needed to bring a degree of continuity and certainty to "Uncertain Times."

To my lawyer who told me to write: The events of this book are made up and any similarity to persons living or dead is strictly a coincidence. He knows that statement is a lie, but is happy I wrote it.

To my children—Jabo, Trick, Gwee and Chibi—for giving me the incentive to stick with a grueling project. I hope that something—somehow, some day—in this book will make them proud…or at least laugh out loud. When it comes to children, I am the luckiest person on the planet.

And, to Gayle, a truly supreme spousal unit. She repeatedly pointed out that I should write down all the stories I loved to tell. I would like to think she told me that because she really wanted me to write a novel. In retrospect, she was probably just trying to get me to quit telling the same stories over and over.

Regardless, thank you, Gayle. You are Widder to my Adj.

Uncertain Times

1

There's a difference between a storyteller and a liar. But for the life of me, I can't recall what it is.

Anonymous

The first twelve words out of her mouth should have been a warning. "Hey, I'm Janie Lou Lauter. You're new in town. I'm a virgin."

Jesus, I hate it when I don't know if I'm awake or asleep? It's 1:22 a.m. and I think I'm asleep.

Realistically, I've got to be awake. Otherwise I wouldn't be able to clearly see the poochey imprints of Janie Lou Lauter's nipples against her tight, purple, rayon cowboy shirt. Or smell the perfume mixed with girl-sweat behind her right ear.

Ten minutes ago I was minding my own business at the Whop the Beaver booth at the Baxter County Fair in Mountain Home, Arkansas, and had just bopped twenty-one consecutive beavers for a new personal record when Janie Lou Lauter walked up and hurled me a stupefying grin.

She bumped my thigh with her hip and said those twelve words that were instantly deposited in my memory bank.

I missed the next thirteen beavers. Beaver-whopping, taken seriously as a recreational endeavor or Olympic sport, mandates intense concentration. Janie Lou Lauter was as distracting as a naked cheerleader at a Church of Christ singing school.

Janie Lou didn't look like a virgin. She looked like someone who liked sex better than a lab rat trained to slurp up synthetic testosterone through a tiny straw.

She had the patent on the word "distracting." It was the way she stood, hip out-thrust, her blue-jeans-encased butt cheeks seemingly trying to bust out of the denim and go in two directions; big eyes, an off-shade blue with golden flakes shooting out from the irises; a double-headful of cotton candy hair; and frontal curves that would make a Rocky Mountain trail jealous. The lips, full, luscious and spit-shined with a small, slick, pointy tongue, had wanger-at-attention appeal.

The plastic carnival beavers kept sticking their little buck-toothed heads out of the nine tic-tac-toe aligned holes to the tune of "Candida" by Tony Orlando and Dawn. "Candida" is a peppy four/four beat. Due to the fact that Janie Lou kept rubbing my left arm with her right breast, I was trying to whop beavers in two/four time. Or maybe three/sixteenths.

Within the first two minutes of our one-sided conversation, Janie Lou told me she was a virgin two more times. By the time another handful of minutes had passed, we had moved behind the tent housing the Half-Man Half-Woman and Alligator Boy freak show. Some red-haired kid with a surplus of snot running from his left nostril took over my beaver-whacking post. I wished him well, hoping he would split open a beaver-head. The carneys hate that when it happens.

Before I could mutter "Whop that beaver!," Janie's red-hot No. Seven flat irons were pressing the wrinkles out of the front of my shirt as we rubbed together in a syncopated version of the Upright Baptist Mambo.

Jesus! Virgin, my ass, I thought.

Rah-wrong, Bob thought back. "*Vah-virgin, her ass.*

It's hard to argue with Bob-logic. As my alter ego, little voice, conscience—call it what you will—Bob's job was to help me steer life's boat through the rocky shoals I usually found abundant time to blunder into. Most times Bob was content to let me wreck the damn boat; on occasion he gleefully gave me subconscious wrecking instructions.

Bob's assigned tasks included keeping me entertained, focused, and thinking in a logical manner. He did entertain fairly regularly. But he seldom kept me focused, and the last time I thought in a logical manner was in grade school when I knifed a spy-hole in the wall separating the girls and boys bathrooms.

Biology was always one of my favorite subjects.

Janie Lou Lauter was one good-looking woman. She was not one of those dewy-eyed, freckled, chesty types that made the Playboy centerfold. She was the type of woman whose picture adorned calendars advertising Harley Davidson motorcycles. Black leather pants. Black-on-black knee-high buccaneer boots with cockroach-killer toes covered by little filigreed-silver caps. Red leather halter top...hanging from a handle bar. One arm draped casually over naked necessities and a couple of other things that started with the letter "n." You know, the *real* reason any man with a normal amount of Y-chromosomes wants to own a big, gnarly road bike.

I checked out Janie Lou and thought dreams can not be this real. Ergo, I'm awake!

Yah-yeah, ri-right! Bob, proving that it *is* possible to make a negative with two positives. I thought about what it was in my psychic makeup that created the only inner voice in the world that stuttered.

I shook my head, flapped my eyes open and shut about a dozen times rapidly and pinched myself to see if I was truly awake or asleep.

Ama-amateur!

Janie Lou was too real to be a dream. With a woman like her, you could forget having to pay big bucks to have a 1,250-pound vibrator between your legs. Bob *fah-figured* Janie Lou would run about 120 pounds. It didn't take much imagination to assume that she could vibrate better than the most expensive street bike.

She looked to be about thirty-five. That put her about ten years ahead of me.

Using some quick reverse math, Bob offered up: *Wha-when she was twenty, yah-you were ten.*

All I wanted to know was where the hell she had been when I was fourteen.

As I was thinking Bob to shut up so I could concentrate, Janie Lou was proclaiming, "I'm a virgin!" for the fortieth time. I wasn't listening. I was busy, prying open the cowboy snaps on her Porter Waggoner-style western shirt and looking for a way to get her out of skin-tight jeans without using a box cutter.

My libido got a mean case of comatose when a girl of about seven came around the corner of the tent and said: "Whatcha doin', Miss Janie Lou?" She was holding a pink-and-blue swirling daub of cotton candy that looked like a bad dye job on a registered septuagenarian at the Rosebud Retirement Center.

"We're not doing nothing, Little Sweet Suellen," Janie Lou said. "I'm a virgin. We're just talking."

"Uh huh," the child said, taking a big gob of cotton candy and putting half in her mouth, the other half being divided in equal parts on her nose and chin. "My momma talks to men like that three or four times a week."

Janie Lou shooed the little girl away using both hands in a forward flapping motion. The movement started a series of rippling patterns that started at her chest and ended up somewhere south of my hubcap-sized belt buckle. She started to button her shirt, stopped, and then reached in with her right hand to adjust the left breast. She plumped it upward. The ripple-jiggle of flesh when it settled back in the bra (which was the exact color of Paul Newman's eyes in "Hud") imprinted itself in my memory cache.

Then again, I had to be asleep because I knew what was going to happen next and if I was awake, I wouldn't know. Right?

Jah-jesus. You're such an eh-idiot!

I reached for Janie Lou's right breast with my off hand. She slapped the hell out of me and yelled: "RAPE!"

I sat straight up in the bed.

Tah-told you! Bob told me.

I'm begging you, Bob: Shut the hell up! I thought, using all my energy and those few brain cells that were awake in the effort.

2

Trying to figure out something that can't be figured out is like feeding a rooster Lay-More feed and expecting to get an egg.

Anonymous

It didn't take me long to shake the sleepies from my eyes and put on a pot of coffee. While it was brewing, I checked out my reflection in the bathroom mirror and was more than mildly disappointed. I told myself I don't look my age, which is fifty-eight. I didn't look a day over fifty-five.

Kah-keep on dreaming.

The face staring back at me is not of the Tom Cruise ilk, but is pleasant enough, even with a nose with a decidedly right-hand bend. A full head of dark brown hair laced with gray, greenish-gold eyes and a smile that a nice lady once called "real" made for, overall, a "reasonable package."

Yah-yeah. Refused dah-delivery. What about the lah-love handles?

Ignoring Bob's early morning asides except to think, "You have to have handles to carry the package," I thought about the dream and Janie Lou Lauter. I didn't like being confused about whether I was asleep or awake. Age. Gotta be age. Janie Lou visited my life more than thirty-five years ago and stayed only a short time. Now I visited her more than seldom through dreams. And stray thoughts pulled her up on command.

Number Seven flat irons. Jesus!

After pulling on a pair of faded jeans, a red and black flannel shirt and my modified photographer's vest with added pockets, I checked out two of my four Canon EOS2 cameras and other equipment. The batteries were good. The vest was loaded with eight new rolls of 100 ASA Fuji film and four rolls of a high-speed film in the special canister pockets on the front.

I dug out the 35 mm., 1.2 lens and the 20-35, 1.7 zoom. I figured those two, plus the 70-300, 2.5 already attached to Betsy, the oldest camera, and the 500 mm, 2.0 on Gertie, my newest acquisition, would suffice for today's work.

Slapping the pouch in back of the vest to make sure the collapsible tripod was firmly in place, I grabbed a cup of coffee in a travel mug and eased out the front door.

I was quiet, not wanting to wake Here Kitty Kitty Moose. Moosie was registered, loved to have her tummy rubbed and weighed 160 pounds. There's something about saying "Here Kitty Kitty Moose" and see a lumbering Great Dane bound out from behind the house that is good way to start any day.

Standing on the porch, sipping coffee, I went over the day's agenda in my head. First, the Poem Board, then breakfast, then a boat ride to a slough off Carter's Chute, where several groups of nesting cormorants were waiting to be immortalized on film.

I was in the middle of a photographic essay on what the guidebooks call "Mysterious Caddo Lake." The lake is a unique body of water stuck like a Nolan Ryan fast ball—high and tight—in the corner joining Texas, Louisiana and Arkansas. The lake was supposedly formed as a result of a giant earthquake in 1812.

An area near a deserted Indian village was dubbed Uncertain by settlers connected to the outside world by the flooded lake, which runs into the Red River in Louisiana. The name of the town intrigues me. When I first saw it on a map, it was enough incentive for me to quit looking for the "perfect" place to "light," as my grandfather used to say, for the four to six months I figured the photo assignment would take.

Uncertain is the only incorporated town in America with a mobile city hall. There's probably a city hall on wheels in some third world country.

Like Zambia. Or Gabon. Or south Louisiana. A single-wide, short-based trailer with CITY HALL emblazoned across the front in red paint slapped on by a shaky hand tells folks they are at the hub of commerce.

For my work as a nature photographer and as "chronicler of environmental happenstance," if I'm in an impress-somebody mood, I wanted isolation. Uncertain certainly had that. Squared. The tiny community (Pop. 192 and on weekdays that seemed generous) could be reached only by a single road that veers off from the community of Karnack several miles up the road, or by water. You could get in the water at Shreveport, La., and snake your way through the sloughs until you hit the main channel and hie yourself on up to Uncertain. Or you could put in on one of three small rivers to the north and west—Big Cypress, Little Cypress, or Black Cypress—and head downstream to Caddo.

There was a time, just after the Civil War, when Uncertain was a hustling, bustling place; it served as a wood stop for steamboats plying their way up the monster lake swollen by a miles-long logjam on the Red River south of Shreveport. The steamboats eventually ended up at Jefferson, about fifteen miles north of Uncertain. At that time, Jefferson was the undisputed cotton hub of post-war Texas. Now the only thing the townspeople pick are the pocketbooks of tourists who flock there for an overabundance of antique stores and a superficial coating of nostalgia.

Some say the steamboats were directly related to the strange name of the town.

Bob was in a thinkative mood:

Wha-what time's the sta-steamboat gonna be here?

Dah-don't know. That's un-un-uncertain.

That story seems as good as any and probably more likely than others that assaulted the ears of tourists and fishermen who came to this isolated place to test their luck with the look-sees or the fish.

I hit the road at a steady clip. The smell of honeysuckle assailed my nostrils, reminding me of a simpler time, when....

Hah-here we gah-go again.

Not going anywhere, Bob. Just thinking *in* loud.

Cah-cute.

The one-lane dirt road was closed in from overgrown natural beds of sour dock, burdock and cattails that proliferated in the ditches that never seemed to be completely dry. The roadway was lined with live oaks, pin oaks, and water oaks, the branches making a natural leaf tunnel.

Filtered sunlight created dabbled patterns on the dirt. The irregular light-and-dark patterns created images, not unlike those in cloud formations.

Today there was a shiny bear with no hind legs, a one-winged eagle, sailboat with only half a hull, and a bunch of little dot-splotches that reminded me for some reason or other of a family reunion of spiked-hair trolls. I was eyeing a particularly intricate pattern that looked like flapping laundry on a line when I noticed the Widder Gleason had not taken in the Monday wash. And here it was Tuesday. In Uncertain, that equates to a local scandal.

Even after only three weeks as her neighbor in the rented hunting lodge I knew what she would say if I queried her about it: "Didn't mean to take them in yesterday. Now they'll just smell two-day's sunshine fresh!"

Hard to argue with sun-logic from a washday widow woman.

I caught myself hoping she would come out of the house and give me an excuse to wave and throw her a howdy. I threw a single, exaggerated wave at the house anyway just in case she was looking through the window.

Duh-dope.

I met the Widder Gleason on my first trip to Uncertain to scout the area and look for a place to live. Her house was only about fifty yards south of the little hunting lodge I had rented. Without a doubt, her house was the neatest residence in Uncertain. Maybe even in all of Texas. Freshly painted a soft beige, the house had off-yellow shutters and a Columbia blue, solid wood door. A short porch went around the front and sides of the house. A white picket fence ran around the entire structure and there were gates, front and back. A separate two-car garage was off to the side. I had never seen either door open.

The woman obviously had a green thumb. Or maybe an entire green hand. Specially shaped beds had more flowers in more colors than Tammy Mae Bakker's eyelids. Not knowing flora as well as I did fauna,

what I saw were flowers in an artist's palate of purples, yell
dark blues, plus off-whites and lavender.

Each bed was edged in some sort of long-stemmed grass; little yellow-topped bushes were strategically placed for emphasis. Red-tip photinias were lined up along the back fence like a line of vegetative soldiers eager for inspection.

Each corner of the fenced area contained tall pink dogwoods, with smaller white dogwoods planted alongside; it was impossible to discern which branches went to which tree. The result was an eye-splash of white-and-pink blossoms that turned heads.

The house had a short porch on its front and both sides; two rockers and a glider swing were complemented with large red clay pots filled with small four-petaled flowers of virtually every color imaginable.

Widder was a relatively short, muscular woman, with broad shoulders. A high forehead set off her prominent cheekbones, sun-streaked hair pulled back into a high-neck bun, and snapping blue eyes. In any other time and any other place, she would have been referred to as a looker. One could tell she spent a lot of time trying not to be a looker. Or even looked at.

When we first met, her hands were red, a shade or two lighter than canned beets; the fingernails snaggledy and not particularly clean; a dark soot-like mark trailed down one side of her left cheek. Her eyes were bright, but with a wary look accentuated by three lines that looked permanently stamped into her forehead; they served as companions to unplucked eyebrows a shade darker than her hair. She had bright eyes that reflected an inner light.

That first day she was wearing a faded, shapeless housedress, with some indistinguishable print pattern and a pair of green house shoes with frog heads on the toes. One frog had a bright red tongue; the other had a small, torn piece of red felt where a tongue once protruded.

"I'm the Widder Gleason," she said when I walked up her gravel sidewalk to introduce myself. "Been a widder for twenty years. Plan on staying that way." Any intentions I might have had were blasted into mental molecules. I nodded and for once Bob was silent.

I thought: How young she looked and how old she dressed and tried to appear. I hinted around about her age—how long she had been here? (twenty-two years), did she have any children? (two), how old were they? (both gone). Despite gentle prodding, she gave out nothing but bare-minimum details. I told her I had four children, all grown-up, but she didn't ask any follow-up questions.

"It seems we raise children just to watch them leave," I said.

Her expression told me the statement scored high on some abstract Dumb Statement Scale.

We ended up talking about the weather—nice now, going to rain before the end of the week when the first fingerlings of summer heat start putting a damper on the cooling effect of the lake—the hunting lodge I was looking at for a temporary home, and a little harmless gossip about the neighbors. She made it plain she didn't mind neighbors if they were quiet and respectful of her property and privacy.

I had dropped by a couple of times since I had moved in. Widder seemed to be always starting out to do something that I gathered she considered important. No more than twenty sentences had ever passed between us.

I took my usual morning shortcut by crawling through the three-strand barbed wire fence across the road from her house and cut across a pasture owned by a "rich oil man from West Texas." No one knew any more that. I had started thinking of the land as Rich's Pasture. Rich hired a local boy, Henery Hills, to watch over the cattle. Henery threw out hay now and then and stayed in an old, mobile home most of the time. Literally. Few people ever saw Henery out in the pasture doing much of anything. Rumor was that Henery fed the cows in the dark. Henery wasn't his real name, of course, just like Widder wasn't Widder's name. His name was Henry, but somewhere in his raising years, someone had added an extra syllable and it just stuck.

About ten cows in the front of the spacious pasture were having a cow meeting—where they all gather up with their heads pointing in sort of the same direction. I tried to pick out the Guernsey with the peculiar white marking that looked like the Golden Arches. Either that or a serendipity "M" painted by a hippie who had done a little partaking of a particular form of vegetable matter. But she and a majority of the herd were out of sight, probably at the forty-acre pond just past the stand of cypress trees to the west.

Cutting the corner sliced off about five minutes on my walk and my path eventually came out just across from Uncertain Bait Shop and Throw Pillow Emporium. John Bob Gibbons and his wife Pearlene were living the American dream. They were doing what they know best and keeping the proverbial economic wolf at bay by what entrepreneurs who have attended financial seminars call *revenue-stream diversification*. From talking to the pair, I came to realize that few people on this planet knew more about minnows, nightcrawlers and crickets than Pearlene and that John Bob could pop as pretty a chain stitch as could be done.

His pillows were first-rate and I was the proud owner of two. One was of a medium size, with one side a slick material that contained swirls of maroon and mauve; the other was a coarser, heavier material on which John Bob had sewn an intricate design.

A blue stream started off at the far left edge of the pillow and serpentined across the front. In the stream there was a jumping largemouth bass and a slightly out-of-proportion blue crane. By the stream bank was an eight-point buck, two does and a speckled fawn, two armadillos and a raccoon. It had cost $12, or about $1.25 a critter, not counting tax.

But my favorite pillow was of a sweeter variety. One side of the pillow was a dark blue and the reverse side was a lighter blue. On the dark blue side, there was a close-up of a boy's face and girl's face. They were kissing, sort of chaste-like, lips all pooched out and leaning in to one another. There was a big yellow moon just over the girl's shoulder. Below the couple were the words:

Man was, is and always will be
looking for a cheap date good enough
to take home to Mama.

I chuckled at the thought of that pillow as I threw a wave at the couple's oldest boy Tilmon who was more than elbow-deep in the minnow-holding tank. He threw a wave back, throwing about a quart of water into the dusty driveway in front of the lakeside store. Tilmon had the largest hands I had ever seen on a human being. They were about the size of Baby Moon hubcaps.

He hello-ed me and said, "There's a new 'un today." I hello-ed back and said, "I figured as much." My walk took me by Butcher's Café, Harlan's Gro. and Sta., Logan Brothers Feed and Seed, and Caddo Lake Guide Service (Tours and Fishing Guides). Vacant buildings in various states of disrepair checkerboarded the small downtown.

At the last vacant building (a faded sign proclaimed it used to be "Gilbert's Small Engine Repair") I cut kitty-corner across from the public boat dock and angled toward the Poem Board.

The Poem Board was a old, scarred blackboard, about four-by-eight feet, that was wired to a magnolia that had a diameter of more than five feet. The tree was not huge. It was bigger than that.

And, as usual, there was a brand new chalked message written in an irregular scrawl.

The littlest dancers
Line up for inspection
In a syncopated fashion.
They approach the barre,
And grip it and rip it
And swing from it
And lean on it
And try to follow instructions.

Who is writing these?

Sah-some nut.

They are oh, so loose,
Despite tight tights
Of varying hues and shades.
Some use tutus as head rags
Or pretend pink hair
Or as an ornamental collar.

UNCERTAIN TIMES

Their en pointe is not perfected;
Their en sit assuredly is.
First attempts at plies
Remind onlookers of a gaggle
Of giant pink frogs preparing to hop.
They don't so much pirouette
As they do admire themselves in the large mirror.

Giant pink frogs preparing to hop?

Gah-good picture, that.

But through it all,
They enjoy and laugh
And squeal and giggle and learn
The initial joy of artistic movement.
For they are the littlest dancers.

I read it once again, studying the rhythm, word flow, and literary images. Good, I thought.
Dah-damn good, Bob offered up.
Better than yesterday.
Dah-different. Bah-but for once you may bah-be right.
As I had every day for the twenty days I had been in Uncertain and first discovered the Poem Board, I and took several picture of the words on the board. I then carefully wrote down the words in a Reporter's Notebook.

Then I read the words again and shook my head. The questions flew like mosquitoes at dusk. Who in Uncertain knows what 'en pointe,' 'pirouette,' and 'barre' even mean? Who around here uses words like 'syncopated'?

Good poem. I agreed with Bob. Yesterday's was decidedly different.

Flipping back a couple of pages in the notebook I read the words left the previous day on the board:

You know the way you felt
Just before you let a belch?
One that roared and one so loud,
One where Mommy said out loud,
"Don't you have any manners, Son?
"Do you think that belching's fun?

The rhythm? Is that what I don't like about this one?

Cah-could be the sah-subject matter.

"I don't want you to run and hide,
"But from now on, please belch outside."
That's just the way that I felt
But I don't think it was a belch.
I think it must be a cough or sneeze,
But it made me check my bony knees
To see if they were still all right
And that my knee skin was really tight.
Because tight knee skin is necessary
To walk and run and be contrary.

Tight knee skin. Who thinks this way?

And tight knee skin should always be felt
About as often as you can belch
Because belching and skin are truly related
And not a subject to be debated.
If you don't belch, and expunge that air
You might blow up and land waaaay over there.
And if you don't have tight knee skin
You might not get to walk back again.
So belch now, Girl, and check those knees,
Expel that air, Boy, and you will feel free

UNCERTAIN TIMES

To walk and run and belch with pride
For belchers and walkers have nothing to hide.

Somebody's been reading Shel Silversteen.
Oh-or Doctor Sah-seuss.

I flipped back another page.

Wildflowers beckon
Rural road travelers
Like carnival barkers
Beckon teenagers in love.
"Step right up and win
the little lady a teddy bear!"
Or
"Stop a while and walk barefoot
Among earthbound bouquets
Before lying down to dream."

Is the same person is writing these? I thought for about the tenth time.
Mah-most definitely, Bob thought.
Different styles for sure.
Mah-maybe they don't nah-know what they are do-doing.
They know.
Sah-same handwriting.

The writing seemed unhurried, even if a tad sloppy. Some words, or even partial words, were printed, others scratched out in a largish longhand. Looked like a man's handwriting. No big loopedy-loops, no cutesy descenders. Straight lines, squared-off loops, straight to the point.

I read the words on the blackboard one last time before heading out across the boat ramp. Few people were on the road this early so I had it to myself. Those who worked in Marshall, Texas, or over at Shreveport were, as my grandfather said, "tail-light gone." Vacationing fishermen had been on the water for at least an hour or more.

A visit to Butcher's Café was a daily ritual. I was a regular since my cooking skills were still at the mix-and-match level and the café coffee was perfect. Strong enough to do push-ups.

The café opened early and closed late, 5 a.m. to about 9 p.m., which is way past the time most folks are closeted inside their houses. The owner, one of the locals told me, was named Herman. He went by the name Hum.

I banged through the screen door and shouted, "Morning, Hum."

"Hmmm," the little, gnarled man with a brand-new gimme hat perched on top of his head replied as he scrapped burned grease probably from this decade off the grill. Hum was probably seventy. Or fifty.

Hum looked like Yoda without the wrinkles and his ears were smaller and not so pointy. His nose was the size of a half-dollar and almost as flat; his George Bush eyes had a wet-twinkle look. His generous mouth always seemed to be in a happy smirk set at the top of a sledgehammer chin. His neck had more waddles than a herd of walking ducks.

"Coffee, bacon, two eggs over medium, wheat toast," I said, sitting down on a tattered counter seat. "Hmmm." He already had the bacon crackling on the clean side of the griddle. Two brown eggs were at hand.

Prah-probably saw you out the wah-window.

"Assuredly," I said out loud.

"Hmmm?" Hum said, turning to look at me. The lettering on the cap front caught my eye: "Bosco's Feed and Seed: Prices Lower Than a Lizard's Lip."

I just nodded. "Nice weather."

"Hmmm!"

A two-day-old regional newspaper left on the counter caught my eye. More killings in the Middle East. Big trial for some big company's CEO. Politicians from one party attacking the president. All the president's men counter-attacking.

Bob started humming "It's a Small World."

Putting the paper aside, I said, "Same old news every day it seems like."

"Hmmm."

Hum drew a cup of coffee in a heavy, white ceramic cup, put it down and then slapped the food on a pale green Melmac plate and slid it along the counter. The bacon was limp, but fully cooked, the way I liked it; the egg whites were perfectly done, the yellows were good and runny; the wheat toast was crisp and evenly buttered.

"Hum, you are a master of the culinary arts."

He threw me a raised-brow look. "Hmmm?"

"Great cook!"

He nodded. "Hmmm."

Bob asked nicely if I would *quit talking to Hah-humm* because he was getting a *hah-humdinger* of a headache. Taking a corner of toast, I broke the egg middles, swirling it around a bit and then slipped the whole thing in my mouth.

Hum raised one eyebrow.

"Absolutely delicious, Hum."

The eyebrow slowly lowered and Hum turned back to scrapping the dirty side of the grill.

Somewhere between the second piece of bacon and the second cup of coffee, the growl of a big, unmuffflered engine hit the café like a strong wind.

Bob's thought squirreled its way inside my head: *Jah-joe B.B."*

"No doubt."

"Hmmm?"

"Joe B. B., Hum. You can hear that truck of his for coming from a long ways off."

"Hmmmhmmm"

In the space of three heartbeats, there was a lot of noise. Truck tires sliding on the café's graveled lot, door opening and closing, boots clomping on the wooden porch, screen door banging open and Joe B.B. shouting: "Howdeee! I'm just so proud to be here." He was a Minnie Pearl fan from way back.

"Come on in and sit a spell, Billy Bird," I said, directing him to the adjoining counter seat. I could do a decent high-East Texas Ernest Tubb twang.

Joe B. B. gave me a look that would dry paint. "Huh?" His face mimicked the question. He had a long face, one that would make Secretariat proud. High, arching eyebrows stuck two inches above sleepy, cat eyes made it appear he was always questioning...something. A too-small mouth, hook nose, a chin so weak it was Popeye before he started injecting liquid spinach topped an Adam's apple the size of an ignored goiter. Jug ears like handles on a cheap trophy finished the picture.

"Cain't sat long," he allowed. "Heading into Karnack to see if they's hiring at Longhorn 'munition Plant. I need some work so's I can fix up my truck."

Without any prodding, Joe B.B., whose full name was Joseph Beebe Beebe (his mama was a Beebe who married a Beebe; he said "no relation" but those ears made a body wonder), said his truck needed two more woofers and bigger tweeters or two more tweeters and bigger woofers. That's what Bob thought later. I wasn't listening.

Joe B.B. could be confusing. Pausing to sip his coffee standing up, he also said he also needed some new straight-pipe cut-outs so he could quit getting "loud-noise tickets" every time he went to town.

"I didn't know there was such a thing as loud-noise tickets, Joe B.B."

"Oh, they got 'em, all righteroo." I got a whole glove box full of them thangs."

Hum stopped wiping long enough to comment. "Hmmm."

Joe B.B. ordered up a couple sausage biscuits for the drive. While Hum was cutting off a couple of sausage wheels, Joe B.B. said, "They got jobs at the depot where you go to work and you get to go on the backside of the depot grounds and you get to blow up little bums and stuff like 'at."

"Hmmm." Me, not Hum.

I hope he meant "bombs, not "bums."

Mah-me too.

"And you can blow up as much stuff in a shift as you can, without paying for the dynamite or B-12 or plastic stuff...."

"C-4 plastique?"

"Whatever. You can take 'at stuff and blow the living owl shit out of little bums and big bums and they pay you money to do it! Wouldn't that be the swellest thing?"

I allowed as how it would probably be sweller than that, then noted with a cluck-cluck and a tsk-tsk that it was getting late and I had work to do. Hum sat down a paper sack on the counter that I knew contained a couple of ham sandwiches, a bottled red soda, two small bottles of water and a bag of chips. Thanking him for my picnic lunch, another short-time ritual of our relationship, I put down a five and four ones, which included a monster tip by Uncertain standards, and headed to the door.

Joe B.B. grabbed me by the arm.

"What 'zactly is it that you do agin?"

"I'm a photographer. I take pictures and hope they are published in books."

"Is there good money in 'at?"

Dah-don't answer that. Wah-we'll be here ah-all damn day.

"We won't if you'll quit stuttering."

"Hmmm?" That was Joe B.B. And Hum. In harmony. Hum took the bass lead.

"Nothing. Sorry. I was talking to myself."

Dah-damn skippy.

"What were you saying, Joe B.B.? Oh, yeah, money. I make some. But I don't do it for the money. I do it because I love taking pictures

and I love spending time in nature without leaving anything behind but footprints."

"Say huh?"

"I get money for doing it and it's fun."

"Oh."

"Hmmm."

Cah-can we please jah-just go?

"Gotta run, guys. See you tomorrow, Hum. Take care, Joe B.B."

"Hmmm."

"I hope I get 'at job blowin' thangs up!"

I gave him a thumb's up and hit the door.

I threw a thought in Bob's direction: I know what you're thinking and

I'm thinking the same thing: Joe B.B. and explosives scare the pee-dowaddles out of me.

Cu-couldn't have put it better mah-myself.

3

Sometimes solitude can get mighty lonely.

Anonymous

It took less than two minutes to get to the boat dock, unhook the rented fishing boat—named *Water Nympho*, and, no, I didn't ask—check the gas and oil, crank the electric starter and ease away from the dock. It took about fifteen times longer to get to the blind in Carter's Chute.

When I first decided to scout the lake I checked around for a guide and several people mentioned Buddy Parley, a member of the local quorum court. The word was that before he became a respectable politician he was a more respectable moonshiner and knew every single log, critter, and cypress knee in the lake.

For a tank of gas and a promise to vote for him if I stayed long enough to register, Buddy spent a good part of two days showing me a goodly portion of the lake. Caddo is not your normal, hit-it-on-the-weekend lake. There are heavily forested bayous, sloughs, and cuts throughout, all of which in some form or other flow ultimately into the more open part of the lake. Cleared channels slice through cypress thickets make watery mazes that can easily confuse any boatman; even long-timers got lost occasionally. Just by looking at it you can tell the lake is an old one. Some of the main trails were cut with slave labor; others were paid by hefty slices of government pork.

Maps of the lake depict it as looking like an exploded appendix. An inverted "C." As seen by a career meth user.

Colloquial names are intriguing and Caddo has its share of interesting and picturesque names for certain areas. I had visited areas known as Red Belly, Carter Lake, Eagle's Nest, Goose Prairie, Old Folks Playground. Kitchen's Creek, Alligator Bayou, Devil's Elbow, Hamburger Point, Pig Pen, and Hell's Half Acre.

Just looking at the lake, one gets the first impression it's just one gigantic cypress forest. There are millions of the hard-center trees in the lake, but other varieties proliferate: Water elm, water oak, overcup oak, cherry bark oak, willow oak, button willow and a goodly slash of swamp privet in the northeast section of the lake. Sweet gum trees are evident on many of the islands and along the main shoreline.

The lake is flush with history, and some of it would be included as background in the book. Potter's Point was named after the first Texas Secretary of the Navy, Robert Potter. When he was in charge of the navy he had five vessels under his command. Potter was the first signer of the Texas Declaration of Independence and killed in a little known conflict called the Regulator-Moderator War. It was like Democrats and Republicans, only with guns. An assassin's bullet struck him down and he was buried next to his wife on a bluff overlooking the north shore of the lake. In 1930 some do-gooder bureaucrats had Parker's remains removed to a cemetery in Austin, the Texas capital. The body of Potter's wife was left on the bluff. Alone.

The first time I read that, the thought spun mini-cobwebs of sadness. Same feeling every time.

In any given week, you can find treasure hunters diving and hand-dredging in the largest open body of water in the lake. In 1869 the boilers of the steamboat *Mittie Stephens* exploded and the boat sank; only forty members of the passenger and crew of the 101 aboard survived. Rumors quickly spread the steamer was full of Yankee gold. More than 140 years later, people still try to pinpoint the location of the stern-wheeler.

The lake is also a recognized hot spot for largemouth bass, white and spotted bass, and crappie. Catfish were also plentiful in certain areas. Fishermen from all over the south make Caddo a regular stop on their trek to fish new waters and set fresh water fishing records.

There's an intricate map most visitors use to navigate the lake. In addition, Buddy showed me the post-and-reflector system that old-timers used to get from place to place. Getting to Carter's Chute from downtown Uncertain was fairly simple: Go due north toward the tallest cypress tree and stay to the left channel where the lake splits at a spit of land shaped like a boot. Stay close to the right bank and take the second cut to the right which weaves back and forth through flooded cypress trees until it empties into the large body of open water called Carter's Chute.

The blind where I was stalking nesting cormorants was about six hundred yards down the left bank just as you enter the chute. During duck season, Buddy and some friends used the blind as a home away from home.

The blind was fairly large, as photo-blinds go, about sixteen-by-eight feet. It was firmly anchored by four, reinforced pilings. Climbing eight sturdy boards nailed into the slightly sloping tree trunk to the left of the blind, and carefully stepping into the entrance accessed it. The plywood floor only swayed a bit directly in the middle and four two-by-fours joined the floor with a tin roof covered in dead limbs. The interior was equipped with a short, lawn chair ($6.28 at Wal-Mart, including tax).

The blind's four open sides were covered with a see-through mesh camouflage material that reminded Bob of the fish-net hose on a stripper who performed under the name The Galloping Tweezer. We caught her act while photographing saltwater crocodiles in Costa Rica.

Wah-we may have caught it twa-twice.

In all my years of hiding out in various and sundry blinds and trying to sneak up on wildlife subjects that one couldn't sneak up on if they didn't want you to, I've never seen a perfect hide. This one was close.

There were three cormorant nests within fifty feet, one each to the east, north, and west. The south side was a wall of solid cypress trees, but even that view had distinct possibilities. I had spotted several alligators of various sizes moving among the cypress knees, as well as a mama nutria followed by two little water trails that I took to be two babies. A piliated woodpecker—known as "Good God" birds in these parts for their sheer size—had been working on a hole for the past several days in a tree on Goat Island, located about seventy-five feet away in the deep shadows of the trees. I was still waiting on the perfect combination of a late afternoon sun stream and the right angle to highlight that photo.

The goal of the current stalk was getting memorable photos of cormorant birds...young, old, perfect lighting. You get the picture. So far I hadn't.

I had been in this particular blind on and off for eight days and had shot exactly six frames. I don't mind wasting film because film and time are the two most abundant and cheap accessories to my curious profession. It's just that, over time, if there's nothing worth shooting, one mostly sits and watches the changing of the sun-shadows and the constant movement of critters, swimming, climbing or flying.

Normally, people afflicted with ADHD seldom end up in a sedentary profession that demands an inordinate amount of patience and quiet demeanor. ADHDers usually end up being motivational speakers, drill sergeants, door-to-door salesmen, abusive Nannies, trial lawyers or carnival barkers. More than a few have wound up as Bible-thumping televangelists. I just happened to also have an extra helping of willpower and was able, over time and with Bob's help, to ratchet down my natural bubbling exuberance when necessary.

It was just a little after 6:30. I concentrated my look-see on the west nest, hoping for a nice, golden-tone shot of a mama cormorant stretching in the nest. Or, maybe, a picture of mama stretching, with daddy swooping in to check out the eggs with a small fish in his long, pointy beak.

Yah-yeah, right.

One can hope, Bob, one can only hope.

I quickly set Betsy on the tripod and focused her in, making sure the motor drive was set on *fah-fast as hah-hell*, as Bob called the four-shots-a-second setting. Checking the view through the finder, all I could see was Maude's head and neck. Maude and Harold were the names given to this bird couple. Naming targets made everything mentally cozy.

UNCERTAIN TIMES

Like most women, Maude had a morning ritual and it started with a long neck stretch—due within the next five or ten minutes—followed by a full extension of her body out of the nest, with full wing extension. I already had a keeper photo of this morning exercise routine, one shot five days earlier with Maude's neck in an S pattern, her wings fully extended with sunlight dripping off each feather.

That one would make the book. No doubt.

Harold hadn't been around for a couple of days but I didn't know enough about cormorant behavior to put any significance to that fact. I figured he was hunting and was coming in early or late. To most watchers, birds of any feather of a particular species look pretty much the same. Like a gaggle of workers in a clean-environment laboratory, all dressed the same, pristine uniforms.

Checking out fauna through either Betsy or Gertie gave me an up-close-and-personal view most folks never enjoyed. Maude had an odd light spot shaped like the state of Nevada with the bottom tip clipped off on the left side of her body, just above the wing juncture. Harold had two tail feathers whose ends looked like they had been dipped in White-Out.

In the other nests were Octavia (light spot over her right eye) and Josephus (always landed with right leg extended and also tended to lean to the right when resting), and Taffy (one odd, blondeish tail feather) and Melvin (extra-long neck and a remarkably darker-than-normal chest.)

Time passed as time does at times like this, like a drugged terrapin. Having rigged up a cable release, it was not necessary for me to keep an eye glued to the viewfinder; viewing all three nests was as simple as swiveling my neck.

On cue, Maude made her early-morning stretch. Nothing spectacular.

A botfly made a dive at my face, but a few swipes with my hand made the fly remember it had another appointment elsewhere.

The weather was perfect for this time of year, about 65 but warming up. No movement in the three nests. Eyes wandering tree to tree along the shoreline, I spied a lonely beaver trailing his watery slipstream near the far shore.

Gotta check that out soon.

Cah-can I cah-come along?

Jesus, Bob.

Settling into the low-slung plastic chair, I let my mind roam, not unlike the mental unexercises I did in high school classes. One teacher called it daydreaming. Another called it escapism. The former conjured up an image of a lazy bum; the latter sounded more, well, acceptable somehow.

In the flick of a gnat's wing I was back on the front porch of the Bartlett homestead, sitting in the white slat swing next to my cousin Jackie. We weren't talking; we were swinging. We were thinking about playing five-hole washers but neither of us had taken the time or used the energy to get out of the swing and go get the washers next to the big magnolia tree, or clean out the five holes set about eight feet from the edge of the porch.

Penny, the world's only spit-eating cocker Spaniel, was asleep in the shade thrown over the half the yard by the largest magnolia.

"Maybe we ought to wake her up and watch her catch spit," Jackie said.

"Or not," I said.

"Or not," he echoed.

"Sides, Uncle Earnest does much better spitting than either of us."

"You're not woofing, pun intended," Jackie said.

"Jesus, that was lame."

"Speaking of lame, where is Unc?"

Uncle Earnest was our great-uncle, Daddy George Bartlett's older brother and a grandkid favorite. About 6-0, he was whip-thin, hatchet-faced, with white hair and hollow cheeks. In the world of Nevada County, Arkansas, he was a dandy. Always wore a clean, pressed blue, chambray shirt buttoned up tight, with blue neat-as-a-pin overalls. Shiny brown brogans over thin, white socks completed the wardrobe.

Uncle drew some sort of government allotment, but didn't have a regular job like Daddy George, who drove a road grader for the county road department. Living as he did with Daddy George and Nannie, Uncle turned over most of his monthly check and did odd jobs around the house for the rest of his keep. He milked, collected eggs, fed the cows and chickens, slopped the hogs, helped put in the truck garden next to the house, and pulled vegetables when requested to do so.

But, whatever he did, he didn't get dirty. I figured it was against his religion, which was somewhere between "a little bit" and "none a-tall."

His main job was corralling and entertaining grandkids, keeping them out from under the feet of the members of the older generation. And teaching Penny to catch spit.

"Hmmmm, Penny," Unc would say and the dog would go into a dog version of an Irish jig, feet flapping all over the place to the beat of some internal rhythm. Unc would then launch a big glob of Garrett's in a high arch and Penny would jump straight up and catch it in mid-air.

Adults thought is was gross. Grandkids thought it was cool.

Uncle Earnest was a favorite of all his nieces and nephews; he set up games and told stories. An expert at mumbledy-peg, Unc could finger-flip a knife to hit a small target with uncanny consistency. No one could beat him at five-hole washers; he could settle a washer in the five-hole with the skill of a short-order cook flipping flapjacks.

And, Unc had a story for every occasion and could alter the story to fit the audience. He was also a teacher. He taught every young male relative to cuss.

He was, by everyone's opinion, a bit strange. He often went "visiting," as a circuit preacher once described it, while his body remained seated on the porch swing. He would be sitting there but his mind was obviously somewhere else. He was also, according to that same preacher, the "only man I ever saw who could walk through a dusty cow lot and not get a speck of dust on his shoes." He didn't walk; he sort of glided with lengthy steps, like he was floating over cotton rows filled with two-foot-tall plants.

Jackie and I were still trying to figure out what to do when Unc quit the house and without so much as a by-your-leave, headed out to the front woods.

It took less than thirty seconds for him to completely disappear in the hardwood and pine thicket.

Jackie and I exchanged looks. We bolted out of the swing and took off at a dead run for the spot where Uncle Earnest had gone into the woods. Edging behind a mock orange bush, we slipped through a nest of tangle vines and crotch-slapping saplings.

There was the impression of a path and we tried to stick to that here-and-gone evidence of Unc's passing. Every ten-or-so steps, we would stop as if by silent command and listen.

Further and further into the heavy woods we pushed, stalking, stopping, listening, starting up again. Then, just off to our right, I caught a glimpse of a movement. Grabbing Jackie's sleeve, I pointed in that direction and we slipped quietly forward.

We found ourselves directly behind a large-leafed serendipity bush and by moving a few branches, we could see Uncle Earnest. He was standing in the middle of a small, twenty-by-twenty clearing. Just standing. Staring at the ground in front of him. A minute. Two.

Finally, he gave a little shudder and walked to the north edge of the circular clearing and stopped, turned to the east and started slowing pacing along the perimeter. He walked almost half-way around, which put him at about a forty-five degree angle to where we were hidden. He abruptly stopped and started unstrapping his overalls. He unfastened both catches and let the overall top drop, where it collected around his ankles.

Hitching up his shirttail with his elbows, he reached around and unbuttoned the rear seat in his off-white longjohns, turned his butt to the southeast and hunkered down like a large, wrinkled toad.

Watching him was a disgusting sight. It was also in the voyeuristic category of watching a fat woman naked; you couldn't avert your eyes if you wanted to.

After a time, Unc reached into his bib pocket and withdrew a couple pages from the local paper, the *Hope Star*. He used them in succession, folding each twice for a double wipe-through. As he completed the chore with each folded page, he flipped it with a practiced flair over his right shoulder.

After the third page, Unc reached into his right front pants pocket and withdrew a white corncob. He wiped his ass—ever so gently—looked at the corncob and heaved it into the woods. Unc got up, affixed his clothes and headed due south out of the woods.

Jackie and I sat there for several minutes, not looking at each other, not making a noise. Finally, I snuck a look in his direction and saw him staring back. We both cracked up. We laughed, we cried, we hurrahed. We thrashed around in the leaves until our sides ached and the laughter had dissipated into mere gaggles of giggles.

Finally, we sighed in unison, got up and walked into the clearing and…just stared at the offering Uncle Earnest had rendered into Mother Nature.

It was not just any old pile of crap. It was a pile worthy of bronzing and using as a paperweight. The finished product even had a curley-cue on top like those hand-did ice cream cones at a big city Daisy Queen.

"That's the damndest thing I've ever seen," Jackie said.

"No argument from here. That's a beautiful pile of shit."

It was Jackie who pointed out the other piles situated at regular intervals around the clearing. Without even realizing it, I started counting and ended up with the number twelve.

The piles were like numbers on a clock. Today's deposit was at the number five position, and as you worked backward counterclockwise, the piles of organic matter were obvious deteriorating at a regular clip.

Jackie stood there a minute. Then he walked out of the clearing, picked up a long, straight stick, swung back into the circle, and stuck the stick hard into the ground.

The stick's shadow angled between the ninth and tenth piles.

Jackie stood there, hands on hips and an I-invented-the-wheel grin.

"It's nine-turdy!"

Uncle Earnest and Jackie had created a shit sundial.

4

Light at the end of the tunnel, my ass!
Don't go in the damn tunnel in the first place.

                                                                       Anonymous

The botfly was back. Along with his speeding motorcycle sound.
Gah—glad you're back. I wah-was getting lo-lonely.
Don't tell me you didn't go along for the ride, Bob. I know better. Now hush and let me get back to whatever it is I'm supposed to be doing.

From the angle of the sun I figured I escaped for about thirty minutes. I checked out Maude and Harold's nest through the camera and still saw nothing but the top of Maude's head.

It's going to be a get-nothing day.
I-I-I'm bored. Cah-can we go check on the bah-beaver?
Bob! Jesus!

There was little or no movement on this particular stretch of Carter's Chute. The water, although it was constantly moving at the rate of about a foot or so an hour, was as smooth as a baby's butt.

Cah-can't you come up wah-with a better cla-cliché?

Biting back a smart-ass remark, I conceded Bob had a point.

Smooth as a mirror. Smooth as a sand trap at the Master's. Smooth as the underside of a Great Dane's ear. Smooth as the topside of a centerfold's breast. Smooth as a new stretch of the Autobahn. Smooth as a professional gigolo's pick-up line. Smooth as....

Jab-Jesus, Adj!

I laughed out loud, which caused Maude to stretch her neck high to check out the noise.

Grabbing the paper sack from Hum's, I unwrapped a ham sandwich and took out the bag of chips and the red coke. Lettuce, pickles, a slab of ham the thickness of a ream of notebook paper, wheat bread. The first bite told me something I already knew but still made me smile: Food, just about any food, including the most simple, tastes better outdoors.

Twelve bites later the sandwich was gone. Crumbs were all that remained in the chip bag and the red coke had been replaced by a bottle of water, which was almost gone.

Tab-time to go in for sab-supplies

You may be right, Bob. This is a wasted trip. I can feel it.

With the sun getting higher overhead and little movement anywhere on Carter's Chute, I descended from the hide, got in the boat and struck out for home. I made a detour before getting to the main channel to a section of cypress trees locals called The Cathedral. I had been there four times now and I knew it needed to be in the book. I had not seen a good angle, lighting or positive framing set-up that could do it justice.

The trees in this particular area were huge, some five to six feet in diameter. Additionally, the cypress knees, the roots that climb out of the murky water and take weird shapes, were prolific and seemed to be taller than anywhere else on Caddo. The multiple knobby conjured up visions of kneeling parishioners in a sanctuary.

In the center of The Cathedral, if one had the balance of a cat or the agility of a spider monkey, it would be possible to walk fifty yards across the shadowed water without touching the water. I had neither.

I approached from the north and stopped just short of The Cathedral. The boat drifted to a stop against a huge tree. Using my hands and a short paddle, I eased the boat just a bit west between to gigantic trees and around a trio of knees I had dubbed Moe, Larry, and Curly. The path seemed blocked but then I noticed a small opening back to the north and paddled to it. Going around a large group of knees I u-turned, swinging the boat back to a southerly direction.

Eh-it's like a cah-cornfield maze.

I was just thinking that, Bob.

I-I nah-know. He moved right into that irritating wheezing, stutter laugh.

A hard right. Left. Right. Left. Right. Right. U-turn. Straight. U-turn. Right. Right.

I stopped and looked around. Without realizing it, I had ended up toward the rear of The Cathedral. While I could see the boat channel about sixty yards back to the east, there was absolutely no way anyone could ever see a path to get from there to here. Or back.

From the inside of The Cathedral looking out the view was drastically changed. The trees seemed to line up like gigantic support posts holding up a light blue ceiling. Light streams filtered through the branches and dappled the tree trucks and brackish water with a stationary disco-ball effect. Ripples from the boat and oar scattered across the surface of the water like Indians running from a cavalry charge in an old John Wayne western. It was pretty, but not spectacular. I needed spectacular.

A lone cloud passed overhead. The Cathedral darkened. I felt it before I saw it. A stream of light cut through a rip hole in the cloud creating a chimney of direct sunlight. From the angle, I immediately realized that the phenomenon would be hidden from the main channel by nearby trees; from the backside it looked like a very expensive special effects manipulation in a sci-fi movie.

Could I move the boat just a few feet further to the east so I could get a slightly different view? No dice. Trapped by a row of knees.

I strapped both cameras to the epaulette snaps on my vest, swapped the telephoto lenses for the wide-angle zoom and eased my legs out of the boat, belly to the gunwale. As water crept over my ankles, to mid-calf and to my knees, I remembered reading 98 percent of the lake was only four feet deep. Bob *rah-reminded me the other tah-two percent* dropped off as much as twenty feet.

With the water right at my waist, I stopped my descent and, balancing carefully with one hand, used the other to put the cameras on the boat seat. I then eased slowly downward. Two buttons high on my shirt, I hit bottom. Feeling the bottom gave me permission to breathe.

Holding the cameras aloft, one in each hand, I crabbed to my right between two knees, being carefully to lift my feet as I moved them sideways in case a below-the-water-line knee was in a tripping position. Four steps. Five. There it was. Framed between two identical-twin cypress spires, with a lead-in row of knees that looked like walking punctuation marks, was an unobstructed view of the sunlight hitting an open spot of water. The water at the center glowed like a vat of gold; beyond the shaft of pure light the water was as dark as a Karachi whore's heart. Leaves and mold motes hovered in mid-air, illuminated by the sunstream. Spotlighted tendrils of Spanish moss gave the impression of the yellow beards of Inquisition judges, leaning forward to view the evidence.

Taking a deep breath, I unleashed Betsy with the twenty-mm. and quickly focused. God! Oh, my God! Almost good enough for the cover.

I quickly cracked off six or seven vertical frames with little variation in angle or exposure. Perfection doesn't need much adjustment.

Wah-wouldn't it be....

Yes, Bob, it'd be neat if some critter would enter the frame.

The word "frame" was still echoing in my mind when a young egret, solid white with bright yellow legs, feet and bill, swooped through a clearing in the trees and quickly settled on a knee just slightly left of center. The very knee I would have chosen to stick a stuffed bird if I were setting up a studio shot.

Having caught the bird out of the corner of my eye about a second before it settled, I think I cracked off a shot, but couldn't be sure. If I shot a frame, the bird might spook. Without taking my eyes off the living tableau, I adjusted the motor drive from single to multi-shot mode and reframed the shot. I knew I had twenty-eight frames left in the Thirty-six shot roll and just pulled down on the shutter release and held it tight.

Sna-snick. Sna-snick. Sna-snick. The frames passed by the shutter like a burst from a toy gun shooting Pez candy.

Four frames. Eight. Twelve. At the first sound, the bird drew to attention. By the middle of the blast, it was getting edgy. By number twelve, its wings were straight overhead and starting a downward pump;

its toes were curled and lifting off the log. The bird rose up and outward. The camera followed its flight. The bird disappeared between a row of cypress trees at about the same time the camera went into rewind.

Six seconds. Seven, tops.

I was exhausted.

Tah-times like this, I'm gla-glad I came along for the rah-ride.

Me too, Bob. Me too.

Dah-did you get it?

If I didn't get that picture I won't come back. I'll leave Caddo, and won't check on the Poetry Board in the morning.

Yah-you got it! Bob paused. *Nah-nah-nothing that good deserves to bah-be seen just by the likes of you and mah-me.*

You got a point, Bob. You do got a point.

5

Juvenile delinquents are not born. They have received a lot of attention to end up that way.

Anonymous

Getting out of The Cathedral was easier than getting in. *If* I had had the services of a squad of Army Corps of Engineers, a couple of industrial chain saws, and a couple of Joe B.B.'s "bums."

It took about fifteen minutes to find the path that I thought I used to get into The Cathedral. It took about two hours to get out. Bob *fah-figured* I was lucky going in. I thought I was even luckier to get out.

It was mid-afternoon when we got back to the dock. When I saw who was loading a boat with boxes being taken from the trunk of a '68 Roadmaster, I almost cruised right on past the dock. Full blast. En route to Louisiana.

Harmony Ledbetter and his brother Bother were as welcome at this point in the day as a mangy, wet dog wanting to cuddle. The Ledbetters were life-long residents of the Caddo Lake area. My research on the lake referred to a prominent section of the lake that had originally been named Ledbetter, but later changed to Red Belly. After hearing about the family, I thought I knew the reason for the change. Several people had told me the brothers had been making moonshine since they were kids and raising hell as long as anybody could remember. The new rumor was that they were expanding their business venture and whipping up some kind of drug at the backside of some slough at the lower end of Carter's Chute. Or Old House Slough. Or Goat Island. Or just on the Louisiana side of lake. The location was changed depending on who was spreading the rumor.

It was too late to make a run for open water since I had already turned toward the dock and cut the engine back. There were several men on the dock, a couple I knew by sight. I figured that if the brothers decided to beat the crap out of me, at least, maybe, there would be folks around to either pull them off or see that I got to a hospital.

I hah-hate....

I know, Bob. Ditto on the back side.

Harmony, backed up by his conversationally challenged, slack-faced brother, was the town bully. Another popular belief was that one of the Ledbetter brothers was the town idiot. Conventional wisdom said they took turns. I hadn't been in Uncertain for fifteen minutes on moving day when I was braced by the pair while getting supplies at Harlan's. To Harmony, I was a new bug to put under his magnifying glass; to Bother, I was a new bug for Harmony to put under his magnifying glass.

That first meeting, they prodded and poked, looking for chinks in my manly mental armor. They had the advantage in the areas of pure numbers, strength, and meanness. In any battle where words were prime ammunition, I figured I was prime rib and they were week-old lunchmeat. The problem was Harmony spoke mostly in single syllables with a few easy two-syllable words thrown in. I don't remember Bother ever bothering to talk much at all.

"Howdy, Photo Man," Harmony threw in my direction as he stacked a cardboard box in the front of a boat. "How's picture takin'?"

"Good and bad. Today, mostly bad."

Lah-Liar.

"Maybe it's bad because of the guy holding the camera," Harmony said. Both Ledbetters started laughing like front row patrons in a Gallagher concert. Sort of nervous, scared-like.

"Could be. You never know."

"Is that the best you can do, Big City Funny Man?"

Determined to get off the boat dock with at least some of my dignity and most of my skin and blood intact, I didn't reply. Just gathered up all my supplies and trash, tied up the boat and started down the dock. All activity on the dock had ceased. Three men standing near a fishing boat halfway down the dock stood stock-still, taking in the confrontation like first-time visitors to a rattlesnake roundup.

Harmony's meaty hand grabbed my right arm and he squeezed harder than necessary. A lot harder. I looked at his hand and his grimy, split fingernails and thought: Tetanus shot. Time for a booster.

His lips split in a cannibal grin. A mental picture popped up: A wolverine sauntering up to a wounded gerbil.

Harmony Ledbetter was, in a phrase, large. Not tall. Large. In Mexico he could have rassled as The Human Gordita. He was about five-foot-eight, but would field dress out at about 280 pounds. He would not be labeled prime choice, however; he was extremely taut and muscular. His whole body looked like a series of carpenters' wrists. Hard as nails. Knotty.

He had an odd, memorable face, like a dead president on money...sort of greenish and one-dimensional. It was a cartoon face, one of those critters who always runs face first into a flat iron or a snow shovel. His ears were slanted forward and the top of his ears seemed to be even with his broken-carrot nose. His nose was tiny compared to his other facial features and tilted upward.

Bob *tha-thought* if he ever got caught out in a rainstorm, he would drown. I thought back that the dreams of the world are built on hope.

Harmony's forehead was huge and a bit lopsided, about half the size of an Edsel grill turned sideways. His lips flopped around like pillowcases on a clothesline. Angelique Jolie lips...after receiving about 35 gallons of injected Botox. His hair was coated in what could only be a derivative of WD-40, and combed—or more accurately "rubbed"—backward, ending in what, in the 1950s, had been called a "duck tail." On Harmony, it was a "baboon's ass."

His brother Bother was about six-foot-six, weighed maybe 170. At least, he would weight that much if he had a 7x75.15 radial under each arm. He was skinny, hairless below his eyes and white as a core sample of Wonder Bread. The only protrusion on his body was his navel, which was showing under a ripped, black, Metallica t-shirt. He was not handsome. His wanted poster probably described him as "dog-ass ugly." Slack-jawed, he was a mouth-breather who looked like he often forgot to breathe and was suffering from advanced oxygen deprivation.

"Nothing to say, Photo Man?" Harmony poked.

I stopped and stared. "Which is it, Harmony, Photo Man or Big City Funny Man? It can't be both. When you give a nickname to someone, it's more socially acceptable and much less confusing to stick with a single nickname rather than run out a laundry list of AKAs. Bother, that means 'also known as.' You've probably noticed that on your arrest sheet. When you choose to call someone by different monikers, you can create the impression you suffer from short-term memory loss and can't remember the nickname you already gave them. That's disconcerting to someone with an I.Q. above single digits."

Harmony was looking at me like a terrier contemplating a rat. Bother was looking at Harmony, apparently trying to get a read on what he was supposed to do and when he was supposed to do it.

"Listen, Mr. Smart Mouth, I…."

"Dammit, Harmony, that's three! First, it was Photo Man, then Big City Funny Man, then Mr. Smart Mouth. I can't answer to all three. I think I like Photo Man best but, then, that just describes what I do, not who I am. I like the way Big City Funny Man rolls off the tongue, but then again, it just doesn't fit. I grew up in a town of about 300 people so Big City just doesn't work for me. I can live with Funny Man because, gawddammit, I am one funny sumbitch, ain't I, Bother?"

My face grimaced. Bob recognized the feeling. I was grinning like that *ah-addled hyena* in the "Lion King."

Bother's look changed to one resembling a baby chipmunk eyeing a snake. Or maybe it was the same look he had had all along. With Bother, one could never be sure. He didn't notice the drool hanging from his bottom lip. I did. I wished to God I hadn't.

"Listen, you, you…"

"You're starting to sound like Bob. Harmony, my good man, didn't your mama tell you not to call people You-You. That's not a nice thing. No one wants to be a You-You. It's a depersonalizing epitaph that creates continuing problems in one's psyche. Now back to the subject at hand: As I stated, I like Funny Man if you'd agree to leave off the Big City part. We might compromise and add Small Town to it. As in Small Town Funny Man. Or even Rural Community...like Rural Community Funny Man."

"EUREKA!," I shouted.

Harmony blinked. Bother jumped about eighteen inches sideways, damn near falling off the dock.

"That's it! Rural Community Funny Man!," I said. "That, I can live with. Smart Mouth doesn't do it for me because—and I'm sure you will agree with me here—the words 'smart' and 'mouth' really should not be connected since, in reality, 'smart' goes with the 'brain,' not 'mouth.'"

I put my hand up to my face, tapping my index finger on my cheek. "How about a compromise: Rural Community Smart Brain. Now, that is the best yet!"

Harmony's eyes had crossed. I squinted and looked closely. No one home. Spooky. His nose, and the hairs ascending from the nostrils, were twitching and while I didn't know him very well, I took that as a good exit sign.

As I turned to leave, Harmony said, "Who's Bob?"

That's two questions I left hanging. Bob asked the other one: *Hah-how can people be so fah-fucking dumb?*

"Ta-Ta, Ledbetter Brothers. Have a marfaburific day and I do hope the sheriff doesn't find out what you have in those boxes. Although It probably would help you get tickets to Convict Dickers Ball."

I didn't look back. Didn't have to. I know when someone is looking mean at my back.

Watch my back, Bob!

Wah-watch it yourself! I move wah-we go home.

The motion was seconded and passed by acclimation.

6

There's a fine line between love and lust. Some people seem to have a knack of always stomping all over that fine line.

Anonymous

After the photo session in The Cathedral and the verbal fisticuffs with the Ledbetters, I was pumped. I got the photo of the century. Or at least the decade. And I verbal-tongued the hell out of the Ledbetters. For this day to get any better I would have to win the Texas lottery, get a National Geographic grant to spend a year shooting chest art affixed to Balinese women, or get lucky in another way that has nothing to do with winning money or getting paid to take a vacation.

Adrenaline is an interesting chemical. It is better that most prescription drugs and way better than anything that can be manufactured in the cargo area of a '76 Chevy station wagon. I was flying high and feeling tight!

Jah-Jesus. You're rah-right proud of yourself, aren't yah-you?

Right you are, Bob. Right you are. My get-nothing day has turned into a marfaburific day, the best day of the year and one of the Top 10 days of my life.

Bob accepted the statement, not thinking another word.

The sun shone on me with a special warmth; I could hear the birds singing for what seemed like miles; roadside flowers emitted LSD-enhanced odors—in colors.

Bob didn't initially query why I stopped walking at a brisk pace and started picking heaping handfuls of blue bonnets, faux daisies, and Indian paintbrushes. In a New York flower shop, the bouquet would have cost at least $40. In Uncertain, it cost me a pricked finger and palmula from a wild rose plant and several uncertain looks from passers-by.

Wha-why are....

I like flowers.

I-I think that yah-you....

Don't think, Bob. It gives me a headache.

It took about twenty minutes to get to Widder Gibson's. I turned onto her gravel walkway and jumped on her porch with the elan of an elan and rapped my knuckles against the screen door jam three times.

Tha-this is a bad...

Nope, Bob. It's a great idea. Go forth and stutter no more.

Tha-that was pla-plain mean.

Sorry. And I meant it.

I could feel Widder looking at me from a widow off to the left but I just stood stock still. The smile on my face was as big as $2 slice of hoop cheese.

Being it was a shade on the high side of warmish, the front door was open; darkness seeped inward behind the screen door. As if by some sort of slight-of-hand, Widder appeared at the screen without noise, without apparent movement. Looking first at me, then to the fistful of flowers, she cocked her head to the right. Her left eyebrow formed a perfect question mark.

"Don't say a word, Dear Neighbor. These beautiful natural offerings are for you. Please accept them as an insignificant token for your hospitality and neighborliness. It's a beautiful day. I've had a marfaburific day and I wanted to share my joy with someone special. Please accept this small gift and I hope this colorful bouquet makes you as happy as it did me to pick them for you."

Jah-jesus!

She looked at me for a long time, her eyes dropping to the flowers every so often. A slight smile crossed her lips, but was quickly hidden by her upraised hand.

"Are you drunk?"

"Yes!" I said. "Yes, yes, and yes! Drunk on life. Drunk on the belief that the stars are aligned for me today and that this is one of the best days of my life. I just wanted to share my feelings of joy with my next-door neighbor. So, I plucked from the fertile loam the best floral bounty that Mother Nature has to offer. I present it to you as a gesture of goodwill and appreciation."

Not a word. She just stood behind the screen and stared alternatively at me and the flowers.

"Those are for me?" she said in a voice softer than a kitten's sneeze.

I lowered my voice to what I considered an appropriate level. "Yes, dear lady, for you. When I saw them, I thought how they needed to be in the hands and home of someone special. They were too beautiful to live and die in a roadside ditch."

"I can't take them." Flat statement. No emotion.

"Why not, pray tell? These flowers were picked with you in mind. If you don't take them, what will happen to them? Don't answer. I'll tell you. I'll strew them along the path from your front door to mine and they will wither and die alone rather than brighten your lovely abode with their color and fill your home with their heavenly scent."

"I don't accept gifts from strangers."

"Stranger? Me? I may be strange, I grant you that. But I'm no stranger. Adnijio Benjamin Franklin Jones, master photographer of the world's beauties, verbal master of mouth-breathing miscreants, plucker of flowers and damn upstanding, responsible and handsome neighbor, at your service." The words were followed by a deep, royalty-in-attendance bow.

A suppressed giggle slid through the screen. I arched my eyebrows to look upwards from the almost-on-the-porch bow. Widder's hand was covering her mouth. Her cheeks were raised upward; her nose crinkled; her eyes laughed.

"Okay," she said, in a no-nonsense tone. "I'll take the flowers, but don't do it again. People will talk. Now give me the flowers and get off my porch."

She opened the screen about a two-hand's-widths and took the pro-offered bouquet.

"Thank you, Kind Lady. Thank you for accepting my humble gift. Now I bid you adieu till the morrow. May your life never experience sorrow and may malodorous floral arrangements from strange strangers be an every day part of your life."

Her face squenched up in puzzlement. "Malodorous? Don't you mean 'ambrosial,' 'odoriferous' or 'redolent?'"

I stood there, thinking. "Yes, I think I do. Regardless, to use your words, in your hand those flowers are more ambrosial that the most expensive perfume. They are more odoriferous than a cotton nightgown sprayed with Fabreze and more redolent than bread fresh from the oven." I bowed again, turned and marched off the porch and down the pathway like a knight on a quest. I could feel Widder's eyes plastered on my blue jean-encased rump.

Wha-what an eh-idiot!

Before I had gone four steps down the road I could hear Moosie raise a nice, alto bay at my arrival. "Moosie, Moosie, Moosie." She quit baying and started barking. I grabbed the mail and went into the unlocked house, shedding my cameras and vest in the overstuffed chair by the front door, laid the mail on the rustic phone table and picked up a bag of doggie treats. Moosie did not require a lot of attention. At fifteen months old and 165 pounds, she was still a growing girl and food was one of her top priorities. Great Danes, even though they are the size of small ponies, don't eat like horses, so to speak. The breed has never been known to founder although they lead the canine world in two decisive categories dealing with flatulence and bodily waste: Volume and mass.

About once a week I dumped a forty-pound sack of Diamond brand lamb and rice food in a twenty-gallon plastic storage container and subsidized it with leftover eggs, bread, spaghetti and bargain basement hot dogs. To Moosie I was the canine culinary king of DogLand.

She was waiting at the back door, tail wagging, and mouth in third gear drool mode.

"Attention!" She quickly threw her haunches on the back porch, locked her front legs, raised her head and pulled her lengthy tongue in her mouth. Rigid, she stayed in that position, with only her eyes moving as they followed my every move.

"Eyes right!"

She snapped her head to the left. My right, which is the way I taught her and it's just a technicality even though Bob thinks *eh-it's a dah-dumb trick*.

I threw her a Liver Snap, which reached her stomach before my hand was back in the bag.

I pointed a treat at her: "Act like my editor."

She started pacing back and forth on the porch, head hanging down and started doing a pitiful whine followed by a series of short, seal-like barks accompanied by weary shakes of her head. The imitation of Deljoe Collinsworth, photo editor of Tabletop Publishing in New York City, was uncanny. Ready or not, Moosie was going to the office Christmas party this year and would instantly become a legend in the publishing world.

After checking her food and running some fresh water in the No. 3 washtub, I went back in the house, opened up the '67 Coldspot refrigerator and grabbed a long-necked Dos Equis from the bottom shelf. Every time I popped the top I had fond memories of a girl I once dated that could pry off a beer cap with her eyeteeth.

The thought of her prying off bottle caps for my friends and me while wearing nothing but a bikini or a crop top and short shorts always made me smile.

Gah-gawd! Yah-you need to get out mah-more!

I am out, Bob. I am so far out that I'm back in. This was one gah-gah-great day!

After a supper of Easy Mac and a warmed up can of generic ravioli, I fired up my iBook and wrote some notes about the day before I showered and got in bed to read.

After about half an hour of trying to concentrate on Gore Vidol's "Lincoln," I realized I had made it through only about twenty pages. On top of that, I couldn't remember much of what I had read. I turned off the light and glanced out the window toward the south. There was a light in one window in the rear part of Widder's house. I watched the curtained window, hoping to see a shadow. There was nothing but a steady light on the light-colored shade.

I could almost see the flowers I had picked in a Japanese-style vase sitting on the nightstand by her bed. I could see her sitting up in bed, reading. Poetry, maybe. More likely a romance novel, *South American Adventure*, *Island Tempest* or some such. Her hair was down, the gentle swell of her breasts pushed the Victoria Secret teddy—purple with yellow trim—up and down in rhythm with her breathing.

Hah-who are you kah-kidding?

You're right, Bob. She's probably sitting there, picking at blackheads while wearing a shapeless shift made out of burlap. She's biting her gnarled, yellow toenails and there's a boil the size of New Jersey on her left butt cheek. I'll even bet one nipple is lodged in her navel right now.

Jah-jesus! Sha-shut up!

I do love it when Bob makes me laugh.

7

Revenge is sweet. Or sour. Depends on whether someone gets hurt or not.

Anonymous

My eyes cracked. I was in my regular seat in the junior history class. The room was in the northwest corner of the two-story brick high school in Avery, Texas. The teacher was the basketball, baseball and track coach. Mostly we studied the history of sports in general, and last week's games in particular. Coach Lawrence Q. Turner drew more Xs and Os on the board than he did events, names and dates.

His classes gave us plenty of time for reflection (which, when I look at it thirty years later, is a form of history) and mischief.

Today, the entire room was buzzing. In about a minute Bridgett Roe was going to get her well-deserved comeuppance. A recent transfer to this rural East Texas school, it was obvious from her first day that she hated the school, the town, and her classmates in general, and the local, tongue-lolling hairlegs in particular. To the boys, she was fresh meat, something new and unusual and a change in dating fare from the local "dating circle," which took in an area of about thirty-six miles in diameter, including the nearby towns of Annona, DeKalb, Clarksville, and Bogota.

Being one of the first to school every day—I had a key to the gym and followed a religious routine of run-and-shoots six days a week—I first saw her when she was dropped off at school by her mom. While most residents of Avery drove around in pickups with rusted-out floorboards or everyday Chevrolets and Fords with nice crops of dings from flying country road gravel, Bridgett Roe arrived her first day at Goat-roper High in a shiny new '59 Cadillac. It was subtle in color, lilac, with chrome spinners and off-beige fender skirts. That car had more chrome on it than a bumper assembly plant; its chrome had chrome trim.

My bottom jaw slapped wide open as this statuesque blonde slid out of the car. The sliding laws of friction had her knee-length shirt sliding due north at a rapid rate. She showed way more thigh than a truckload of cut-up chickens. It was a lot less than I wanted to see.

She planted her feet and her dress slid back where it was supposed to be. I gave her a welcoming once-over. Twice-over, actually. Long, blonde hair in a Veronica Lake hide-and-peek; neck of Audrey Hepburn proportions, chestworks that if her head were locked in at noon, her breasts in a bullet bra would be showing nine and three respectively. Her ankles and calves matched up perfectly with nightly wet dreams.

"Good day, Fair Maiden," I said as I East Texas-sauntered up to her side of the car, thumbs stuck firmly in the top of my jeans, arms akimbo. "But what light from yonder window shines. It is the moon, and you, Fair Maiden, are the sun."

She looked at me like I was a cow that had just been sledgehammer-whomped at Bushmill's Meat Market.

"What?"

"Welcome to our humble school. Allow me to introduce myself: Adnijio Benjamin Franklin Jones at your service. My friends call me Adj. Is this beautiful creature driving this pristine chariot your mother? Can't be! Way too young and beautiful to have a daughter as old and beautiful as you."

A barely suppressed guffaw erupted from the shadows of the car. "Watch this one, Bridgett. He's got a gift of gab and isn't afraid to use it."

Bridgett! I liked that. It rolled off the tongue like sweat off a hay hauler's chest in mid-July. We didn't have a Bridgett at our school. Names of the feminine gender tended to run toward country mundane. We had a Lorene and Corene (twins), a Nancy or two, several Maries, June, Sybil,

Glenndora, Jo Vita, Ruby, Doylene, Velda, Ouida, Sarah, Gloria, Wanda and a Delaphene. There were, of course, the normal ratio of Marys, Joyces, Kays, Anns and Deannas. We also had a Wynona and two Yvonnes, one pronounced E-vonne, and the other Y-von-ey.

No Bridgett.

"Yes, fair Bridgett, do watch me. How about watching me up close and very personal at a movie Friday night? I'll watch the movie and you can watch me. I have a car and everything," I said, pointing with pride to my '57 black-and-white Ford Fairlane with a Thunderbird Interceptor engine, twin pipes and muffler cutouts.

"See, Bridgett, I told you you'd make friends," the woman in the car said smilingly as the Cadillac started moving toward the front gate.

Bridgett quickly affixed me with a look akin to the one Miss Ima Williams gave me in third grade when I stuck a banana popsicle inside my pants just to see how it would feel. Her eyes flashed. Snapped, actually. She smiled. My stomach did two outside toe-loops and a reverse one-and-a-half camel with a twist.

She licked her top lip, lazily wetting it left to right and back again. I fell in love with her tongue.

When she spoke, her voice was melted sugar-butter. A sort of Scarlett O'Hara on laudanum.

"Movie? Friday night? With you?" Pause. Lip-lick. "I'll never be that desperate. I'd rather sit home and wash the cat."

She waited for a snappy comeback but there was none. My brain pan was awash in silent shadows, vocal chords frozen.

Wash the cat? Who washes cats?

With ten words, Bridgett had turned from a perky-breasted goddess to a certified SUB—stuck-up bitch.

Who does she think she is? A snooty cat-washer, that's who. In these parts, at that time in my life, I was a highly sought-after companion for weekend rendezvousing, movie-going and submarine-watching exercises. Bridgett was asked out about forty times the first day at school, accepting none. Those that asked her out and were summarily rejected joined the SUB-hating clan. To the girls, she was competition and, therefore, instantly was labeled "the skanky bitch trying to steal our men."

UNCERTAIN TIMES

In a community where mental entertainment for testosterone-ridden males was mostly confined to bragging about sports prowess or made-up conquests of non-existent teenage queens from distant communities, it didn't take long for a small group to come up with the perfect plan to put the newcomer in her place.

After school Cowboy and Turnip Melbrook and myself put out eleven live bait-traps along known game trails in the prolific woods that bordered area tomato and cucumber fields. Over the next three days, we caught six rabbits, two skunks, and an armadillo. The rabbits fetched two bits each from a family where the father was on permanent disability. It was a bargain for both sides. The skunks were released via a long pole and short rope with a minimum of "stank" getting on any of us.

The armadillo had a date.

Thursday morning, early, the three of us broke into the school well before first bell by climbing up the rusted fire escape slide that connected to the library. The armadillo—Mr. Revenge—was pulled up in its cage via a long hemp rope. Without turning on any lights, we located the right locker and poked Mr. Revenge with a ruler until it crawled out of the cage into the locker.

The word of our prank spread quickly and about fifty students were lounging around in the second-floor hallway, waiting for Bridgett to arrive, open the locker, and get greeted by her best new friend.

There was only one hitch in the plan: She didn't come to school that day.

Various plans for getting the armadillo out of the locker were brought up and discarded. All were deemed not quite right because most ended in the distinct possibility of getting caught and getting paddled by the principal, a heavy-handed authoritarian who seemed to delight in wielding The Board of Education, as he named the one-by-six board with the whittled handle and tape-wrapped whopping area.

It was impractical to wait after school and extricate the armadillo; the first games of the Dimple basketball tournament were that night and practically the entire town would be at the game. That included all possible armadillo-getters.

"She'll be back tomorrow," Turnip Melbrook said. "It'll be just as good then as today. What's the worst thing that can happen?"

That argument made sense, in a convoluted sort of way. But it had two elements that made it the plan of action, or inaction, as the case might be: SUB would still be surprised out of her prissy drawers and we might not get our asses busted by The Board of Education.

The next morning, again, the hall was double-crowded with onlookers just waiting for SUB to arrive. The first bell rang, sending students to class. Jewlynn Crank happened to look out the second-floor window and reported seeing the lilac Cadillac pull up in the parking lot.

"She's coming in late!" The word among spread the students like cold sores in a household with one drinking gourd. "She's here!"

The history class was the first room at the head of the stairs. Everyone watched as Bridgett slumped up the stairs and disappeared from view in the direction of the lockers. Ten students got up at the same time to use the pencil sharpener affixed to the wall near the door.

The line had just started forming when there was a scream. Elsa Lancaster's wail in *Bride of Frankenstein* rattled off the school's molded-tin ceiling.

Students fought to get through the door and into the hall.

SUB was sitting on the floor, her back against the north lockers, her legs stuck out in front of her. She was flailing her feet like the tines of a thrashing machine in high gear. The armadillo was obviously in a state of distress and was attacking her Mary Janes with a single-minded kill-and-destroy intent.

Bridgett's white skirt with yellow polka dots, and the uncountable layers of petticoats under it, bunched up around her hips. Flashes of red panties and white thighs swirled around as she kicked her legs in four/four time. The rhythm of survival. Supine Celtic clogging.

The letters F, R, and I flashed by on her red girl-briefs in a psychedelic artwork of lust. I was still contemplating the F, R, and I when a male teacher broke out of the crowd with a wastebasket and slapped it down on the armadillo. The edge of the trash can caught its tails, and one of Bridgett's toes in the process, breaking both.

The armadillo shrieked. Bridgett screamed. All the girls and about half the boys screamed in a non-harmonic crescendo. It was a sound inspired by Dante's Inferno, but instead of people being caught up in a river of shit, people were caught up in the tableau of a mad armadillo attacking a long-legged blonde in her perfectly fitted, red **FRIDAY** panties.

A stray piece of sheet rock was used as a lid and the armadillo was quickly removed. With help from a few girls, Bridgett removed herself from the hall and sat on the front steps, holding her knees in her locked arms. She just set there, crying and rocking until her mother picked her up a half-hour later.

Cowboy, Turnip and I made a pact to confess and apologize to Bridgett on Monday. We never got the chance. Word filtered back that she quit school and went to live with an aunt in St. Louis.

Sadness is a lonely emotion, especially when one realizes that a specific goal in life will never be reached.

I knew I'd never get to see her panties for the other days of the week. I had only seen half of **FRIDAY**. I longed to see all of **SATURDAY**. Every single letter.

From the packages at the Hub General Store in nearby Clarksville, it was common knowledge **SATURDAY** panties were black.

My favorite color.

8

Being tactful works...
except when it doesn't.

Anonymous

Sometime during the night, a thunderstorm came in over the lake and the drum-roll of distant thunder pulled me out of the dream about drooling, pissed-off armadillos wearing red panties.

Watching nighttime storms bluster has always been one of my favorite free things to do. That and watching sunrises and sunsets. And seeing naked women jog on a South Pacific beach with nary a single bounce in sight.

This storm was building up to be a good one; lightning traces lit up the southern sky in irregular patterns. It reminded me of a rock concert I caught in London. The electrical system blew and all the concert-goers thought that the showers of sparks, three loud explosions and screeching speakers were part of the show.

Moosie gave a short bark, then another one, this time a little lower, more gravelly. I went into the kitchen and peered out the back window.

In one particularly bright lightning burst, my eye flicked to a strange shadow cast in the back yard. It was like a large bowling ball, or one large bowling ball and a smaller one on top. Like a snowman.

Wha-what the hah-hell?

I had the impression of the shadow throwing something in the backyard.

Moosie!

I shouted some strangled noise at the top of my lungs and ran back to the hall, grabbed my Ithaca .410 shotgun leaning against the wall. I sprinted for the back porch, screaming whatever came to mind as loudly as possible.

I didn't turn on the back porch light, knowing it would ruin my night vision and make me a target for whatever was outside. "Moosie!" I yelled as I hit the door running. It was between lightning flashes and all I could see was black. I fired off a shot straight up in the air. Sounding authoritative is uncertain situations is never a bad thing.

The rain kicked up a good imitation of a waterfall. Rapid lightning flashes illuminated the yard and surrounding area is disconcerting patterns of light and dark. Moosie was to my right, standing, head down. A flicker of movement went behind Widder's house and was gone. I fired a second shot high in the general area of the shadow for effect.

Running over to where Moosie stood, I saw her chewing something, swallow and then try to pick up something else from the ground. "NO!" She stopped and looked at me, picked up whatever it was on the ground and trotted toward me, chewing as she came.

I grabbed her throat with my left hand and squeezed forcefully, trying to force open her mouth with my right. She tried to get away from the attack but I wrestled her to the ground. Forcing my right hand into her mouth, I grabbed what felt like a piece of meat and jerked it out, ripping a finger and the back of my hand. I could feel the cool rain mixing with something warm.

The next lightning flash revealed I was holding a chunk of meat the size of my fist. Throwing the meat over the fence, I grabbed Moosie's ear, twisted and she willingly followed me to the house. Inside, I grabbed a squeeze jar of mustard from the Coldspot, forced the tapered cap into her mouth and squeezed hard, stroking her throat with my other hand at the same time.

She gagged, but swallowed and I dosed her again. This time she gagged for real and I discovered an unsung trick she had down cold: Projective vomiting. The contents of her stomach first hit the bottom of the refrigerator, the floor and then my bare feet. Again. Again. And yet again. Along with the bile came up half-dissolved dog food chunks and three large pieces of barely-chewed slabs of meat.

I tried to give her another dose of mustard but this time she was ready to fight. There are three things that man was not meant to fight and a pissed-off Great Dane is one of them. The other two? An ex-wife that happened to be a professional knife-thrower and an IRS agent with hemorrhoids.

I knew without knowing the meat was poisonous. I thought I had gotten to her in time to prevent much absorption of the poison. Should I take her to the vet?

"I'd take her to the vet."

Not Bob. Widder.

I looked up from my seated position on the ragged linoleum floor and Widder was framed in the doorway to the hall. She was standing there, in a white, cotton gown that looked like it had come right out of a washtub. The filtered light from the bedroom silhouetted her and the gown was as transparent as onionskin paper in a wedding invitation.

Her hands had been at her sides. Now they fluttered up and crossed themselves over her chest. Her fingertips brushed the ends of her wet hair. It was crinkly and hung past her shoulders.

"Poison," I said.

"I figured," she said, removing one hand from its crossed position and pointing at the mustard container on the floor. I caught a glimpse of a very youthful-looking, proud-as-punch breast. She recrossed her arms. I wanted her to point again.

"Do you see my car keys?"

Without uncrossing her arms, she looked around the kitchen and turned slightly and looked in the hall. The bottom half of the gown swirled like a Seymore scarf and now I wanted her to turn and point. With verve and feeling.

She disappeared and hollered back, "They're here on the table by the door."

UNCERTAIN TIMES

Grabbing Moosie by the ear, I started to lead her out of the kitchen, when Widder said, "Wait." She pointed to my hand, which was dripping blood on the floor and on my pants. "Go clean up and change," she said. "Bring me some First Aid supplies and I'll fix you up."

I started to protest. Her look told me not to bother. She walked over, took Moosie by the ear and clamped down tight. I quickly went to the bathroom, took off my pajama bottoms and jumped in the shower, rinsed off and checked the hand wound. It wasn't bad. I slipped on some old khakis from the floor of the bedroom, a stained t-shirt advertising smokeless tobacco and a pair of slip-ons. I went back in the kitchen toting a small red, plastic First Aid kit. Moosie was sitting there, looking up at Widder adoringly. I tried not to look too closely at Widder. Sometimes my eyes have a mind of their own. Like now.

Telling Moosie to "stay," she took my hand, held it under the cold spigot of the kitchen faucet and then dried the wound on a dish towel. After slathering on a heavy coating of antiseptic ointment, she wrapped the hand quickly in gauze, which she split and tied into a nice, neat knot facing the palm of my hand.

"Thank you," I said, maintaining eye contact. Or low neck contact. I grabbed Moosie's ear and led her out on the porch. Widder followed close behind and I wanted to give her a hug for several reasons but her body language was clear: Ain't interested.

"I'm going to take her to the vet's. Thank you for coming by. Did I scare you with the shouting and shooting?"

"Take care of your dog. We'll talk tomorrow."

9

Dogs and cats are alike. They both have their place. They just don't like to stay there.

Anonymous

Ear-leading Moosie to the car was a breeze. Putting her in the back seat was an impossibility. Moosie was a shotgun dog and after balking and whining considerably, she eagerly hopped in the passenger seat when I opened up that option.

As I was starting to pull away, I saw Widder coming down the porch steps, waving like she was a front-row spectator at a Veteran's Day Parade. It was still dripping rain, but the storm had moved on to the east. It was too dark to see anything but a dark object against a darker background. Why hadn't I thought to leave the porch light on? She opened up the back door and set a large plastic Wal-Mart sack in the floorboard.

"The meat chunks from the kitchen floor. Thought you might show them to Doc."

I had never thanked anyone for handing me sack of upchuck, but I did just that. As I started to back the Jeep out, she said, "Wait!"

She opened up the passenger's front door and, dodging Moosie's attempts to lick her to death as best she could, she rolled down the window.

"Dogs like fresh air. Moosie needs lots of fresh air."

With the dome light, I could see her. A lot of her. The nightgown was a scooped-neck affair and it was scooping to beat the band. I could see all the way down to her navel.

"Thank you. For more than you'll ever know," I said.

She smiled as she moved her left hand up to put a dent in the nightgown scoop.

I thanked her again before tearing out of the driveway. I rolled down my window and the wind poured in.

It was about a twenty-minute drive into town. When I got to the Ben There-Don That's store—two brothers, Ben and Don Woosley opened up a little dry goods store, and one or both of them came up with the name-pun that was the catch-line for a few feature stories from major Texas papers—I checked my cell phone. It registered a reasonable signal.

Hitting 411, I quickly raised a sleepy-voiced operator, had her check the computer for a number for Racehorse Higgins, the local vet. Home, not office. My first day in town, I had cruised Marshall until I came across Racehorse's office. Took Moosie in for a pre-emergency checkup.

Racehorse was in his mid-fifties, with billowing white hair that resembled a feather pillow with worn ticking. He was big and loud and pear-shaped; his light-hazel eyes were teardrops turned sideways; his ruddy complexion was etched by acne scars lined up so neat they looked like they had been plowed using a laser guidance system.

His first words were endearing: "Look at this beautiful Great Dane. I dearly love Great Danes."

I gave Doc copies of Moosie's puppy chart, but he insisted on starting his own chart, examining her from wet nose to wagging tail. He pronounced her "one healthy, beautiful female Great Dane." For Moose, and me, it was vet-love at first sight. When your dog is the size of a newborn Clydesdale, it's important the vet be likeable.

After the examination, Dr. Higgins had turned his attention to an ailing parrot and I went to the counter to pay. I remarked to the stern-faced clerk how impressive the vet was. "The first words out of his mouth were 'I love Great Danes.'"

Without looking up, without, seemingly, even moving her mouth, she said, "He says that to all the dogs. And cats. And all other critters, walking, crawling and flying."

The 411 operator quickly looked up the number and patched me through. After four rings, there was a click.

"Do you know what time it is?" A glance at the dash clock told me it was 1:15 in the a.m. "It's 1:15 a.m., Doc."

"Good. You can tell time. Now, dammit, this better be an emergency." The voice tailed off at the end like he was trying to go back to sleep."

"It is, Doc, it is. This is Adj Jones. You know, Moosie the Great Dane's owner. Somebody poisoned her."

"Moosie! Somebody poisoned Moosie! I just love Great Danes. Where are you now? How is she?"

"About ten minutes out, on the highway near Josey's Ranch." Glancing at Moosie, I said, "She seems okay. She has her head out the window and her ears are flapping in the breeze."

"Watch the road and be careful. Don't go to the clinic. Bring Sweet Moosie directly to the house." He gave me instructions that even I could follow.

Sha-she's gonna bah-be fine!

I just realized Bob had been AWOL during the crisis.

Where have you been, Bob?

Di-didn't want to bah-bother you.

Never a bother, Bob. Never a bother. Speaking of Bother and his jerk-brained brother....

Lah-let it go for now. Mah-moosie first.

I found Doc's house without any real problems, only making one wrong turn. Hitting the street leading to Doc's house, the headlines did an arching sweep. Doc was at the curb of the third house on the right, holding a brown briefcase-looking bag.

He opened the passenger door before I got the car stopped and Moosie bounded out like a cobra-spooked mouse. She tore a trail around his front yard, stopping to sniff a rose bush, a small magnolia, assorted flowers in the front bed and finally finished the loop and came back to the car.

"Poisoned, you say?" Doc said, watching Moosie act like a dog.

"Think so. I've got several chunks of meat someone threw over the back fence in a plastic sack in the back seat."

"What did you do when you found her?"

"I don't think she had it in her very long. At least from the size and condition of the meat. I dosed her with a squeeze bottle of mustard. Two doses, in fact."

"French's or store brand?"

Wha-wha-....

"What?"

His smile was clearly visible from the nearby security light. "Just a joke, son, just a joke. I don't see what else you could've done or anything else I can do. If she was poisoned, she certainly should be showing the effects by now. She would not be feeling this perky, that's for sure."

Moosie was chasing and jumping at a big moth that was darting up and down in front of Doc's house.

"What should I do?"

"Get her home and put her outside. Don't give her anything to eat tonight, but make sure she has plenty of water. Feed her something light in the morning. Scrambled eggs or some watery oatmeal or even a combination of the two. I'll have the meat checked out and get back to you late tomorrow or the next day."

"If she's okay tomorrow morning, I'll probably be on the lake. I'll call you when I get back."

"That's fine. Come here, Moosie!" he said, squatting down on his heels. She bounded over to him, knocking him over and washing his face.

"I love Great Danes."

So do I. Jesus, so do I.

It was just a little after three when we started home. Moosie had apparently enjoyed everything about the evening except the mustard stomach douche.

Sha-she's okay.

I know, Bob. But I'm not.

Riding back to Uncertain I didn't think a thought to Bob. I was raised to believe in certain values and to treat people and animals in a certain way, with respect, with caring and, for the right ones, with love. Of course, I had made my share of mistakes in all categories. I knew what values I treasured and followed and I never intentionally physically harmed another person or animal in my life since I had graduated from the torch-the-ants-with-a-magnifying-glass stage of youth. Poisoning a dog was about as low-down as a person could get.

I thought of what could have happened if the storm hadn't awakened me, if Moosie hadn't barked, if I hadn't seen the shadow in the lightning flash, if....

Jah-Jesus!

He can't help them, Bob. He wouldn't even if He could.

10

*Cheap joys. Cheap thrills.
Bring 'em on!*

              Anonymous

 The road back into town was after-rainstorm dark. The wetness swallowed up security lights from isolated houses. The car's headlights seemed to drop into a dark horizontal hole about 100 feet or so in front of the car.
 The only sound came from dog ears flapping in the wind. Thoughts drifted from the pebbly roadway in the headlights. The storm had raged. Moosie was poisoned. Widder came over and offered far more support than she probably realized. Doc was great. Moosie was going to be fine.
 Inside, I was still not all right. A hot ember burned steady and not even thoughts of Widder in that wet gown cooled the feeling.
 Widder in that gown. Holy Matilda! I could still see her standing in that doorway, the light flowing through her gown like golden fingers, caressing her legs, hips…sides of her breasts.
 Letting out a long, slow sigh, I turned onto what I laughingly referred to as the Uncertain Turnpike and bumped through a series of freshly slung asphalt patches the county road crew put down last week. It was the

type of job that County Judge Paul Pirtle would refer to as "major road improvements" in his re-election campaign material next year.

I slowed down as I approached the Poem Board. As the headlights swept over the board, I thought there was a new verse on the board; the length seemed different from yesterday. But I couldn't be sure. It's late. I should go home and get Moosie settled. But I wanted to see if, despite the recent rain, a new verse had been written.

I pulled to the side of the road, put the car in park and left the lights on and motor running. Reaching into the glove box, I fumbled around until I found a mini-Maglite, gave Moosie a pat and got out.

Using the light to maneuver the ditch, which still had about a foot of water running in it, I flashed the beam on the board and read the new words, which were blurred from the rain:

No noise assails me
Except for the krick-krick of the fire.
No wind blows through the trees,
No scraping of branches
Outside the house.
What I am not hearing
Must be the silence of the limbs.

I read it again. What the hell? Who is writing this?
Mah-my thoughts exactly.
I read it again, this time aloud.
"Somebody is really having fun," I said.
And yah-you are lah-loving it!
I went back to the car, got a piece of scrap paper and a stub pencil, went back to the board and, holding the Maglite in my mouth, wrote the seven simple lines. After double-checking the words and promising myself to come back in the morning and shoot a photo to add to the collection, I headed home.

It was obvious Moosie liked her late-night adventure, but she was ready for bed. After drinking about two quarts of fresh water I ran in sink-size tub and giving me a sloppy kiss, she headed for the tool shed where I had put down an old sleeping bag for a bed.

I was not looking forward to cleaning up the mess made earlier in the kitchen but was not only surprised but a little shaken to discover the kitchen was sparkling clean. Mustard puke. Blood. Cleaned up. The dirty dishes, cups and glasses that seemed to accumulate every other day or so were washed and in the elevated plastic drain. The kitchen floor had not just been wiped down, but mopped. The counters were sparkling clean.

Wah-what....

Widder.

No shotgun. I checked the hall closet and there it was, sitting in the front left corner, barrel up.

Then I noticed a white sheet of paper on the small table at the front door. Flicking on the overhead bulb, I picked it up.

Mr. Jones/Adj

> *Hope Moosie is okay. Didn't get any bad feelings so I'm betting she's fine. Didn't think you'd mind if I cleaned up a bit. I know if the situation was reversed, I'd sure appreciate it if somebody cleaned up that mess at my house. Ha!*
>
> *I checked the backyard and picked up two pieces of meat. They're in my refrigerator if you need them.*
>
> *I said we'd talk tomorrow and since it's already "tomorrow" as you are reading this, that doesn't mean "now" tomorrow but, now, "later" today.*
>
> *I get up early and I always have coffee on. When you get up, come on over if you don't have something more important to do.*
>
> *Celestial*

Sah-Celestial? Who in the hell eh-eh...

Widder.

Jah-Jesus!

Took a peek at the wall clock. 3:35. Four hours until I would feel right about going next door to drink coffee with...Celestial.

One more look at the back door of the cabin convinced me that Moosie was tucked in for the night; one more peek at the house next door convinced me Wid...er...Celestial was tucked in for the night.

The cool sheets and tacky velour comforter felt almost as good as feather-massage by a specially trained sect of geishas on a Japanese island where I had once spend four months shooting photos for a spread on whales.

I propped a pillow against the headboard and sat up, with the sheet pulled up tight to my chest and thought about the day's events. Was it just today that I shot the egret in The Cathedral? Seems like a week ago.

Lah-longer.

Good night, Bob.

Gah-good...ah, you know.

My mind was a cluttered closet. The confrontation with Harmony and Bother at the dock, the thunderstorm, Moosie's close call, Widder showing up.

Widder showing up.

Thinking about her in that wet, transparent gown, with wet hair and bumps in all right places.... The vision of the flash of flat stomach through the scoop-vent of her nightgown was enough incentive to touch myself. Instantly I was hard. I closed my eyes and gently rubbed myself, thinking of nipples and thighs and hips and wild hair and wet, plush lips.

Satisfaction came quickly and completely. Release was welcome; no guilt attached.

After cleaning up, I took one more look out the window, saw lightning in the distance and thought that it would rain again before morning, rolled over and was instantly asleep.

I think I remember Bob saying, *"Jah-jesus"* but if he did I never got past the "Jah" part before sleep hit me like a blacksmith's hammer on a hot horseshoe.

11

Trying to change a woman's mind is like whistling up a dead mule's ass.

Anonymous

Missy Gilmore was sixteen and a virgin. Every boy in the county had tried to rid her of that stigma. And every strikeout was duly noted on God's score card.

Science was to blame for Missy's virginhood. Like many girls in the early '60s, she wore a girdle but not to just flatten and shape; her girdle protected her virginity like chastity belts did for medieval maidens. I started dating Missy because of the mystique of virginity. I wanted to get rid of mine; my friend Cowboy told me to do that I needed a partner.

Missy was no prude. She liked kissing and upper-body touching and her hand found its way into my pants by our second date. And she didn't mind having her lower body parts rubbed through the girdle. In fact, she insisted upon it. Rubbing between the belly button and knees was, is and always will be fun. But rubbing those places through sticky plastic-like material is like rubbing a shaved pig's ass. You rub something. You feel something. But...what?

It was a moonless night in May when I was girdling to beat the band with Missy in the front seat of my Ford Fairlaine. I had secured an entrance to the top part of the girdle with my right hand and was in that sucker about wrist deep when she inhaled sharply—out of lust or as a defense move, I never knew—and my hand cramped. The pain was akin to circumcision with a rusty butter knife. The inside of her girdle was like an oven; her stomach was sweatier than a tomato picker in August.

Later that night I made a pact with God never to go girdling again. I was a basketball player and had almost lost my shooting hand to a woman's undergarment.

12

*It's not that men are from Mars and women are from Venus.
It's just that men are stupid.*

Anonymous

A single sun stream shooting through an opening in the big patch of cypress trees to the east caught my left eye. The eye opened, apparently by itself, causing considerable pain. I rolled over, snuggled down in the covers and commenced to go back to sleep.

Bah-better get up.

Not now, Bob. I had a rough night.

Fah-fine. Don't drink coffee wah-with....

My eyes popped wide open. The bedside Baby Ben read 6:20. I had a coffee date with Widder.

My thoughts quickly turned to Moosie. I grabbed the jeans from yesterday, some scruffy moccasins and headed to the backdoor. I opened the door and Moosie was standing there, ears forward in her "happy" look, tail wagging at a fast calypso beat. I fluffed up her ears and got down on my knees and gladly put my face in the way of a massive wet tongue lick.

Mah-moosie!

She's fine, Bob. Couldn't be better.

I pulled a big metal bowl out of a cabinet and filled it with water, which Moosie attacked with vigor. While she was wetting down a large portion of the back porch, I popped four eggs out of the container in the fridge, cracked them open a skillet. Remembering Doc's instructions, I got out the round cardboard oatmeal container, put about a cup in a bowl, ran a half glass of water from the faucet, mixed it up and dumped the gray mess in with the eggs.

I let the *eggs porridge* sit for a spell while I put on the coffee. Cup in hand, I stirred up the mess up again, added a bit more water and set the heat to high-medium. A couple of pieces of bread went in the art deco toaster.

The egg-oatmeal gruel looked simply awful, like clumpy mud bubbling in Yellowstone Park. Bob thought it looked *dah-dog scrumptious.*

The first cup of coffee was about half gone when Moosie's breakfast was ready.

Opening the back door to call her was wasted effort; she was sitting at the door, tail wagging to some unheard rhythm of serendipity.

She attacked the food. A bouncing rear end pronounced the mess excellent.

I refilled my cup and headed to the bathroom. The electric Timex hanging on the wall showed 6:57.

A short, double-hot shower scalded off dirt and dead skin cells. As always I lathered up and shaved in the shower. Hadn't used a mirror in years; shaved by feel. After toweling off, I selected a pair of Docker khakis and a muted vertical-stripe, dark beige, light beige, permanently wrinkled, six-button Columbia short sleeve shirt. Leather skids with a loppy rawhide bow completed the casual-but-elegant look.

As usual, there was not much I could do with the hair. With four cowlicks and too much time between barbers, my hair pretty much did what it wanted to do.

7:18.

It's too early to head over there, I thought.

Sha-she's up!

Maybe, Bob, but I don't want to appear too eager.

Jah-jesus! It's coffee. Not a sah-sex romp!

I didn't know I had a choice. So, Bob, I'll take the Sex Romp for two hundred dollars!

To waste a little time, I picked up yesterday's mail, which included a copy of the *Uncertain Times*, a local tabloid newspaper that had as its motto: *Published when we want to, not published when we don't*. In the three-plus weeks I'd been in town, this was the second issue I'd seen. The other one was in a pile of magazines near the fireplace and had a date of last December.

It was an interesting publication in a look-at-the-wreck sort of way. There were stories about the county quorum court, written in chronological order, like they were taken from the minutes of the meeting; pictures of big fish caught on Caddo were splashed about; tidbits concerning the Uncertain Volunteer Fire Department pancake breakfast or beautification committee doings. I also learned there was a planning session for the Uncertain July 4th boat parade. It was located under a heading: "Tids and Bits."

In the first issue I had noticed a local column by a Millard Ghormley and looked to see if he was a regular contributor. His column—*"Talk is Cheap…and Here's About a Nickel's Worth"*—was at the top of Page 4.

While there was no picture of Millard with the article, from his writing I thought I had him pegged: In his seventies, short, hump-backed, no teeth. He had dentures he seldom wore. He considered himself a country philosopher and didn't mind stating his opinion in a straightforward, inventive manner.

The headline over the column caught my attention. The introduction held it.

The world is in one helluva mess!

(Millard Ghormley is a pineywoods philosopher who is older than dirt and is starting to feel the years and the wear and tear. He is to the point where he uses Preparation H on the bags under this eyes to "shrink them up a mite." He used to put his teeth in a glass of Efferdent at night, but now he just throws a tablet in his mouth each morning and shakes his head. He is suffering from Dunlap Disease: His belly has done lapped over his belt buckle. But he still has an opinion on just about everything and he writes an occasional column for the Uncertain Times.)

Well, the world is in one helluva mess.

I said that during WWII. Or maybe it was later I said it.

I said that during the Korean War, which the politicians called a "conflict" on account they couldn't justify nor afford a war.

I said that during Vietnam.

And I said that the entire eight years Clinton was president.

Heckfire, I even said that when the only two choices we had for president back in Ought-Ought was Junior Bush and Albert Gore's dumbest son.

It gets pretty durn bad when all you got to vote for as leader of the free world are the offspring of two old, worn-out (in the case of one of them, dead) politicians.

And I say it again: The world is in a helluva mess.

Let's get one thing straight right off: I'm not afraid of anthrax or terrorists. I decided that I wouldn't be afraid of anything I can't see. And since half my relatives can't seem to find my house, I don't think terrorists are going to spend too much time looking for me either.

It's all a matter of what I used to call substance over fantasy until I got too old to remember to call it that.

I kinda abide by the O'Hara philosophy of dealing with trouble. Scarlett O'Hara. The Gone With the Wind hellion. Well, she had the right idea: "I'll just think about it tomorrow." Do that long enough and just about every problem or trouble goes away.

Worked for me real good on Wife No. 2. I kept thinking about what to do with her and one day I came back from a bowling tournament and she was gone.

Now Wife No. 3 is a different story. Can't get shed of her for shucks! She's one of those women that if I packed up and left, she'd pack up her stuff and tail me out of the house.

Saves us both a mess of trouble if I just stay put.

Anyway, this war on terrorism is plumb wearing me out. I get tired of watching them little bombs shooting out of pipes every night on television. I get tired of hearing about body counts and listening to politicians try and excuse it all.

UNCERTAIN TIMES

And I get tired of commentators commentating on what happened that day and guessing what's going to happen tomorrow.

And I'm real tired of hearing about anthrax and botulism and watching them people with turbans dancing in dusty streets burning our flag in one picture and then going to pick up free U.S. food packets we hand out like Cheese Whiz in a welfare line.

You know, some folks really believe in the ideals of the good ol' USofA. Remember when we went bombing the bejeezus out of Afghanistan and Iraq after the Muslim maniacs used four airliners as missiles and killed more than 3,000 people here?

Now this is the weird part: After all that happened, we dump more than 50,000 food packets across those countries and are still sending in food in trucks to both countries right now. I've seen those people gobbling up that U.S.A food like it's a Happy Meal with two free prizes in every sack instead of one!

My neighbor Maure Finley said that is the dumbest thing he has ever seen. He said, "If the situation were reversed, and midflicked Afghanistan or gaphacked Iraq was bombing us with their one, good, gitblathered biplane, and they dropped pre-packaged rice curry or squatgnatted camel meat down here in East Texas, who would take a chance and eat it?"

He's got a point.

There's also something wrong with watching Americans at war in some foreign country from your living room one minute and, quicker than Dan Rather can get a new hair-do, the next you are watching a commercial for a feminine hygiene product. Don't matter which product. They all look as scary as the war pictures to me.

I didn't know too much about those things when I was younger, and I don't need to know anything about them now.

The only commercial that I give one hoot in Hades about now is the one that makes Bob Dole look like a smiling idiot while he holds up a little diamond-shaped blue pill.

I asked Maw if she thought I ought to give that Viagra a try. She fixed me with a look similar to the one she gave Bessie the milk cow when she put a manure-encrusted foot in the pail (Bessie, not Maw) and said,

"Do what you want. But don't include me in any of your sex schemes."
Some things never change.
That's the same line she's been using for the past thirty years.

Yours 'til next time,

Millard Ghormley

I was chuckling at the end, wondering if at what age I might need Viagra. Maybe I'll get Widder's opinion.

Don't think it, Bob. It was a joke.

7:25.

I got a pair of scissors and cut out the Ghormley column and put it in a side pocket of one of the two soft-sided briefcases I always carried on assignment.

The boys back in New York won't believe this, I thought.

I tha-think he wri-writes good.

Well. I think he writes well.

Mah-me too.

Going out the front door, I turned right instead of left toward Widder's and went to the side of my house where a dogwood was in full bloom next to a flowering red bud. My Swiss Army knife easily sawed through a couple of dogwood limbs and three red bud limbs well-clustered with blossoms. Adding one sprig of wisteria invigorated all of the colors.

Sha-she's got all that in hah-her yard.

It's the thought that counts, Bob. You, of all psyches, should know about that.

Walking around to the front of Widder's house, I felt like Alfalfa trying to get a date with Darla; I stood at her door and slicked down my hair with one hand.

Before I had a chance to knock, the wooden frame door with the large window swung open.

"Wondered if you were going to make it," Widder said.

"If I'm late, I'm sorry. If I'm early, I'm sorry," I said. "We didn't set a time but Bob... I mean, I thought you got up early."

"Six o'clock seldom sees me in bed," she said, throwing open the screen. "Come in."

It took a couple of seconds for my eyes to adjust to the dark interior. The view was well worth the wait.

Widder was standing in the hall, left hand hanging by her side, the right folded behind her with her right hand holding her left elbow. She was wearing a white, slick-type t-shirt with a pocket, dark blue slacks, and white sandals. Her hair was down and pulled back from her face with two hair clips that could have been made from oyster shell or plastic made to look like oyster shell.

She was looking down slightly and watched me with her eyes rolled upward slightly upward.

I let my eyes move over her body and saw the clear imprint of her nipples embossed on the t-shirt surface.

"Let me shut the door," I said, "You must be getting cold."

Tha-that's jah-just dumb!

I know. God, I know.

"It *is* getting a bit chilly in here," she said and a hint of a smile touched her lips. She crossed her arms. "Come on in the kitchen. The coffee's ready."

I took a second to glance around the entryway. A small shelf to the right of the door held an antique mantle clock and a small framed pressed flower. An old secretary's table was under the shelf and a Japanese-style vase of fresh flowers added color to the darkened room. Two books that looked fairly new were set to the left of the vase and a single pin from am antique Parlor Ten Pin set was set next to the books as sort of a *faux* bookend.

Across the hall was a low-slung antique day-bed and over it was a watercolor of a patchwork quilt draped casually over a high-backed rocking chair.

"Coming?"

Following the sound of her voice, I turned to the right and went through a small sitting room that seemed crowded with old, overstuffed furniture and through a doorway to the left that led to the sun-filled kitchen.

"Sorry. I was just looking around. I can see you like antiques."

"The past sometimes gives us a look at the future. Some things were better in the past and never should have been changed."

"That's true."

She cocked an eyebrow. "How so?"

"I, uh, was just agreeing with you."

"Do you do that often?" she asked.

"Do what?"

"Agree with women."

Musing for half-a-heartbeat: "Every chance I get."

A big smile. "I like that in a man."

Walking to the counter, she said, "Cream? Sugar?"

"A little of both, please. But here, I can do that."

"I don't get to wait on a man very often. Sit and I'll fix your coffee." It was not a suggestion. An order. A nice one.

She poured the coffee from the plastic electric percolator with four or five small, pastel flowers running around the top. I studied her closely as she added sugar from a soda fountain shaker and milk or cream from a small pewter pitcher. It seemed that her accent and speech patterns were decidedly different than earlier conversations. Smooth, no East Texas drawl overtones.

I studied her face, which looked scrubbed. Almost shiny. She had on a little make-up I guessed, but could not be sure; that meant she was very good at it or my eyes were going. She didn't use eye-liner. A sprinkling of freckles slide across the top of her cheeks and across her nose. Didn't recall seeing them before. Her lips were thin, and shiny with just a hint of neutral lip gloss.

She was not beautiful and sultry in the lingerie catalog kind of way. But she definitely had something special that caused people to look. She seemed to suck the air right out of a confined space.

I guess I took a big breath, because she looked up sharply and knitted her eyebrows. "Are you okay?"

"Sure. I think I just forgot to breathe."

She grinned, crinkled her nose, shook her head.

Yah-you are so sma-smooth.

"Thank you, Wid... Celestial!"

That smile again. "For what?" she said as she started to walk over the small wooden kitchen table with a tray with two tiny cups sat on matching saucers.

"Oh, for inviting me for coffee."

"You look like a big coffee travel mug type of guy to me," she said, pointing to a chair, directing me to sit. "I hope these little cups are okay."

"Actually, I do drink most of my coffee from travel mugs. Seems I don't have many opportunities to drink from real china."

"Imitation china, I'm sure," she said, "but I bought them at an estate sale and I really like the pattern."

The tiny cups were decorated in a traditional Blue Willow pattern, with a Japanese garden, a stream, the necessary willow tree and a couple of blue swallows or doves or Chinese vultures hovering over the stream.

I took a tentative sip. She laughed at my expression.

"What was that look?"

"I, well, I guess I'm surprised. I've been all over the world and I don't think I've ever had a better tasting coffee. Unbelievably rich. Smooth. It's great! Of course, I'm comparing it to the Folger's I brew every day at the house. Even though I put a bit of Lusianne with chicory in it to give it a bite, it's pretty ordinary."

Another sip had me shaking my head.

"This is very, very good coffee."

She gave a little curtsy, grabbing the ends of an imaginary skirt and bending ever so slightly at the knees. "Thank you, O' World Traveler."

"What brand is it?"

"I don't think you've ever heard of it."

"Try me."

"Guess."

Smiling, I shook my head. "Do you know how many coffee plantations there are in the world? Don't tell me you grow your own beans on one of the islands in the lake?"

Her smile matched mine. "Nope, not even close. It's actually from a little plantation in Costa Rica."

"Café Britt? Doka Estate?"

"My, you are a world traveler. Close in distance, but not in taste."

She got up and walked across the kitchen to a small cabinet, opened and withdrew a small, silver bag. I watched her backside as it glide-bounced to the cabinet.) On the return trip, I looked at her eyes. While thinking about her backside.

She put the bag on the table. Café Tres Generaciones. AAA Peaberry. I studied the label. In small letters, near the bottom were the words "Doka Estate." Inwardly I grinned.

"Why are you smiling?"

"Oh, nothing. I've never heard of this plantation. Where did you hear about it?"

"I spend a lot of time on the Internet and I came across Tres Generaciones (she said the words smoothly but with a mild twang). I read up on the plantation and got them to send me a two pound tester order. Been getting a regular quarterly shipment ever since."

"Internet? You spend a lot of time on the Internet?"

"Just because I live on Caddo and isolate myself because it's my choice does not mean I don't want to know more about what's going on in the rest of the world." Her voice had an edge to it.

Crawfishing time in Texas. "I'm sorry. That was an insensitive remark. I didn't mean anything by it. Swear."

There was a sewing basket on the back side of the table. I quickly opened it up and plucked a needle from a pin cushion. "Here," offering her the needle. "Stick this in my eye. I'm a brute and I deserve it!"

Jab-jesus!

She grabbed the needle out of my hand, pointed it at me in a theatrical fashion.

"Stick a needle in your eye!" she said, shaking her head. By the time the chuckles had subsided, the coffee was cold. She picked up both cups, poured out the dregs in the sink and picked up the coffee pot.

"If you don't mind, I'd like to try this cup black."

With a sideways glance and an imperceptible nod, she refilled the cups, brought them over and sat down.

She casually propped her chin in her left hand.

"So, tell me about yourself."

"That's about as open-ended a question as I've ever heard. I'll make you a deal, tell me about you first and then I'll talk about me."

She sat there for a spell before she started talking. Born in California, married at seventeen to a pipefitter, had two sons within two years. Her husband died, leaving some insurance money. She picked up the boys and moved to Caddo Lake more than fifteen years ago and moved into the house that had been the homestead of her late paternal grandparents. Her sons were twenty-one and twenty; one was in the Air Force, stationed in South Texas; the other attended a small college in Kentucky on a scholarship, part academic, part soccer.

"I know your name is Celestial Gleason, but is Celestial your first or middle name?"

"Middle."

"Maiden name?"

"McLaughlin."

"Okay, here's a game I like to play. Your first name starts with a letter in the first part of the alphabet, from about L or M forward, probably A to E."

Her face screwed up in an expression of intense concentration. "It does. How'd you know that?"

"I don't know. It's a game I've been playing since college. I had to write a paper and the assignment was to come up with an original theory. Somehow I came up with the name deal and it seems to work about eighty percent of the time.

"So," I said, "what's your first name?"

"If you're so smart, guess."

"That's not part of the game."

"It is now."

"Nope, can't do it. Too many names, not enough time. I would say, though, that it starts with a C or D."

Again, the screwed-up face.

"C."

"Camille? Camille Celestial McLaughlin?"

Smile…and a shake of her head.

"Candace?"

Dead square miss.

"What is it?"

"Charlena."

"Charlene Celestial McLaughlin?"

"Not Charlene. Charlen—ah!"

"Charlena Celestial? Did your parents hate you when you were born?"

"They didn't, I don't think. I was named after two maiden great-aunts who had money. My parents thought they might cash in playing their own version of the name game. Eventually, my aunts died, leaving cash and property to a non-profit organization."

Pretending to think about that, I said, "I guess that was nice."

"Yes, I hear the Bide-a-Wee Pet Cemetery in Carmel is really a very nice place to put Fido or Fluffy."

My face was split by a smile-plank. "They gave the money to a pet cemetery?"

"I went there once to see where the family fortunes went. I've got a picture of the entrance if you'd like to see it?" she said.

"Now, okay, how'd you get your name?"

"Jones? Well, Charlena Celestial, my great-great-grandfather was Heinrich Johannsen and when he came through Ellis Island...."

Waving off the story with a flick of her hand, she said, "You know what I mean. Adnijio Benjamin Franklin Jones. Not your everyday name, now is it?"

"I was actually named for a Scrabble word."

"No!"

"Yes. Dad was playing in an anything-goes Scrabble game in St. Louis when he put down six letters connecting with the 'I' in 'peninsula'—adnijio. Another player bet him fifty dollars there was no such word and Pop convinced him there was, thus winning the bet."

"I've never heard of the word. Is it really a word?"

"It is now," I said. "Pop told him that 'adnijio' was a Greek musical instrument that was kin to a Turkish musical instrument, the 'lerter.'"

"Lerter?"

"That's not a word either. But Pop told the guy that he liked the word 'adnijio' so much that it was what he was going to name his first-born son.

UNCERTAIN TIMES

I was born three days later and I was named 'Adnijio' after a fictional musical instrument from Greece and 'Benjamin Franklin' for the dead president on the fifty dollar bill Pop won in the bet."

"You are lying!"

"Why would I lie about something like that? Where did I get that name then?"

She pursed her mouth and knitted her forehead. "I think Adnijio is a nickname for 'Admonition.' You remind me of a mild, kind, yet earnest reproof. I believe that's the proper definition. I also think you should be cause for a cautionary warning."

Wha-what does she do? Sah-sit around and read the deh-dictionary?

"Cautionary warning, eh? Actually, I kind of like that. It makes me appear dangerous of something."

"From what I heard about your confrontation with the Ledbetter brothers yesterday, you may not be dangerous, but you could certainly be in danger. And it's a fact that you are not very smart."

"You heard about that? How'd you hear about that?"

She just sat there, looking at me and shaking her head. "Where do you think you are? This is Uncertain, Texas, population 100 and something. Everybody knows everything that happens around here. I had four phone calls within an hour after you got back yesterday. Mr. Jones...."

"Adj, please."

"...Adj. The Ledbetters are not nice people. They are bullies, at least Harmony is, and since Bother is mind-melded to him, they both are on the stupid side of dangerous."

"I've found that bullies, for the most part, are cowards. When confronted...."

"They sneak around at night in the rain and try to kill dogs."

"There's that. I'm planning on taking care of that today."

"By doing what?"

"I'm going to the sheriff's office and file a complaint."

She gave me a dumber-than-a-burned-stump look. "Adj, you're not from around here. The rules for home folks are different than they are for other people. The chief deputy for the county is Bill Ledbetter, Harmony and Bother's uncle. Sheriff Twiddle is married to their first cousin, Letta

Lynn. They are on the inside; you are on the outside. It's a fight you can't win."

I mulled that over, sipping the last inch of coffee from the tiny cup.

"Sometimes it's not winning that matters. Sometimes you just have to come out even."

Wha-what the hell does that mah-mean?

"What does that mean?" Widder said.

"I don't know exactly. I was trying to sound sophisticated and manly."

No smile. No laugh. Just a quick shake of her head.

Glancing at the clock, I was surprised at the time: 9:06.

"Look at the time, I'm sure I've overstayed my welcome…"

"Not at all. I've enjoyed talking to you. So, what's your plans for the day? Going to the lake to shoot some photos?"

"Nope. Taking the day off. Want to keep an eye on Moosie and just relax. Yesterday was a tough day all around. Today, though, has started off rather nicely."

I got up and started toward the front door. I stopped, turned and looked at Widder: "Would you like to get some breakfast at Hum's?"

She shook her head slowly. "Not a good idea. People would talk. Besides, it's way past breakfast time."

"Lunch?"

"Goodbye, Adj."

Then I remembered something else: "Do you have a piece of chalk, by any chance?"

"A piece of chalk? What for?"

"Well, I went by the Poem Board last night coming back from Doc's and there was a good poem on it, but the rain was starting to do a number on it. I just wanted to make sure it's still on there. By the way, how long has the board been up there?"

Widder said, "Only about a year or so. One day it was up there, wired to the tree, and a poem was on it."

She went to a old school desk set along the entryway back wall and rummaged around for a short time, finally withdrawing a short piece of light blue chalk.

"This do?"

I nodded and pocketed the chalk.

"I do have one more question for you before you go," she said. "Which do you prefer to be called, 'Photo Man,' 'Smart Brain or 'Rural Community....'"

That's as far as she got before she saw the look on my face and had to lean against the entryway wall to hold herself up as the laughter slapped the back of her teeth in syncopated swells.

13

Most liars are dumb. Those that aren't, are dangerous.

Anonymous

Walking away from Widder's house I could have been walking on tiny clouds; my step was that light and the feeling was that special.
Eh-it's just that you've been coo-cooped up too long.
Could be, Bob, could be.
I walked the normal route to what passed for downtown and ended up at the Poem Board. Three men I knew by sight but not by name were standing around the board, obscuring it from view as I came across the pasture and crossed the fence, road and ditch.
"Good morning," I hello-ed. "New poem?"
"Don't know," one elderly man wearing faded overalls and a brown felt hat said. "Rain got it."
"It's different, I'd say," one of his companions said. "Length seems off from yesterday."
I walked over toward board and they parted obligingly. There were a few words scattered here and there, and more than a few partial words, but the overall literary effort was incomprehensible. I pulled a handkerchief out of my back pocket and wiped the board. Pulling the chalk and a scrap of paper out of my front left pants

pocket, I started writing. The men didn't say a word until I had finished.

No noise assails me
Except for the krick-krick of the fire.
No wind blows through the trees....

Must be the silence of the limbs.

"So, you're the feller writing them words every day," the third man said, looking me up and down.

"Cain't be," another man piped up. "He ain't be around here long enough."

"No, sir, it's not me." I said. "I just liked this poem. Read it and copied it down early this morning."

"I just don't get this one. It don't make no sense."

I started off explaining about puns and how "silence of the limbs" was a play on words from a movie, but their faces.... I settled for, "This one is pretty deep at that."

"That your big dog that was poisoned last night?" one of them asked.

Hah-how'd they....?

Small town, Bob. Real, real small town.

"Yeah, but she's fine. Doc fixed her up."

"Heard you fixed him up first. Doc told a feller who told me you gave your dog a couple of doses of mustard and probably saved his life."

"Her. Moosie is a bitch. She's seems to be doing fine."

"Anybody that'd poison a dog is just plumb low-down," one man said. The other two nodded in abject agreement.

"So," the tallest of the men said, "you didn't write this here writing?"

"No sir, I just copied it down last night and rewrote it so folks could read it."

"So," the same man said again, "you gonna fight Harmony and Bother?"

I assured them I was not going to fight anyone. It wasn't my nature or my style.

"Hurrrumph," one hurrumphed. "It's about the only nature or style them two have. Well, one anyways. The other one's so dumb he'd shit in his hand." The others nodded like those toothpick-stabbing metal woodpeckers for sale in truck stops along interstate highways.?
They introduced themselves—Hy, Thompson, and Glenn Alan ("Three N's, two L's")—and offered their hands.

Leaving the men standing at the Poem Board, I headed to Hum's. He was behind the counter, scraping the grill. Five men were in the back booth, drinking coffee. "Sorry I'm late, Hum. Got hung up this morning. Is it too late for breakfast?"

"Hmmm," he hummed as he snatched down some eggs and spatulaed some bacon, moving three slices from the back of the grill to the hot middle. In less than two minutes, he slid my usual breakfast in front of me and I dug in with vigor.

"Good, Hum. Excellent."

"Hmmm."

The front door creaked. By the look on Hum's face, I knew it wasn't Ed McMahon with a big check. I didn't turn around but Bob *tah-told* me later I hunched my shoulders a bunch and tensed up more than a mite.

"Well, well, well, look who's here. If it ain't Big City Smart Mouth," Harmony said in his distinctive sandpaper-on gravel-voice. "How you doing, Big City Smart Mouth? Or better yet, how's that big dawg of yourn?"

Remembering what Daddy George had once told me—"There's a time and a place for everything. Smart people pick the time and the place."—I sat there, stone-still, except for shoveling food in my mouth. Didn't taste it. Just chewed and swallowed.

"Look, Bother," Harmony said, "Big City Smart Mouth has done and gone deaf on us. I asked him how his big dawg was and he didn't answer. Maybe he don't got no dawg no more."

Twin hee-haws of forced laughter slammed against my back. The noise was like two water buzzards fighting over a fish.

I turned slowly and looked directly at Harmony. No words. Just sat on the stool, staring.

Out of the corner of my eye, I saw Hum ease into the kitchen. I hoped to God there was a phone back there and he was calling someone who might be interested in not seeing someone get killed. The five men in the corner were quiet; all ten eyes turned toward us.

"What's the matter, Big City Smart Mouth? Ain't so Smart Mouth this morning. Cat…or daid dawg…got your tongue?"

"You're out of the loop, Disharmony. Moosie is fine. Fit as a fiddle. Whatever poison you used was old and gone to seed. Didn't work. You're so dumb you can't even poison a dog right."

"Old? It wasn't old. Why, I…." Then he caught himself, and his voice jumped up a couple of octaves. "You think you're so damn smart! Your dawg be daid! You so dumb you don't even know a daid dawg from a live one!"

"Damn, Disharmony. Get the words right. It's 'dead dog.' Not 'Daid da-hog.' Makes you sound all hickified and redneckish. But think whatever you want to, Disharmony. What you think or what you do don't mean shit to me."

Showing more bravado than I was feeling, I turned back to my plate and shoveled in a big helping of eggs. I hoped, like Bob, that I could keep them down.

Bother: "Why's he keep calling you Dish Hahmony, Hahmony?"

Harmony growled in response, "Shut the fuck up, Bother!" I could see the brothers in the mirror on the wall to the left of the grill. They were just staring: Harmony at me, Bother at Harmony.

Harmony nodded his head and they both hit the door, nearly tearing the screen off its hinges in the process.

I let a breath whoosh out that I had been holding since the last decade.

The men at the back table began to whisper. Hum came in from the kitchen.

"Call the sheriff?" I asked.

"Hmmm."

"Think he'll come? And, if he does, think it'll do any good?"

"Humm."

This time, with this situation, in this town, Hum and I were in perfect agreement.

I finished my breakfast in short order, told Hum I didn't need the sack lunch today, that I was taking the day off but that I'd probably be back for lunch later.

"What's the special today?"

"Hmmm."

Yah-your favorite.

Just so it wouldn't seem like I was running off to hide, which is exactly what my head and feet had been planning, I walked to the back and asked the men if I could pull up a chair. "I've got some thoughts on how we can all work together to help the economy, secure world peace, and make sure the Lingerie Bowl is a permanent part of sports broadcasting."

They welcomed me into the think-tank. For the next 20 minute or so, the group—me listening, them talking—decided that if a Republican didn't win the next presidential election, then a Democrat would. They also agreed that Reagan was a better president than actor and that having Movie Moses as head of the National Rifle Association was the smartest PR move since the real Moses made sure that parting-of-the-sea bit made the final edition of the Bible.

I finally thanked them for their hospitality and hollered at Hum, who was somewhere in the back of the café, as I dropped a wad of crumpled dollar bills on the counter. I marched out, making sure my back was straight and my gait steady.

There was no sight of the Ledbetters' truck. I thought about going home and checking on Moosie, but figured even Harmony and Bother weren't dumb enough to go to my house in broad daylight. I headed north on the road. I figured a long walk would do me good.

The entrance to "Harlan's Gro. and Sta." was about fifty yards down the road. Two old pumps sans credit card slide-ins, sat out front. A straight-across porch was flanked with several old, wooden soft drink crates and two cane-bottomed chairs. Usually all are occupied by members of the local fiddle-and-whittle club but with a brisk off-the-lake wind blowing, the early morning nippy air had probably driven them inside.

Or, maybe, Rayon Finnigan was holding court. Rayon was the town storyteller. The first time we met, he found out I was from New York and wanted me to find him a "first-rate legal lawyering fella" to represent him in a lawsuit against fabric companies that were using his first name "to make clothing and some such."

He had, he said, a good legal case for "name infringement." I told him I would check on it.

That first meeting he told me and anyone within hearing distance about an idea he had for manufacturing buzzard wing ceiling fans. "Materials is cheap," he said, "and those fans would raise quite a wind storm."

I opened the screen door and stepped inside. It was dark and cool. Four men were sitting around a checkerboard set on a hand-made slat-board table. Harlan Harlingen, the store owner and operator, was waiting on a bonneted lady who lived three or four houses the other side of me. Miss Baxter? I acknowledged everyone with a single umbrella howdy, and nodded to Miss Baxter.

I found an empty Dr Pepper crate one aisle over by the magazine rack and dragged it over to the edge of the table and sat down.

Rayon looked at me to make sure I was settled and said, "I'm glad to hear your dog is going to be fine. As I was saying: Did I ever tell you about Johnson T. Boyles's youngest son, Percival, who we all called Pusy?"

Everybody head-swung in the negative and Miss Baxter decided she had business elsewhere, leaving the store like her dress was on fire.

"First off, it ain't pronounced the way you think it is, but in the running sore sort of way. Well, Pusy wanted to go in business for hisself instead of being a flower box painter for the Garden Spot Flower Box Company over to Waskom. He was pretty good at painting flower boxes if he had only straight colors or if the design was nothing more than a dandelion or petunia. Anything exotic like a English rose or a tattered-edge violet and he would have to throw down a dose of laudanum or three just to keep his hands from shaking. He had a good case of the nervouses, is what he had.

"Anyway, Pusy decided to open him up a store, a sort of combo taxidermy and income tax emporium. He said he knew enough about income taxes since he paid them regular, and he was learning taxidermy out of a county extension club brochure, *Taxidermy and You, The Ins and Outs of Innards*.

"He thought the idea of two businesses was a good one. He had seen an article about 'diversification'" in *Mind Your Own Business* magazine. That was put out by his cousin-in-law's brother, Jay Ned Powellette. His name weren't really Jay Ned. It was Jed Ned. But he couldn't abide people hollering out JED NED, so he shortened up the Jed to J. and added a "ay." I heard one of the uncles, Uncle Jed, I believe, cut him slap dab out of his will. He didn't have nothing to give away when he was jerked to Jesus, but it was the principal of the thing."

He stopped and took a swig from a half-empty ROC bottle.

"Pusy had a name picked out and everything for his business. It was, as I recollect, *Pusy's Permanent Critters and Income Tax Service*. When the sign guy came by to put up his sign on the mobile home he bought at the sheriff's auction a while back, Pusy showed him where the sign would go and what size he wanted it and what it would say. Then Pusy went to do his laundry at his mama's. Which meant he took it to her and left it there while he had a beer at Poole's Pool Hall.

"I just realized this story is getting longer than Rev. Waldo P. Weiner's sermon on the mount. You might remember that one. It was about Lady Godiva and her horse and how too many men have gone to Hell just wishing they had been that horse."

I realized I was shaking my head. Nervous twitch.

Bob was not amused. *Jah-jesus!*

"So, Pusy got through beering at Poole's and bee-lined home. His sign was done but somehow the sign guy misunderstood what he was supposed to do and this is what the sign said: Pussy's Pematu Crackers and Incon Tack Serbus.

"Oh, did I mention Pusy had a hairlip and lisp-ped something terrible?

"Anyway, Pusy made him come back and redo the sign, but he could only negotiate a eight-letter renewal deal. The final sign said: Pusy's Critters and Incom Tack Servus. He got the sign guy to wipe out "prematu" as one letter.

"He said he did not have a problem with the final version since it was mostly correct. The only problem he has had is to tell Mr. Boy Don Dilkins the Three-I one hundred and eleven times that he don't sell saddles and bridles. The fact Mr. Boy Don don't have a horse does not seem to be the point. 'Tack is tack' he would yell every time he would pass Pusy's shop.

"And every time, Pusy would yell back" 'Taxes, you damn fool. Taxes.'"

All the men politely snickered. A couple slapped their legs.

"That's a good'un, Rayon," one man said. "That's a good'un."

Thanking Rayon for the story, I went over to Harlan and told him I needed a few things and rattled off a short list, which included dog treats, couple cans each of green beans and corn—kernel, not creamed—a bar of soap, head of lettuce, a tomato, four thick slices of sandwich bologna, two big slices of Monterrey Jack cheese and a loaf of wheat bread.

He wrote down the items and said, "Need a good pocket pistol?"

Wha-wha....

"Excuse me?"

"Pocket pistol. Carrying gun. I've got a good .32 and a .38. Let you have them cheap. Can even borrow them if you've a mind to."

"No, no, thank you. Just the groceries will be fine."

Harlan nodded and went to get a box and gather up my order.

Why on earth would he think....

Ha-harmony and....

You're probably right, Bob. You're probably right. Jesus! This *is* a small town!

I didn't want to tote the groceries home on foot so I told Harlan I would be back with the car. "Need to fill up anyway."

I was at the door when Rayon started another story. I needed a laugh in the worse way, so I plopped back down and settled in.

"Ya'll heard the story about the horrible accident that my Uncle Bubba had? Well, in case you did and forgot it, Uncle Bubba is the daddy to my Cousin Bubba. Anyway, he broke both his kneecaps in a tractor wreck. Durn thing flipped over on him as he was trying out his new six-row planter. Just so happened the sixth row was over a drainage ditch and Uncle Bubba lost his traction, not to mention his tractor, and the thing turned over on top of him. Cousin Bubba went to the scene and found his daddy's tractor was in pretty bad shape.

"Uncle Bubba's knees were mangled, crushed and broken and they called in a kneeologist from Shreveport name of Sinjin or Sinjin or something like that. He's a foreigner; his wife has one o' them red dots on her head.

"Now, the story goes Doc Sinjin had just received new bifocals and couldn't get his eyes focused properly so during the operation he attached all the good parts of Uncle Bubba's knees backwards. They now hinge toward the front. He is going to be able to walk, but he'll need a mirror to see where he's going since he now walks backwards. And sitting in a chair is a tad difficult, because he has to sit face first. The family don't eat out much because not many places have a counter high enough. The only one that has a high counter is the Neck of the Woods Cafetorium on the east side of the lake, but to get there you have to take a boat. Boat-sitting with backward kneecaps is not something Uncle Bubba has mastered yet."

He stopped and took a swig of Mr. Pibb.

"It could be worse, I suppose. He could have really screwed up his tractor."

I couldn't resist: "Your Uncle Bubba had his kneecaps reconnected backwards?"

"Boy, that shows you was listening. Anyway, Cousin Bubba doesn't like hospitals so he just waved to his daddy from the parking lot while Uncle Bubba was confined. Cousin Bubba can't stand the smell of that hospital antiseptic or whatever that gag-smell is.

"Wait a minute!" he said. "I just had a stray thought. Is something that is antiseptic, *against* septic?"

We all exchanged looks. The kind of looks condemned prisoners shyly slide to one another on execution day.

Rayon took a deep breath and plowed on, switching gears faster than Dale Earnhart Jr. at Turn 3 at Darlington.

"Papa has been trying to figure out a way to speed up the rotation of the earth and tilt it slightly on its axis to keep America in perpetual sunlight to 'darken out all them Commies,' as he puts it. Plus, he figured, by having sunlight all the time, he could not bring in three crops a year instead of the one he never does bring in now.

UNCERTAIN TIMES

"Mama and me pointed out the problems with that venture, however." He started ticking off numbers on his fingers.

"One, with perpetual sunlight, roosters wouldn't know when to crow.

"Two, Jay Leno would be on in the middle of the day.

"Three, it would really kill the drive-in theater business.

"Four, instead of plant workers having day, swing and graveyard shifts, they would have day, day and day shifts. No one would know when to show up.

"Five, what would we do without a Saturday night?

"And, six, it would change our language something terrible. Here's a example of a conversation between two buddies:

"Where are you going today?"
"You mean 'today' today or 'tonight' today?"
"'Today' today."
"I don't know. What time is it?"
"Nine o'clock."
"A.M. or P.M.?"
"What difference does it make?"

"See what a hassle that would be?" Rayon said, pulling a two Adam's-apple-bobbing gulp from his soda.

"Papa finally saw the light of day about that proposal and withdrew his request to speak to the joint Houses of Congress," Rayon said.

Not a word was spoken. We all looked at each other for the umpteenth time since the story got in high gear. In a move that could have been choreographed by Tommy Tune, every man-jack stood, said mutual goodbyes, waved gaily, and quit the store.

Proof positive that sometimes you can get too much of a good thing.

14

An oxymoron has nothing to do with cattle and idiots, with certain exceptions, of course.

Anonymous

The day was gorgeous and not even that last gawdawful Rayon story could diminish the sense of rightness that comes from a spring day smelling crisp from a nice rain mixed with the heady smell of wild flowers.

I had just stepped onto the county road out of Harlan's parking lot and was so engrossed with looking at the living potpourri along the roadside ditches that I didn't hear the car approaching.

The blast of a siren stopped my heart and created an involuntary slam-down, hard-pucker of the anus.

Fah-fuc…!

"Jesus!" I screamed as I jumped about a foot straight up.

At least I thought it was straight up. I landed in mid-ditch, which was about eight feet sideways from where I had been standing.

A blue-and-white car squatted in the middle of the road. It had an expensive set of gumballs on top and a blue-and-silver logo on the front door closest to me: "Sheriff, Harrison County."

There was a man sitting behind the wheel. He looked big—full-grown cow big—and he was laughing something fierce. He had on mirrored, wraparound sunglasses; a well-chewed toothpick hung from the left side of his mouth. His face was well-padded and looked like a pasty sofa pillow. His big red nose was in the approximate position of a pillow button. Attached slightly off center.

"Something funny?" I asked rhetorically.

He shook his head and stopped laughing long enough to blurt out: "Man, I wish you could have seen you jump? It was truly something special." Then he commenced to laugh again. It was not a jovial sound. It was the laughter of Praetorian guards as they made fun of Christians being hauled out to the Coliseum to entertain a few lions.

"Glad you liked it. Consider the preceding act my contribution to the local law enforcement ball," I said, climbing out of the ditch. He stopped laughing and the sunglasses stared mean at me. "I heard you were Mr. Smart Mouth. What I heard was right, I reckon."

"You must be Sheriff Twiddle."

"Yep, and you are Mr. Smart Mouth, a.k.a., Adj Jones from Atlanta. Georgia. Not Texas."

"I guess you're here because of me being harassed by Harmony and Bother Ledbetter."

"Well, not exactly. I'm here because those same two local citizens have filed a complaint against you for harassing them."

Ah-a joke, right?

"Not now, Bob."

"Name's Johnnie, not Bob. Sheriff Johnnie Twiddle to you. And I'm the one that'll be giving the orders, not you, that's for durn sure."

"I'm sorry, I was just thinking out loud. What's this about Harmony and Bother filing a complaint against me?"

"Yep, called it in just a while back. They said you were badmouthing them, cussing and all and that you threatened them with bodily harm."

I just stood there, looking in the window, not saying much. Not breathing much either. In situations like this, if I breathe I tend to get riled more than a smidgeon.

"Well?"

"Well, what, Sheriff?"

"What's you got to say for yourself?"

"About what?"

He opened his door and got out, hauling a dark blue Mountie hat the size of a tractor seat with him. He took his sweet time to unhinge and stand up and adjust his hat on his head. It was one of the biggest heads I'd ever seen this side of a National Geographic special on elephants. He was on the north side of six-foot-five and would not have been described as lean by any stretch of the imagination. He might be soft in some places; he looked tough and hard in most of the others.

While he was getting out and adjusting, I noticed that there was a gaggle of spectators standing on Harlan's porch. Just standing. Staring.

"Let's finish this conversation down at the jail," Sheriff Twiddle said.

"Sheriff, I'm a newcomer to the area and I know that the Ledbetters live here, but those two poisoned my dog last night...."

"Poisoned your dog, you say? Last night, huh? Of course, you reported it right away as an eyewitness to the crime?"

"No, I was coming in today to report it. But...."

"And you saw the Ledbetters poison your dog. Is that what you're saying?"

"They poisoned my dog. During the storm last night I saw this shadow cast by lightning...."

"Let me get this straight. You want to press charges against a shadow and claim it was the Ledbetters?"

"Sheriff, listen, I know you are related to Harmony and Bother...."

"Stop right there! Are you saying that because of my relations, I might not uphold the law to the best of my 'bility?"

"No, I think you do the best of your 'bility, but what I'm trying to say is...."

"First thing off, don't say one other gawddamned word. Second thing, shut up now and keep that smart mouth of yours shut. I do the talking here, not you. I'm the law, gawddamit, and I will give the orders.

"First order for you is to leave the Ledbetter boys alone and quit harassing them. Second order is...well, I can't remember the second order. Oh, yeah, if you do harass them boys again, I'll arrest you good and proper. And I've got just the cellmate in mind for you. Around these parts we call him Fudge-packer Higgins, if you get my meaning."

I thought of about two dozen snappy comebacks that would cut him off at the knees and leave him in the road with bloody stumps. Bob reminded me that *Twah-Twiddle* was toting a big-ass gun. All I had for weapons were some goathead stickers on my pants from my jump in the ditch.

He took off that thirty-five-pound hat and got back in the car and drove off slowly, scanning me with those sunglasses as he passed.

Damn! His head is huge! I'm not having a good day, Bob. First Harmony and Bother. Now Sheriff Twiddledeedumb.

Yah-you're not doing such....

I was pissed and didn't have the patience to wait on Bob.

I know, Bob. I am not doing a very good job of winning friends and influencing people.

It took about five minutes longer than usual to get home. I kept stopping and staring at the clear sky and thinking how'd I get in this mess and how'd I get out of it short of packing up my gear and heading east.

I was passing in front of Widder's when she came out on the porch and waved me in. I opened the gate and walked up close. Not to hear her, necessarily. Because I wanted to. She said, "You just can't stay out of trouble, can you?"

"Good news travels fast around here, that's for sure."

"What'd the sheriff want?"

"He wanted to welcome me to town and to commend me on my ability to mingle and get along with the local folks. I also think he said something about my incredible talent as a picture-taker."

She put her hand up, cupping her chin. "Hmmm."

"That's exactly what Hum said." She tried to hold it in, but a smile finally found its way to her lips.

"Don't take the Ledbetters or Twiddle for granted."

"Don't worry. I don't think they will give me the opportunity."

I told her I decided on the walk home to take Moosie into Doc's for boarding. "No sense in giving those knuckleheads an opportunity to finish the job."

It seemed to me—probably because I wanted it to seem that way—

that neither of us wanted to break off the conversation, but I had some running around to do.

"I had an idea this morning. How would you like to come out on the lake with me tomorrow while I look for some stuperific pictures to take?"

Her smile was sweet...and fleeting.

"Can't say I've ever seen a stuperific picture being taken. Or the photographers who take them." She paused and looked sad. "How do I know that if I go you won't disappoint me and take some absolutely benign photographs."

"You roll the dice, you take your chances."

A new smile drifted away. "People will talk, you know."

"I'm sure they're already talking. The gossip in this town seems to be on real time. So we might as well give them something to talk about."

"I have been cooped up for a while. Getting out would be nice. What time?"

We settled on six a.m. She again nixed a breakfast stop at Hum's, saying that was pushing the Caddo gossip bubble too hard. "Don't worry about breakfast or lunch," she said. "That'll be my contribution."

She didn't ask what time we'd be back. That pleased me for some reason.

I walked to the house and got in the car, drove back to Harlan's, picked up the groceries and added a twelve-pack of bottled water, a small bag of ice, and an assortment or sodas before heading back.

After putting the all the groceries and ice away, except for doggie treats which I left in the car, I let Moosie romp through the house and put her in the shotgun seat for the ride to town. I thought I saw a curtain move on a front window at Widder's but couldn't be sure.

As I opened up the door to get in, I happened to glance down the street and saw what I thought was the nose of Sheriff Twiddle's Grand Marquis. It was sticking out of a driveway at an empty hunting lodge about four to five houses down the road.

I stood there for a minute, rubbing Moosie's ear and thinking to Bob. He didn't like what I was thinking but that was no surprise. Inner voices can be a pain in the head sometimes. Bob usually like to be a pain way south of there.

I ran back in the house, pulled a long-necked Dos Equis out of the fridge, opened it and emptied it in the sink, rinsing out the inside of the brown bottle several times. Getting a cold Barq's Root Beer from the fridge, I used it to refill the beer bottle.

Tha-this may be rah-real dumb!

Life is for living, Bob. And I wanna live!

Yah-you're a nut!

I sauntered from the house toward my car, making sure the double XX logo on the bottle was visible just in case Sheriff Twiddle had a pair of binoculars and was smart enough to figure out which end to look through. Taking a big swig of root beer from the bottle, I made a big production of making a loud "Haaauuuuuu" sound and then wiping my mouth with my free hand.

Jah-jesus!

Quiet, Bob. The curtain is going up.

Jogging over to Widder's I didn't even have to knock before the door opened.

"Take a sip of this, please," I said.

"It's a little too early for me."

"Take a tiny sip."

She took the bottle and tipped it just enough to trickle a little of the contents into her mouth.

"Root beer?"

"*Correctamundo, Cherie*! If I get arrested for DWI or something, would you be a witness for me and tell exactly what was in this bottle?"

"Are you going to do something dumb?"

"That's what Bob said."

"Bob?"

"Never mind. Do you always answer a question with a question?"

She smiled and my heart did a couple of quick push-ups. "Do you always answer a question with a question after someone answered one of your questions with a question?"

Bob tried to diagram that sentence in my head. I felt a baby migraine coming on.

"I'll take that as a 'yes,'" I said, sprinting to my car.

I spilled some of the root beer on my pants as I worked to get Moosie to her side of the front seat of the car, but figured I could write off the cleaning bill by chalking it up to "entertainment expense" on my next year's taxes.

Backing out of the driveway, I made sure to take mini-sips from the bottle every five feet or so before straightening out the car on the road and heading toward down, at a very, slow rate of speed.

I was chug-a-lugging from the bottle when I passed the sheriff's car but I didn't have to go to all the trouble: He already had his bubble gum machine whirling and he hit the siren for effect as he pulled behind me.

I dutifully pulled over after gesturing wildly about where I was going to pull over and finally did…in Harlan's parking lot. The same gaggle of men as before, with six or seven additions, were on the porch, goggle-eyed and silent.

Sitting in the car, I kept sucking from that bottle as I watched Sheriff Twiddle get out of the car and adjust that garbage can lid-sized hat on that big-ass head. He walked toward the car with what I assumed he thought was swaggering authority. It looked more like the lead clogger in the River Dance of the Water Buffaloes.

"Get out of the car and bring your license and registration. No funny moves," he said loud enough for the men on the Harlan's porch to hear.

"Yeth thir," I lisped, taking another sip, toasting the men on the porch in the process. No one openly acknowledged the gesture.

The sheriff stepped back quickly as I threw open the door, but I just grinned like the lead clown in a circus act. I handed him the car registration and my license. And took another sip from the bottle.

"Being a know-it-all Yankee fella and a registered smart-mouth, I wouldda thought you'd by-gawd know every thing about the local laws and such," Twiddle said, loud and in a tone that meant to convey he took his sheriffing duties seriously. "You forgot to check on a little liquor law hereabouts called the 'open container law.'"

"Waz that, Little Sheriffee?"

He grinned. It was not a nice grin. More like a picket fence that had been the victim of a rock-throwing crowd. The missing pickets didn't bother me; the moss attached to those left did.

"You can't have no open container of alcohol while operating a motor vehicle. Looks like you broke the law. That means, Smart Mouth, your ass is mine and I'm a lawnmower."

I had been slumping and hanging on to the side of the car for support. I straightened up.

"Sheriff Twiddle. I'm not trying to be overly critical here but when you are using language to make a point, it's preferred to use the correct verbiage to create the proper word images. You said to me—I think I've got this down right—'Your ass is mine and I'm a lawnmower.' The correct words should have been 'Your ass is grass and I'm a lawnmower.' 'Your ass is mine and I'm a lawnmower' is nonsensical. It's like saying someone has a big head and saying something like, 'Your head is huge and I need to go take a dump.' It makes no sense. The two parts of the sentence, as well as the thought, don't properly connect."

Sheriff Twiddle's mouth was open; his pupils shrank to the size of dried lentils. He shook his head and spittle flew quite a distance in two directions. Moosie in khaki.

"Smart Mouth, you just don't learn. Hands behind your back. Now."

"What's the charge, Sheriff?"

"Sassing the law. Drinking in public, you damn fool. I'm charging you with violating the Texas open container law and anything else I can think of between here and the jailhouse."

The sound of a car tires on gravel didn't cause either one of us to back down.

"Since when is it against the law to drink soda pop, Sheriff?"

"Soda pop, my ass, Boy! That's Dose Sekee and you're going to jail. Hands behind your back. Now! I'm not telling you again and just between you and me, I hope you don't do what I tell you 'cause I'd dearly love to beat the living shit right out of you."

"Not today, Sheriff." I held the beer bottle up high. "This is not beer," saying it loud enough to be heard by the men at Harlan's. "Root beer."

"The hell it is!" Twiddle grabbed the beer bottle and put it to his nose and sniffed, reminding me of a one-nostril bloodhound with allergies.

A strange look came over his face and he took a sip from the bottle, spitting out the contents on the dirt driveway.

"What the hell do you....?

"I always put my root beer in empty beer bottles, Sheriff. Makes me feel like such a (I threw my arms out and twirled around like Julie Andrews in "Sound of Music) maaaaan."

Laughter flowed off Harlan's porch and across the parking lot.

The sheriff's Strange Look was replaced by Evil Look. He tipped up the beer bottle and poured the contents on the ground. "I say it was beer, Smart Mouth. You're going to jail."

"Take me away, O' Law Enforcement Gendarme Extraordinare. But I must warn you that I took the precautions of having a number of local citizens (*wu-one is a number!* Bob thought*)* sample the contents of that bottle before I put myself willingly in your disgustingly simple trap. All will testify at my trial, which will be held after I sue you for false arrest—and I will insist upon a trial—that the contents of that bottle were revealed to you and that you poured out the evidence of my innocence. A false arrest charge right before your re-election run might swing quite a few votes one way or the other. Boy, that would look splenderific on your resume. Now, arrest me, Sheriff Johnnie Twiddle, or go forth and sin no more."

On that line, I threw open my arms in a decent imitation of Jesus on the cross.

The crowd on the porch started yelling and applauding. At least they did until sheriff turned his attention in that direction. To his credit, Sheriff Twiddle analyzed the situation, got in his car, after taking off that bird bath-sized hat, and left. Quickly. Siren and lights off.

The applause and laughter started anew. I gave a little nod in the group's direction, hoping that the gesture contained the proper amount of humility. I glanced over his shoulder and saw Widder standing at the edge of the store's driveway, leaning against an old Willys Jeep. Her hand was over her mouth and she was shaking. I couldn't tell if she was laughing or crying.

Another mystery. The first was I couldn't figure out why I was not feeling happier about my splenderific performance.

15

Good news travels fast, bad news faster, unconfirmed rumors faster than that. The fastest traveler of them all is damn lies.

Anonymous

Widder was shaking her head when I sauntered over. She looked up and her eyes were glistening. If that was a smile playing on her lips, I've seen better smiles on disfigured corpses.

"What'd you think of the show?"

"I had already thought you were a big showoff, but now I know you're full-fledged crazy."

I-I agree hah-wholeheartedly.

I didn't answer immediately. I just looked down at the dirt and scuffed it up with the toe of my right Reebok running shoe. I said, "There are times when some people, people like me, simply have to do whatever they can to disencourage the status quo."

"Disencourage? Do you make up words for the fun of it? Disencourage the status quo? Does that mean you're a born rebel?" The good smile was back. Sort of.

"I've been called that. But I like to think that part of my job on earth is to pop the ego bubbles of pricks and prickettes."

"Prickettes? There are really 'prickettes' in the world you live in?"

"Oh, assuredly. Some of the biggest pricks in the world don't even have them. But they have the natural mental accoutrements that qualifies them to be in the prick family," I said.

Shaking her head, she said, "If I understand this correctly, it is your job to identify and deflate these pricks and prickettes wherever they may be and with whatever mental tools and gimmicks you have at your disposal?"

I couldn't have said it better myself and told her so. Bob was impressed with her insight and threw me that thought. Nothing fancy. Hanging verb ball.

The silence was overpowering. I could feel the eyes from the crowd at Harlan's sweeping over the scene.

Widder broke through my thoughts. "I think your passenger is ready to go. Past ready."

Moosie's head was out the driver's window and she was into deluge-drool mode. Half the car door was wet.

Disgusting.

I told Widder I'd see her early tomorrow and headed to the car.

Shouts from Harlan's porch came fast.

"Good luck."

"Drive careful."

"Take care."

I waved at the gathering and told Bob: Don't take much, Bob, to become a folk hero in one's own lifetime.

Yah-you're a superhero. Sah-super Dummy!

I shooed Moosie to the other side of the car and slid through a puddle of slobber to get behind the wheel.

Jah-jesus!

Bob, a wet ass created by a faithful friend is better than a whipped ass created by an asshole.

Spa-spare me. Tha-that's just dumb!

Waving a casual-we're-nothing-but-mere-acquaintances-honest! wave toward Widder, I headed the car toward town with a good feeling in my heart and a song on my lips.

And a cold sliver of fear somewhere south of my gut.

UNCERTAIN TIMES

Doc was more than willing to board Moosie.

"I like Great Danes!" he said for the thirty-third time. "I'll take real good care of her. She's a big ol' baby, aren't you, Sugah?"

Moosie gave him a lick that started on his shoulder and ended at his hairline.

"Doc, Moosie likes just about everybody, but she is really attached to you."

"When I was a kid," Doc said, "I brought home every animal you could think of that was native to this area. Squirrels, armadillos, 'coons, rabbits. Even had a baby coyote once. Mama made me get rid of it when it got big 'cause she was 'fraid of it. Didn't limit myself to furry critters either. Birds, snakes, frogs. If it was alive and wiggling, I adopted it.

"I brought in more baby animals than you could count. I remember once Poppa saying that he could not believe I could find that many orphaned animals. But I knew he knew I was getting those critters by robbing nests and burrows. Looking back, I regret taking those babies from they nests and burrows, but I look at it as training for what I do now: Trying to make sure all the animals are taken care of good and proper."

Neither of us said much for a while. I wanted to tell Doc what he had done was okay, but knew he didn't need my approval.

"I got the report back from the lab," Doc said.

"What kind of poison? Strychnine?"

He nodded. "Probably from rat poison, D-Con or something similar. It was mixed with some feeder material, they call it." He paused. Then, "There ought to be a special place in hell...."

"There is, Doc. There has to be. Life wouldn't make much sense if there wasn't."

We just sat there, him rubbing one of Moosie's ears and me the other. Moosie broke the mood by giving us both a big slobbery kiss. I gave Moosie a big hug and tried to get her to sit and "give me five." She looked at me with that lovable, patented huh-look.

I got in the car and headed back to the lake. Just as the Marshall City Limits sign blew by the window, I had a thought and turned around and backtracked to Doc's. He was all ears as I explained what I wanted and then wrote down a name and address on a piece of paper.

I looked at the paper. James Mitchell. The address on the piece of paper was only a couple of blocks away.

As is the custom in many small towns, this lawyer had taken up residence in a large Victorian mansion. It was a three-story affair that was white clapboard with dark green shutters and enough landscaping to qualify for a botanical garden. The secretary assured me that if I wanted to wait, I could see the attorney in due time.

I parked on a nice Italian leather couch in the waiting room and picked up a largeish tabletop photo book: *Amazon River: River of Life...and Death*. In block letters at the bottom right corner was the photographer's name: A.B.F. Jones.

Although I knew every detail of every photo in the book, I flipped through it, trying to look at the offerings objectively.

Hah-hard to do.

Mighty hard.

With only four or five exceptions, the photographs were exceptional. Lighting, subjects, exposure...all top quality. I grimaced at a couple of the "filler" photos, pictures that normally would not have made the book but were needed to fill in spots in the narrative or illustrate a point. The Amazon book was one of my earlier efforts, and I thought proudly how later books had used fewer filler-photos.

There was no one else in the waiting room and I couldn't see anyone out in the reception area. Pulling a Bic from my pants pocket, I opened the front cover and quickly scribbled these words:

> *To Attorney Mitchell:*
> *Lawyering and photography are similar in that both professionals of the respective arts sometimes are called upon to make something from nothing.*
> *A.B.F. Jones*

Tha-that's cah-corny.

I thought you were going to think *"caca."*

Tha-that too! Ah-and egomaniacal.

Ten minutes later I followed the receptionist through a mini-hallway maze into an office about the size of a racquetball court.

Mitchell was sitting in a throne-like leather chair, leaned back with a pair of lizard cowboy boots up on a desk that could have been the delivery box for a small Buick. He was on the phone but pointed toward a chair to the right side of the desk.

Once seated, I noticed the chair seemed shorter than normal, about two inches or so. I eased my head to the side and noticed a small, three-inch platform custom built on the other side of the desk. To give Lawyer Mitchell some height advantage.

I'm sitting here and he's on the phone. Double-billing his time, I thought. Phone call and me.

Cy-cynic.

Realist, too.

The lawyer's spiel filtered through the Bob-talk: "My client is hurt, gawddamit. Real hurt. I know the limits of the insurance company and that's not going to be enough. We're going to trial and I will have a jury that will stick a big, bad punitive damages award so far up your ass that you'll be pleased to have someone dig it out with an excavator. Think about that picture and get back to me with a settlement offer by Friday."

He hung the phone up with a slam and reached across the desk to shake my hand. He was short, no more than five-foot-six. I like short lawyers with Napoleonic complexes. On my side. Most of them are meaner than hell.

Waving his arms like a over-caffeinated maestro, he said, "Got off the phone with Doc a few minutes ago and he outlined your problem. What did you do to piss off our illustrious sheriff?"

Knowing this conversation was costing me $125 an hour or more, I summarized the last couple of days in less than ten minutes. Or about $20.40 worth.

"You may have a problem in representing me on retainer," I said. "I know you have to live in this town...."

"Stop right there," Mitchell said. "First, I hate that sumbitch Twiddle worst than a bout of Mexican clap. He's useless as tits on a boar hog and plumb mean to boot. He's been in office a dozen years now and I've sued his sorry ass about one time for every year in office. I'd sue him more if I could. I also got a big-ass settlement about five years ago in an injury case that pretty much set me up for life. If I don't win another damn case, or even take one for that matter, it don't make no never mind to me."

He stopped and reached behind him to a coffee pot and refilled a cup off his desk. The writing on the cup said, "If you hire me, you hire the best!" In a practiced move that looked unpracticed he turned the cup so that the writing faced me.

"What do you want from me?" he asked, knowing but putting it on the record just the same. Time, in his case, was money. Tick and double tock.

"I want you on retainer so that when, not if, Sheriff Twiddle puts me in his jail, I spent the least amount of time possible in there. And that I have representation quicker than a pond darter."

"Done. Next."

"Well, for now, that's about it, I guess."

"This is an attorney-client privilege thing, so feel free to tell the truth, which is something I don't hear too often in this office. Did you threaten the kill the Ledbetter brothers? Don't make no never mind to me. Them two are as useless as eighty-year-old, saggy-titted twin whores in a Fifth Avenue brothel. I just need to know."

Damn, rumors in this part of the world travel faster than the flick of a gnat's wing.

Yah-you need to wah-work on your clichés.

"Nope. It was the other way around."

"Figured as much. Do you have a need for personal protection?"

Wha-what is he....

"Excuse me?"

He looked at me like I was a slow relative holding up the fried chicken line at the homecoming buffet.

"Do you have a gun? Do you need a bodyguard?"

"Oh, personal protection. Got it. That may be a little premature, don't you think?"

"I know this county. You don't. If I thought it was premature, I wouldn't have brought it up. Here," he said, reaching in a desk drawer, "take this and keep it handy." He plopped a Glock nine millimeter on the desktop along with a full box of shells. "You lose it and I'll charge you double out of the retainer."

I looked at the gun like it was a rattlesnake. "What about carrying a concealed weapon? Twiddle would love...."

Mitchell let out a whoop and holler. "Hell, Mr. Jones, this is Texas! Anybody that don't have a gun is a gawddamned liberal tree hugger or gay or both. Being a big city photographer, I figure you are a liberal, but I know you ain't gay, since you're sparking the Widder Gleason and all. Hell's bells, boy, I've got two teenagers and they both are packing! And one of them is a girl!"

"Sparking the Wid...?"

He eased a piece of paper across the desk and said, "To put your mind at ease, sign this."

It was an application to carry a concealed weapon, already approved with a name I didn't recognize.

"This is for Harris County, down in Houston. The sheriff there is a friend of mine and he hates Twiddle more than me and you put together. He used to work for him and knows the man is crookeder than a dog's hind leg that's been broke in three places by a runaway Harley. Son, when you sign, you're legal to pack heat."

He smiled a long, slow smile. Bob figured that *sma-smile* cost me about $4.67.

After assuring Mitchell I knew how to use the pistol, I signed the form and he had the secretary make copies for his files and to fax to the Harris County Sheriff's Office. He handed me two copies.

"Keep this permit on you at all times, and keep one in your car." he said. "But even if you forget, it's still legal. If you shoot anybody, make sure there are witnesses even if you have to make them up. Remember you were provoked even if you weren't. Shooting somebody outside your house and dragging them inside is still an accepted practice in Texas." He gave me a $1.32 wink.

We shook hands one last time after I assured Mitchell that my agent Mark Goodlaw would wire transfer a thousand dollars to his office account later in the day. The secretary quickly wrote down the bank transfer numbers. When I got to the car, I made the call on my cell and was assured the transfer would be taken care of before end of business.

"Do I need to tell Mark anything special about the transfer?" Becky, his assistant asked.

"Tell him it's preventive maintenance."

"He'll want to know more than that," she said.

"Knowing and wanting to know are two different things. Let him chew the cud on that for a while. It'll be good for him."

"Chew the cud?"

"It's a colloquial expression. If he doesn't know what it means, tell him to go to Google and look up rednecklingo.com."

"This is a joke, right?"

"I don't think so. Thanks, Becky. Talk to you later."

Mah-Mark will call bah-....

Before we get home. That's why we have Caller ID, Bob.?

I figured it would only take the usual twenty minutes to get home but then I realized it would take longer. I caught myself driving slow, looking behind every shrub, tree, billboard and in every driveway look for mid-level executives for Sheriff and Company.

About five miles from Uncertain I spotted an unmarked brown Chevy that had pulled out of a side road. It quickly came up on me, but slowed down to match my speed, hanging back about fifty yards. Two silhouettes in the front. Couldn't see if anyone was in the back. Forms indistinguishable, but not Harmony and Bother unless the driver had lost about fifty pounds off his head weight, and the passenger was really retaining a lot of water.

Keeping a close watch on the car was easy. Forgetting about its presence was not. I thought about the Glock in the glove box and regretted not loading it at Mitchell's. The distinctive chirp of the cell phone broke into my thoughts. The Caller ID digital readout told me it was Mark. Letting the phone lay unanswered in the console cup holder was a no-brainer. Trying to explain the unexplainable to my agent was not high on my agenda.

I breathed a little easier...or, more factually, started breathing again...when I hit the Uncertain City Limits sign. The car pulled into the abandoned Board Foot Lumber Yard. Someone had Xed out the "a" in "Board" and added an "e" between the "r" and "d" and changed the double-o's into "e's".

There are some bored people in Uncertain.

Nah-no pun intended, rah-right?

Pulling into my driveway, I killed the engine and went to the trunk and pulled out a couple of garage rags, wet them down with a half-empty bottle of water on the seat and wiped down the Jeep's passenger door. I'd read that dog slobber has enzymes that can cause paint to fade or kill small furry animals or something.

Better safe than sorry, Bob.?

Bah-better you than me.

I am *you*, Bob. You are *me*.

Dah-don't remind me. Tha-that's just damn dah-depressing.

16

Symbolism is used to illustrate points. Sometimes coincidences are turned into symbols to make the story better.

Anonymous

Opening the door, something stopped me dead-still. There was a presence in the house.

There was a fragrance hovering in the disturbed air. Magnolia blossom. No. Wisteria, maybe, with a touch of pear blossom. Or possibly Secret deodorant. Definitely feminine, which definitely meant not Harmony, Bother or Twiddle.

"Hello. Anyone here."

No answer.

Then I saw it. Above the small mantle was a painting. Caddo Lake, or at least a very small section of it. Maybe the east side of Goat Island, but no way to be sure. I stared at the painting, which was framed in what looked like old barn board. The shadows off the cypress trees were precisely dark but also contained an enormous amount of detail. Tree bark, tendrils of Spanish moss, hidden in the canopy of close-knit trees, a patch of water hyacinths half in the sunlight, half tucked in the shadows. A cormorant was in the middle of a sweeping left turn, preparing to skirt the edge of the cypress trees, or maybe heading home to a nestful of hatchlings.

It was good. Very good. Full of intricate detail.

It was then I noticed a small envelope below the picture. Inside was a small note.

> *Noticed your walls are a bit bare. I hope this brightens up the room. Keep it if you want to; return it if you don't.*

It was signed in a small, cramped hand: *C.C.*

I wanted to rush over and thank her profusely—more than once—in a very special boy-girl kind of way. Bob suggested that waiting until the next day might be better. He had a point. No sense in appearing too eager.

To hell with that! I went next door and knocked three times on the screen door. Nothing. Three more knocks and a short wait assured me she wasn't there. Jogging back to the house, I got a sheet from an old reporter's notebook and with my Bic wrote a small thank-you note:

> *C.C.:*
>
> *You are indeed a woman of many talents. Thank you! The painting is perfect and I wouldn't give it up for less than $100. If you could only cook, you'd be the perfect woman.*
>
> *Adj."*

I left the note stuck in a corner of her front porch screen, went back home, fixed a sandwich, got a beer and went out in the back yard. I took *Lincoln* with me. I sat leaning against the lightning-stuck tree in the yard for several hours, trying to read, mainly thinking.

My concentration level was nil. Trying to make sense of the thoughts racing through my head was like trying to work on a stock option deal while sitting on a topless Bahamian beach. Rehashing the events of the day, plus thinking about spending some quality time with Widder tomorrow had me stretched tighter than a thong on a fat girl.

I finally gave it up went back in the house, had a glass of Alice White merlot and a Tylenol P.M. The combination changed my mind-etchings from seventy-eight rpm. to forty-five. Sleep slipped up on me like a mountain lion on a sheep herd.

It was a couple of days before Easter.

On a whim I drove to south Arkansas with my convertible top down and the wind whipping my hair like a cat o' nine tails. I cut south from Prescott, through Laneburg, to Sutton.

Landmarks flashed by like black-and-white newsreels with the occasional broken sprocket.

The courthouse where Daddy George served on the quorum court. The pond where he and I sat under a huge pine tree more than forty-five years ago, catching catfish using apple peel for bait after we ran out of bacon. The farm where we drove to in a battered pickup to see a crew drilling an exploratory oil well. The overgrown lane leading to a shotgun house where, when I was ten, Daddy George let me pick out a pig he wanted to turn into meat for the smokehouse.

Harmony Church, where a slew of relatives are resting, zipped past on my right. I eased onto the narrow road to Sutton and a half-mile later, turned down the pebble-rock-and-sand lane to Nannie and Daddy George's house.

The place has changed a little in the past fifty years. Aunt Wonder and Uncle Gene put another shotgun addition on the original, simple structure. They did a beautiful job matching the exterior of the original house.

I sat there in the car, looking, listening and welcoming the feeling of peace that I always experience when visiting there. A smile stuck to my face like a peel-and-press sticker from a quarter machine at the grocery store.

Daddy George and Nannie were no where to be seen, but I could feel their presence, see their touches everywhere…in the cleanliness of the place, the beautiful spring shrubs, the picture-perfect magnolias framing both sides of the front porch. I could almost hear the small herd of cows lowing to be fed, the chickens squawking in the back yard, Penny, the age-worn cocker Spaniel, yipping at anything that moved.

I took my shotgun and pistol out of the trunk and headed up the lane to the Long Gate (or Lawn Gate as some relatives call it). The pathway was shaded by balanced rows of magnolias Daddy George let me help plant and water four decades or so ago.

The eighty-plus acres of the Bartlett Place was overgrown to the extreme. A geographically challenged logger clear-cut a large part of the tract years ago. He was supposed to have logged a farm somewhere down the road and ended up cutting a section owned by one of my cousins "on an accident," as my Aunt Martha Gertene would have said. Scrubby trees and vines had made a successful invasion. The main road to the back of the place was still clear enough to maneuver. It was up this road that I walked.

A fat, droning bumblebee popped up and I followed the sentinel up the path. On a sandy flat past the old home place, myriad tracks popped up like dandelions in the spring. Armadillo. Raccoon. Deer. Dog.

I checked out the prints closely, remembering the many times I had done exactly the same thing as a youngster walking beside my grandfather. One deer track in particular was interesting: The track slid just a little off a little mini-hillock of sand, creating the impression the animal was startled. "This track is fresh," I thought out loud. "Early this morning."

Then I stopped, thought about what I had muttered.

Nearly fifty years ago, in approximately the same spot, I had stopped with Daddy George while he grilled me about tracks in the sand. I had said about the same thing about a deer track: "Early this morning, I reckon," I recall saying.

Without batting an eye, Daddy George said, "Maybe. Or yesterday. Or the day before. Or last week since it hain't rained."

Still shaking my head at my attempt to "read tracks," I followed the two-lane trail past the Sand Field—my grandparents had a big truck garden here—to the Duncan Field. It was there, according to local legend, that some cattle thieves were hung and buried before the turn of the Twentieth Century.

With the pistol in my belt and my shotgun slung across both shoulders and held firmly in place by my arms draped casually across the stock and barrel, I wandered through the hardwood thickets near the back of the place. I was looking for Daddy George, thinking about lost youth.

Stepping into a clearing, the sun at my back, I glanced down and saw…my shadow. The gun was over my shoulders, my hands dangling off each end. "Hmmmmm. Looks like a man on a cross," I said out loud. I stopped, stared and remembered that Easter was approaching. I thought about the reason for it and gave silent thanks for my life and everything in it that makes it special.

Making my way to a small, rocky hill near the northeastern edge of the property, I found a rock and sat down and just watched and listened to the slow, easy sounds of spring.

I was thinking about the time Daddy George and I went looking for a cow that had busted through a rickety section of fence, when he appeared beside me. He didn't say a word, just sat down beside me and ruffled my head, the way he used to do a half-century ago.

We didn't talk; there was no need. We just sat there, sharing mental memories, smiling more than a little, shedding tears, more than a few.

It started to get dark and I reluctantly got up and walked a few steps before I turned to tell him goodbye.

But, as I knew he would be, he was already gone.

I walked back to the house, trying to match his stride and walk in his footprints every step of the way.

I sat up in bed and looked around the room.

2:35.

Fluffing the pillow, I laid back down, willing a re-run of the dream. Daddy George died more than twenty years ago. But he was never more alive to me than on that not-so-distant Easter weekend.

17

Time. Sometimes there's just not enough of it. It makes no difference which clock you're looking at or what time zone you're in.

Anonymous

It was 5:15 when I got up and put on the coffee. Packing up for the day was fairly easy as most of the equipment I carried was always sitting by the front door. As I was pulling an extra lawn chair out of the back of the hall closet, I spied an self-inflatable mattress rolled up tight in a corner and decided to throw that in as well.

If Widder got tired and wanted to take a nap....
Jab-justification is for losers. Yah-you qualify!
Please control your cynicism, Bob. No ulterior motives here.
I-I must have missed the nah-news.
What news?
Huh-hell froze over!

After telling Bob that I was going to figure out a way to work overtime to get rid of him, I went about my gathering and packing. With the small ice chest, extra fold-up lawn chair, camera bags and two dry boxes. and small plastic sack of munchies and goodies, it took two trips to load up the car.

5:54.

Widder opened the door before I hit the porch.

"Everything is right here," she said, pointing to behind the door.

From my perspective, everything I needed was standing right in the doorway. Widder was wearing a pair of dark blue Columbia travel pants that could be converted to shorts with the slide of a couple of zippers, an off-white, air-vent Columbia shirt with sleeves that could be rolled up and buttoned the high side of the elbows. The shirt was open and tied in a knot at her waist. A long acrylic-y looking, thin, bright orange, extended halter-top went from above her breasts to below her navel. Covering the good parts. A sturdy pair of Rockport walking shoes and a floppy straw hat completed the look.

Her hair was pulled back into a ultra-short, bouncy ponytail and her neck looked extremely eatable, or at very least, lickable. It vied with her lips in both categories.

You look great!

Suh-say it to her! Not mah-me!

"You look great!"

"Thank you, kind sir. Then I accomplished my morning objective."

I grabbed a large, wicker picnic and picked it up with more than a little effort before I noticed it had a painting on the side. The filtered morning light coming through the door was dim but I was able to make out another Caddo Lake scene, this one I recognized: The Cathedral. Even with the waviness created by the bumpy wicker, the detail was astonishing.

"You did this." Statement, not a question.

"I can paint on anything," she said matter-of-factly. "Baskets, saw blades, tiller blades, barn board, toilet paper...."

"Toilet paper! You paint on...."

My eyes were wide when I saw the mouse-grin pulling at the corners of her mouth.

"Gotcha!"

"Big City Smart Mouth just got put in his place by beautiful Small Town School Marm," I said.

"School marm? You think of me as a school marm?"

Backtracking faster than a skunk-sprayed hound, I said, "Yes. The kind of school marms that all young boys like to think about when they are in bed at night, all along with their fantasies. You know, the school marm that helps you enunciate your vowels by pinching each side of your face with a hand that has a perfumed wrist attached to it and pursing rosy-red, luscious lips to show you how to sound them out."

"Let's see: Quick on his verbal feet. I like that in a man. Verbose to the extreme, perhaps, but usually the conversation is, at the very least, mildly entertaining."

"Verbose? Me? Verbose? Me?"

She looked at the ceiling of the entryway, setting herself in a musing pose. All she needed to do was tap her lip with an upraised index finger to complete the image. "Tends to repeat himself at times," Widder said. "That's not a good trait."

"Repeats himself? Me? Repeats himself? Me?"

She looked at me and pretended to talk into a small microphone: "Ultra-sensitive to criticism. When confronted with fact-based psychological evaluation, tends to get defensive." She made a big show of turning off an imaginary recorder.

"Defensive? Me? I'm not defensive."

I loved the way she laughed, not the small tee-hee, suppressed giggle usually stereotypically associated with a woman on a first date. She was prone to a from-the-belly, honest laugh that I associated with people at ease and having fun.

I looked at her closely as we started to carry the supplies to the car. "Fact-based psychological evaluation? I can't tell you how many times I've heard those very same words since I came to Uncertain."

"Now you're making fun of my home town and all my friends." Her voice got more nasally, tinnier. "Frogs a-goshen! Time's a-wastin', as they say, so let's get to those pitcher-taking places and snap some shots. Er you ready?"

"Frogs a-goshen? Where did you come up with that one?"

"There you go again!" she said. "Answering a question with a question. Or in this case, questions, plural."

We started stacking stuff in the Jeep and Widder said, "There was an old woman that lived out in the lake named Hannah. No one seemed to know much about her but she had no last name, just Hannah."

"She had an old pirogue that she rowed over to the back of Harlan's for supplies ever so often. I met here there one day and we just got to talking. She was a hermit in every sense of the word, but she had this special glow about her. She was smart. She was obviously lonely because she started docking the boat behind my house and we'd walk to Harlan's and carry her supplies back, talking all the way."

Widder paused. "I asked her several times if I could come visit her at her place—where ever it was—and she always changed the subject. She did say one time that she didn't want anybody else to see the life she had chosen.

"Anyway, when she would get excited or tickled or, sometimes, just couldn't pick out the words or phrase she wanted she'd say, 'Frogs a-goshen!'"

"Frogs a-goshen!" I said, mulling the words over as I secured the basket, a small cardboard box, some sort of hard-sided case and two plastic grocery sacks in the back of the Jeep. "Gosh a-mighty! Heavens to Betsy! Good God Gertrude! Do you think it was used like those expressions, except that it was her special, made-up phrase?"

I held open the passenger door so she could slide in. She gave me a small nod and said, "Actually I do. I think it was a coined phrase that was distinctly her's. I think it was the only thing she really owned."

I shut the door gently and went around and got in, started the car and was backing up when Celestial said, "The last time I saw her which was, oh, about two years ago now, she said, 'Whatever you do, Celeste, don't you never turn into me.'"

Celestial looked out the front window and said in a low voice, "Don't you never turn into me."

I drove to the Poem Board and stopped, got my reporter's note pad and camera, attached the flash unit I always kept in the bag and got out. A new poem was scratched in chalk on the board and I struggled to read the words in the light glow coming out of the east.

I felt Widder sidle up to me as I read the words out loud:

UNCERTAIN TIMES

Sidesaddle Slim and the Bronco Kid
walked in out of the gloomy night
They were looking for grub and looking for love
and wanted to do it up right.
As they stepped into the dusty saloon
and cast their eyes about
Slim saw a woman in distress
and it made him turn and shout:
"Lookee there, Kid," he cried in a panic
as he watched a woman turn blue
"That woman is going to choke to death
and there's nothing nobody can do."

"This is different from all the others," I said.
"There's no pattern to the poems that I can see," Widder said. "Ever."

"Not if I can help it, Slim,"
the Bronco Kid cried out as he ran
To the woman's side and he whispered in her ear,
"Don't you worry none, Ma'am."
"Why I can save you sure as you're born
and soon you'll be good as new."
And he stretched his arms around her waist
'cause she was a-turning mighty blue.
Quick as a cat, with a twist of his hand,
he jerked off her belt of rawhide
And jerked down her jeans way past her knees,
and swiped his tongue up and down her backside.
That choking woman jumped about eight feet high
and let out a bellowing yell,
Then she turned, red in the face and slapped the Kid.
And you knew it stung like hell.
Then she slapped him again for good measure
and left the bar in a huff
If the Kid was looking for love from this rescue,

that cowboy was plumb out of luck.
"What in the world are you doing, Kid?"
Slim looked at his friend with disdain.
"That woman might've been mighty nice to you
if you hadn't gone plumb insane!"
The Bronco Kid rubbed his cheek and gave a smile
and uttered this famous line:
"All I know, Sidesaddle Slim, is that hiney-lick maneuver
will unchoke 'em every time."

As I read the last line, a peal of choking gurgles started way down low in my gut and gallivanted its way out upward and outward. "Sorry. Nervous laughter, I guess." I looked at Widder. She was intently studying the words.

"Are you embarrassed?" I asked.

"Give me a break, Big City Smart Mouth. Embarrassed? I grew up in a family of three brothers and lived among rough men most of my life. It'll take more than this little ditty to embarrass me."

I studied her for a heartbeat then said, "What would it take to embarrass you?"

Her eyes twinkled; her top lip quivered. "More than you'd ever believe or think of."

I turned back to the Poem Board and read it again, this time silently. "This is driving me crazy. What drives this person to write these? I'm starting to think these are written by a schizophrenic or a troubled poet with multiple personalities."

Widder remained silent as I wrote down the words in the notebook and checked it several times to make sure I had all the words right. After I took a couple of pictures using the flash, I turned to Widder: "Is it just me or are these poems or literary offerings or whatever they are really intriguing?"

She looked at the board and back at me: "Intriguing? A good word. I've read every single one of them since the board first appeared. I've come up here and written down the words every single day except when I'm out of town for some reason or other. Then I get Harlan or Miss Baxter to write them down for me."

She was silent for a moment. "They've gotten better since the beginning. More variety, that's for sure. Most of the early ones were about love and family and nature. Some of those were obviously written in a hurry and there didn't seem to be much thought put in the words or structure. Or maybe there was and I just missed the signs."

"I would really like to see the early ones sometime," I said.

"I thought you might," Widder said, smiling. "I heard you were taking photos of the board and writing down the poems. I brought a few of the early ones along today. They're in the picnic basket."

We loaded up and drove the short distance to the dock. The boat was loaded with supplies and camera equipment in short order with a minimum of talking. Widder did arch a quizzical eyebrow at the rolled up air mattress, but I just shrugged and broke eye contact.

Sma-smooth.

We were well out in Caddo, heading toward the Carter's Chute blind, the boat's motor running about half open, when I asked Widder: "Whatever happened to her? Hannah, I mean?"

She was quiet for a few seconds, the wind whipping her pony tail. "I don't know. She usually came to town about once a month or so. One day I realized I hadn't seen her in quite a while so I asked around down at Harlan's and to others who live or work on the lake. No one had seen her.

"I even asked Harmony to please keep an eye out for her since he and Bother are out on the lake all the time. He just gave me a good once-over and said he would. Didn't put much hope there; he was more interested in what was under my shirt than in finding Hannah." She paused and looked at a coot trying to get airborne near the shoreline.

"I went to the sheriff's office and filed a missing person's complaint but the deputy I talked to just laughed and quit writing when I told him who it was I was reporting as Missing." He said, "That crazy old swamp bitch? Why'd you care about her?'" Her accent was right on. "I honestly didn't have a good answer so I just told him 'Because I do.'" She paused and turned in the seat to face me, the wind at her back. Edges of her pony tail licked at the edges of her lips. I don't ever remember before being jealous of hair.

Widder looked at me, nodded her head slightly to the right and smiled. "What are you thinking?"

"Why are you asking?" As her face started to darken at my question-following-a-question gambit, I smiled and said, "Gotcha! I was thinking how I'd like to be those stray strands of hair caressing the edges of your lips."

Turning back to face the front of the boat, she threw a look over her left shoulder and solemnly said, "I've made a mistake. Take me back to the dock."

"Wah-wah-wait." That was me, not Bob. "I-I-I deh-deh-didn't..."

Her eyes suddenly sparkled. "Gotcha!" was all she said before turning back to face the front.

My heart started beating again. My eyes roamed over her body, starting at the juncture where her butt and the boat seat met, moving up to her decidedly feminine waist, to her smooth back (no bra snap bulge) and on to her neck and hair.

Yah-you may have mah-met your match.

"That's a scary thought," I said.

"What is?" she said, turning slightly on the boat seat.

"I was just thinking out loud."

"You tend to do that a lot."

"Comes with the territory, I guess. Being alone a lot, I tend to talk to myself," I said.

"It's not the talking to yourself part that makes you crazy," Widder said. "It's when you start answering back."

Uh-oh. We're in deep doo-doo.

There was never a doubt in my mind, Bob.

To Widder: "Well, if that's the criterion for sanity, I know I'm as sane as you are."

She threw me another one of *those* smiles.

It took the usual twenty minutes or so to get to the Carter's Chute blind and another five or so to unload the boat and haul the gear up the leaning tree ladder. The chore was simple with two people; a majority of items were hauled up on the end of a slightly frayed ski rope I had thrown in for that express purpose.

Telling Widder to wait in the boat, I climbed down the ladder in what I hoped was an exhibition of sheer masculine athleticism, but I realized was probably a silly display of a fifty-eight-year-old former jock trying to impress a member of the opposite sex. I didn't fall off the ladder and kill myself or knock Widder into the lake, so Bob thought that was a distinct *pah-positive* sign.

"Why'd you come down?" Widder asked.

"Just being the gentlemen that I am," I said. "Wanted to make sure to follow you up so I could catch you if you fell."

"Catch me if I fell? Catch me how? It's a board ladder nailed to a tree! How are you...."

Grinning at her like one of the Cheshire cats in Alice in Wonderland, I said, "Climb the damn ladder, Woman! We're wasting daylight."

"Oooohhh," she said, coyly. "I like domineering men." Then she said something as she turned her head away to being the short climb.

"I'm sorry. I didn't catch that."

She paused with one leg hiked up on a step. The movement caused the fabric of her pants to stretch tightly across her left butt cheek.

"I said, 'You just came down to get behind me so you can stare at my ass on the way up.'"

Pah-perceptive.

"That's unfair," I said. "I could just as easily have stayed in the blind and looked down your top as you climbed up. I assure you my intentions are totally dishonorable."

"That's what all the boys say."

I did watch her ass all the way up and I was rewarded for my chauvinistic avocation when, three steps from the top, she paused, her right foot high on the next to last step, and gave an exaggerated butt-waggle. That move would have guaranteed her a spot in a traveling carnival's hootchie kootchie show.

Luh-lust or love?

They usually come in that order, Bob.

By the time I made sure the boat was tied securely and climbed into the blind, Widder had set up housekeeping. The extra lawn chair was set by my old standby; the picnic basket, the ice chest and sundry sacks were arranged along the blind's east wall; my camera bag and the dry boxes were to the left of my chair, where I always put it when was alone.

She was standing, looking to the west at Maude's nest. Without a word, she pointed. Without a word, I nodded. She went back to staring, hands on hips.

The western sky was light, light blue. Errant streams of sunlight were piercing the thick stand of cypress. It took less than a minute to ready both cameras for the day's shoot and as I sat down, I grabbed Widder's hand and gave a little tug.

She glanced at me and smiled a small, happy smile and eased into the bright, pink plastic lawn chair.

She leaned toward me and instinctively whispered: "Pink? I like a man who's secure in his masculinity."

"It's pink because it was on sale. And because it was the only color left."

I pointed toward the closest nest and leaned over and whispered in her ear: "That's Maude." You could see her neck and head rising out of the nest of branches. "I think she has some eggs ready to hatch. She's been very attentive lately to detailing the nest and Harold has been working overtime to deliver extra food." While I was talking, the warm air from my mouth bounced off the side of her head and assailed my nostrils.

She nodded. "Maude and Harold?"

"Maude and Harold."

I pointed to the nest to the left. "Octavia is usually in that nest, but she's gone fishing. Her nest-mate is Josephus but he's not very reliable. Over there," I said, pointing directly behind us, "are Taffy and Melvin. Taffy seems to be doing fine without too much Melvin-help, if you know what I mean."

"Independent woman."

"Exactly. The photo I'm looking for is early morning with the sun just topping the cypress trees behind us. This time of morning the sun gives off...."

"A golden glow," Widder said. "I know. I'm not much of a

photographer, but I do paint. Capturing the right light nuances in a painting is just as important as in a photograph."

A strange look glanced off her face. She closed her eyes and pinched her brow:

"Her light sucked from her in the breaking dawn.
Never was dawn so welcome as that pale,
Faint glimmer in the cloudless, brooding sky!"

Opening her eyes, she reached up and closed my mouth.

I gulped and took a deep breath. "You know Montgomery's 'The Watchman?'"

It was my turn to reach up and close her mouth.

Grinning like a ten-year-old preacher's son who farted during benediction, I apologized for my condescending attitude. "It's one of my favorite poems. Please excuse me prattling on about poems and photography. I don't have a lot of opportunities to talk about what I do to too many people, much less beautiful school marms who paint. I guess you can say I was trying to impress you."

She snuggled down in the chair. "Well, let's just say you succeeded. I like honesty. Haven't had much chance to see it in my life."

It was a line that I didn't follow. Didn't know if I should. Or even wanted to.

I took my eyes off Widder for just a moment to check on Maude. She was doing her stretching thing, swaying gently from side to side, wings out, long bill waving back and forth in a hypnotic rhythm.

I reached over to touch Widder's arm and Missed about six inches to the right, finger tapping her left breast. From the pressure I figured my finger made a temporary depression about three-quarters of an inch deep, about to the first digit. Without outwardly showing any embarrassment, I pointed with the same baptized finger toward the nest, while grabbing for the camera with the 75-300 mm. zoom lens with my other hand.

Just barely visible above the edge of the nest were the tops of two (No, three!), little fluffy heads. Baby cormorants were snow white when first born; gradually the top feathers darken to almost black.

Studying the scene through the camera lens, I adjusted the focal length slightly and steadied it about just slightly under 300 mm. That frame provided enough room to get the entire nest with Maude standing upright.

Widder poked me in the chest in the approximate area where I had poked her and I saw her pointing upward. A lone cormorant was about a hundred feet out, almost directly in front of us, keeling over in a long swooping dive. Without thinking, without looking, I ratcheted the lens back a few millimeters.

Betsy was already set on rapid-fire mode so I quickly checked through the lens to make sure the nest was properly framed, popped it up to focus on Harold, waited to a count of two and hit the shutter release.

Harold hit his mark as if he were a Broadway professional. As the shutter started firing at four shots per second, he flared his wings and for the first time I could see he had a large crappie in his beak. His left leg was out straight, his right one pulled up slightly, apparently allowing for the angle of his turn and the angle he was going to hit the edge of the nest. Maude instinctively hopped over a foot or two from the landing pad and spread her wings as a welcome gesture.

Three little heads popped up out of the nest on the ends of scrawny necks and three mouths opened in perfect synchronization. Harold made a perfect, slow one-point landing, with his trailing foot hanging in mid-air momentarily, while he balanced himself, then plopped down for stability.

Harold laid the fish on the top of the nest in front of Maude. Without hesitation, she speared its side with her bill slightly open, snapped it shut and twisted, tearing out a small piece of flesh. Harold stood in the background, preening.

The chick closest to Maude got the first piece and she worked her way down the line, making sure each chick got its fair share.

The camera was rewinding long before the scene was over so I reached for Gertrude, but Widder had already anticipated that move and had it at my elbow.

I quickly let the automatic focus do its work and started rat-tat-tatting through the second roll, this time with the 500 mm., which closed in on just the mama-and-baby feeding exercise.

Less than ten seconds later, I felt the canister start to automatically rewind. For the first time, I looked at the scene without the camera in my face and I knew I had one, maybe two, keeper-photos.

"Thank you," I said softly to Maude and Harold and their three chicks. "And, thank you," I said, turning to look at Widder.

"Watching you was absolutely amazing," she whispered. "For the first time, I think I know how I look when I get engrossed in a painting or when…." She stopped and looked at the ceiling of the blind. She closed her eyes.

"When you what?" I asked.

"It's not important. What is important is that I was with you when you took that picture. I saw what you saw. When I see it in your book, I will know what it meant to you to take it. I will know what you were doing at the precise moment you shot the picture. I will know what you did to get what you worked so hard to get."

I suddenly realized how tired I was and how I just wanted to sit down and cry. Concentrated mental effort, bolstered with an adrenaline rush for short periods of time, can be exhausting.

"I don't know if I've ever said this to anyone before," I said. "Or maybe I just realized it. But it's times like this when my mind becomes one with the camera and the scene. I see the scene in frames of captured light through the lens. But even after the film is gone and I put the camera down, I can see each and every frame very clearly.

"I think I have four to six photos that could go in any book about birds, Caddo Lake or cormorants in general. There's the initial shot or two of Harold sliding through the incredibly blue sky with the morning sun layered on his wings; there's a three-or-four shot series of him landing with Maude's wings outstretched and the chicks going nuts for food; there's a shot of Maude ripping the fish apart and then feeding the babies."

I paused and then added, "I hope what I think is there is there."

Eh-it's there.

"Don't worry," Widow said, "it's there." She reached over and took my hand and held it gently, tickling my knuckles with her thumb. We watched the Maude and Harold show for a few more minutes. I reloaded both cameras and got some extreme close-ups of the middle chick's head as Maude shoved fish parts in its gullet. It's not an original shot, but always a crowd-pleaser.

"Did you mention you had some breakfast?" I asked, pausing between pictures.

Immediately there was some faint rustling behind me and then a soft hand rested on my arm and Widder pushed me into my chair. She put a thick paper plate in my lap containing two biscuit, scrambled egg, and sausage sandwiches. I took a bite. Homemade biscuits. Fluffy eggs. Good even cold. Sausage with a hint of sage and paprika.

Chewing the first bite for what seemed to be an inordinate length of time, I swallowed and said, "Life doesn't get any better than this."

"Maybe it does," she said, handing me a cup of hot coffee she had poured from a stainless steel thermos. No cream. No sugar.

Leaning back in the chair and propping my feet on the short blind wall, I took another bite. "I was wrong the first time. It doesn't get any better than *this*."

"Sure it does," Widder said. "Either it does or you're mighty easy to please."

Conversation took a break. The breakfast sandwiches and coffee—plus keeping tabs on Maude and the chicks—occupied the time. Harold was off hunting again. I shot a single frame of him jumping up, wings up high to pop down and catch a draft as he almost literally fell away from the nest toward the water got my adrenaline flowing again.

It was not spectacular—more Gilligan than Skipper—and I told Widder so.

After we polished off the sandwiches and most of the coffee, I checked the other nests and started looking for other photo possibilities. The sun was climbing fast and the flat light of mid-morning to late afternoon was not usually conducive to picture-perfect pictures. The sky contained not a hint of cloud cover.

Widder pointed out a lazing alligator about seventy-five yards away. It didn't offer up any award-winning photo images. I picked up a little movement in the nearby grove of cypress trees. A nutria was swimming in its breed's straight-line method.

"I bet he comes out of the woods in that little nest of knees near that biggest tree," I said. "Then he'll go across the lake until he gets to that closest bunch of water hyacinths."

"You're on," Widder said, following my finger as I pointed out the landmarks. "What's the bet?"

"I'll think of something."

The nutria, just as he (or she) had done about nine a.m. almost every single time I had been in the blind, came out of the cypress grove right behind the little knee nest, skirting the north side, and headed straight for the water hyacinths I had pointed out.

"You lose," I said with authority. "Pay up!"

"Pay up? What was the bet?"

"The bet was that the winner would receive a kiss from the loser."

"That was the bet, huh?"

"Yes, ma'am. And winners never cheat and cheaters never win," I said.

"What if a person knows something is going to happen before it happens and then bets on the outcome. Isn't that cheating?"

"Nope. Not at all. That nutria could have been gobbled up by that little ol' alligator before he even reached the water hyacinths."

"So I have to kiss you because the water rat ran the maze the same time it has before," she said.

"Yep. Unless you're a welcher."

Her hands glided up to my face and she pulled me forward. My eyes closed and I could feel the heat generating from here body as she stepped closer.

Then she kissed me. Right on the forehead.

My eyes snapped open like a steel trap snaps shut.

Widder was leaning against the near blind wall, holding her sides and laughing loud enough to cause Maude to get fidgety.

She was trying to talk and laugh at the same time. "Eh-if yah-you could just see your fa-face!" She sounded like Bob.

Jah-jesus. Sha-she sounds...."

I felt my face flush. "That wasn't the bet. That was not the bet!"

The laughter ran its course. "You said the loser had to kiss the winner. You won. I lost. I paid off the bet."

"A kiss on the forehead does not count in any civilized society as a kiss."

That set her off again. Finally, she said, "This isn't a civilized society. This is Baxter or Marion County, Texas."

"A bet is a bet." I was on the edge of heavy-duty pout mode.

"Maybe you better learn to specify your bet."

I looked at her. Then I smiled. Taking my right hand, I vigorously rubbed my forehead where she planted the kiss. Then I took my hand and kissed it expansively, open-lipped and with sound effects. Without opening my eyes, I licked my open palm, from the wrist all the way to the fingertips and back again.

You're nah-nuts!

Widder was laughing again and between giggle spouts, she said, "Okay, I give! Uncle! Tickle lock! Calf rope!"

She took my fresh-licked hand and poured some water out of a bottle across the palm. Untying the big knot of her shirt, she wiped the hand dry. Her movements were hypnotic.

With no warning, she kissed my palm. Icy fire formed where her lips touched my skin and raced along veins and arteries to touch every part of my body.

She stopped, which restarted my heart. "How was that?"

"Eh-it wah-wah…." Now I sounded like Bob.

Her right index finger slid up to my lips and shushed my stammering. She pulled my head down. Her lips touched mine and the feeling was lighter than a floating spider web on the morning breeze. Her tongue lightly flicked at my lips, a darting moth hovering over a steady candle flame. My eyes automatically closed and she increased the pressure of her lips to mine. Without realizing it, my arms were around her, crushing her to my chest and our lips were sliding, slithering, sensuously vibrating. Our front teeth touched as her tongue flicked at the roof of my mouth. All I could think about was undoing zippers and popping buttons.

My hand started sliding from her back…and just as quickly as it began, the kiss ended. I opened my eyes as she stepped back. If this scene were in a romance novel, she would have been described as "dewy," with beads of perspiration dotting her forehead and upper lip.

UNCERTAIN TIMES

She signed deeply. "Okay, now, how was that?"

I smiled and fell into the pink plastic chair. "The only think I can say is 'Wow!' And, let's make another bet, this time double or nothing."

"What we both need is a cold shower. But how about settling for the last of the hot coffee?"

I needed something, anything. Coffee was not even on my Top 100 list.

18

Life, as we know it, can change without us even knowing it.

Anonymous

The coffee was still hot. It was just barely on the south side of scalding. It burned my mouth in a good way. Grabbing a bag of fruity orange slices from one of the plastic bags, I offered one to Widder.

"My favorite," was all she said, as she took two and stuck one in her mouth. I instantly was a little pissed off that part of me was jealous of a stupid candied orange slice.

"How da ya ee yo swiceses?" she asked, between rhythmic, chomping mouth movements.

"I just realized that I like to bit off little sections that are divided by the orangey lines and eat them one at a time."

Widder, who was definitely doing some heart-rate pumping jaw calisthenics, slurred: "I usted ta at thum that wah. Buh now Ai jus kinda mulch thum up wid my teef en swaddo tha ho thang."

"I assume you mainly do this when you're alone and not out somewhere alone with a handsome world-traveler?"

"Yeth. Dis is a 'ception."

We sat there for a long time, not talking, just watching the nests, occasionally checking out the sun as it crawled across the sky.

Harold finally came back and took a turn at trying to feed the babies. You could tell their sharp little beaks punching in the air made him nervous. Nothing to get excited about. Sun pretty much overhead and mid-day shadows are conducive to wasting film.

Widder dug in the picnic basket and I was just getting ready to tell her I wasn't hungry yet when she pulled out several sheets of paper. "Early versions from the Poem Board," she said. The second orange slice disappeared in her mouth and was subjected to immediate and vigorous mastication.

Mah-mastication is a guh-good word.

Shut up, Bob.

The poems were written neatly on a lined notepad. There were five in all.

I leafed through the pages, reading the first one out loud.

Time
With you
Is like the rising tide.
It slowly, methodically
Covers my heart and soul
With wave after wave
Of lasting feelings of love.

Time
With you
Is like the rising sun.
It breaks through the darkness
And illuminates my soul,
Allowing me to accept
The lasting feelings of love.

Pausing, I looked at Widder. Her head was back, eyes closed. She opened the eye closest to me and the pupil slid over to my face.

"What?" she said.

"Nothing. Just a nice sentiment."

The eye slowly closed.

Time
With you
Is like Christmas morning.
It allows my childlike spirit
To emerge and grow
And respond naturally
To lasting feelings of love.

Time
With you
Is like a full moon.
It shatters the darkness
With its velvet light-streams
And paints surreal pictures
Of lasting feelings of love.

I read it again, silently. letting the visual images caress my psyche. There was a special feeling in that poem. It was amateurish, sure, but not hastily thrown together. The second one was shorter and I also read it out loud:

Pumping iron,
Pumping iron,
Puffing legs and blowing up arms.
Pumping iron,
Pumping iron,
Trying to get some muscles.

Some girls want men with breasts like girls.
That's real hard to understand.
But men work to get those girlish breasts
And still look like a man.

Bee-stung,
They look to me,
As they pump and primp and sweat.
But I guess that has to be okay with me
Since they could crush me plumb to death.

"What do you think?" Widder said, before digging with one finger at a stray piece of candy stuck between her molars.

"Don't know yet. I'll tell you in a minute."

No. 3 was different. I read it silently, then aloud.

Life swarms with
Leaders,
Complainers,
Suck-ers, suckers
And followers.
For God's sake,
Be either 1 or 5
For they are the only ones
Who can laugh.
That trait will benefit
Their children,
For they shall
Inherit the mirth!

I suppose I was shaking my head at the last line because Widder said, "What?"

"They shall inherit the mirth? That's a great line. Who is writing these?" She turned to see if there was any activity in Octavia's nest.

The next one I read in a whisper, then repeated it aloud. With emphasis.

Is there a God?
God! There is!
Is there a God?

It's a question God expects,
Thus answering the question.

This five-line ditty deserved several readings.
I-I like that wah-one.
"I really like that one," Widder said, turning her head and fixing both eyes on the poem in my hands.
"Then it's unanimous."
I turned to the last one.

Systems churning
Think-tanks yearning
For the ultimate score.
CEOs salivating,
Groupies gravitating
Till they can take no more.
Deals extreme,
Listen! The screams!
Of the monied whores.

What am I missing here? Are these gawddamned good or just gawdawful?
Mah-maybe both.
"What?"
I looked up at Widder. "I'm sorry. What?"
"No, I just said 'what?' You had the strangest look on your face."
"I can't figure out for the life of me if some of these are really good or all of them are really, really bad." Pause. "Or is it that I'm a bad judge of poetry. I'm no expert, but I read a lot and I love to read poetry on occasion when I'm in the mood. A glass of wine, roaring fireplace, snowflakes coming down like tiny pillows, a good woman curled up on the floor rubbing my feet…that's a good time to read poetry."

She set up as if stabbed in the butt with a blunt darning needle. "A good woman curled up…?"

"Yes, but forget that for a minute. You can play that part some time but not now. We try and build up a fire in here and we're burn the damn blind down. It's not going to snow on Caddo anytime this century and the closest thing to wine we have is (I opened the ice chest and withdrew a bottle) a half-full bottle of grape-cranberry juice. The point is: Is this good poetry or not?"

She settled back down.

"Why couldn't it just *be*. Why does it have to be judged?"

After a pause to consider the statement and the question, I said, "People are judgers. It is something that most of us can not *not* do. People look at my photos and they either like them or they don't. They may not see the nuances of light or the selective focus that I think makes it a good photo. It may be the greatest picture of a snake ever taken, but if some person has an aversion to snakes, to them, it's not a good picture. Some old biddy drives by your yard and judges whether or not the landscaping is nice. Harmony and Bother judge me and I judge them."

I paused and Widder gave a little rotating hand signal, which, I surmised, meant "go on."

"It's human nature to judge, well, virtually everything we come in contact with," I said. "We look at people and made judgments about the way they look, dress, comb their hair, walk, talk and communicate with body language. We look at companies and either like their products or don't. We look at Web sites and find them user-friendly or absurdly difficult."

"You have a good point," Widder said, picking up another orange slice, then putting it down. "We even describe people that way. For example, if I were describing Hum I would say he always wears a blue-and-white checked shirt, can cook simple foods well, and doesn't talk, just goes 'Hmmm.'"

"How would you describe Harmony and Bother?"

Her lips pursed for a second or two: "Little boys lost."

"No, seriously, how would you describe them?"

"I was being serious. Those two never had a chance, When I first came to Caddo about twenty years ago, they were just boys, hightailing it from place to place on two old, ratty bicycles. Bother has always seemed slow; the rumor is his daddy threw or knocked him against a wall when he was just a baby. His 'sin' was crying when his daddy was trying to sleep off a drunk. It's always been Harmony and Bother; see one, see them both, for as long as anyone can remember. You know they are only in their early twenties?"

"That can't be! Nobody can get that mean in less than thirty years, minimum."

"It's true. Neither one of them caused much trouble till their mamma left when the boys were about ten and twelve. Bother's the oldest."

"I thought he was the younger of the two."

She looked out toward Maude's nest and smiled. She pointed and I tracked her finger to see the three chicks, heads up, scanning the sky for mamma, poppa, and food, in that order. I looked back at Widder and winked.

Wah-winking is ah-overrated.

"Most people think that. Harmony has always taken care of Bother," Widder said. "I'll bet he's been the Alpha male since he was crawling."

"You said their mamma left. What happened?"

"Hiram Ledbetter, the boy's daddy, just told everyone Althea—that was her name—'runned' off. Said she hitchhiked to Shreveport and caught a bus north. The sheriff at the time did some poking around, but 'caught a bus north' is the official story."

"So, when did Hiram die?"

"He didn't. He's still alive. Lives down a lane off the Marshall highway. Has a small cabin that is pretty much built right up against the lake. The boys still live at home."

It took a while to process this information.

"How'd they get those names," I asked. "I assume their real names are not 'Harmony' and 'Bother.'"

Widder took a sip of water. "'Harmony' is a family name. I've heard that several men and women in the Ledbetter clan were named 'Harmony.' The story is that when Bother was born, he was premature. Hiram supposedly looked at him and told his wife, 'If you can't have 'em no bigger than that, why bother?'"

"Jesus! Lots of people have a hard time growing up. Most of them don't turn out just plumb mean. When I look in Harmony's eyes, it's like there's nobody home. I swear I can see all the way to back of his head. Empty. Cold."

"I know. I've seen, or not seen, to be more precise, the same thing. It's different with Bother. Everyone who meets him thinks he's retarded. And, in a way, he is. But he made good grades in some classes at school. That is, until Harmony decided to quit school and took Bother with him." Anticipating my next question, she said, "They were in their mid-teens when they dropped out of school and started working at odd jobs around the lake."

Tons of thoughts waded around in my head like a stork convention. I must have tuned out because I looked up and saw while Widder had been talking, she had also been busy making sandwiches. She handed me two pieces of wheat-berry bread that had a slab of ham on it the size of a forty-five rpm. record and about as thick as a regional telephone book.

"This is a real man sandwich," I said, thanking her for the thought and the effort.

"What does that make me, then?" she said, flashing a heart-stopping smile with a fenceful of teeth. She pulled a similar sandwich to her mouth and took a huge bite. I gave her a thumb's-up and said, "You're just one of the guys, Miss C.C. You're a man, all right, a WO-man!"

The sandwiches, canned Nestea and a big bag of baked chips occupied us. I took the opportunity to study Widder. She was leaning back in the chair, happily eating her sandwich and stopping only occasion to get a sip of tea and a chip.

She was not a dainty eater, at least not in this setting. She attacked the meal but not in a sloppy or uncouth way. No bird nibbles to make an impression. It's a sandwich! Eat the damn thing!

Without realizing it, I laughed, causing her to look my way. She asked a question by arching her eyebrows.

"Oh, nothing," I said. "I was just admiring the way you are enjoying that sandwich."

"I am probably giving the impression of making a pig of myself, but I'm at the point in my life where honesty is more important than just about anything. This is a good sandwich; why play with it? Eat the damn thing!"

"My thoughts exactly and that's the truth."
Sha-she's starting to wah-worry me.
Why?
Tah-too perfect.
I'm not worried, Bob. Just a mite scared.

19

The courting dance of humans is the funniest thing on the planet and proves beyond any doubt that God has a sense of humor.

Anonymous

"How would you describe me?" I asked after the last bite of sandwich had been washed down.

"Too early to tell," Widder said. "And, I think, you are much more complex than you let on. You have a shield up most of the time, too. I haven't figured out why it's there and what caused it."

"I don't have a...."

"Yes, you do. Now hush and let me finish." She popped a potato chip in her mouth. She didn't immediately chew it. "Ah lak to suk ahff tha saht."

Lucky chip. Luckier salt.

For once, Bob agreed with me.

She swallowed. I swallowed and if Bob could have swallowed....

"Are you married?"

"Wha..." I had just taken a drink of tea and got strangled.

"It's a simple question: Are you married?"

"No. No. Was once, but no longer. Did you think I was married?"

"It doesn't matter what I think. What does matter is the reality of the situation. I didn't think you were married, but I've thought that before and was wrong. I just wanted to make sure. Do you have a name and number that I can call to verify your marital status?"

I blew tea out my nose. "Wha…? Ah-ah-are yuh-yuh-you serious?"

Widder's nose wrinkled like a new calico dress. It looked like her freckles were trying to mate. "Gotcha!"

"Well, stop it. I'd hate for my obituary headline to be: "Famous photographer dies from drowning in a can of Nestea."

Her laughter made me think of a set of graduated bells in a little church in the interior of Peru. "Don't worry, it won't. In the *Uncertain Times*, your death notice headline would read "Big City Smart Mouth Dies While Courting School Marm."

"Is that what we're doing? Courting?"

She gave me a look that made me think "Stupid" was tattooed on my forehead.

Jah-jesus. Yah-you are such idiot.

What does that make you, Bob?

That shut him up.

"Tell me about your ex-wife?"

"I married her for all the wrong reasons. She married me for different, but still wrong, reasons. She was, in a phrase, knock-down, screaming gorgeous. She was the perfect woman for a teenager's wet dream. Tall, blonde, athletic, smart, witty." The last word tailed off.

"What went wrong?"

No apology for her curiosity. None expected.

"Everything. Before we got married, there was every sign that the match would be a disaster, but I ignored them. She had an ex-husband and they were umbilically knotted together in some strange sort of psychological dance. She told me a thousand times that her ex would always be her best friend. I hated it when she told me that. I wanted to be married to *my* best friend. They both had master's degrees but he was a frustrated hippie-type that quit teaching college and decided to be a farmer. Even though he came from a farm family, I thought he was a lousy farmer. That's probably just my prejudice showing."

UNCERTAIN TIMES

I paused to allow questions, but Widder did the hand-circling motion again. She popped in another chip. I had another internal spasm.

"He was not happy, no matter what he did. Up and walked off and left three wives. With two of them he just left a note on the table. 'Gone,' Have a good life.'"

"You're not serious?"

"Dead serious. Don't know the exact words on the notes, but the sentiment is there. He was always searching for something, someone, better. He was very intelligent. Book smart, at least. He read all the time. He actually told me once that he enjoyed plowing while reading books by Chaim Potok." I ate a chip. "Have you ever read Potok?"

Widder waited to answer until she took a swallow of tea. "Once. At least I tried. I'm not good with book titles, but this one was something like *The City of Lights* or something."

"*The Book of Lights.*"

"That's it. It bored me silly. Have you read it?"

"I tried to read it. Couldn't get past the second chaper. The only book of Potok's I ever made it all the way through was his first one, *The Chosen*. On the International Scale of Book Boredom, with ten being 'bored to tears and contemplating suicide,' it was a twelve. But I did learn a little about what I think drove my ex-husband-in-law...."

"Ex-husband-in-law?"

"The triangle in the relationship was as weird as a carnival freak show. That's what Bob named him after the first year of marriage."

"Bob?"

"A friend. A...close friend. But, anyway, back to the point. What was the point?

Oh, yeah, reading the book helped me to at least halfway understand why he was the way he was. Potok has a re-occurring theme about father-son or father-family relationships."

Widder said, "What happened to your ex-wife?"

"I was on assignment in New Mexico seven or eight years ago and I got a call from the wife of my ex-husband-in-law. She said she caught the two of them at a seedy motel in the Arkansas Delta."

"He was married." A statement. Not a question. "What did you do?"

"I called my wife, let her hang herself with a couple of lies and said she had ten days to file for divorce or I would make damn sure that every single dollar we had or had saved would be spent on attorneys."

Silence. Then Widder said, "And she filed."

"And she filed. Money meant more than saving a relationship."

She picked up my hand and started rubbing the back of it with her thumb. "You're still hurting."

"No, not hurting," I said. "It's sadness I feel. No matter what I did, it was never enough. Wasted time. Wasted effort."

Widder said, "Where is she now?"

"She died. She remarried her ex when she got sick. She always said that she was going to die young, like her mother and grandmother. Both of them died in their early forty's; she was just over fifty." Pause. "Sometimes, you wish for something long enough and hard enough, you get what you want."

She didn't comment and I turned to look at her. Her eyes were on her hands, which she now clasped in her lap. Now it was her turn to let out a deep sigh. "Sometimes when relationships are bad, people search for some positive outlet as a form of escape."

"Or negative outlet."

"True," Widder said. "Or negative. But I like to think people are inherently good. It gets me in trouble sometimes, but I still like to think that way."

I tried to figure out how to phrase the thought that was nuclearizing in my head.

Nu-nuclearizing? Wha-what kind of....

Dammit, Bob!

"Please take this the right way," I said, knowing that was a horrible introduction line, "but you have isolated yourself in Uncertain. From what I've seen, you've pretty much withdrawn from society as a whole, with notable exceptions." I ended the open-ended comment/question with an elaborate sweep of my arm to indicate the current surroundings.

The silence was interminable. Finally, she said, "I was just thinking about that. You're right, of course. I can't take offense at what you said since it was just a minute ago I was talking about placing such a high value on honesty. When I came to Uncertain, I was running away, from a bad situation. And, probably from life. I found the area restful, even peaceful. For the most part. Living in my grandparents' home gave me a connection with the past while allowing me to live in the present."

"If you don't mind me asking, what situation did you run from?"

"Bad marriage." Widder laid it out. "Bad life. Bad everything. My husband was abusive, physically and emotionally. He was always unhappy with life the way it is and was always trying to change it. When events didn't turn out the way he wanted, he started pointing fingers and placing blame."

"So you up and left—where was it?"

"California."

"So you up and left California and came to Uncertain By God Out In The Middle of Nowhere Texas. Did you decide to come back home after your husband died."

"Nope. A year or so before. I just up and came back to my parents' funerals. Both had died in a car wreck. I stayed a while to settle the estate and take ownership of the house. I never went back."

"Your husband? What was his name?"

"Bob. That's why I asked who Bob was a minute ago. It just sort of startled me when you said the name."

"Okay, Bob then. He didn't come after you?"

"To be honest," she said, "I think he liked the freedom that he had when I was back here. And I kept making excuses for not coming home. Then after six months, I filed for divorce. That's when the rotten eggs hit the fan."

"Rotten eggs?"

"I started to say 'shit hit the fan but I'm trying to make a good impression here."

"So, what happened when Bob came to get you?" I said. "That's what happened? He came to get you, right?"

"That's right. Only he didn't make it. He took the southerly route from California to Arkansas and made a stop in El Paso. Crossed over into Mexico. His body was found in a back alley in Juarez. Stabbed. Robbed."

"And your sons?"

"They have the best of their father and I like to think, some of my better qualities. They both look like Bob. They have his gift of gab, can talk cats out of trees. I believe both of them have my creativity. Or, better stated, creative spirit. They are bright, well-adjusted, and I don't have to worry about them making it in this world."

"What about the future?"

"Who knows? It's not here yet. In fact, it's never here. When it gets here, it's the present."

"What about the next minute?"

"Don't know. It's not here yet."

I eased up in the chair, put my hands on her closest thigh, leaned in and kissed her lips. Not like before. Different. Not better. Different. A short, sweet kiss. Nice.

As I started to pull back, she grabbed me by the right ear and pulled me back, pecked me on the lips.

A whisper. "Thank you. Just…thank you."

20

Friends of assholes are always other assholes.

Anonymous

The thought of kissing Widder crossed my mind a second time. Then re-crossed it. The thought was broken by the sound of a sputtering boat motor. While boats came by the blind occasionally, most of the waterway traffic was early morning or late evening. Mid-day visitors were an aberration. Usually too hot, fishing not good and not good for sight-seeing since most of the critters were cubbied up, resting. Or hiding.

Getting up to look back at the entrance to Carter's Chute, I could hear the motor straining a little bit making the twisty-twirly curves of the channel. Widder didn't get up for some reason. For some reason I didn't want her to.

I made out two men in the boat when it flashed out of Carter's Chute from the east.

Bob's thought was a little panicky. *Hah-Harmony and Bother.*

It wasn't. It was two middle-aged men. Both had full beards and looked hard. Matching anvils.

As the boat turned directly to the blind, I could see both had on light shirt-jackets. One had on a chambray shirt; the other a dark sweatshirt with the letters "ten" visible between the folds. A wad of waders and a Styrofoam cooler occupied the center well between the seats.

I threw them a wave but got none in return so I moved to the north side of the blind and pretended to look at something in that direction. Out of the corner of my eye, I saw the man in front point in my direction and the other one nodded. The driver cut back on the power and the boat eased up next to the blind. The passenger grabbed the closest gunwale in my boat and pulled their boat up tight.

I put my hand down flat below the side wall of the blind, telling Widder to stay put.

"Morning."

"Mornin' back to ya," the driver said. "Somebody said there was somebody out here sitting up housekeeping in my brother's and me's blind."

"Buddy Parlay set me up in this blind about three-four weeks ago."

"Don't care for him. Didn't vote for him neither. I'm saying that's our blind. You calling me a liar?"

I didn't say anything but had to shush Bob before he got started.

"Are you deaf?"

"Not hardly. Well, I'm about through today anyway. Think I'll load up and head back to the dock. I'll get ahold of Buddy this afternoon and get this whole mess straightened out."

The two men exchanged quick eye contact. The talkative one grinned.

"Nope, that's not what gonna happen atall," the boat driver said. "You be trespassing and in these parts, trespassers get taught a lesson." Turning his head to his passenger, he said, "Elrod, how far is it you reckon back to Uncertain?"

Elrod studied on that a bit and said, "Ridin' in a boat or swimmin'?"

Both men hooted like they'd gone to the circus and seen their first elephant.

Elrod reached over and started untying my boat from a blind leg.

"I wouldn't do that, if I were you," I said, trying to put menace in my voice.

"Well, shit, you ain't me, Big City Smart Mouth, now, are you?"

He was still working on the knot when the first shot hit the water next to the boat. Elrod jerked his hand back like he had been moccasin-struck. The boat driver hunkered down between the back and middle seats. I jumped straight up and hit my head on a roof support. I was holding my head and trying to hold back tears when a second shot blasted by my right ear. Two thoughts emerged simultaneously: 1) I'm shot!; and 2) I'm shot twice!

"Gawddamn!" I screamed. I opened my eyes just in time to see Widder aiming for a third shot. She was holding a gun that General Patton could have put to good use against Rommel in Africa in World War II.

I checked out the visitors with one eye. The driver was reaching under his seat and another shot from the pistol rang out and a hole appeared between his feet. It was immediately followed by a small, wondrous fountain of brackish water.

"Fuckamighty, Widder! Have you gone half batty?"

"Unhand that rope, Elrod. And I mean now!" Elrod dropped the rope to our boat like it was a hot andiron. "Beryl, crank up that motor and get the hell out of here."

Beryl looked up and a scary grimace hit his face like a claw mark. "Yeah, Widder, or what?"

"Or I'm gonna put the next bullet through your zipper and the one after that through your motor and if you think you can swim or walk out of here without bleeding to death, then just go ahead and do what you gotta do."

I looked around for something manly to do but came up empty. I wasn't a fifth wheel; I was a sixth wheel that was flat.

Beryl finally let the smug grin slide off his face. But you could tell he wanted more than anything to make Widder eat that gun, after first making her eat something much more personal.

The gun in Widder's hand didn't waver. Even from my angle, I could tell it was aimed right at Beryl's zipper. About fourteen teeth down from the top.

Tha-that would hurt.

"This here ain't the end of it, Widder. You know that." He licked his lips while looking in the general direction of Widder's chest, which were prominently encased in that orange halter top between the folds of the white cover-up.

"Oh, it's the end, Beryl. It's the fucking end. Now get the fuck...I apologize for my language, being a lady and all. Now get out of here and tell your stupid-ass cousins that they're too stupid, chicken-shit, or lazy to do their own dirty work. And be sure to tell them that their dickless stand-ins got *runned off* by a little woman with a big-ass gun. Be sure and tell 'em, Beryl. 'Cause when I get back to town, I'm telling everybody I meet. The first thing I'm gonna do when I get back to town is go to Harlan's and put up a fucking poster telling what went down here today. Then, just because you pissed me off royally looking at my tits, I'm going to take out a full-page ad in the *Uncertain Times* and tell every fucking person on the entire fucking planet what worthless hinny-hole punchers you two are."

Hah-how much cir-circulation you figure that paper's gah-got?

Beryl looked as mean as a pit bull on short chain and shorter rations. Elrod just looked puzzled. Beryl reached for the starter cord, when Widder's next words froze him.

"One more thing, Beryl. If you ever think about trying to hurt me or Mr. Jones, I swear I will find you, cut off your nuts and stuff them down your throat. It makes no never mind to me if you're dead or alive when I do it. Think about it, Beryl. It's Texas! A woman can shoot a man—or two of them, three if she's a mind to—claim they tried to rape her and get off without even having to go to the courthouse. Hell, for killing you two, I'd get a fucking medal and a key to Uncertain."

Then she fired another shot that hit between the two boats and showered both men with a wall of water.

"Now, GIT!"

"You're fucking crazy, Widder?" Beryl said as he pulled on the cord. Three pulls it took to start the boat. Beryl cranked down on the throttle and turned the boat quickly toward the exit channel, yelling at Elrod to find something to "plug the gawddamn hole."

I looked at Widder and she reached up and closed my mouth with the fingers not holding the hand-cannon.

Then she swivel-butted the gun and handed it to me. She batted her eyes like an ingénue in a silent movie. "Would you please take this big, ol' gun? Why, I do de-clare, they just plumb scare me to death."

21

Whoever said size doesn't matter is either blind or just plain stupid.

Anonymous

I took the gun and was amazed that I could even hold it. It was the biggest handgun I had ever seen. It was about the size of an Army trenching implement.

Looking at Widder, I said, "Hinny-hole punchers?"

"I was mad. It was the best thing I could come up with at the time."

My eyes went back to the seven-pound pistol I was holding. Without being asked, Widder recited: ".45 caliber, Smith and Wesson revolver. Single action. Holds six rounds. Ten and three-eighths inches from end to end with a five-inch barrel. Hogue rubber combat grip that has been sanded down to fit my hand, then resealed. Satin stainless finish with Patridge front sight and black adjustable back sight. I put a dot of White Out on tip of the front sight so I could find it quickly."

She reached up again and closed my mouth.

Sha-show her your guh-gun.

"I've got a gun."

"I'm sure you do, Big Boy. Oh, you mean *that* kind of gun. I know. Nine millimeter Glock. You got it from Mitchell."

She reached up a third time to close my mouth.

I stood there, with my mouth closed, looking at the gun and then at Widder.

"Do you have any questions?" she said, batting her eyes fast enough to give a hummingbird flight.

"Do you want to make out?"

22

Sometimes life is like a movie. Other times it's like a movie trailer.

Anonymous

After Widder stopped laughing, we decided that heading back to Uncertain was probably a wise move.

The extent of conversation on the subject went something like this:

Me: "Let's go to town."

Her: "Sounds like a plan."

In the middle of picking up stray pieces of chips and throwing them in the water as a Caddo Lake variation of chumming, I stood up, frowned, and said, "Cousins?"

Widder kept gathering up stuff. "Elrod and Beryl are first cousins; their mamas were sisters. And their granddaddy and Harmony and Bother's granddaddy were first cousins. So that makes them fourth or fifth cousins to each other, which around here means they get invited to reunions and homecomings."

"Where did you learn to shoot like that?"

"Taught myself, actually," Widder said. "I ran into a little trouble when I first came to Uncertain so I went to town, bought me a gun and practiced, practiced, practiced."

She anticipated my next question. "I bought the biggest gun the store had for a reason. I wanted everybody and their brother to know that the Widder Gleason had the biggest damn gun in the county and wasn't afraid to use it. If I could have bought a bazooka, I would have."

"What...? How...? What I mean is...."

"I used to practice for five minutes every morning behind my house. I put up targets on a cypress tree back there—well, actually, it's a stump now—and just blasted away. Usually started in about seven every morning, about the time the crowd hit Harlan's and Hum's for C&C."

"C&C?"

"Coffee and chatter. I figured they'd hear the gunfire and pass the word that 'Widder's practicing again'," she said.

"You mentioned you ran into trouble when you first came back," I said. "What kind of trouble."

"A couple of men came 'callin',' as they called it. I didn't want them 'calling' but they wouldn't leave. I wanted to make sure that the next time they came 'calling' and I asked them to leave, they'd leave."

"What men?"

"What men what?"

"Came calling?"

"Hiram Ledbetter was one."

I had a million follow-up questions but didn't ask any of them. The look on her face plainly asked me not to.

When everything was as packed as it was going to get, Widder climbed down the stairs to the boat and I started lowering items to her using the frayed rope. Not trusting my camera bag to the rope (or, for that matter, Widder), I put my head and left arm through the strap and eased down the plank ladder.

I decided to take the air mattress, but left the extra chair.

"How come you didn't go down first and check out my ass?" Widder said.

"Seen that. Thought I'd check out some new scenery."

"And?"

"A little change in scenery is good for a body. High mountains or deep valleys...I like 'em all."

She tried to hide a sprouting smile.

"You want to get that extra chair?" she asked.

"I'll leave it. Maybe I'll have another visitor over to the house sometime."

"Maybe. Never can tell. Always good to be prepared. That's my motto."

Mine too. Now.

The boat ride home was a nervous one. My head swiveled from side to side like an oscillating fan. Widder was tense; her hands were tightly clinched in front of her.

We had just emerged from the curvy channel from Carter's Chute when I noticed something for the first time over at the west shoreline. I angled the boat over that way and told Widder, in response to her question, that there was a possible picture that I needed to get.

Cutting back on the throttle, I slid the flat-bottomed boat gently over a patch of pussy willow onto a grassy patch of dirt without making a single punny remark. Bob *ah-applauded* my restraint.

I got out Betsy and unscrewed the lens, popped the water-tight medal camera case and popped a thirty-five mm. macro out and clicked it in the camera base. "Come with me," I said, more as a plea than an order.

Widder took my hand and gingerly stepped from the boat to the shore. It was hard to imagine that just minutes before she was holding a gun the size of a howitzer, blasting holes in boats, and cussing like a drunk with Tourette's.

"What'd you see?"

"If this is what I think it is.... It is. It's a tickle tongue tree."

"Tickle tongue? Is this is a ploy to get me into a conversation about sex?"

"If it was, would the ploy work?"

"There you go again...."

We finished the line together: "Answering a question with a question."

"I've lived here for a long time. I've never heard of a tickle tongue tree," Widder said.

"It's also called a toothache tree. It's from the *Rutaceae* family, genus *zanthoxylum* and the species name is *hirsutum*."

I reached over and gleefully pushed Widder's bottom jaw up to touch her top. "I may not have as big a gun as you, but, Baby, I do have a lot of useless trivia floating around in my head."

I explained that the tickle tongue tree got its name from its natural ability to dull pain. "Indian tribes used it as a mild anesthetic. Here," I said, breaking off one of the wide-based thorns, "I'll show you. Stick out your tongue."

Widder did. Quickly. At me. Then it slid it right back in, like a scared turtle hiding in its shell.

"Come on, Woman! Be a man! Take your medicine. If you don't stick out your tongue, I'm going to tell all the folks in town that when Elrod and Beryl showed up, you cowered in the corner of the blind and wet your pants."

That did it. She stuck out her tongue, but only after giving me a *frog country* bump on my shoulder muscle from a fierce hit with an extended knuckle from her tiny fist.

"That hurt," I said, rubbing the raised knot caused by the contracted muscle.

"Good. Now let's get on with it."

She stuck out her tongue and this time she kept it out, I touched the raw side of the thorn to her tongue and rubbed it back and forth before tossing the short, sharp spiny thorn aside.

A few seconds later she said: "It's tingling!"

"*Voila!* Tickle tongue."

I explained that all parts of the tree are poisonous if ingested. That didn't set well with her until I explained that merely rubbing a thorn's backside against her tongue did not contain enough poison to matter.

"Indian women would take a bunch of thorns and grind them up and make a poultice and pack it in wounds and even on large bruises."

"How do you know about this? Like I said, I live here and have never heard that."

I explained that extensive research on an area always was the first step to tackling a photography project. "And," I said, "this tree is a relative of a similar type tree that grows down in the Amazon basin. That one, though, can either take away all pain or kill you, depending on the time of year."

Widder looked at me with a strange smile.

"Are you trying to impress me because of what happened back at the blind?"

Sha-she's smart.

"Probably." Pause. "Maybe." Pause. "Damn skippy. What happened at the blind was a new experience for me. I mean, I've stared down headhunters in some of the most unexplored areas of central South America. I've taken a picture of a charging rhino as it went right by me at 35 mph. I've taken close-ups of a swarm of piranhas tearing apart a bird carcass. But I've never been rescued by a woman. It unnerved me a bit, I'll admit."

"You've stared down headhunters?"

I nodded. Then: "Gotcha!" Followed by an evil, maniacal laugh with my own special end zone dance. The entire routine was punctuated by a mime spike of a mental football.

Chanting "Who's No. 1! Who's No. 1!" was a bit over the top but as Bob clearly thought, *Ya-you needed to get your sa-self-esteem back.*

Widder started laughing and couldn't stop. That just egged my performance to a higher level, with more exaggerated dance moves, hip thrusts and Indian war whoops.

She grabbed my hand as I danced around her and jerked me down beside her. I inadvertently on purpose fell against her and my momentum caused me to bowl her over and me to, sort of, fall on top of her.

Our laughter continued until it didn't. Just as she was taking in a big breath, I kissed her. With purpose. Her arms went around my neck and I prayed the kiss would never end. It did, finally, but not without at least one of us trying hard not to let the moment escape.

"That was nice." That's all she said.

I helped her to her feet and as I was reaching back to grab her hand, she hauled off and hit me hard in the same muscle she did before with the same damn knuckle.

The knot that rose this time was twice as big before.

"Damn, Woman. That hurt! Would you quit that?"

"If you ever show me up again, I promise you I will tickle tongue your ass until you beg me to stop."

My tongue beat her to the verbal draw.

"Is that a promise?

23

Building friendships is hard work. Why, then, does it sometimes seem so darn easy?

Anonymous

It only took a few minutes to get a close-up photo of a tickle tongue spine. I chose one that was in front of an empty bird's nest. The thorn was in perfect focus and the macro's field of vision put the bird nest very out of focus, but still recognizable. It was not a great shot but was a decent filler for the book.

During the process, Widder asked questions and I let her look through the lens to see what it was I was trying to capture. I told her to crack off a frame or two and added that if any she shot were good, I would try and work it in the book and give her credit.

"Pickup line?" she asked.

"Of course."

Holding the camera like it was a hot anvil, she quickly shot 10 or 12 frames.

"Just like a woman: Give them an inch and they'll take a mile."

"Just like a man: Show you an inch and claim it's a mile."

Ah-are you that slow or is sha-she that fast?

Fuck you, Bob. And the psyche you rode in on.

Tha-that answered mah-my question.

The trip back to town was uneventful but there were a couple of boats tied up at the dock and several scatterings of men were huddled on it. One of the men I met earlier at the Poem Board—Thompson—waved as I guided the boat to an empty spot, and motioned for Widder to throw him the rope.

"Thanks, Thompson. Appreciate it." Widder indicated that she'd haul stuff out of the boat and hand it to me. She had untied the knot in her shirt and buttoned it up tight over the halter-top.

As we transferred gear onto the dock, I said to Thompson, "How long did you rodeo?"

He leaned back on his heels and looked at me, his expression hinged somewhere between quizzical and plumb strange.

"'Bout 30 years, on and off. The 'off' times was when I was banged up."

"Calf-roping, and I'd say, probably, riding bareback broncs?"

"Some bull-ridin' too," he said. "Although those bulls scared me something awful." Several of the men had moved closer to us. Sometimes sound carries good around water; sometimes it just swallows it up.

"You ever rodeo?" Thompson asked.

"Nope. Too scared to even try just about every event," I said, smiling and winking, "except maybe the Grand Entry."

Several of the men hooted, and Thompson said, "How 'bout barrel racing?"

"Nope, not for me. I was a NRA photographer for a time in college and even spent a year on the circuit shooting pictures on assignment. Saw some girls take some nasty spills barrel racing."

"That's a fact. How'd you know I was a cowboy?" he said. "That was a long time ago."

"I didn't notice it the first time we met," I said, "but coming into the dock, I noticed the way you were standing: Thumbs hooked into the tops of your jeans, legs set wide apart for balance. But when you half-hitched that rope in two seconds flat, and flipped your hands in a miniature 'all done' sign, I had a real good notion you didn't practice that on boat ropes."

He smiled. "Glad you're back safe," he said. Tipping his short-brimmed, straw hat to Widder: "Ma'am."

Back safe?

"News travels fast hereabouts," Widder said, thumbing at Bart's and Irv's boat set away from the others in the pussy willow shallows. Half-sunk in the mud. Half-full of water.

Bah-beryl and El....

"Whatever."

"What?" Widder said.

"Nothing. Thinking out loud again."

The group of men wandered off, some heading toward Harlan's, a few going in the direction of Hum's.

Widder said something low and grumbly.

"What?"

She looked at me and shook her head. "Winning friends and influencing people. You have this gift, you know, of finding a connection, a bridge, so to speak, with people. I'll bet you can go up to just about anybody and start up a conversation and find out more about them in a minute than most people could in a month."

I didn't answer right away, mulling over the supposition. Picking up the ice chest and my camera case, I said, "You're right. Or, at least, I'd like to think you're right. I like people, genuinely like them. Or most, anyway. I have always believed that people, if they work hard enough and work together in communicating, they can find something that connects them."

She picked up double handfuls of sacks and we walked down the dock toward the sparse parking lot.

"When I was a kid, I worked for paper in north Arkansas and I went out on assignment to do a feature photo page on a hermit. An honest-to-God hermit. This guy lived three miles off a dirt road way back in the Ozark Mountains. He was mostly self-sufficient, growing or killing his own food and lived in a dirt-floor cabin with a pack of dogs.

"A county employee directed me to the trail to house and I headed in by a faint foot trail. About a mile or so in, I heard barking and baying by what I took to be 100 or more dogs. The sounds got closer and closer and, being the sane person I am, I shinnied up a big oak tree. I was sitting on a big fat limb when, seriously, 20 to 30 mixed-breed dogs ran up, all slobber-jawed, and started clamoring around the tree. This tall, gaunt man with a beard down to his waist just sort of materialized under the tree.

"'Who are you and what you be wantin'?' was what he said. "Why're you up in that tree?"

"'Adnijio Benjamin Franklin Jones is my name and I'm sitting in this tree admiring the beauty of the countryside,'" I said. "Then I gave him the spiel about working for the paper and wanting to do a story and photo spread of him, but he didn't say another word. Just stood under the tree with all these dogs milling around and looked at me.

I paused and shook my head as the memories slapped away.

"The whole scene was surreal. Here I was in the middle of nowhere, sitting in a tree trying to talk to a hermit who had more dogs than a big city kennel. I realized I needed to find a connection and find it quick.

"'That's a good beard you got there,' I said. "'I sure wish I could grow a beard like that, but mine's kinda patchy.'"

"He pulled on his beard a minute or two and then said, 'Better get down outta the tree. I got two dogs that er pretty good climbers.'"

"The short version is I spend the entire day with him, got a good interview and some great pictures and, to this day, it was the best interview and life-experience I ever had. If you don't count Beulah Mae Phillips in junior high who taught me how to French kiss."

Widder laughed and said. "Remind me to send that girl a thank you note."

Her head cocked to one side. "That whole story came from a little comment about being able to talk to people. Adj, you are a wonder. Bet you talk to people on elevators, too," she said as she marched toward the car.

Dah-damn, she's gah-good.

Thompson was leaning on my car, which was up on concrete blocks. Being a quick study of my surroundings in general and automotive engineering in particular, I noticed there were no tires on the vehicle.

"Come on, Widder, Mr. Jones," Thompson said, motioning to his old pickup next to the car. "I'll give you a ride home."

I guess my expression gave him an opening. "Somebody slashed all four of your tires," Thompson said. "Some of the boys got 'em off and took 'em to get fixed. We'll get 'em back on and you'll have the car back sometime tonight."

"Who…"

"Don't know, exactly. You can guess, though."

After loading up the back of Thompson's truck, we piled in the bench seat and were home quickly. I was riding shotgun, and slid out when he pulled in front of Widder's. She grabbed a bag and the picnic basket and I told her I'd bring the other stuff over later.

She nodded, fixed me with a serious look and walked toward the house. My eyes followed part of her all the way into the house.

In my driveway, I knew better than to offer Thompson payment for the ride, but said sincerely, "If there's ever anything I can do for you, let me know. I'm serious."

He nodded. "Now that you've mentioned it, there is something if it's not too much trouble."

I nodded and he looked embarrassed, rubbing a chin covered with white stubble. He took off his hat and brushed a callused hand through his hair, let out a sigh.

"Well, I got a girl out in California and she's been wanting a pitcher of me." He paused as if he was never going to utter another word.

"You've got a girlfriend that wants a photo and you want me to take one for you?"

Durn fool. That was the look Thompson gave me, but it softened quickly. I've always admired a man who could suffer fools lightly.

"Girl," he said. "Daughter. My daughter is in California and we don't get to see much of one another. I'd like to send her a pitcher."

"Consider it done, Thompson. I'd be honored to shoot some photos for you. How about tomorrow morning, fairly early. I could meet you at Hum's for breakfast about seven, if that's okay."

He mused on that for a moment. "Seven is kinda late for breakfast, but that'll do. If it's okay, could we meet in the parking lot. I will be dressed up and all and don't want the fellers making fun of me."

Deal. And done.

24

The word "gullible" will always have an "I" in it.

Anonymous

I checked the mailbox by the road; it was cute, the shape of a small, red-and-white barn. Little barn doors open easily for insertion of mail. The barn is attached to a large-link welded chain in the form of an "S" that had been painted silver. I thought it was cute when I rented the lodge. The cute had worn off; now it was countrified tacky.

There were two bills—electric co-op and one for the house phone, which I seldom used, but was required to keep on and pay the bill as a condition of rent. Two circulars were on top of the haul—one for a regional grocery store, the other for a charity golf tournament. There was also an invitation addressed to a "Wendell Hinson" for a wedding in West Texas from people I had never heard of. For that matter, I had never heard of Wendell. There was also a box of slides from previous shoots and I set them aside.

I also checked my cell phone, which was laying on the table in the entryway. I never took it on shoots. The ringing could disturb the subjects. I also didn't take it because there is no signal in most areas of Caddo.

The "missed message" signal was blinking and the Caller ID function vomited the information with a couple of thumb punches. Eight calls, all from my agent Mark Goodlaw.

Oh-only eight?

He must not be feeling well, Bob.

Before thumbing the redial mode for Mark, I looked up Doc's number and checked on Moosie. She wasn't at the vet's, the receptionist informed me. She was at Doc's house. "He just loves Great Danes," she said. The receptionist's name was Portia, she was forty-six, a native of Romance, Arkansas, married, and her husband Don had piles. They act up more than normal, she offered up, "worser when he hits the hot sauce on his pintos."

Although conceived in the South, even Bob *ah-opined* that sometimes Southerners simply give out too much information.

Dreading the next few minutes worst than an ice water enema, I hit the call-back function. After three clicks, a buzz and a eeee-ooooooh, a disembodied and echo-ey voice said," Goodlaw, Williams and Sonoma. How may I be of service?"

"Oh, excuse me," I said. "I was looking for Hoodlum, Liar and Thieves. I must have the wrong number."

"Mr. Jones! It's so good to hear your voice," Matilda Tooey, the agency receptionist shouted in my ear. Truth be told, Miss Matilda has a crush on me. It does not matter she is sixty-ish, plumb in an I'm-a-material-tester-for-the-Polyester-Institute sort of way, and is a living monument to the hairstyle known as Texas Big Hair. I use her infatuation to my advantage at every opportunity. You know, James Bond and Miss Moneypenny.

"Matilda, love. How you doing? Are you still my sweetie?"

She tee-hee-ed just as she always did and went immediately into her Efficient Secretary mode. Just as she always did. "Mr. Goodlaw has been trying to get in touch with you. He's very anxious to talk to you. He said something about you being in jail and needing bail money." Lengthy pause during which I hummed the first bar from "Bridge Over the River Kwai."

"Have you been a naughty boy?"

"No, but I certainly could have," I said. "I've been slaving night and day searching, searching I tell you, for the perfect picture, one that will get me international acclaim. No! Strike that! Intergalactic acclaim! I want the universe to know I'm a better, a much better, photographer than Snooky Tooeylicker from the outer moon of Jupiter."

All I could hear was heavy breathing.

"I'll put Mr. Goodlaw on right away." More heavy breathing, a sigh, then a click. The next sound was another click and the sound of someone blowing a nose, presumably their own. Bob surmised it was a *sha-she* because it was alto nose note. I bet him it was Mark. Stuttering psyches are lousy gamblers.

"Adj, my man," Mark said. "Where in the world are you? How are you? Are you okay? What's this about you being in jail? Did you get the bail money? Taken any good pictures lately?"

That's why I don't often return Mark's calls. He wears me out before I ever get into the conversation.

"I'm in Uncertain, calling from my house. Everything is fine. I'm not in jail. It wasn't bail money you wired, it was a retainer for a local lawyer just in case I do go to jail. No good pictures. In fact, I'm thinking about swapping in my camera equipment for an old blackboard and just stay here and write poetry."

"Always the kidder. Hey, Harry, Adj is on the phone. I just told him he's a kidder. Isn't he a kidder? Adj, Harry said to tell you you're a kidder."

Silence.

"Adj?"

"What?"

"Are you there?"

"There where?"

"What?" Mark said.

"What?"

"No, I mean what's going on?"

Pause. Then I said, "I was waiting for you to tell me that Harry said I was a kidder?"

"What?"

"I was waiting for you to tell me that Harry said I was a kidder?"

"I did. I did. I said, 'Harry said to tell you you're a kidder.' I said that."

Pause. Then I said, "But then you didn't say it. You told me Harry said to tell me I was a kidder, but then you never told me Harry said I was a kidder. That's the part I was waiting on."

"What? Never mind. Okay, here goes: Harry said you're a kidder. Is that good enough?"

"No."

"Why not?"

"I've got a question."

"A question? What question?"

"Who's Harry?"

"Harry? Who's Harry?"

"That's my question," I said. "Look in the picture phone, I'm signing it in Braille. Whoooooo's Haaaarrrrry?"

"You know Harry. He's my new partner, Harry Abercrombie. You haven't met him? Oh, that's right, you've been shooting alligator asses in Miscreant, Arkansas, for the past several 13 months or something. Harry just joined our firm last week. You'll like him. He graduated from Yale and plays tennis. He has a wife named Bunny."

"I graduated from East Texas State University and always thought Yale graduates made locks. And I hate tennis. Makes me sweat. Does he ever do Tai Bo nekkid? Now, that's an exercise for you."

"I'll ask him. Hey, Harry, do you..."

"Mark, forget it. Oh, and nobody has a wife named Bunny. Be too confusing for the kids at Easter. Anyway, I'm getting a headache. So let me get this straight. I used to be a client of Goodlaw, Williams and Sonoma. Now I am represented by Goodlaw, Williams, Sonoma and Abercrombie?"

"Yes, sir! We're growing like a wildfire in a dry Idaho canyon."

"Nice imagery. When's Fitch going to join the firm? I heard Fitch was coming aboard."

"Who's Fitch?" Mark said, his voice going up at least an octave.

"I don't know. It's your firm. You mean you don't know about Fitch? Haysus Christo, Mark, if you don't know about Fitch and you work there and I know about Fitch and I am stuck way the hell out here in Malfeasance, Mississippi and I know about Fitch, it makes me wonder—did I tell you I know about Fitch?—what kind of people I have as agents."

"Calm down, Adj. I'll check on this Fitch thing and get back to you. Okay?"

"Okay, Mark, okay. That'll be fine. I really want to be a client of Goodlaw, Williams, Sonoma, Abercrombie and Fitch. It's kinda catchy, if you know what I mean. Add two more partners named Barnes and Noble and you will be the talk of the town."

I could hear him thinking over the phone.

"Mark, don't bother to call for a couple of weeks. I'm going in-country. I'm going to embed myself in an alligator clutch. Planning to live in an alligator suit for a couple of weeks. That's the only way I can think of to get some close-ups of the Caddoan alligati mating ritual."

"Jesus, Adj. Caddagonia gators. That sounds dangerous." Pause. "You got a gator suit or do you need us to help track one down?"

"Got one. There's a woman that lives near me, just down the road in Lollygagger, Louisiana, who is a alligator skinner and taxidermist. She also a part-time bartender and makes a helluva Tequila Slim. Or is it a Cleveland Fancy? I forget. Anyway, she took my measurements yesterday and the suit should be ready by the weekend," I said. "Mark, you know, it's the damnest thing: I wear a forty-two long in a suit, but in an alligator suit, I wear a twenty-seven stubby."

"No, I didn't know that, Adj." Shouting away from the phone: "Harry, did you know…?"

"Gotta go, Mark. I got a call on the other line. Bye, I'll check in next week. Give my love to Tooey and tell her we'll get married when the geese fly east."

I hung up the phone, marveling at the fact that I actually had an agent and that Mark was it.

A sound behind me made the hair prickle on the back of my neck. A dark shadow on the far wall made them stand at attention. Remembering that my gun was in the camera bag still in the car didn't make the hairs lay down.

Just like in the old vaudeville act about "going to Niagara Falls," slowly I turned…and…Widder! She was standing in the open doorway, shaking her head. Her smile made Julia Roberts's seem like a smirk.

Jah-Jesus.

"Jesus! Scared the hell out of me!"

The zippered long pants, orange tube top and white over-shirt were gone. Replacing them was a loose, dark beige dress covered in tiny, five-pedaled flowers. Magnolia blossoms, maybe.

Mah-magnolia? Yah-you're such an idiot!

She leaned up against the door jam and started ticking items off on her fingers: "Malfeasance, Mississippi. Lollybattle...."

"Lollygagger."

"Excuse me, Lollygagger, Louisiana. Abercrombie and Fitch and Barnes and Noble. Alligator suit. A woman who's an alligator skinner and part-time bartender. Is there really a drink called a Cleveland Fancy? 27 stubby." Pause. "Oh, yes, who's Tooey and why are you going to marry her?"

"Awfully pushy for a one lunch date, don't you think?"

"One date, but it was for breakfast and lunch. If you'd played your cards right, maybe it could have been breakfast, lunch and dinner."

"What will I have to do for breakfast, lunch, dinner, and breakfast?"

She ignored the question and asked one of her own: "Do you know the difference in being 'naked' and being 'nekkid?"

I shook my head.

"If you're nekkid, you're up to something."

Without being asked, Widder came in, shut the door and went into the main room and sat in a big chair framed up with deer horns. It was as ugly a chair as I've ever seen.

"Bet you didn't know I made this chair," she said, lovingly rubbing the deer horns intertwined to make the arms.

"Yeah, right," I said, "and Jesus turned water into wine 'cause the drive-through liquor store had run out of...." I stopped short. She had the most serious expression on her face and I started thinking about doing some serious backtracking.

Bob was way ahead of me. *Yah-you just can't keep yah-your mouth shut.*

"Did you really make the chair?" I asked.

Silence. But the look she threw me spoke volumes.

I studied the chair. I had been standing by the doorway but walked over to the chair and gave it a closer inspection. Even though I had been in the house more than a month, I had never sat in the chair, with the exception of a test-sit the day I arrived. I couldn't be sure a certified horn extraction person would be on duty at the county hospital emergency room.

"You know, I've never really looked at this chair before, but now that I've looked at it..."

"Gotcha!"

My face scrunched up into a tight little ball. My first thought was that this Widder Gleason cute shit routine was about to get real old, real fast.

"You didn't make the chair." Statement. Not a question.

"You really think that I would even be associated with making anything associated with dead animals?" she said, getting up and waving her arms around like the blades on Quixote's windmill. "Why don't you put this in the shed or something?"

"It's not bothering me where it is. But now that it's been put into my psyche, I'm sure I'll dream about getting gored by a horny chair that comes to life."

"Maybe I'll borrow part of that dream," Widder said, sitting back down. She batted her eyes like a hottie at a mall shoe store.

"I've got some dreams I'd like to share with you," I said.

"You silver-tickle-tongued devil, you. But enough of this double entendre talk, I came over to talk about Harmony and Bother and Elrod and Beryl."

"What about them?"

"They are like woodlands mushrooms after a summer shower. They pop up all over the place," Widder said. "There's no telling what they might do."

"Well, I know for a fact that one, maybe two, of them are holding a grudge against me because I'm a registered smart mouth. I know at least one of them poisoned Moose. I know that the two new ones were humiliated today by a widder woman carrying a gun the size of rock star's ego," I said. "I guess we can deduce from those facts that, from their perspective, they'll be hell to pay."

Widder had settled back down in the horn chair and was

absentmindedly stroking a spike with two fingers and the thumb of her left hand. The action was hypnotizing.

"Adj!"

"Huh? What?"

"I asked you a question three times."

"Sorry, I was just thinking about starting a charitable foundation for people with gout. It's such a misunderstood ailment."

Widder got up and headed toward the door.

"Where are you going?"

"Home. It's obvious you're not going to take this seriously."

"Sit down in the horny chair. I promise to behave." I went over to her, offered her a crooked arm like we were going to the prom or something. She ignored it and walked back into the room, sat and started stroking the spike again. Watching her rub that horn made me think of the supper scene in the movie *Tom Jones*. Go figure.

After she got settled and her temperature dropped somewhere below boiling, she said, "When you were ignoring me a while ago I asked 'How are you going to protect yourself?'"

I thought about it for a spell. "I guess I'll lock up everything tighter and keep the gun handy. What else can I do? I can't report anything to the sheriff, that's for sure."

From the look on Widder's face, my answer was not sufficient. "Why don't you come over and stay at my place?"

My head was nodding before she got through with "my" and her lips started to pucker on "place."

She said, "It might work for a couple of days, until the word gets around town. And that is going to be a problem. I'm a widow and you're a traveling man, so to speak. People will talk."

"Wid...Celestial... Is it okay if I call you C.C.? Celestial makes me think of a group of singing angels named The Celestial Choir."

"C.C. makes me think of the old Mitch Ryder song, 'C.C. Ryder' but C.C. would be fine. It's got to be the initials though, not something cutesy like CeeCee or SeaSea."

Wha-what's the difference in Sah-C.C. and....

Bob, please!

"It is a fact that people will talk whether I temporarily stay over at your house or not," I said. "After all, we spent the day together hidden inside a blind deep inside Carter's Chute."

She nodded at the logic. "I guess the question is: How much gossip flak do I want to take?"

Silence.

I spoke first. "Let me ask you a question: Would it make you feel better or safer if I came over and slept on your couch? You don't have a horny couch, do you? I couldn't be in the same room with such a contraption, much less sleep on one?"

"Not horny," Widder said. "Crushed velvet. Dark blue."

"Do you have satin sheets to put on it when guests come over?"

"I did have, but the last time Harmony came over to spend the night, he insisted that he take them home, give them a good washing and then return them to me. He never brought them back and rumor has it he swapped them to the madam running the Hello Sailor Motel down in Galveston for unlimited female companionship on nights and weekdays."

"Sounds like a wireless telephone monthly plan."

"It is," she said, "only you get screwed *before* you get the bill."

Tah-touche!

Where were we?

Tah-to her, not mah-me.

"Where were we?"

"I don't know," she said. "And I don't know what's wrong with me. One day of taking snapshots of birds, eating slab-ham sandwiches and shooting and cussing at fraternal rednecks has driven me crazy."

"Taking snapshots? Well, I hardly think that what I do is taking…"

"Are all Big City Smart Mouths so defensive?"

"Yes, assuredly. Oh, and about your day, you forgot about getting kissed down to your toes?"

"There was that."

"How about if I just come over after dark and sack out on your crushed velvet couch? Since I will not be in my own bed and have my own bankey, you may have to rub my head until I go to sleep," I said.

"Not likely. And I'll let that obvious pun just slide on off into verbal oblivion."

"Not changing the subject," I said, "but would you like something to drink?"

"What have you got in a nice merlot or shiraz?"

"Bottle or box?"

"Bottle, if you have it."

I got a bottle of Anne White merlot, class of ought-one, out of the refrigerator and dug out the plastic cork with a misshapened and slightly bent corkscrew I found in a drawer in a motel in Cheyenne. Wine is a good companion when you are trying to shoot nesting sand cranes. I found two clean glasses, put the bottle and glasses on a small tin tray that had a picture of Santa standing on a rooftop with a sack slung over his back, and popped back into the living room.

Widder's position had changed only slightly. She had tucked her legs up under her, which pulled the flowered pattern tight over her buttocks. There was no panty line. Bob *cah-compliment*ed me on my power of observation.

"Pebbles or Bam Bam?," I said.

"Excuse me?"

"Do you want to drink wine out of a Pebbles jelly jar or a Bam Bam jelly jar? I usually drink my wine out of Pebbles but if you want Pebbles, I'm sure Alice White would taste just fine in Bam Bam."

"Pebbles, please. You take Bam Bam. I think it's good for a body not to get too hooked into systematic rituals and routines, don't you?"

"Yeah, sure," I said, as I poured Alice into Pebbles up to her belly button. Pebbles, not Alice. To prove I was still in charge, I poured wine in Bam Bam up to his eyeballs.

Widder held the glass and turned it slowly in her hand, looking at it. I imagined she was looking at the ambient light filtering through the rich, full-bodied wine.

"Have you ever noticed that Pebbles only has one pupil."

"I didn't know Pebbles was a teacher."

"Pupil. Eye," she said, expertly signing the statement by pointing to her eye. "Doofus." She didn't feel a need to sign that word. It is the same in any language.

"What are you talking about?" I said, sidling over to the chair and bending over the back and looking over her shoulder. The dress' scoop neck was defying gravity, clinging to her high chest like a baby spider monkey hanging onto its mama. Tape. Definitely tape.

Oh-or heavy stah-starch.

"Now, that's a possibility."

"What's a possibility?" Widder said.

"Uh, uh, in the paint imprinting process, someone forgot to dot the eye, so to speak." Glib of tongue, fast of thought. Yea, team!

Pebbles did have only one eye, the right one. Even though she was turned slightly to her left, her left eye was clearly visible. It was just as clearly pupil-less.

"I had never noticed that before," I said. "I believe that a vast majority of people look at things but seldom see them. I like to think that's because of what I do for a living. I look *and* see. But I had never noticed that Pebble was one pupil short of a pair."

Widder looked up over her shoulder at me, reached up with her free hand and patted me on the cheek. Actually she tried to pat me on the cheek, but since she was looking sort of backwards, the "pat on the cheek" was more of a "slap on the ear."

When Widder looked up at me, I naturally looked down at her. When she raised her arm to pat or slap me, the dress material naturally scrunched to the middle, causing it to bulge out slightly more than slightly. No bra. I checked. Thrice.

"Hot diggidy damn!"

"Are you okay," Widder said.

"Yes, right, sure. I just had a eureka! moment. Or should that be 'an eureka! moment?'"

Silence.

"Well?" she said.

"No, nothing about a well." Widder slapped me lightly on the arm. "Oh, by your 'well?' you mean 'and?' or 'so?' I 'hot diggidy damned' because I was thinking about a picture I want to take that would go great in the book."

"What?"

"Excuse me."

"What picture did you (she started signing again) think about to put in the book?"

D*ah-don't stutter. It's a dead give-a-wah-way.*

"Tah-thompson. Hah-he's coming by tomorrow to have me take his picture for his daughter out in California and I thought, with his face and hat and all, that it might be good to figure out a way to shoot him to put in the book."

"That was your eureka! moment?" she said.

"Yep. Didn't sound nearly as good voiced out as it did when I thought it."

"Voiced out? Do you always talk like that?"

"Only when I'm nervousing, and I'm real nervousing right now."

A laugh splashed against her teeth. Bob *ah-agreed.* Angels would kill to own that laugh.

"Nervousing? What are you nervousing about?"

"About shooting Thompson's picture tomorrow. It's really important, you know, that he get a good picture to send to his daughter. I mean, she lives in California. Do you know how far it is from Uncertain to Lodi?" I was still standing behind the chair hoping for another cheek pat when she swiveled completely around in the chair. Her knees were now against the back cushion, both hands were gripping the horny arm rests to keep her from tumping over backwards into the floor.

"Adj," she said. "What's wrong with you?"

I thought about what would happen to her, and the dress, if she tumped over, but I didn't really want her to get hurt or anything, so I sidled around the chair and sat down cross-legged, on the floor. Using her hands for leverage, she swiveled her butt around and sat facing me, her legs crossed under her in a quasi-yoga move. Squatting Frog? Constipated Gerbil? I forget which.

"You," I said.

"Me?"

"You."

"Why?"

"There's a lot happening right now," I said. "Harmony and Bother. The evil cousins, Leroy and Jerome...."

"Elrod and Beryl."

"Yeah, them. The sheriff. I really have this feeling that things are not going well right now in the friends-hugging-friends department. And now you are caught up in it. And I...."

Cah-cat got your tuh-tongue?

"And...."

"And I like you and I don't want you to get hurt."

With some little deft hand moves, she levered herself out of the chair, legs still crossed, and eased down to the floor. I was certain that maneuver took some high degree of upper body strength. I was about to ask her about it when I remembered the way she handled that artillery piece this afternoon. The question died a natural death.

Our knees touched. Warmness spread through my body like liquid fire. Not really fire. More like warm hot chocolate. I guess I was looking at our touching knees because she picked up my chin with her left hand kept lifting until our eyes met.

"Adj."

I didn't speak, hoping she would say the word again. She didn't because there was no need.

She stood up out of the Posturing Toad position without putting her hands on the floor. She simple *stood up* and walked to the door.

"Come on over any time you want. I'll make up the couch." Then she was gone.

I got up shortly thereafter, but not without pushing, leveraging and prying my butt off the floor by using both hands and the chair arms for support. A forklift would have been helpful. Sitting on the Horny Throne, I marveled at the speed and simplicity of the relationship Widder and I seemed to be building.

Com-complicated!

"Truer words were never thought, Bob." I said it aloud and with feeling.

25

Don't blame others for your mistakes. But, then, who else is there to blame?

Anonymous

Widder had been gone only a few minutes when I got tired of cogitating, went to the refrigerator and picked up the lone tomato in the crisper bin and a Dos Equis off the top shelf. After grabbing a salt shaker and opening the long neck, I headed out the back door, crossed the short back yard, went through the back gate and walked the thirty yards or so to the water's edge.

There was an old, half-dead water oak near the lapping water-waves kicked up by boats somewhere out in the lake. The tree had a perfect backrest hacked out of its truck from an apparent long-ago lightning strike. I settled in and stared at the water. Without giving it much thought at all, I took a bite out of the tomato. I sprinkled a little salt in the raw, open wound. Fresh tomato washed down with Mexican beer. Not much can beat that combination.

Eating a tomato like an apple was a small tribute to growing up in Avery, Texas in the fifties and sixties. Back then Avery was known as "The Tomato Center of East Texas." When the Jones family arrived in Avery in 1953, the population sign read: 332. When we pulled up roots 10 years later, the sign read: 332. Avery was, and is, a stable population town: Every time a baby was born, some man left town.

Bob knew all the jokes and loved telling them: *Wha-we grew up in a tah-town so small that....*

Ah-avery didn't have a vah-village idiot. Wha-we all took turns.

Tha-the city library only had ta-two books. And wa-one ne of them had been cah-colored in.

Eh-it was a poke-and-pah-plumb town. Pah-poke your head out the wah-window and you're plumb out of tah-town.

Eh-it was a sixteen-mile dah-drive to date someone huh-who wasn't a relative.

Yuk. Yuk. Yuk. Let's give it up for the Stuttering Redneck Psyche.

During the dead of Texas summer everything green in Avery turned brown and everything brown turned a deeper shade of brown. Heat stroke was as common as sweat bees. When East Texas was at its hottest, the population of Avery jumped from 300-barely-plus to more than 2,000 as an ever-changing army of immigrant farm workers arrived to pick tomatoes and cucumbers, or haul hay. It was the only time of the year when residents actually locked their doors when the sun went down. And wedged chairs under the door knobs. After letting the dogs in the house for the night.

Avery was a good place to grow up if you were a creative kid that could imagine arranged hay bales as being a medieval castle or a bedraggled bicycle being an Indy car. It didn't matter that everybody in town knew exactly what you were doing when you were doing it, because that was a given in all small towns. It was written in the Avery town charter, Section Twenty-nine, Paragraph Seven, under the heading "Knowing Everybody Else's Business."

I sat under that Uncertain tree, eating that tomato, drinking that beer, thinking about growing up in Avery, realizing that there was no place in the world I would have rather have been reared. And also realizing that thinking about Avery kept me from thinking too much about the situation—make that *situations*—at hand.

Harmony. Bother. Edsel and Betelgeuse or whatever the hell their names were. Sheriff Badass Lardass. All bothersome.

Widder. Bothersome, too. In a different way.

I decided to tackle the hardest potential problem first: Widder. There was something there all right. I knew it. Bob knew it. I think Widder knew it. What I didn't know was what we, jointly or singly, were going to do about it.

I liked Widder. Instant attraction. Bob *rah-reminded* me that it wasn't actually instant, but somewhere slightly past instant. The first impression was one of curiosity, not interest. He was right and I acknowledged his contribution with a mental hug. I was rewarded with his impression of Stuttering Elvis, which always made me mentally chuckle: *Tha-thank ya. Tha-thank you vah-very mah-much.* Bob had The King down pat.

I sat there as last rays of the sun slid below the horizon and behind the tree on which I was leaning. I felt myself slipping away. I embraced the darkness. On all levels.

It was August, late afternoon. It was hot and I was mightily pissed off.

Melvin the Echo had just hit me flush in the face with a splattering of fresh meadow muffin. That battlefield tactic was dead-set against the rules of war. In the continuing Supreme War of the Cattle Cookies, slimy, wet or slightly damp field fritters were not allowed; patties—heave-ers or flingers—were supposed to be bone dry before being brought into battle.

"Damn you! Damn you to hell, Melvin the Echo, you pond scum-sucking dog's ass!" I said, wiping at the chunky, slimy, green mess off my face.

"You're dead, Adj," Roy Boy sang out from the top of the Galloway barn. "That miss-aisle killed you deader than that three-headed embalmed cat at the carnival last year."

"You're so stupid, Roy Boy, *and-HUH*," Highpockets said as he wandered out of the barn, pulling on the waistband of his Jersey Gent jeans. He stopped tugging only when they were nestled nicely and neatly three fingers under his armpits. Highpockets had his heart set on becoming an *and-HUH* preacher like the ones you could pick up on the radio early, early on Sunday morning. The ones that say stuff like "Your going to Hell—*and-HUH*—if'n you don't give your soul to the Lord—*and-HUH!*"

"You can't kill a Mighty Trojan, *and-HUH*," Highpockets said, "with a wet pile of cow crap, *and-HUH*. It's against the rules, *and-HUH*." Highpockets was known by his parents and the teachers at school as Eugene Gene Jenkins Jr. He was the local school superintendent's son and in that capacity he was expected to set an example for his peers. He made straight A's in school, F's in peer-ing. He was known as Gene Gene or Gene-Squared for a time. Highpockets was his official nickname.

He said he had a calling to be a missionary in the "African Bongo" and practiced his preacher *and-HUH*s constantly. "Gots to be ready when the call comes, *and-HUH!*"

"Maybe I can't kill a Mighty Trojan, *and-HUH*," Roy Boy said, hiking his pants up to imitate Highpockets', "but you can sure, *and-HUH*, send one home smelling like the ass end of a Guernsey, *and-HUH*."

"You're going to hell, *and-HUH*, in a hand basket," Highpockets countered, pulling his pants up once again.

"*And-HUH*, hell in a handbasket, *and-HUH?* What in the hell does that, *and-HUH*, mean anyways?," Roy Boy said mockingly.

"Does this mean the game's over? I'm hot!" That came from Shadow Wren who was still in the barn, hiding out in the Royal Treasury Stall One, guarding the King's Ransom.

One by one the High and Mighty Golden Trojans and the Exaulted Greek Army Extraordinary DeLuxe came out of their places of hiding. I continued cleaning my face with a handful of white t-shirt.

"There's three things in life I don't want ever to happen to me," I said to no one in particular. "Two of them are getting hit in the face with cow shit what come from a cow that has been eating sour dock and thistles and the other one is to have some ass-wipe wipe his cow shit face on my new shirt."

"Hey, dammit to hell and back," screamed Little Leroy, "that's my shirt." He jumped on my back and started pummeling me with fists no bigger than half dollars. Laughter crackled across the meadow as the armies collided in a writhing body splash-pile. Some one picked up a nearby cow pile and chucked it into the group; it landed with a dull thud against the left cheek of Melvin the Echo, who bellowed like a turpentined dog. Coming to Melvin's defense, Roy Boy ran to the barn and picked up a bucket of hard patties and started heaving them in every direction. Some hit, most missed. The war was back on!

We Trojans fought our way back into the castle and part of the Greek Army retreated to a mountain of hay bales about thirty yards away. The rest slid around the side of the barn to get in attacking position. Or, more likely, to get in the shade.

The object of this game was relatively simple: One army took control of the castle and guarded doubloons and jewels and gold and the like. We had just recently added virgins to the mix of things worth guarding. While one army was counting gold and figuring out what to do with the virgins, the other army tried to take the castle and its rewards by mass attacks, stealth, or plain lies. A "kill" was recorded by a direct hit of a missile, i.e., cow chip, to the body from the navel to the shoulders. When a combatant died, they were out of the game. A non-lethal hit—leg, arm, foot, head, gonads or "lubbocks", as Melvin called the ass-end—meant you took a break long enough to get a drink of water.

I always wanted to be a Trojan and finagled a spot in that army whenever possible. I had older, mouthy cousins and they had mentioned Trojans a time or two. I didn't know what they were, but I thought they were dirty and knew they were secretive. or something to help me later in life.

The Trojans Army in that particular battle consisted of me, Chicken Ghormley, Highpockets, Willy Ray, Shadow Wren and one of the two Gilfoy twins, either Sammy Smiles or Allie Bammy. They looked just alike. One was a southpaw, but no one could remember which one.

The Greek Army fighters were Melvin the Echo, Billy Three Names, Mark Markett, Little Leroy, Roy Boy and The Gospel According to Paul.

Chicken was called Chicken because his given name was Charles and he didn't like to be called Chuck. Willy Ray was William Randolph Foster and Billy Three Names was called William Hampton Harrison by everybody except his pasture army buddies. Shadow Wren was so nicknamed because he was so thin he didn't cast one. Sammy and Allie had to take turns playing the game since their daddy, Big Johnson Gilfoy, set a rule that one of them had to be at work at the farm every day. Samuel Adolphus smiled all the time, but then, so did Allie Sampson, also known as Ally Bammy. Ally Bammy was born in Georgia and some halfwit thought Allie Bammy was a better nickname than Allie Georgia. It might have been me.

Little Leroy would have been the maximum height for a certified midget if he would grow about three more inches. Roy Boy just rhymed. The Gospel According to Paul was a name given to Paul Nightengale by an older cousin who one caught him preaching to a penful of chickens in his grandparents' back yard. Most times we just called him Gospel or Preacher Paul for shot.

In this particular fracas, we Trojans were entrenched firmly in the castle and were not likely to be forced out anytime soon. Hay bales blocked both the front and back doors and cardboard boxes were filled to overflowing with missiles. Chicken was up in the loft with plenty of ammunition; he had only to watch the front swing door; the back one had been wedged shut.

It was getting hot in the barn and the Greeks were laying a whole bunch of sieges. Tree shade was in abundance in the pasture and every Greek, it seems, was more interested in not getting heat stroke than winning the rights to a virgin.

"It's hot," Chicken said.

"Damn hot, *and-HUH*," Highpockets chimed in.

"Are ya'll ready to quit and go to the Galloways and get some ice tea and something to eat?" That was from the Gilfoy twin who was here today.

"We're the Mighty Trojans," I reminded the troops. "We are here to save the day."

"I love it when Adj gets going," Willie Ray said. "He sounds just like that Mighty Mouse song."

As if struck by a maestro's baton, they all sang in unison and disharmony, "Here I come to save the day!"

I got deadly serious. "Men, it's hot." Echoes and agreement all around. "But are we men or are we mice?"

"Mighty mice, *and-HUH!*" Highpockets screamed.

"I've got a plan how we can win the game and go to Galloways for shade, tea, and pie."

We hotly discussed the plan. The temperature in the barn had to be 110 or higher.

The treasure was kept in an old checkered cardboard suitcase called the Treasure Trove. The team that held the Treasure Trove at the time everybody wanted to quit won that day's battle. In the Treasure Trove was a broken axe handle, some plastic doo-dads someone won at last year's county fair, a broken mirror, hair comb with only two teeth, and an old Baby Ben clock that has stopped working a decade or two past.

Me and Highpockets took out all the items while the others were slicing a big hole in the end of a hay bale stuck way back in the rear stall with a couple of pocket knives and a broken hoe blade. The treasure was installed in the hole and the hole was then re-packed with hay. That bale was marked with a loose grease rag stuck under one of the twine bindings and put under two other bales to hide it from invading hordes.

We didn't really have a virgin yet so there was no need to actually find a place to hide one.

Even though he was as thin as a thermometer, Shadow was the fastest runner in the bunch. He was designated as Protector of the Treasure Trove.

The plan was simple: Shadow, carrying the suitcase, would run out the door lickety-split, heading for the Galloways, which was about 200 yards due south. The remnants of the Trojan Army would yell at him to come back with the treasure. The Greeks would charge after Shadow, opening up their rear guard, which would then be attacked by the Trojans.

The treasure would be safe. We would win. Iced tea for everyone.

"Listen, Shadow," I said, "the secret is for you to draw their fire but not get killed. So kinda run sideways to them. Don't show them your chest or back. Oh! Oh! I just had a good idea. Hold the Treasure Trove over your back and just run away from them. They can't kill what they can't hit. When they run after you, we will attack with the vengeance of a mighty horde."

"You said a bad word, *and-HUH*," Highpockets said.

"Horde, you damn *and-HUH* fool," I said. "Not whore! Jesus!"

"Father, forgive him, *and-HUH*, for he knows exactly what he do, *and-HUH!*"

I wondered what the penalty was for slaying a potential preacher.

Somebody suggested we tie the Treasure Trove to Shadow's back and that sounded like a good addition to the plan. Some hay twine and three minutes later it was a done deal.

Everybody secured a supply of hardified pasture pancakes, some in old buckets or tow sacks,, some stuck inside half-buttoned shirts. After one last look-around, Chicken came out of the loft and Shadow put his running face on. We pushed open the door and he went through it like a dog track rabbit.

He hadn't gone ten feet when the Greeks noticed the action and they immediately got up, grabbed ammunition and started flinging it. The back armor worked to perfection, as Shadow angled away from his pursuers. We were just about to charge after them when a trailing piece of hay twine got tangled up in Shadow's left foot and down he went, coveted Treasure Trove on top of him.

The Greeks, the merciless bastards!, were on him like a pack of ravenous wolves and began pelting him at close range. We charged out of the barn, chunking up a cow shit hailstorm.

The first one killed with a rib hit was The Gospel According to Paul. Melvin the Echo caught a clumpy clod right in his left armpit as he raised his hand to throw. Billy Three Names went down next when two missiles hit him square in the chest. Mark Markett got off two quick shots, taking out a charging Highpockets, then I got him with a hummer that hit him just south of the Adam's apple. Little Leroy screamed "Calf rope" and huddled on the ground. He was pelted prone. Roy Boy stood his ground and took me out with a hard hit to the stomach. Chicken got Roy Boy with a handful of hard little missiles that had the short range of a shotgun.

The only surviving battleteers, as Little Leroy liked to call the group, was Chicken, Allie or Sammie...and Shadow.

Although hit maybe a thousand hundred times, not one registered hit was certified a killer strike. When Shadow had fallen, he hit chest first, and the suitcase slipped forward, covering completely covering his back. If ass hits were counted as kill shots, Shadow would be dead 10 times over.

The Trojans were victorious. The Treasure Trove was safe from pillagers and plunderers. The virgins were still in the castle somewhere waiting for us to do to them whatever it is that warriors were supposed to do. We were all tired, hot, sweaty, and happy.

It didn't take long to get to the Bartlett pond. There, clothes were discarded. Fights with water and cool, soft mud replaced concrete-hard cow shit.

Later, after iced tea and pie at the Galloways, we all headed home, splitting up at off-shoot cow trails, heading in a general direction of the individual homes of the tired soldiers.

It was late, the sun low. A not-so-hot breeze had picked up, signaling, maybe, a summer shower later.

I smiled, raised a hand in salute to the last of the soldiers and headed back to my grandparents' house.

Feeling free, feeling victorious…and smelling, faintly, of *Eau de Bovine*, with just a hint of clover.

26

Life is not simple. Those that think it is are simple.

Anonymous

The noise sounded like it was coming from inside a fifty-five-gallon drum, tinny and vibrating.

I was still walking down the single path cow trail toward the Bartlett place and....

"Adj. Adj."

Something was pulling on my sleeve, which I thought was rather odd since I was not wearing a shirt.

"Adj."

Opening my eyes, The first thing I saw was the ghostly tendrils of the Spanish moss hanging from a nearby tree limb. As my eyes focused, Widder's face, hair hanging down around it like a golden halo, moved into view from the right.

I blinked several times, attempting to bring her into focus and failing. I then realized it was dark and her face was in deep shadow. Her hair was coated with an eerie bluish cast. I looked to the right, remembering to check for drool on my lips, and looked directly into the biggest full moon I had seen in years.

"Adj."

"Yo. Right here. Present and accounted for. What time is it?"

"About nine. I started to worry when you didn't come over and went to check on you. When I checked the house and you weren't there, I got worried."

"No, I'm fine. I just came out here to think and fell asleep, I guess. What time is it?"

A sparkling half-chuckle flowed over her tongue. "Nine. At night. Wednesday. You're in your backyard, leaning against a tree talking to C.C. Gleason. You were going to spend the night with me, remember?"

Spend the night with Widder!

I jumped straight up, snapped to what I assumed was an attention position and saluted. "Yes, Ma'am, Col. Wid… C.C. Private Jones ready and volunteering for the assignment."

"You're like a Great Dane puppy, just plain goofy. You are going to sleep on the couch, remember?"

Parade rest, followed by an over-abundance of non-military slumping.

She put her hand on my shoulder. "Why don't you go in and freshen up and then come on over. I've got some supper warming."

I eased myself off the ground gingerly. Old injury to back, plus too many sports activities over too many years had created pains where I didn't even know I had places.

"Need some help?" the statement had a smile half-hidden in it.

"No, thank you. I always get up slow. Helps the blood balance itself in the body. Learned that from a Tibetan monk a long time ago."

"His name wasn't Arthur Itis, now was it?"

I looked at her and liked what I saw. The moon hit her full on, and the way the moonlight slid over her body and around…. Well, I thought and Bob *ah-agreed* that is was like a visual concerto. Soft strings, melodious flutes. The moonlight created flowing shadows interspersed with intense light areas on the short, robe-like wrap she had on. The darkness swallowed up about half of her, the back half, but that only served to punctuate what was visible.

Sha-shut your mah-mouth.

I did, just as her right hand moved from her side in an upward motion to do it for me. Widder's hair was down, straight with a little "That Girl" flip at the end. It brushed against her shoulders. Lucky hair. It seemed impossible that it was just this morning that I had kissed those lips. She put her hands on her hips and took a defiant stance.

"Okay. Enough lollygagging. You can do that when you're back home in Louisiana. Get in the house, wake yourself up, clean up, and come to supper."

With that she turned and stalked away at an angle toward the back of her house.

The moonlight illuminated the other side of her and I'm sure my mouth dropped open again. She had pulled the wrap tight (On purpose?) and her backside undulated in a bomp-bomp-bump rhythm. It looked like....

Dah-don't say like two pah-puppies fighting in a sah-sack. I-I'm begging you!

Jesus, Bob. You are no fun.

Thinking about Widder and food, in that order, I jogged to the house, threw off my clothes and hit the shower. I washed every place one time really good and preferred places twice. I even used the fragrance soap I had picked up at the Peabody the last time I was in Memphis. For some reason, I like rubbing the heads of those little ducks on my body until their little, soapy necks break off.

As usual, I shaved in the shower without use of a mirror. It's easy to pick up such traits during week-long stays in hides and blinds from Tibet to Uruguay. Ten minutes from the time Widder left, I went out the front door and saw my Jeep was parked in the driveway. There was a note under the windshield. I plucked it off and went back to the house to read it.

> *Here's your car. You owe me $200 for new tires.*
> *Thompson.*

Two hundred dollars. Good tires cost more than that. I put the note on the entryway table, went out into the night and forty-seven steps later I knocked on Widder's front door.

"Come on in," she said.

As I hit the porch, the smells from the kitchen hit me and the front door and the floodgates of my saliva glands opened at the same time.

I walked through the small room off the entryway and into the bright light of the kitchen.

Widder was at the counter, still wrapped up nicely in what looked like a lounging robe of some sort. It was dark blue with imprints of what looked like stamps and was made of some shiny material. It was still as short as I remember from the back yard.

She left the counter and came toward me.

"You look...." was all I got out before she reached me, eased up on her tiptoes and kissed my cheek.

"Nice. Yes, I do. And thank you." She paused as she gave me a toes-to-hairline once over.

"You look nice, too," she said, giving me that Debbie Reynolds eye-batting routine. "And you smell good, too. Brut would be my guess." As she turned, she mumbled something that sounded like, "lots and lots of Brut."

Tah-told you.

"Did I put on too much?" I asked.

She turned slowly, pinching her nose between her thumb and forefinger. "What makes you think that?" she said in a Betty Boop voice.

Laughter bounced around the small kitchen like a verbal Bouncy Ball.

She motioned me to sit. The table was an old-fashioned, swirled-tile pattern popular in the 'fiftys. With its mortised, metal edges and top pattern of mixed swirls of yellow, gray and white, it would be worth $1,000 or more in an artsy furniture dealer's loft in New York's East Village. I thought the table was *so Widder* and said so.

"There's something soothing to me about certain types of furniture," she said without turning around. "And music. And clothing. In furniture I like period pieces, but am not crazy about true antiques, although I have quite a few family pieces."

Pause. I just looked at her, at the little ripples coursing through her body that were the results of whatever she was doing at the counter.

"I like funky stuff, you know, art deco clocks and bright colors that don't really match, the blues and greens and yellows. That table makes me think of my parents and grandparents. That table has been right there, set against that wall, for as long as I can remember."

She turned around and came to the table bearing two Fiesta plates. "Green or blue?" she said, indicated the plates in her hand.

"Blue, if you don't mind."

"I knew you were going to say that."

"Oh, yeah? How?"

"I don't know. There seems to be something about the color green that is aversive to some people. I don't entertain much, as you can imagine, but every chance I get, I always do the green-blue thing and no one ever picks a green plate."

I mused on that, but not for long. My blue plate was loaded with food and I was hungry.

Broasted chicken breast with charred flakes of something on top. Black-eye peas. Thin sliced potatoes cooked in a broiler or oven, then sprinkled with grated cheese. A hunk of cantaloupe, still in the rind. A sprig of parsley was stuck right in the middle of the plate. She walked back to the counter and returned with a couple of saucers bearing a chunk of cornbread the size of one of my size thirteen shoes. Butter was running out both sides.

"I'm hungry, but this is ridiculous. This is more food...."

"Shush! Eat what you want to. I didn't load your plate up to make you eat it. I loaded it up to make the presentation of the meal symmetrical."

"Ahhhhhh. So, is that one a womanly wile trick to seduce hungry suitors."

Leaning her head forward, she rested her chin on her bend right wrist. She studied my face for a couple of heartbeats, then said, "Is that what you are? A suitor?" Pause. "Do you think I'm trying to seduce you?"

"Wah-well," I stammered. "I-I wah-was just trying to mah-mah-make conversation."

Jah-jesus!

She leaned back, never taking her eyes off my face. She took a healthy bite of potato, stuck it in her mouth and chewed with purpose.

"You know what I think?" she said. "I think you are smitten with me."

Pause. Followed by a longer pause.

"And I don't think I would have to seduce you."

All I could think of to say was: "Smitten? Me?"
Yah-you're tongue is getting more sah-silver by the mah-minute.

The conversation picked up considerably after the first few trial bites. The food was excellent. I asked about the seasonings. I told her I was not a good cook, but I like to dump stuff in a bowl or pan and mix it up and see what it tastes like when it's done. I could tell she's a cook, while I am a certified, pedestrian dump-and-mixer.

Widder learned to cook by watching her mother, and by simply getting in the kitchen and "playing around." She said between bites the only rule of thumb she tried to remember when experimenting was to "balance spices and ingredients by remembering that opposites attract."

Quizzing her on that point, she said, "If I decide to add something sweet, I add something sour or hot. For example, a pinch of sweet paprika requires a squirt of lemon juice or a dash of hot mustard."

As I mixed a forkful of peas and a bite of cornbread, I wrote myself a mental note to try that the next time I decided to cook something rather than run down to Hum's.

"You said you cooked?" she said.

I acknowledged enjoying puttering around the kitchen, making up recipes, eating the ones that work, dumping the ones that don't. Moosie appreciated my mistakes, I said.

"When did you start cooking?" Widder said, then filled her mouth with cantaloupe.

"After my divorce, I really had a lot of time on my hands. I didn't want to just chow down on fast foods, so I started messing in the kitchen. Even though I seldom use recipes, I have about a hundred cookbooks back in my house in Atlanta. I think it's fun to find a great recipe, get the gist of it and then close the book and," I said, throwing my hands in a dramatic, drag-queen fashion, "have fuuuuuun!"

Her hands flew to her mouth and she started giggling like a Catholic school girl approached by a raincoat flasher.

My age compared to her's? My feelings at this particular moment? Not a bad mental analogy.

When we were at the stage in dinner when the utensils were clanging regularly against the plates, Widder apologized for not having any dessert, but offered coffee as a substitute. I saw that the coffee pot was unplugged and begged off.

"I have a good substitute," I said, "getting up and heading to the door. "Be right back."

Less than two minutes later, I walked in the door holding an unopened bottle of Bailey's Irish Crème that my agent had shipped to me several weeks ago. The note on the card was typical Mark: *"A touch of civilization for the best photographer on the planet! Any good pictures, yet? Mark and the Gang!"*

Best photographer on the planet? Mark didn't know at the time I had raised my professional sights. Maybe Matilda had told him by now.

"I hope you like Irish cream," I said. "It's one of the most soothing and relaxing liqueurs I've ever found."

"I do and I agree with your assessment." She pointed to the kitchen counter over by the refrigerator. A half-empty bottle of Bailey's was half-hidden behind a clear canister jar.

"Well, darn! And here I was thinking I was being cool and sophisticated. Here's the alternate plan: Let's drink some from your bottle and I'll leave this one here for future suppers and talkathons."

She took the full bottle from my hand and swapped it with the tapped bottle. She poured too short arms in two small glasses with fluted bottoms. Smuckers, maybe?

"In case you're wondering why I'm serving you Bailey's out of jelly jars, my good crystal is packed away with my good dinnerware and the silver candelabra. The butler had the key with him and it's his night off."

"Don't you just hate when that happens? Besides, where I grew up," I said, taking the glass from her and raising it in a toast, "this was good crystal."

"Would you please make a toast?" she said. "I would just like to hear what comes out of your mouth at a time like this?"

Jah-jesus!

"Jesus! Don't go out of your way to put a guy on the spot or anything.," I said, thanking Bob for the introduction. Quickly, my mind starting doing a variety of exercises. It was on one-legged jumping jacks when the thought "world peace" came to mind and just as quickly rejected.

I raised my glass, nodded my head toward her and said, "Life, love, laughter." We touched glasses. Our hearts touched without any outside assistance.

27

There is "sleeping" and then there is "sleeping." Me, I prefer "sleeping" to "sleeping."

Anonymous

We lingered over the Bailey's, relishing the warm feeling it produced. I chanced a glance at the wall clock over the sink when Widder was talking about a tornado that hit the lake area several years back, causing a lot of damage and throwing up a log barricade in one particular area of the lake.

11:22.

Nah-no wonder we're tah-tired.

I tried unsuccessful to stifle a yawn, but Widder caught the back end of it, smiled, leaned over and put her hand on my arm.

"Come on, Sleeping Beauty. Time to get you to bed."

That was the best news I'd heard since I found out Widder was going to protect me from Elvis and Bateau this morning.

We picked up the dishes, I tried to so some preliminary cleaning, but she said to just stack them in the sink.

"Tomorrow. There's always tomorrow," she said.

Taking my hand, she led me into the small living room, through the entryway and down the hall. She opened the first door on the left and flicked at an old-fashioned dimmer switch. Not her bedroom. Not any bedroom. A small parlor, apparently turned into an office. There was a computer against the wall behind the door. A small, obviously antique roll top desk filled a good portion of the wall on the wall facing the door.

The walls to the left and right were both covered by bookshelves that went from floor to ceiling. Facing the door was a wall of windows, the windows that faced the lodge. Below the windows was a couch, converted into a bed with sheets, light acrylic blanket, puffy pillow, and comforter.

"I hope you can be comfortable here."

I nodded, thinking that would convey a positive response, but my face must have given me away.

Stepping in close to me, Widder held both my hands and said, "Adj. I'm an honest woman. In every single way you can imagine. I am having powerful feelings right now. About you. About us. I could just throw caution to the winds and give in to those feelings. To hell with the possibility of being hurt. Live for the moment."

I nodded vigorously.

"That's not me. Never has been. Never will be."

Didn't say a word. Don't remember breathing either.

"I don't know where this is going, Adj. Neither do you. I know that regardless of what happens, one or both of us stand a chance of getting hurt. That's not what scares me. I've been hurt. I survived."

She paused and punctuated it with a healthy sigh. "You're going to leave here someday soon."

"C.C., dammit! There are...."

"Shhhhhhh. Let me finish. You're going to leave here soon. You may not want to when the time comes. But you will. You can no more change who you are than I can change who I am. You don't know me even though you might like to think you do. I probably know you too well even though you would probably disagree with me," she said.

"This place is where I live. No, it's the place where I am *alive*. It is part of me. I can't foresee any circumstance where I would leave it. Not for money. Not for love. This place, these people, this house, they saved me when I needed saving. I owe them...my life."

She bowed her head and whispered, "I owe them."

The speech was followed by an uneasy silence during which I became aware of her thumbs gently rubbing the backs of my hands.

"Go to bed, Adj," she said. "Think of me. Dream about me. Because I'm going to be thinking about you."

She dropped my hands, turned and went out the door, closing it gently behind her.

A few seconds later I heard another faint click as another door shut.

I stood there. Numb. My mind racing out of control. Hurting. Wanting to cry but refusing to give in the feelings.

Tha-that was swah-sweet!

Jesus! Shut the hell up, Bob. Not another damn thought!

An hour later I was still wide awake. I was lying on my back, hands behind my head, staring in the darkness, when she came to me.

The door creaked, a silent motion floated in to the room. Widder leaned down, brushed her lips through my hair and whispered, "Come with me."

We went to her bedroom and by the light of the filtered moon, she motioned me to the inside of the old, double sleigh-bed. She unbelted her robe and let it fall to the floor. I couldn't see what she was wearing, but it looked short. Shorter than short. Like a handkerchief with no hem. If she had worn it to Harlan's, she would have been arrested. Or at the very least, stoned by Missionary Baptists.

She eased into bed, kissed my eyelids. "Hold me. Please, just hold me."

Then she turned her back to me and snuggled backward until she was touching me in every place possible to touch in that position. The classic, Victorian position called *spooning*.

Her right arm found my right arm and pulled it around her, leading my hand to her breast, which was covered by something softly cotton. She left it there so, I thought, neither would be lonely. She pressed my palm hard against her. "Thank you," she said.

"For what?"

"You know."

She was wrong. I didn't know.

UNCERTAIN TIMES

The full moon was filtered by a coverlet of high clouds. The defused light etched the countryside like a dim-bulb beacon.

I was thirteen and in love. Not puppy love. Real, heart-pulsating lusting love. Love so hot your blood damn near boils, and your insides feel like they are passing through a power-train auger.

How could life be any better than this? I thought as we passed the Turner barn on the church youth group hayride. Here I am, sitting next to Wanda Blankenship, who was a year older and one of the prettiest girls in Red River County, Texas. I have it made, I thought to myself, almost wriggling with the image of being in love with Wanda. We're holding hands. She's squeezing my hand every now and then, even if it is sweaty.

The church group had piled on the wagon about six o'clock on a mild autumn evening. The old, sputtering John Deere tractor had jostled us about three miles out in the country to a deacon's house, where we played badminton, horseshoes, and croquet. We had consumed prodigious amounts of hot dogs, hamburgers, chips, and soda pop. A mountain of s'mores had topped off the outing.

Now we were almost back to town and I could hardly wait until we arrived at the church. Wanda had agreed to slip off from the group and meet me behind the big elm tree in the darkest part of church property. We were going to kiss, grope, and grapple. I slid just as close to Wanda as I could, giving her hand a squeeze, which she immediately returned. No one could see; our hands were wrapped in a fold of her dress, which billowed all over the place. There was a time when six or nine petticoats served a purpose.

We were only a couple of blocks from the church when the wagon went under one of only about ten street lights in the whole town. As the light appeared from behind a gigantic oak tree, I glanced at Wanda. She was looked away from me. I eased forward and noticed Jerome Dillard looking directly at her. Glancing down, I saw Wanda's left hand intertwined with Jerome's right hand.

This can't be happening! She's in love with me! It doesn't matter that Jerome is a year older than me, the same age as Wanda! It doesn't matter that he's a freshman starter on the high school basketball team! I love Wanda and Wanda loves me!

Without waiting to arrive at the church, I threw aside Wanda's hand and jumped from the wagon.

But there is no street to stop my fall. I plunge into blackness, arms flailing, legs kicking. I'm screaming but there's no sound....

I awaken to what feels like a mouse nibbling at my cheek. I try to brush it away.

"Adj. It's me. C.C. You had a bad dream. Turn over and go back to sleep."

I follow the instructions to the letter.

This time, Widder snuggles me, getting as close as she can. Then she struggles to press closer.

I swear I can feel her nipples double-dotting my back.

Bob said it was my *eh-imagination*.

Bob was wrong.

28

If life is funny, why are more people not laughing?

Anonymous

I was back at Sutton, in the double feather bed in a side room that used to be a porch. Years back the porch had been enclosed to accommodate a live-in relative. I smelled bacon and knew that Nannie was up, that the fires were lit and that it was....

"Are you going to sleep all day, Slugabed?"

Not my grandmother. Widder.

I opened the eye closest to the voice and saw her standing provocatively in the doorway. Actually, she was just standing, right arm upraised to lead on the door jam, left foot canted across the right. I just threw in the provocative part because it felt like the right thing to think since I had just slept with her.

She had on pale yellow shorts, a dark blue t-shirt and flip-flops. I don't know if she was wearing any undergarments although I tried mightily hard to see if she did.

That last thought did it: I had morning wood.

What time is it?

Lah-late. Ah-ask her, not me.

Before I could get out the question again, Widder said, "It's after seven. I know you like to get up early and get on the lake. I started to wake you, but you looked like such a little boy, all scrunched up in the covers. Want some breakfast?"

"Little boy? Me? You need glasses. Thick ones. I would love breakfast. Is it ready?"

"It'll be about ten minutes." She smiled. "You have time to go down and check on the Poem Board, if you hurry."

I waited for her to leave the room so my physical condition wouldn't embarrass one or both of us, but she just stood there, smiling.

"Would you please get out or at least throw me my pants so I can get dressed?"

She put on a fake pout and stomped her foot. "Boy, you are not a fun date. One roll in the hay and you get grumpy."

"Roll in the hay? You're going to be committed, you know that! My God, woman. Thirtysomething and don't even know the difference in a roll in the hay and a freaking sleepover. There are special cells for people like you where they put women who tease men, lead them on and then make fun of them for not performing when, I will assure you, if they had been given the chance, they could have performed admirably."

Her laugh was musical. The world quit spinning.

"I wouldn't have gotten out of bed so early but you poked me out."

She turned, took a short step, stopped and actually waggled her ass at me. Waggled! Ass! At me!

Poked? Poked her out? Did she say I poked her out of bed?

Yah-you were mean to me last nah-night.

I accept your apology. Don't let it happen again.

It took less than three minutes to throw on my jeans and shirt, find the bathroom and do the essentials, making sure to put up the seat and lower it at the appropriate time, holler "I'll be right back" to Widder, run next door, pick up Betsy, and fire up the Jeep.

The two-minute ride to town was uneventful, but I kept an eye out for Twiddle and the Boys just the same. They must be sleeping in.

Poked her out of bed? Jesus!

Grabbing Betsy and the notebook out of the glove box, I parked the car on the side of the road and jumped the ditch to the Poem Board.

I wouldn't classified the writing as a poem. Hell, I didn't know what it was.

Being wise
Is the end result
Of doing dumb things in a wise manner.

Being successful
Is the ability
To do dumb things
And get away with it by succeeding.

Being dumb
Is the ability
To screw up a good thing
Even when aided by success and wisdom.

The thought hit me like a mental cattle stampede: Why did I immediately think the writer was communicating directly to me?
Prah-probably because of number tha-three.
Probably.
After writing the poem down I snapped off a couple of pictures, got back in the car and started home. I stopped in at Hum's to apologize for not getting breakfast two days in a row.
"Hmmmm," he said, waving off my apologies.
"I'll be by tomorrow. Promise."
"Hmmmm."
Was it just me or was Hum's humments getting longer?
As I was heading out, Thompson was heading in. "Thank you for taking care of my Jeep. I got the note. Two hundred dollars is too cheap for those tires. How much did they really cost?"
Thompson tipped back his hat, rubbed his chin. "George Alvin down at Tire City gave you a deal when he heard 'bout what happened. Two hundred is just fine." I had a couple of hundred dollar bills squirreled away in my wallet, dug them out and handed them to him.

"I owe you," I said, turning to the door.

"Nope. That ain't the way I see it."

Back at the house, I stopped long enough to brush my teeth and toss my shirt from the night before in the dirty clothes hamper and exchange it for an old advertising t-shirt.

I knocked on the door at Widder's and she hollered something I couldn't make out, but that I was sure meant "come on in." It did and she seemed genuinely glad to see me.

She was standing at the kitchen counter again and the effect her wiggles and vibrations from stirring and blending were exactly the same as last night: My favorite two H's: Hungry and Horny.

She glanced up, stopped wiggling, vibrating, and undulating and poured a cup of coffee and brought it to me. Black. She started to turn back to the counter, did a double take and said, "Turn around."

I spun in a 360 and she said, "What's on the back of the shirt."

I sipped the coffee as I turned halfway around and, using one hand, stretched the shirt tight and backed up closer so she could see the design clearly.

The entire back of the medium-yellow shirt was a map of the Middle Fork of the Salmon River in Idaho, complete with names and degree of difficulty on all the major rapids.

"You've been on this river?" she said, following the main river down my back, using her fingernail. Digital Magic Marker. Goosebumps popped up on my arms.

"Only once, but I've been on the Main Salmon about eight or nine times."

She read off the rapids and just the mere names made me smile.

"Devil's Tooth? House Rock?"

"Big rocks right in the middle of the channel."

"Weber. Waterfall Creek. Earthquake. Porcupine. Haystack. Jack Creek. Are these big rapids?"

"The little numbers underneath the names are the difficulty. Rapids run from 1 to 5, with a 5 being the most difficult. On this particular river, there are three or four Class 4's, which can be very dangerous at certain water levels," I said.

"Do you kayak?"

"I wish I could say 'yes' and impress you, but I mainly ride in the big boats and scamper around on the shore and take pictures. I tried a topsider kayak a couple of times, but I'm a little tall and top heavy. Kept tumping over. The water on the Salmon is real cold and it can wear you out in a hurry. Besides, I'm a pretty lousy swimmer."

"Scamper? You? Scamper?"

"Well, okay, walk mostly. But if I come across a snake or a marmot killing ball, I can scamper to beat the band."

"Marmot killing ball?"

"Yeah, that's a story I made up when I damn near fell off a cliff over the Main Salmon one time. I was maneuvering around in some loose shale and put my hand on a ledge to support myself on an incline, when this horrendous noise came from the ledge. I jumped, of course, and slid down the shale and came within a couple of inches of pitching headfirst 80 feet down onto big boulders."

I paused for effect. "The guides tried to tell me it was just a little old marmot letting me know I was its territory. But the way I tell it, it was a marmot-killing ball. That's where the critters all stand up, back to back, hook their little legs together and roll with nothing but claws and teeth slashing and gnashing at their intended prey."

She shook her head in disbelief, then turned me around and looked at the front of the shirt: *Warren River Expeditions, Salmon, Idaho. No telephones.*

"Thought you said this was the Salmon River?"

"It is. Warren is Dave Warren, the outfitter and a friend."

Widder informed me breakfast would be ready "in a few," and popped something yellow in a skillet in the oven.

"I'd like to go whitewater rafting," she said. "That would be fun."

"I always go with Warren on the Salmon. I've been on the Snake River, the Colorado, and a river down in Costa Rica. I met Dave years ago when I was doing some travel writing to make extra money. To tell the truth, he is a kind of super hero to me."

Widder threw me a quizzical expression.

"Not in the Spiderman or Hulk sense, but in the way he figured out one day what he wanted to do with his life and just went out and did it,"

I said. "One day he was working for a big oil firm in Houston; a week later he was working in Idaho to set up a whitewater rafting and hunting guide service."

I paused to take a sip of coffee and Widder did her "keep going" hand thing.

"What's neat about Dave is how he treats his guests. He coddles them if they want to be coddled; he lets them pitch in and row or cook or put up tents or set up for supper or whatever they want to do. Plus, he's one of the funniest people on the planet. But I'm not for sure he knows it."

"Such as?" she said.

I thought for a minute and told her about the time Dave's father Sam, a retired forest ranger, was rowing for him. Sam was in a big raft with two women in their seventies.

"At the time, Sam was about sixty-four and nice-looking in a rugged, Terry Thomas-gap-toothed sort of way. I was riding with Dave in a boat behind Sam and the women," I said. "Sam's boat disappeared around a sharp bend and when we got him back in sight, Sam was floundering in the water and one of the women was trying to get back to the oars. And there was a nice-sized rapid coming up."

Widder had stopped what she was doing and leaned against the counter, her arms crossed under her breasts. She was just standing there, looking. What's this sudden fantasy about wishing I could be different body parts? Now it was arms.

"Well, what happened?"

"Dave didn't change expressions, didn't change the rhythm of his oar strokes. He just looked at the situation and deadpanned in a low, gravelly voice: 'Hmmm. That ain't good.'"

Widder hooted. "You ARE KIDDING!"

"Nope. Swear to God. He later said there was no reason to get excited. There wasn't a damn thing he could do. He said if Sam got out and didn't die, it'd make a good, funny campfire story. And if he died, it'd make a good story to tell at the funeral." I stopped to sip the coffee.

"So I assume the women and Dave's father didn't die or you wouldn't think the story was so funny," she said, turning once again to the counter.

"Nope, a lucky bounce wave caught Sam and literally threw him toward the back in the boat. He lost his hat though and since he only had about eleven hairs, when we caught up to his boat, he was grousing about terminable sunburn.

"I happened to have an extra baseball cap and dug it out of my gear for him. It was University of Arkansas hat with a big A on the front with a frothing Razorback running through it. Sam took one look at the hat and tossed it back. "Rather burn than be caught with that on my head," was all he said.

"I didn't understand what the big deal was since the hat he had lost was some little-billed wool-type thing that made him look like an over-the-hill French pimp."

"Maybe he's Jewish," Widder offered.

"Jewish?"

"Jews. Pig. Pork. Hel-lo-0-0! For a sophisticated, world traveler, you can be pretty dense, you know that?"

Gah-got ya!

Spying a couple of plates and utensils on the counter near where Widder was cooking, I jumped up and started setting the table.

In the next minute, Widder shoveled peppered bacon and biscuits on a couple of plates and put them on the table. Getting a pitcher of orange juice from the refrigerator, she indicated I was to pour.

By the time two glasses were filled and put next to the plates, she had extracted a small, iron skillet from the oven and put it on the table on a ratty oven mitten decorated with a litter of appliquéd calico kittens looking out of a basket.

The skillet's interior was a cornucopia of color: Yellow, red, green, orange.

"What is this?"

"Skillet omelet," she said, bringing two paper napkins to the table and sitting down. "Eggs, milk, butter, onions, four kinds of bell pepper, onion, chopped up bacon and spices. Easiest thing I know to whip up for breakfast."

Using a metal spatula, she levered out half the omelet and slid in on my plate. I tried a bite. "Either I'm hungry or this is really, really good."

"Thank you, Overnight Visitor. The cook appreciates all compliments regardless of ulterior motives."

I let the line slide since I figured she was primed for a little morning-after *tete a' tete*.

Mah-morning after? Mah-morning after what?

Bob, don't you have something better to do?

Tah-times like this, wah-wish I dah-did.

I took another bite of the omelet and followed it up with a bite of buttery biscuit. I noticed Widder was sitting with her elbow on the table and her chin stuck firmly in a hand-cup. She was staring at me.

"What?"

"Where do you go?"

"Go?"

"Go. What is about the word 'go' that escapes you? For a second or two there, you were someplace else. Your facial expression changes and you 'go' someplace. I've seen it a couple of times now. Where do you go?"

"Go?" I sounded like a scratched record that needed a new needle.

She didn't say a word. Just sat there. Staring.

Putting down my fork, I sighed. Then I looked directly at her face and said, "I... There's... Okay. Okay. I spend a lot of time by myself. Hours, days, even weeks. There are many times when I'm in a hide for hours on end and try not to move, to make a single sound. That's difficult for most folks, but even more so for me."

"ADD?" she asked.

"Probably, even though I've never had a diagnosis. Probably could throw in the "H" for good measure. When I was a kid, there was no ADD or ADHD. A kid out of control was simply 'a handful' when they were little, a 'juvenile delinquent' or 'mean little shit' when they were bigger. To be honest, I was probably a couple of handfuls from two up till about twelve. Then I became Avery's token juvenile delinquent. While I was full of mischief, I don't think I was ever a certified mean little shit."

I took a sip of coffee. Cold. Without a word, Widder got up, took my cup, poured out the dregs in the sink, refilled it, brought it back and sat down.

"You? Delinquent? I don't believe it." Her expression said she did.

"It's true. There are too many stories to back up the assumption. I got by because I was smart. But I was always getting in trouble. Couldn't sit still, couldn't concentrate. Drove teachers, and my parents, to distraction. Later, when I decided to get into the photography business, I was smart enough to...." I looked at Widder. "Are you sure you want to hear this?"

Her chin was back in her hand. She nodded.

"...figure out I didn't have the patience to sit and watch and wait without, well, some sort of crutch."

"Crutch?"

"Crutch. Well, not exactly a crutch, but help, assistance, in making it through those times when I needed to just sit and listen and watch and focus. I don't always do...well by...myself."

Another sip. Widder took the pause-time to refill her own cup.

She did the hand-thing again. The first couple of times, it was cute; now it was bordering on irritating.

Ah-are you sure yah-you want....

"One day, when I was a about fourteen, I was in a stand of woods near my house using my dad's old Topcon camera, trying to get some candid photos of cotton pickers without them knowing I was there. I had set up in a small deer stand and that been there for several hours, waiting for something more exciting than picking cotton to pop up in front of the camera," I said.

I took a sip of coffee to give me time to figure what the direction I wanted to go.

"It was one of the worst experiences of my life. Hot, tired, smelly. Eating crackers and chips and drinking hot water. I knew there was no way I could sit in that stupid blind for another minute without going crazy. Then...."

Widder's eyes were wide. I wasn't for sure she was breathing.

"Bob showed up."

"Bob?"

"Bob."

She waited. I squirmed.

"Who's Bob?"

"I don't know exactly. Bob is... Bob. He's my conscience, I guess.

Maybe my inner voice. My...friend, companion, alter ego, amigo, partner. Hell, I don't really know who he is, what he is. He's just Bob. I just know that there have been times that without Bob, I would have gone crazy sitting behind some damn tarp in some country that's hard to pronounce, trying to get a picture of some animal that few people even think about, much less care about."

I finished the cup of coffee, glanced at Widder' cup, picked them both up and dumped the sludge in the sink. Refilled them from the Faberware percolator. Unplugged it.

"Thanks," Widder said when I handed her the cup. "Why 'Bob?'"

"I don't know. It's just like he just popped in one day when I needed...something. He came. He never left."

"No, I mean, why the name 'Bob.'"

"Oh, I named him after my favorite fishing cork when I was a kid."

"That's a joke, right?"

"I don't think so." Then I grinned.

"Seriously, why 'Bob?'"

"I don't know. At first, he was just 'the voice.' You know, 'The stupid voice is back.' I started to call him Bob after singing a song in my head one day—'When the red-red-red robin comes bob-bob-bobbing along.' Somewhere in the middle of the song he thought something to me and it's been Bob ever since."

"I hope you don't mind my questions, but this is very interesting." She didn't wait for a comment. "Does he just talk to you, or give advice...? What does he do exactly?"

I thought about that for a spell. "Bob is sarcastic, mainly. Smart little remarks to keep me on my toes, keep me thinking. Sometimes he has poignant points to make; other times his comments are dumber than a box of hair."

I waited for a verbal slap-back from Bob. Nothing.

Widder caught my expression. "Did Bob just say something?"

I felt really stupid talking about Bob and told her so. "No, but I was expecting him to. I think he's pouting."

"Bob pouts?"

"Oh, yeah, and he's quite good at it. Sometimes when I need him most, he is pouting and refuses to talk to me. Stutters, too."

"Stutters? You made that up! Bob doesn't stutter?"

"He honest-to-God stutters. I've thought a lot about why he stutters. I think it's to slow down my thinking processes, making me wait for the reward, so to speak," I said.

"So, let me get this straight. Bob is a voice that stutters, a disembodied alter ego that pouts. And, I assume from what you said, you can't control Bob. Bob is his own man, or voice, or whatever he is"

"Absolutely. What's the point of having someone, or something, to talk to if you control everything that's said?"

She mused over that for a time. "I think I like Bob. He can come visit me anytime."

Hah-hah-hah ah-ah-and HAH!

Widder was like a terrier thrown in a cage with a rat. She was holding onto this conversation and was not about to let it go.

"What does Bob say about me?"

Gah-good one.

"Not much."

Lah-liar!

"I bet he does." She got up and twirled around. "Look at me. How could he not comment on this?"

Now that I looked at her closely, she wasn't really that good looking. She was too short and her shorts were too loose. And her skin lumped up in the strangest places. Is that cellulite on her left thigh?

Jah-jesus! Yah-you're such a loser.

"Sometimes **Bob** gives too much advice. Sometimes **Bob** won't shut up. Sometimes **Bob** sticks his nose, if he has one, in places it **doesn't belong**."

"He just talked to you, didn't he? This is so…neat. So," Widder said, sitting back down, "then he does talk about me."

"Not so much about you as about me and what I am doing or feeling about the situation," I said.

"And…." followed by that hand-rotating thing again.

"He mainly takes your side."

Her eyes widened. "He does! Really?" She giggled. That really pissed me off. I tried to hide it. Didn't I need to be somewhere else, doing something?

She said, "He really takes my side?"

"Just about every damn time. He really can be a pain in the ass."

"I don't think he's a pain in the ass. I think Bob is smart and funny and cute."

Bob's stutter-cackle started at the base of my skull and bounced around inside my head like a motorized Super Ball.

I could feel a migraine coming on. A major screamer.

"Can Bob hear me when I talk?"

"If I can hear you, Bob can hear you."

"Does he know everything I do?"

"If I'm there, Bob is there."

"Even last night, in bed, when you were asleep?"

"Wha—I don't know. What are you talking about?"

"You know, Bob. Right?"

"What are you talking about?"

Yah-yes, C C. I-I know. Eh-it's our secret.

After silently cursing both Bob and Widder, I helped clean up. Just as the last dish was dry, she gave me a peck on the cheek and shooed me out, saying she had some work to do.

"I want to talk about last night," I said as she pushed me gently toward the door.

"I don't. Talk to Bob."

I went back to the lodge and wandered around thinking. Bob was closeted somewhere, not thinking. I started thinking about dusting, but decided instead to check in at Harlan's, then take a ride out in the lake. No serious shooting, just a look-see ride. I needed fresh air.

At Harlan's seven men, mostly elderly, mostly in overalls or khakis, were sitting out front when I pulled up. I saw Thompson sitting at the edge of the group. I hadn't noticed earlier but he was dressed in pressed khaki pants and shirt, and wearing what looked like a new felt hat. His brown brogans were as shined as brogans can get. I grimaced when I remembered I was supposed to shoot his picture early this morning.

Motioning him away from the group, I apologized and told him I was out early and simply forgot about taking his picture. "Let's go back to the house and I'll get those pictures now."

"No hurry, Mr. Jones," he said. "I figured you was busy." Then he winked.

"Let me pick up a few things and we'll head back."

"Take your time." Wink.

Must have the pink-eye, I thought as I turned to go into the store. That's when I saw Rayon sidle up to the group, pull up a Dr Pepper case and sit down. Bob *bah-begged* me to run away. I couldn't. Listening to Rayon was like driving by a shirtless four hundred pound man on a riding lawnmower going over a terraced lawn. You could not *not* look.

"Did I tell boys about my idea for Bible School toys? It's a winner, I tell you, a winner!" he cackled, settling in for the story.

"You see, I got this idea to hammer out some plastic toys 'bout some of the great stories of the Bible. One of them toy sets would be *Jonah and the Whale*. People could order a kit, which would give 'em a plastic whale, a plastic Jonah, a plastic boat and a little timer. During the telling of the famous Bible story, you would feed Jonah to the whale and set that there timer. In three days, every body would gather around and get all the kids you could find and let them watch the whale puke up Jonah. They'd be this little, tight spring that would upchuck Jonah across a Sunday School room."

He stopped to slap his knee and hoot.

"They's more. The Bible's full of possibilities. Hebrew Children in the Fiery Furnace. That's got lava rocks and comes with a Zippo lighter. Daniel in the Lion's Den. How 'bout Samson in Delilah? Did I say I was looking for investors?"

He cracked himself up one more time.

"Boys, the Southern Baptists would love it. And if the Missionary Baptists had any money, they'd love it too! And them Pentecosts? Hell, they'd buy them things up by the truckload. Can't you just 'magine them Bible School convicts watching that whale puke up Jonah! Now that's really education if they ever was such a thing."

He looked around at the group.

Not a word. Dumbstruck. Except for Bob.

Jah-jesus!

Bob, there's some things even He can't do anything about. If He could, He'd already done it,

29

Ask and ye shall receive. Or not.

Anonymous

Harlan was waiting on a customer that I didn't recognize so I wandered around the aisles, looking for…just looking. A new shipment of sunbonnets was neatly stacked on a middle shelf. They conjured up the image of my grandmother, elderly and stooped, watering flowers in old wash tubs or slowly attacking weeds in her garden with a short-handle hoe.

Dresses, women's shoes, bolts of material, all caught my eye, before I realized that I was "shopping." For Widder.

I shivered just a tad but willed the fear-feeling with double willies to pass, which it did without much of a grumble. I was looking at a case of "play-pretties" as my grandmother used to call them—fancy geegaws and fake, shiny jewelry—when my eyes fell on a photo album that was under a quilt on a low shelf. Glancing at Harlan, I caught his eye and motioned I'd like to go behind the counter. He smiled, nodded twice and went back to counting change.

Behind the counter, I eased the quilt out, laying it on the counter behind me and picked up the album. It had a leather cover, dark blue, with gold, embossed trim that squared itself around the page in a series of connected curlicues and swirls. Flipping through it, I figured it would hold at least a hundred 4x6 photos. Replacing the quilt, I took the album over to Harlan, who was finishing up on his last sale.

"I forgot that was even back there," Harlan said, eyeing the album.

Brushing a little—no, a LOT—of dust off one corner, I asked the price. He thought a minute, then said: "Twenty dollars."

"Nope."

"Too high?"

"Too low." We settled on thirty dollars.

He wrapped the album in heavy brown paper and tied it expertly with twine spun off a thimble-shaped ball in an antique wire cage screwed to the counter top.

I slipped him a twenty and a ten, and two ones and some change for tax, picked up the package and went to round up Thompson. Rayon was starting another story (this one about a cousin who was bedridden with the "hivey epizootie"). His audience had shrunk to two. One old man had his eyes closed; the other one I knew was stone deaf was smiling and nodding and nodding and smiling.

Thompson was standing out by the Jeep and I motioned him to hop in.

"I couldda followed you in my truck," he said.

"No need. I don't mind running you back. Unless, of course, I run into Rayon again."

"I been listening to his stories since afore the lake was dug. And, I swan, I never heard him tell the same story twice."

"Fertile mind. Fertilizer," I said.

"That there's a good 'un," he said, without changing expressions.

At the house, I asked him he wanted something to drink, a cup of coffee, maybe?

"Two cups of coffee, maybe, if it's no bother."

I put on the coffee while Thompson made himself at home in the living room. He was snuggled down in the horny chair, leaned back and apparently relaxed. He unconsciously stroked one of the upturned spikes.

"Sorry about the furnishings," I offered as an opening to conversation. "It's rented, you know. And I just took it 'as is' since I won't be here for too long."

UNCERTAIN TIMES

"I used to spend a lot of time in this here cabin, when there was not much down here excepting a few old-timers and fewer hunting cabins. I lived in town back then, working for the railroad. Hell, back then, everybody worked for the railroad. Did a little mussel diving on weekends to help make ends meet. I always liked this place. Helped built it, you know."

I didn't know and told him so. Then, "Mussel diving?"

"Yep. This lake used to have truckfuls of freshwater mussels. Had pearls in 'em, too. Not good 'uns like they got elsewhere but still good enough for fake jewels and such."

"And you built this cabin?"

"Yep. That would have been about 'fifty or 'fifty-one. Me and 'bout four other fellers took vacation time and holidays and slapped it right up. We used it nigh on to forty years before just about everybody died off excepting me and Luke Gilfoy. We sold it to a group of rich men over to Tyler. Divided the money up between all the original families."

I thought about how knowing a little history of the place made it seem more homey, somehow. Told him that, too.

He sat there, smiling, rubbing on that damned spike sticking out of that chair arm.

The coffeepot stopped gurgling, so I fetched back two big travel mugs of coffee.

"Black? Or do you like something in it?"

Thompson motioned for the cup. "Coffee ain't coffee lessen it's black. With anything in it, it's Bosco."

Bah-Bosco?

I moved to lean against the hand-hewn mantle, telling him I liked the layout of the house. "Everything is so convenient. The only think I haven't gotten use to is that chair. It's kinda spooky, with all those dead deer horns sticking up all over the place. Somebody must have liked it. I just think it's dog-ass ugly."

He stopped rubbing the spike and smiled at me while taking a long, slow slurp of coffee.

"Good coffee, Mr. Jones. Can taste the chicory."

"Adj, please."

He shook his head. "That I can't do. You stay around here for twenty-five years and I'd be obliged to call you Adj. Folks like you just passing through, Mister will have to do."

"Then I guess I'll just have to call you Mr. Thompson."

"Nope, that won't do. Not at all. Thompson. That's who I be here in Uncertain." He stopped rubbing that spike and looked at me. "Mind if I tell you a story?"

"Please do. I love stories. Fancy myself as a storyteller on occasion."

"Storyteller like Rayon down at Harlan's?"

I forced ahoot and said, "Not hardly. Most of mine at least have a germ of truth to them."

He settled back in the chair and closed his eyes.

"Back about forty years ago, I reckon, I went to a school thing where kids got up and sang songs on the stage. The whole durn town was there on account there weren't much to do back then except go to church, sit on the porch, whittle and the like. I went in with the Missus—she passed on December of aught-aught. How that woman wanted to see a new century roll in." He paused, shook his head, then continued. "I got there early as I'm a mind to, just to talk to folks and see who's there, that sorta thing."

He took a long sip of coffee, then said, "This woman I had seen before, but never talked to, sat right down by me and said 'Howdy' and I howdy-ed her back. That was about the beginning and the end of our talking. The program started up and the mayor got up and said some words and then the superintendent of the school hisself got up and said some words. Then he introduced a big old woman who he said was a music teacher from around these here parts, but I'd never heard of her. She commenced to singing the National Anthem." He pause to take another slurp.

"I swan!" he said. "That woman took to caterwauling and I didn't know if she were singing the National Anthem or doing a Bovarian war chant. It were the worstest thing I ever heard, afore then and till now." Another sip of coffee preceded a healthy clearing of his throat. "When she finely quit killing that bag of cats her lungs were squeezing, I leaned over to the woman next to me and said, 'Somebody should of told her she lost her voice somewhere on the way to the meeting. Maybe we can go help her find it after."

Another sip of coffee.

"That woman looked at me, smiled real purty-like and patted me on my knee. Then, real lowish, she said, nodding her head toward the woman on the stage, 'That's my mama.' Then turned back and never said another word."

After a healthy silence, I said, "So, Thompson, how long did it take you to make that chair?"

He graciously accepted my first apology and rejected the eight or nine that followed. I started gathering up some equipment while we talked about Uncertain history, upcoming events, where the crappie were biting…regular chit-chatter that people do when they are trying to morph from one conversation to another without appearing to do so.

Bob said he admired my *ap-aplomb*. I didn't even know Bob knew what aplomb meant. I thought I did, but wasn't sure.

I picked up two heavy-duty spotlights from a trunk under the bed, two long extension cords from the closet, Betsy and a couple of lenses that I stuck in photo vest pockets. We went in the backyard, with Thompson helping me spread the cables out to the big tree near the water. I had him lean against the tree while I set up both lights, one to his left and about head-high, the other to the right, slightly higher.

After jockeying them around for a bit until I got the right balance between muted floods and filtered sunlight, I took a couple of test shots, checking angles and settings.

Sah-something's missing.

Yeah, Bob. And I think I know what it is.

"Stay right there," I said to Thompson.

I ran into the house and went straight to the horny chair. It was a heavy sucker, for sure, but I managed to get it up so I could support part of the weight on my thighs. The trick was to find a resting-place that didn't have a spike sticking out. I manhandled it through the kitchen and out the backdoor before needing a short rest.

Horns kept sticking me every time I'd move. A different strategy was definitely in order. The only places where the spikes were in quasi-control were the seat and back. Placing my hands on both arms, I put my head in the crease between the seat the back and pulled with my hands and straightened my neck until the chair was resting uneasily on top my head.

Yah-you look like Rah-robin Williams as Mork.

Bob, if you're not going to help, shut up!

Thompson started chuckling when he saw me trying to maneuver the chair through the back gate. By the time I eased it off my head and onto the ground, with Thompson grabbing one side before I skewered myself, he was still chuckling. "This'll be worth a couple of good days of conversation down at Harlan's," he said.

"If you tell about this, it'll make us even for the remark about the chair," I said.

"I never did like owing nobody, and don't much like anybody owing me," Thompson said.

We pushed the chair over next to the tree, but just a little off-center so part of the background would also be the curtain of Spanish moss hanging from every tree limb in the viewfinder.

Thompson seated himself, removed his hat and proceeded to hitch up his face in a goofy grin. I obliged him and shot a picture.

"Thompson, let's do something a big different," I said. At my instructions, he put back on the hat, tilting it just a little so the shadow from the spotlights weren't as visible, kinda slumped to his right in the chair. He crossed his legs and put his right hand flat against the chair's arm, while propping his left hand on his cheek.

Just as I got ready to shoot, that goofy grin spread across his face. I shot the picture.

"Thompson. Close your eyes. Relax. When I say 'three,' open your eyes."

Working for the railroad all those years, he was good at following explicit orders. On 'three,' his eyes opened...and the companion goofy smile was again captured on film.

A cha-challenge.

Oooooooo, yeaaaah.

"Relax a minute, Thompson. I want to switch lenses. He noticeably relaxed. I pretended to fiddle around with the camera, but didn't change anything.

He was watching me closely when I glanced over to my right, toward Widder's, then snapped my head back around. "Don't look now, Thompson, but Widder is sunbathing."

His head didn't move, but his eyes started slowing moving to his left. Three frames later and I knew I had just shot the best pictures that had ever been taken of him. Or ever would be.

Thompson was no longer cutting his eyes sideways to see Widder; he was standing…on the chair, trying to look in her backyard.

"She ain't there," he said.

"Must of gone inside when she realized we were here."

"Nekkid, you say."

"Didn't say."?

"Bet she weren't all-the-way nekkid. Still a mite chilly for that."

He helped me get all the cords rolled up and the chair back in the house and thanked me for all the time, coffee, and conversation.

On the drive back to Harlan's, knowing he wanted to know, I told him I'd send the photos off today or tomorrow and have them back next week.

"Thanks," he said, getting out of the car.

"And if it's all the same to you," he said, "I'll just think that I saw Widder sunbathing nekkid. Makes a whole lot better memory thataway."

30

There's no such thing as a secret. Just ask anybody.

Anonymous

As I was dropping Thompson off at Harlan's, I handed him a pre-printed addressed envelope containing the film I had shot over the last week and asked him to tell Harlan to send it off. "I have a credit balance, so it should be okay." I drove the short distance down to the dock, parked in a shady spot that was going to be shady the rest of the day and started carrying camera gear to the boat. I had the boat loaded when I noticed there was a hole in the top of the motor cowling.

It looked like someone had punched a hole though the metal cover directly into the top of the motor. Screwdriver, maybe. Might be something bigger. The sharp end of a tire iron?

Jeb Huckaby, a middle-aged man I knew from around town, who was rumored to be on disability from the Mo-Pac Railroad, wandered down the dock toward me. He was a small man, about five-six, and couldn't have weighed more than 135. He had tiny features, small hands and smaller feet. Size five or siz. He was dressed in overalls and stained t-shirt that at one time could have been white. He was carrying a large plastic bag with thick handles; *Estee Lauder* was printed on the side in simple black letters. From the smell, I knew the sack wasn't full of perfume samples.

"Somebody done punched a hole in your motor."

"Jeb Huckaby, right?" He nodded. "Seems like you pinpointed the problem all right."

"Where you headed?" Jeb asked.

"I was going to a blind to check on some nesting cormorants. Not now. Not today."

"Hope you don't mind," he said, shuffling some dirt around with his foot. "I noticed the motor and told Harlan. He called Trapp's Small Appliance and Motor Repair. Tim or Mary Ann one'll pick the motor up and have it back good as new tomorrow. If you'd allow me, I'd be pleased to take you out in my boat. No charge. Just feel like getting out and getting some fresh air."

He pointed with a slight nod of his head in the direction of a grove of trees skirting the lake behind me. There was Sheriff Twiddle and a deputy, leaning against a big tree, laughing their asses off. The front left fender of their patrol car was barely visible behind a nearby cypress.

"Jeb, I would be obliged to you for a lift to the blind and back."

With Jeb toting two of my waterproof ammo boxes, I managed to get the small ice chest and the waterproof suitcase off my boat and back onto the dock. His boat, a fancy metallic red, top of the line Ranger, was tied at the end of the dock. Sheriff Twiddle and his running buddy quit laughing when we didn't head to the parking lot. They looked downright mean when we got on Jeb's boat.

"You reckon this is a smart move, taking me out?"

"Not hardly," Jeb said, checking the gas levels and untying the stern line. He eased the boat away from the dock and idled it about ten feet from the dock before he spoke again. "When it comes to Twiddle, I just use two words most times."

"And…" I said, finding myself doing the Widder-keep-going hand thing.

"FUCK 'IM!" he shouted. Loud.

Jeb then slapped the throttle level full down, and the roar of the 200 hp. Evinrude threw us both backwards.

I hoped to God Twiddle heard Jeb's last phrase. From the look on his face, Jeb did too.

Twenty minutes later, we were easing past The Cathedral and, as always, I marveled at the way man sometimes imitates nature in building things, or, sometimes, tearing things up. Squint your eyes just a little bit and you could almost see a big city skyline, or the columns of rice silos imitating a big city skyline.

"This are a special place." That was all Jeb said.

"I took a picture here a couple of days ago. When I get the proof back, I'd like for you to see it. Shot it from the back side."

His initial expression was one of puzzlement. He said, "Sounds like a plan."

Right after we left the dock and hit open water Jeb asked about what blind I was checking on, and when I said "Buddy Parley's," he nodded before I could add "on Carter's Chute." At the end of the winding channel leading to Carter's Chute, Jeb turned left and opened up the throttle and the boat literally leapt forward and bounced high twice before settling down for a slick-as-owl-shit ride across the mirrored surface.

"She'll get," he said.

I think I nodded. I was holding on so tight to the chair bottom and focusing on not flying through the air if the boat went airborne again, that I couldn't be sure whether I did or not.

All of a sudden, Jeb cut back all the way on the throttle and the boat settled lightly in the water.

The blind was gone. Only four charred stubs from the leg supports remained. Pieces of charred lumber bobbed gently on the water's surface.

"Somebody sure got it in for either you or Buddy," Jeb said. Pause. "My money's on you."

Jah-jeb's money's sah-safe.

There was not enough time for me to rebuild the blind by the time all the chicks in the three nests were hatched and learned to fly.

"I gather you had some more work to do here?"

"Yeah, I did. About three or four more good days would have been nice. But what I really hate is that Buddy's blind was torched."

"Buddy's lived here his whole life," Jeb said. "He'll piss and moan for a couple of days, but he'll have it back up before duck season. Count on it."

"You know what really pisses me off?" I said. Jeb waited, then finally broke down and said, "What's that?"

"Now I have to go buy two more damn pink lawn chairs."

Jeb laughed an honest laugh that I've always associated with people who sleep well at night.

He eased around the blind, carefully avoiding the charred chunks of lumber and headed to the far shore. "You got any gator shots," he said.

"Not yet. I've shot both gators and crocodiles in other places around the world but these on Caddo are skittish."

"Hard to sneak up on, too. You ever seed a gator jump?"

"Jump?"

"Yeah, like straight up, outta tha water."

"I've seen shows on the National Geographic channel, but I've never actually seen one jump."

"Gators can jump. Run like a dog with tin cans tied to its tail too. But only for a short sprint. People think gators are slow and mean. They ain't always slow and they ain't always mean. They are gentle with they eggs and young'uns. I seed mama gators take they babies in they mouth with a head hanging out of them big-ass teeth and carry them around gentle as you please."

Jeb eased up on throttle and edged the boat down a narrow channel between huge cypress trees.

"Where're we going?"

"A place. A place I thought you might like. You'll see."

For the first time I noticed the rubber bumpers added to the edges of the boat. He needed them in the channel. There was no way the boat could make it down the squeeze-in channel without hitting trees and knees. Because, I assumed, the depth of the water was so shallow, Jeb wasn't using the big motor; a small trolling motor attached to the left rear side of the boat pushed us along so slowly it seemed like we were merely drifting.

He stationed me at the front with a long, metal-shafted boat paddle with a hard-plastic blade, the kind normally used for whitewater rafting, only longer.

I guess I chuckled because Jeb said, "Whatcha laughing at?"

"Just thinking. The last time I used one of these paddles, I was going down a big rapid called Elk Horn up in Idaho in a paddle raft with six other crazy people. I was screaming, 'I'm gonna die!'"

Jeb gave a polite laugh, or it could have just been a hiccup. It was apparent he didn't see the irony.

"How many people know about this place?" I asked to get the conversation back on an even keel.

"A couple. I've brought some friends back in here, mainly to show out, if you know what I mean?"

"I've done that a time or two myself."

"Not meaning to be nosy, but was that what you was doing with the Ledbetters and Twiddle?"

Jeb had stopped the boat dead still. He looked at me over his right shoulder, his head swiveling around like a barn owl.

There was no malice in his face or in the question and I didn't try to force any into it.

"Yes, Jeb, that's exactly what I was doing, showing out. But I don't think I did it for the reason some folks might think I did. I didn't do it to impress people, but to embarrass the Ledbetters and the sheriff. I'm almost sixty years old and, for some strange reason or other, I have always thought it was my special calling to puncture the bubbles of trained and professional assholes and pricks."

Yah-you're expanding your dah-descriptive repertoire.

I paused, reached down beside the boat and, using my hand as a skimmer, wiped away the top layer of stagnant water mixed with algae. I scooped up a handful of the cleaner water underneath the scum and wiped my face.

When I straightened up, Jeb was still looking at me, eyes locked on mine. He was waiting.

"I don't know if you will believe me or now, but I'm not a fool. I know what people like Harmony and Bother and the sheriff are like and what they can do. No hero, either. That's for sure. I just hate people that make it their life's work to create situations to make other people feel uncomfortable and then work overtime to make them even more uncomfortable," I said.

I waited for a response. There was none. His only reaction to my speech was to sit up, swivel his butt around so that he faced me. Then he went back to staring, elbows on knees.

"When I was a kid, I was tiny. Real small and, well, almost frail. I didn't start growing until after I was sixteen. Shoot, when I got my first driver's license, I was five-eight and 110 pounds. People picked on me all the time. Big kids, little bullies, it made no difference. Hell, I even had a girl call me out one time."

Jeb's face split in a grin, but he dropped his face in an attempt to hide it. When he raised back up, the stoic expression was plastered on tight.

"The summer after I turned sixteen I grew. Six inches in two or three months. I didn't fill out until much later, but the height gave me confidence to, at the very least, stand up to the bullies of what was then, my small, small world," I said.

Bob started humming the familiar Disney tune, which was more than a bit distracting.

A big splash off to our left caused us both to look in that direction.

"Big lunker, I imagine," Jeb said.

I opened up the ice chest and offered him a bottled water.

"Not often I get to drink water that didn't come outta a well," he said, uncapping the bottle and taking a healthy swig.

"Didn't now, either. I buy bottled water and usually refill them from the tap in the house, which is hooked to a well."

He shook his head, grinning. "Damn fine water." Then, "Damn fine," for emphasis.

"I've learned that when you're thirsty, all water is sweet-tasting. Brush aside the mosquito larvae and get down with the animals and quench your thirst."

"You done that?"

"Many times. Not proud of it. Not bragging. Just a fact of life for me. A person trying to succeed at what he's good at will do just about anything to maintain that success."

"Like Harmony and Bother?"

The question shook me more than a little bit. Harmony and Bother? Successful?

Heh-he's got a point.

Yes he did, and I told him so. Those two qualified as A-Number 1 assholes. Looking at it from that perspective, there were very successful assholes.

Jeb changed places with me and asked if I would keep the tail end of the boat straight by using the paddle to pry off trees, knees and stumps.

He then stood in the front of the boat and moved it slowly from tree to tree using only his hands. Reach. Grip. Pull. He had small arms, smaller wrists. But when he pulled, the tendons popped up on his arms like hackles on a threatened dog. No way I'd ever agree to arm-wrestle him.

"You worked for the railroad, right?"

"Yep, twenty-six years until a platform I was working on gave way and I hurt my neck and back."

"Do you mind if I guess what kind of job you did?"

"Guess? No, have at it. It ain't no secret,"

"Well, this is just a guess, mind you, but I think you used hand tools, probably a hammer or something that required a hard grip. Not a sledgehammer for driving spikes, though I bet you are no stranger to it."

He stopped the boat's forward motion and turned at looked at me.

"How'd I do?"

"If it was a nail, you'd hit it plumb center. I was a forge master at the machine shop. Spent a lot of time making parts that were broke, fixing them that could be fixed, making new ones if they couldn't. As I said, spent twenty-six years at the Mo-Pac yard, all but one of them with a hammer in my hand."

He shook his head. "How'd you know?"

I pointed toward his hand. "Tendons from your hand to your arm. Lots of hard work in those hands."

He tightened his right into a fist. The tendons exploded to attention. He shook his head again and just looked at me.

"Want to see me show out again?"

"You got to go some to beat that 'un."

"Jeb Huckaby. First name Jeb or Jebediah?"

"Jebediah."

"Do you have a middle name?"

"Two of them. First one is...."

"Don't tell me! This is part of the trick. I've never had practice with double middle names, but let's give it a shot. Are either one of your middle names 'family' names, names for some relative that may be unusual?"

"One is that name of a uncle. He's dead."

"But it's not a family name that is a last name, like Galloway or Higgins or something like that?"?

"Nope."

"Okay, Jebediah Huckaby, your first middle name starts in the last half of the alphabet, from M to Z; your second middle name starts in the first half of the alphabet, A to M."

He studied on it for what seemed like quite a spell.

"Jebediah Zachariah Keening Huckaby."

"*Voilà!,*" I said, raising my hands aloft in the universal sign of 'good job.' Or touchdown. "It's just a game I played with in college. It's a great exercise at parties. And the interesting thing about it is that it works about eighty percent of the time or higher."

He pondered on that for a time. Then I had a thought.

"Wait a minute," I said, "I thought you said your names are not family names. What about Keenin?"

"Keening. It's gotta 'g' at the end. My mama gave me that name," he said, quietly. "It was in a poem book. She showed it to me when I was little. It was something about the 'quality of keening is not narrow.' She just liked the way it sounded. I guess I'm a mite lucky. Coulda named me 'Narrow.'"

"Keening," I repeated, letting the word roll off my tongue.

"The quality of keening is not narrow.
It ranges freely, back roads and low roads,
A violin heard from a window at night
A silent rubbing, a tune you cannot place...."

Jeb looked in my direction, then shook his head and smiled at me with his eyes.

"How do you know that poem?"
"My mama read poetry, too, Jeb.
Buh-but doesn't 'keening' mah-mean...?
Yes it does, Bob. I move we keep the meaning to ourselves.
Bob sulked up then *sah-seconded* the motion.
It passed. Unanimously.

"We about there," Jeb said as the front of the boat entered a small clearing of about six hundred square feet. There was a indention into the small clearing to the right and that's where we headed, using just the oar to push the boat forward.

There was a big, leaning tree at the end of the nipple of water. It had a funny-looking platform attached to the tree with what looked like a very long trace chain, or, maybe, four or five smaller ones intertwined. It was comprised of a simple floor structure, with ten two-by-fours slapped together and connected by an underpinning of crisscrossed pieces of lumber. Two lengths of chain came down from higher up on the tree, wrapped under the floor and disappeared around the back of the tree.

Jeb rowed the boat past the tree, then asked me to swing the back end around so that the boat faced the opening. The space was tight, just wide enough to do the job.

There were six boards nailed to the back of the tree, making what I now thought of as a "Caddo Ladder."

"Now's here's the tricky part," Jeb said. "We got to get your stuff up on that deck without falling in the water."

He looked at the boxes and the case and suggested I "take just what'll you need, no more." He hadn't said, but I assumed I was going to shoot a jumping alligator, so all I needed was three things: Betsy and two lenses—70-300 mm. zoom and 20-35 zoom; enough film to shoot jumping alligators; and not to fall off that small-ass platform.

Nos. 1 and 2 I could take care of; No. 3 was still up in the air, so to speak.

I already had on my vest so I loaded up the cartridge slots with film, put the extra lens in a roomy button-down side pocket and buttoned Betsy's strap to the epaulette fastener. For good measure, I included a small digital, which I hooked to my right shoulder. I buttoned the vest up halfway, putting Betsy and the digital inside, where they fit snuggly and wouldn't bounce around. Both cameras were on, ready for action.

"I'm going up first. When I get up there and give you the high sign, come on up." I nodded and watched as he scaled the ladder like a jacked-up spider monkey. When he started up, I was just taking in a breath; I was still taking it in when he nimbly stepped on the platform and motioned me up. I wondered what he could do if he wasn't on disability.

Dah-don't try and out-macho hah-him.

Bob, please just shut up. Jesus!

I have never been afraid of heights. That's been a blessing in some of the places I've been and crazy things I've been accused of doing. This was a little different. It was only about fifteen feet up, but, dammit, I am damn near seventy...

Sah-sixty.

...whatever, and if I fell and don't get impaled by a malaria-carrying cypress knee, I'd probably fall in a nest of alligators and...."

"You coming?"

"Yes. Jeb. Coming right up. I was just deciding the best way to get up there: Jump up on the platform with a single bound or use these cute little boards."

I didn't look to see his reaction. Bob said he was *sha-shaking his head sah-sadly*.

In the end, I just climbed the damn thing, coordinating my climbing rhythm like members of the coconut tree-climbing tribe in eastern Borneo...right hand/right foot, left hand/left foot. Jeb was standing at the top with his hand outstretched when I hit the last board. He latched onto me and I fastened my hand around his wrist. I could swear I grabbed a gnarly oak limb.

I opened my eyes and I was witnessing an exception to a rule of perspective. Objects far away look smaller than up close. This platform was smaller than it looked from the boat.

"Here," Jeb said, handing me a small chain that I had seen holding up porch swings. "Wrap it around your waist a couple times." I started to comply and then thought about how a body wrapped in chains would stay at the bottom of this lake for a long time.

Jeb must have seen the look in my eyes because he took me by the shoulders. "Mr. Jones, if I'd wanted you dead, I sure as hell wouldn't a gone to all this trouble. I'd just popped one in your conk and dropped you in the middle of Big Lake."

Conk? Who uses the word 'conk'? That was a favorite word for author Richard S. Prather, author of the Shell Scott mystery novels. Growing up, I spent more time with Shell than I did with girlfriends. Not by choice, but as an alternative. Shell always got the girl. Always.

"Did you ever read Shell Scott mystery stories?"

Jeb stopped wrapping my waist with the chain and stood straight up. "You just plain spooky, you know that? I must have got every one that guy…what's his name…?

"Richard S. Prather."

"That's him! I got every one he ever wrote I tell you. Howdja know that?"

"He's always been one of my favorite writers, "I said. You said something about shooting me in my 'conk.' That was a word used by Shell Scott."

He looked at me with a hint of a smile. "It's sure a small world."

In Uncertain, it's smaller than that.

After wrapping my waist with the chain, Jeb threw one end around the Tree, adroitly avoiding putting out an eye in the process, then used a little fast-snap metal clip to attach the two loose ends together.

"Now, you're not going nowhere, even if you fall."

"Fall? I'm not going to fall. Fall?"

Without another word, Jeb swung around me on the chain like a g-string stripper on a pole and went down the ladder faster than he came up.

First thought was he's going to leave me chained to this platform and then him and all his friends are going to come back and take target practice.

Without looking at me, Jeb said, softly from the boat, "I'm coming right back up."

Gathering up the *Estee Lauder* sack, he was up beside me about three seconds later, rocking the platform more than a tad in the process.

I didn't know which to hug, Jeb, the chain, or the whole damn tree.

Bob was absolutely no help.

Balancing on about six square inches of platform, Jeb opened the sack and removed a smaller grocery sack. Inside that sack were two plucked chickens and bits and parts of other unidentifiable critters. A small, yellow ski rope appeared from Jeb's back pocket and he expertly tied what looked like the back half of a motorcyle-sliced raccoon to the rope.

"Gator bait?"

"Yep."

"How long for them to get here?"

"They already here."

Reaching into the small sack, he took out a handful of offal and flung it toward the water. It hit with a flat splash and lay on the surface of the water. WHOOSH! The surface of the water erupted as an alligator—a big alligator!—broke the surface, snatched at the guts and did a roll or two for effect.

"Sumbitch!" That was me.

"Yep." That was Jeb.

Dah-do it again! That was Bob.

"So," Jeb said. "Ya get a good shot? That's only chance you'll get."

"What? Whoa. No. That's not it! Tell me that's not it!"

He actually laughed out loud. "You're a sight, Mr. Jones. You crack me up. Now, get ready, here's the good part."

After testing the chain to make sure I wasn't heavier than a porch swing and my Aunt BetAnn, I inched to the edge of the platform with Betsy at the ready as Jeb slowly lowered the carcass.

"First couple of times," he said, "you gotta put it near the water to get 'em excited."

For the next several minutes, Jeb "excited" two or three alligators pretty good, but I wasn't happy with the photos because of the angle wasn't right.

"Now they excited," Jeb said. "You ready to go?"

"The angle's not right," I said. "I need to actually get out over the shot and shoot directly down as they come up without the rope being in the way."

He thought about that for a minute, then unhooked me from the tree and gave the chain a few more wraps around my waist. The feeling was like you get after Thanksgiving dinner at your grandparents' house. Heavy. Tight.

He took the loose ends of the chain and wrapped them around the right-hand chain supporting the platform and urged me over to the edge. There he fastened the metal clip, securing me to the chain.

"Lean out on that chain. Use it for support."

Lean out there? On a chain?

Bah-big baby. Remember Uganda?

"That was twenty years ago, Bob!"

"Jeb. What was twenty years ago?"

"Oh, I was just thinking that I did something like this in Africa one time. I let some bushman strap me into a hinny sling and him and twenty-seven of his brothers hauled my ass to the top of this six hundred-foot-tall tree to shoot a nest of scorpions."

"Why?" he said.

"So I could be prepared to shoot a photo twenty years later of a jumping alligator on Caddo Lake."

I took off the digital and hung it around Jeb's neck. Then, leaning out on the chain and supporting my weight on my right side and shoulder, I checked Betsy, aimed down and said, "Make 'em jump, Jeb. Make 'em jump high!"

The next ten minutes were among the most exciting in my life as a photographer. Jeb was a master of the lower-and-snatch, lowering the meat to about two to three feet above the surface and then hauling it up a little as a gator made its run across the short opening, getting up speed for the jump.

I came to the conclusion there were three separate alligators, two about six to seven feet in length and one that was about eight or maybe a little longer.

After finishing one roll, Jeb grabbed my belt and pulled me back upright, where I quickly reloaded, put the film away and resettled myself on the chain.

I instinctively knew I had two shots worthy of inclusion in the book. One with a smaller alligator literally hanging onto a piece of meat almost totally out of the water; in the other, the larger alligator had just started his jump, and I had close-focused to capture the moment his head broke the surface. That shot—water droplets frozen in mid-air, the gator's mouth wide open, left spooky-yellow eye staring…at nothing…was imprinted on film. And in my brain.

Pah-page three of the bah-book?

Maybe cover, Bob. It's that good.

Jeb was down to his last chicken. I got set for one more good series. Thirty-six shots left. Rapid fire.

I gave him the signal and he lowered the chicken.

When the chicken was a about three feet off the surface of the water, two gators broke the surface and I started firing away. They were belly to belly and they came up out of the water, mouths wide open, reaching for the prey. I had the telephoto lens zoomed in fairly tight and cranked back on the focal length just a little…and slid off the chain.

All I remember was looking at the gators and then looking at the tops of the tree and then looking up at the sky. The sharp snap of a chain as it dug into my back embossed a picture on my brain.

I was gator bait.

"BOB!" I screamed but it was Jeb who leaned over the edge. He was holding the little digital camera and clicked off a shot.

He didn't say much, only, "They ain't gonna believe this back in town."

Quick as a will 'o the wisp, he dragged me up onto the platform and steadied me against the tree.

"You okay?"

"Shit, no! I'm not okay. I damn near died! I would rather get stewed and cooked and sautéed by headhunter pygmies than get chewed on by an alligator. I would rather Harmony cut out my liver and feed it to Bother while keeping me alive on Beanie Wienies than…."

Jeb handed me a bottle of water, which I took and which I drank till it was gone.

"Damn! That scared the crap out of me."

"Hope not," Jeb said. "If it did, you not riding home in my boat."

I didn't laugh. I did smile.

But I didn't mean to. The thought passed through my mind that I might never smile again.

Bob didn't think a word. He knew better.

I had made a move to go back down the ladder when I noticed one gator sitting just below the water's surface, facing the tree. The shadows of the trees had lightened as the sun started its fast slide toward the horizon. Little pennant flags of sunlight slipped through the almost solid tree fence, putting an interesting light on the water's surface.

I took Betsy and popped her to maximum focal length, framing just the gator's head. As the light played over the water, subtle colors became dynamic. The slight scum had swirled around where the alligator has surfaced.

The first photo was great. The next three or five were even better. I turned off the cameras and stowed them away.

We were already back in the boat and about to head out when I remembered the digital camera. As Jeb watched, I turned it back on and popped up the last image.

I looked at it in amazement and motioned Jeb to come on back. He looked at the small image and if there was ever a bigger smile on a human being with a small mouth, I couldn't imagine it.

The digital had done all the work, and with its medium wide-angle lens, my body, hanging face-up with the chain wrapped around my waste took up most of the frame. My hands were thrown out wide, feet way apart. My mouth was open in a silent scream. Just to the right of my left ear was an alligator, mouth open, making a jump for that chicken. It looked like it was coming right for my head.

Nah-now that's the cuh-cover.

Maybe, Bob. Yeah. After I'm dead and gone.

Jeb took the long way back home and I just sat back and enjoyed the ride. He told story after story about the lake, some I had heard or read about, some brand new. By the time we got back to the dock, it was, as my grandfather was fond of saying, "Half past plumb dark." The lone light bulb nailed to a single post did two things: Gave us just barely enough light to see to unload the boat and attracted every bug in East Texas.

Jeb helped me carry the stuff to the car. He noticed and mentioned there didn't seem to be "no hole in the car motor...at least far as I can tell from the outside."

I shook his hand, saying, "It's been a pleasure." I meant it.

"Yep. It was a pretty nice afternoon." He paused, then grinned. "I been recollecting on our talk today. I been thinking about that tree in Zymaneer or wherever. Six hundred feet, huh? That's a mighty tall tree. Wouldn't mind seeing that one myself."

I said, "A good story is never harmed by exaggerating."

"Lying, neither," he said. He paused again, then said, "I told you I weren't going to

charge you for the ride."

I waited.

"Well, I changed my mind. I just want one thing."

Uh-uh oh.

"If I've got it or can get it, it's yours."

Bah-bad move.

"I want one pitcher that I took of you hanging on the end of that chain. I truly do. I been to twenty county fairs and three taffy pulls, been so drunk I saw hobgoblins and once a flying magnolia tree. But, I swear on Granny Elum's Bible, I ain't never seen one thing that beat that pitcher."

I started to offer him a hundred dollars instead but I knew he wouldn't take it.

Tha-thousand, neither.

The car started without blowing up. Bob thought that was *nah-not a bad way to end the dah-day.* It was approaching nine when I finally got the car unloaded. In the bathroom, I stripped off my shirt to check the damage done by the chain. My chest was badly bruised and a regular crisscross pattern of abrasions circled my midriff like a case of terminable, but extremely structured, shingles. I couldn't see but part of my back but to an untrained eye, I thought I might need reconstructive surgery.

I had just reached into the fridge for a beer, when I heard a mouse knock at the door.

I turned on the porch light. Widder stood there, swatting at a bug.

"Since when did you start knocking?" I said, holding the door open so she could squeeze through without the bug.

"Don't want to seem too pushy." Then she saw my stomach and chest. "What in the world happened to you?" she said, turning on the entryway light for a better view of the damage.

I gave her a real short version, leaving out the alligator nipping at my head part.

She rubbed her fingertips gently across my chest. If that alligator had walked into the room right that second, I would have kissed him on his big, hard-as-rocks lizard lips.

She smiled, batted her eyes, and said, "Want me to kiss it and make it well."

She was really starting to piss me off. Here I was standing in the hallway without a shirt on, I was quickly running out of breath from holding in my stomach, and she was teasing me. I said, "I've got a much worse abrasion on another part of my body if you're really in a kissing mood."

She looked askance.

"For your information and contrary to popular belief, "I said, "a kiss has no medicinal value. You know, Missy, there was a girl in high school like you. Teasing Tina, we called her."

"But you liked her, right?"

"Yep. Still do. Now, back to that you-don't-want-to-be-pushy line: If you package that line, it'd sell big at the National Liars Convention."

She went into the deluxe edition of her demure act, Scarlett O'Hara as a recent graduate from Miss Ruby's School for Wayward Man-Teasers. She placed one hand across her chest, slid one knee over in front of the other, and batted those eyelashes long enough to lasso fleas. "Why, sir. You do me a great injustice. The only time I'm pushy is at the supermarket with one of those little ol' squeaky-wheeled cahts."

"Don't give up your day job." I took a sip of beer. "By the way, how's your painting going?"

"Going. I got a lot done today. I heard about your motor. Other than shooting alligators, what did you and Jeb do?"

I guided her to the kitchen, fetched her a beer. We sat down at the table and I filled her in, again leaving out only the part where I did a stint as gator bait so Jeb could get a good picture.

She liked Jeb's remark about Twiddle, then she said, "I wish I could have seen the jumping gators."

"I'll send the photos off tomorrow and will have them back in a couple to three days."

"That's one thing I wanted to talk to you about. I've got to be out of town for a few days and was wondering if you'd watch my place," she said.

"Is something wrong? Family? How long are you going to be gone? Can I take you to the airport? You're not going to drive, are you?"

I beat Bob to the mental outburst. My God! I was starting to sound like my agent!

"No," Widder said, "nothing like that. I'm taking some of my paintings to a gallery for a show. I'm flying out of Dallas, so I'll drive over there early in the morning and leave my car at the airport. I don't know how long I'll stay. I have to meet some people and make 'nice'. I'm sure you know the drill."

"Yeah, I do." Pause. "I must've missed something here. I didn't know you were a world-famous painter. I thought you just sold your paintings locally or something."

She gave me the kind of look one would give a half-wit beagle. "No, Silly, I'm not famous. It's just that this gallery owner saw my paintings in the lobby of First National Bank in Longview and contacted me. She wants to see how they'll play in New York."

"New York City?"

"The very one. You heard of it?"

"You have a showing of your paintings in New York City?"

"Yes. But why are you acting like…."

I waved my hands in a version of a spastic flamingo trying to get airborne. "You're going to have a showing in New York City. A showing for your paintings. And you are acting like you're going to Harlan's to have a soda with the boys! Aren't you excited?"

That giggle again. This one started vibrations deep in my chest. A hand covered her mouth. I wanted to be that hand. Come on, Adj, *be* the hand!

"You are just being silly. It's not like I'm going to New York and come back to Uncertain as a famous painter. This is a one-shot deal and I think it'd be fun. Be happy for me."

I thought about that. "It'll be fun and I am happy for you. But...."

"But what?"

I tried to will my face into a portrait of chagrin. "I would have liked to be the one to show you the Big Apple."

"Okay, Adj, here's the deal. You look after my house while I'm gone to New York this time and I promise to meet you there some day and let you give me a tour."

I've always heard the expression "and my heart soared," but never knew what it meant until that moment.

"What?" she said.

"I think my heart just soared."

She gulped down the last three swallows of the beer in the most unfeminine manner and finished the act with a rousing "aaaahhhhhh."

I picked up both bottles and headed to the trashcan.

She came to me and pressed her body to mine. She touched me in all the right places with all her right places. Her kiss was beery-sweet, and absolutely perfect.

"If I didn't have these bottles in my hands...."

"Why do you think I picked this time to kiss you. My mama didn't raise no fool."

She walked to the door and waggled her ass at me. Waggled! Again!

She looked over her shoulder and winked.

"I'm going to miss you," I said.

"I know. Bye, Bob."

Bah-bye.

31

Hating something ain't hard. Loving something you hate is.

Anonymous

Widder was back in less than two minutes, this time to give me some liniment to rub on the abrasions. She also brought along an envelope, which she put on the hall table. "Key to the house," she said.

My attention was focused on the bottle. A thickish solution was in a dark brown bottle with no label. By holding it to the light, I could tell it was about half-empty. This morning, I would have thought it was half-full, but I was tired and not in an optimistic mood.

"What's in this?" I didn't particularly care, but Bob was curious.

"Eye of newt and balls of bat, plus a few other things I had laying around the house."

"Balls of bats?" I looked her square in the eyes. "I know who's got those bat balls and trying to grow them into elephant size."

"Sweet talk like that is going to get you somewhere if you just keep it up." She flapped those too-long eyelashes.

I grumbled low, hoping she'd hear: "Teasing Tina."

"Rub this on tonight and wear a t-shirt to bed. Do the same thing for a couple of nights. It'll get better quick."

"What's in this…besides newt balls and bat eyes?"

"I really don't know. That was what my grandmother used to doctor us with when I was a kid. It seemed to work pretty good."

"Grandmother? Didn't you say she was jerked to…had passed on? How old is this stuff?"

"Do you ask questions like this when you go to the doctor?" she asked.

"No, but at least he knows what's in the medicine he's giving me." I uncorked the bottle and sniffed. It was so old it had a cork!, I thought to Bob. He said I was an *eh-ingrate*. I took a bigger sniff and I swear my nose hairs caught fire.

"Haysus Christo! Widder, this stuff will eat straight through my skin and kill me deader than Bother's brain."

She took the bottle, daubed a little in the palm of her hand and held it up for me. "See! No hole!"

Without warning, she slapped the liniment on my chest and started rubbing.

I jumped. My skin was more than a little tender and the liniment was a bit chilly. After about thirty seconds of her rubbing my stomach and chest, I started looking for that alligator to come through the door. Another lizard-lip kiss was definitely in order.

Two more handfuls of liniment later, she had rubbed all the way around my torso. I had already made a conscious decision to buy some stock in the company that made that damn swing chain and leave a little something in my will for Jeb.

She finished, went to the kitchen and washed her hands.

She turned and looked at me, standing across the room, leaning on the door jam.

She walked over, reached up and kissed me gently on the lips, carefully avoiding contact with the liniment-lathered skin.

"Thank you!" she said over her shoulder as she walked out the door.

Teasing Tina was an amateur compared to Widder.

Later, I was lying in bed, on my left side, looking out the window at the barely lighted landscape to the north of the house. The half-moon. The one where the top half of the Energizer Bunny's head is dark, bathed the yard and nearby trees in a dull-silver shroud.

For some reason, it reminded me the front yard looking east from my grandparents' house. In my mind the cypress trees were replaced by magnolia, elm, and pine.

In the next instant, I was walking up the lane to the Lawn Gate down at Sutton with a halter rope in my hand. Walking alongside me was my cousin Gary. We were going to find Tony, a gentle old horse that Daddy George still used for plowing. Tony was always easy to catch; a mouth-smacking sound and an open hand would always convince him he was due a treat.

We found the old black-and-white horse down by the pond, lazing under the shade of a big pine, asleep maybe, since he was standing on three feet, with the front left relaxed and canted over the right hoof.

Easing up on him, I whispered, "Good boy" and grabbed a handful of mane. As expected, he wheeled and jumped a step, picking me off the ground in the process and swinging me around. He quickly settled down and accepted the rope halter sans bit. Gary gave me a leg-up and I reached down and hauled him up. He was younger but weighed more than I did, so he used my rigid foot as a stepladder.

No adult ever worried about the grandkids riding Tony. He was docile, like a long-legged cow on Quaaludes.

(Every time I think of the word "Quaaludes" Bob recites his favorite part of a Shel Silverstein poem:

"*...rah-ready for animals, women or mah-men,
She's doing Quh-quaaludes again.*")

Tony would gee and haw with just a touch of the rope on his neck or a gentle heel kick. Of course, we always wanted him to gallop, but Daddy George opined as to how his galloping days were over "back when Roosevelt was president."

Didn't know Roosevelt. We liked Ike. Just like everybody else.

Despite our rib-thumping attempts to get Tony to get up to a slow trot, he just ambled up the lane from the pond to the main two-run road that ran through the place.

Usually we just rode Tony rather than walk, but today he was going to be put to work as a toting mule.

Gary and I had decided to built a castle back in a stand of pines over near the Estes place. We had absconded with an entire roll of hay twine from the barn that weighed too much to lug the half-mile back in the woods. We managed to carry it from the barn to the Lawn Gate without getting blessed out by an adult and to that spot is where I pointed Tony.

Gary slid off the horse's back and retrieved the hefty twine ball and together we eased it up behind me. He remounted, this time behind the bundle, and we headed out.

The site we had chosen for the castle was deep in a pine grove, a forty-by-fifty-foot opening completely locked in by fifteen-year-old pines. We tied Tony to a nearby tree, hauled the twine to the center of the clearing, and set to work.

The engineering concept was amazingly simple. Tie the twine off to one tree and then run the twine from tree to tree at about head-high level, creating a canopy of hay twine. Branches and pine needles added to the top would create the castle's roof.

Our calculations were off slightly. The one huge ball of hay twine only covered about half the clearing.

"We need more twine," Gary said, hot, sweaty, and gasping for breath in the airless pine thicket.

"You definitely have the genius genes of the family," I snapped. Forty-five minutes later, we had returned to the barn, gotten another hay twine ball, stopped by the house for cool water, told the various relatives who took time to ask that we were building a fort, told two younger cousins to 'Eat dirt and die!" when they wanted to come with us, hopped back on Tony, picked up the twine and went back to the fort.

More than two hours later, the fort's roof was complete. The gathering of branches, leaves and pine needles and placing them in the proper place took another hour.

Gary and I sat in the middle of the finished castle, breathing hard, trying to suck the warm humid air that hovered in the confined space into our lungs. The effort was a tussle.

"Think we can sleep out here tonight?" he asked.

"Can't think of a reason why not. It's our castle and it's a prime place for sleeping."

Unhitching Ol' Tony, we climbed back on and let him walk gently back toward the barn, but when he got in sight of it, he started to trot. His bony back was like riding a rail full of nails. Bouncing a foot high off his back, we both cupped our hands over our privates to protect our respective tiny family jewelettes.

I sawed on the rope halter but it did nothing but make Tony mad and he increased his gait. I sawed back harder and got his head turned at about a 45-degree angle and I thought I had his feet turning when I glanced up and saw the hanging saw vine right in front of me.

A saw vine is dotted with hundreds of tiny thorns spaced like teeth on a crosscut saw.

Before I had a chance to bail off, grab the vine or do much of anything, it hit me square in the neck. The thorns dug in and I was dragged backwards. My butt hit Gary south of his stomach and he decided to go with me. We both slid ass-backwards off that horse, with Gary hitting the ground first. He had time to put up his knees before I landed on him; his bony-assed knees drilled twin holes in my back.

We both lay there, gasping for breath, watching Tony's broad ass heading toward the barn. Gary noticed the blood. That saw vine had done a number on my neck. My plucked-chicken-scrawny chest was covered with blood. It looked like I was wearing a red sapphire necklace.

I panicked. I ran for the house, hollering at the top of my voice for mama. I hit the back porch screen, barged in the kitchen through the well porch and screamed: "That sumbitch damn near killed me that time."

Mama was bending over the sink, her back to me. She turned and jammed a bar of lye soap in my mouth quicker than a swooping hawk. I fell to the floor, gagging.

It was then that the gaggle of kinfolk noticed the blood running out of my neck and down my chest. My grandmother then uttered words that are etched forever in family lore: "Don't you think you ought to see if he'll live first before you soap 'im for cussing?"

The women folk jumped on me like a gaggle of chickens on a June bug stampede. "Women dearly love to save people," Daddy George would later tell me. "It's born in 'im, like reminding men folk to change their drawers. It's a wonder more women ain't preachers."

The men folk did what men folk do when women folk get in a dither: They headed to the porch. To discuss important things. Cattle prices. What's good for ticks and chiggers. The weather. What not.

Mama shooed off all the relatives and had me wiped off quickly. She cleaned my neck twice, adding hydrogen peroxide the second cleansing. Then she went to Dad's overnight kit and got out the Styptic Pencil, wetted it and daubed it directly on the neck wounds. That stung worse than a kamikaze hornet attack. I screamed and hollered and jumped around. She just grabbed me by the ear and showered down on it until I begged for some more doctoring. Pretty please. With sugar on it.

I saw Aunt Wonder coming with the brown Tincture of Iodine bottle and I prayed to God, Mama and anybody else within hearing distance not to iodine me. "Does no good to holler before it's put on, Adj. Save the hollering for after," Aunt Wonder said. She had a mean streak when she was young.

I swear if given a choice I would have taken two more saw vine cuttings and three more styptic pencil daubings rather than one swipe across the neck holes with iodine.

Mama consoled me a bit before she administered the iodine: "Hold on tight. You know, this serves you right." Then she added for good measure: "You know this is going to hurt you more than it hurts me."

Meanness ran in through the Bartlett clan like water in a roadside ditch after a frog-strangling rain.

I am convinced that if torture of prisoners of war were to include a small cut and a small daub of iodine on it, there's not a soul in the history of this planet that wouldn't blab their guts out in the first five minutes of captivity.

Daddy said later he was walking up the lane toward the main road and I screamed so loud, it scared him. He started to run back to the house, thinking Mama was beating me with a plank with nails in it before he stopped to think that couldn't be happening. Too many witnesses.

After two good daubings, Mama turned me loose. I hit the back door and ran around the house three times before the pain dully out.

UNCERTAIN TIMES

I stopped at the front porch, panting like a hard-run dog needing water. I sat on the edge, my feet tailing in the dirt.

"You must be growing up, Adj," Uncle Jack said. "You just ran around the house three times. Your record's four." He was trying to be funny. He failed.

"Where were you when Tony dragged you off?" That was Daddy George.

"We were just on our way home and that stupid horse drug me under a saw vine."

"Not too stupid," he said. "You're the one that ended up on the ground."

I turned and, aiming the question at Daddy and Uncle Bill, asked if we could spent the night in "our castle in the woods."

Daddy had no objections. "Gonna be a nice night," Uncle Bill surmised. "That sounds like a plan to me."

"Where is this castle?" Daddy George asked.

"In a pine thicket near the Estes' place. It's real neat, got a roof and everything. It's a great castle."

"I'd like to see this castle," Daddy George said. He stepped off the porch and all the men folk tucked in behind him.

Daddy George called for me and Gary to join him at the front of the pack. He held both our hands on the short trek.

When we got there, the men, one by one, complimented us on the construction of the roof and the meticulousness of the layout.

Daddy George didn't say much after checking the twine tied to the trees and putting a hand on the roof to test its strength.

"It's okay if we stay here tonight then?" Gary asked.

"Yep, it's fine," Daddy George said. "One night won't hurt. But tomorrow, you two figure out a way to rewind all this twine and get it back in a useable bale 'cause I will be needing it come haying time."

With that he turned and headed to the house.

Defining moment in a person's life come at the durndest times.

Daddy George had just taught me a life lesson: It doesn't take long to hate something you loved just a minute ago.

32

Isn't it a wonder that when you want to be alone, that's the time when everybody shows up?

                 Anonymous

I opened an eye. The dawn wasn't yet breaking; it was, however, cracked.

I got up, stretched, scratched and put on a robe with a fancy Hotel Nairobi crest. I waited until the coffee was almost through bubbling and poured a cup. I walked out on the front porch to smell the morning air and to get in some more stretches. I stopped in mid-stretch.

Pulled up tight behind my car was a county sheriff's car. A tall, thin man got out, put on his blue Mountie hat and sauntered up the porch. He was about 6-foot-3 and couldn't have weighed more than 165 pounds. And that would be if he was carrying an anvil.

His right hand was interlaced with his left and not close to his gun.
Pah—positive sign.
Maybe he's the state fast-draw champion.
"Morning."
The greeting lay fallow.
"Just wanted to make sure everything was fine."
"Fine. Everything is fine," I said, copying his accent with the extra-

hard 'I' in 'fine' as best as I could. I didn't do a very good job. My throat was still sleep-scratchy.

"That coffee smells good."

That statement didn't sprout a single sprig of meaningful conversation.

He raised a hand and pawed at his chin. "Mr. Jones, I'm Andrew Shupe. I been a deputy in these parts for more than 20 years. I worked for three sheriffs so far because I can do things 'round the office nobody else can do. And, not to brag, but folks like me."

He waited for a reply. He came up empty-handed. I stood there, leaning on a support post, sipping my good-smelling coffee and hoping he drowned from over-active drool glands.

He ahem-ed and then a-hawed. "Mr. Jones, I work for Sheriff Twiddle, but of course you knowed that. What I wanted you to know is I been ordered...well, not me, but the whole crew...to follow you and watch you."

He stopped, looked at me and swallowed. His Adam's apple bobbed like a fishing cork attached to a hook just hit by a shark. Then he said, "I axed why and got shot down, so to speak. I just want you to know that I don't got a reason one to have a problem with you. From what I hear, you ain't done nothing to harm nobody except rile the sheriff and Harmony and Bother." Pause. "Which, most times, ain't too hard to do."

There was a longer pause this time. A thinking look latched onto his face. "I just want you to know that you got nothing to fear from me. I'm a churchgoer and I believe in God's word. Meanness ain't in my Bible and I'll do whatever I gotta do to keep the Word."

"You want a cup of coffee?" I said. "It's fresh."

"Would be obliged. Can't hardly think of nothing that would taste so good right now."

I invited him in. Deputy Shupe hesitated, then took off his hat and followed me.

Bob was wondering something about him being a *spa-spy*, but I pooh-poohed that notion. If anybody wanted to spy, they could do it when I was gone.

When he had his cup of coffee and was settled at the table, I asked him why he was confiding in me.

"Some folks would say I was unloyal to Sheriff Twiddle. My mama and daddy and the Good Book all say not to follow false idols. Twiddle is my boss; he ain't my God. What he's doing is just not right. But I will follow orders up to a point while I'm taking county money because I need my job."

I nodded, got up and refilled my cup, bringing the pot to the table and refreshed Shupe's.

"So I'm going to be watched, right?" He nodded. "Just watched? That's all."

"For now. To tell the truth, that might not be all. Twiddle is out to clean your clock for making him out a fool down to Harlan's."

"I didn't make a fool of Twiddle. He did that all my himself," I said.

"I know that and you know that. We ain't what counts here. All Twiddle's got is a title and a gun. Without them, he's nothing. He'll do whatever he's gotta do to keep both. Count on it."

We sat there for quite a while, each with our thoughts.

Shupe broke the silence: "I used to spend a lot of time in this lodge when I was a kid."

"I got a little history of the cabin from Thompson. You know him?"

"Everybody knows Thompson. He gets around."

Shupe finished his coffee, thanked me and got up to leave. As we walked through the living room, I asked him, "Deputy Shupe, your honest opinion now: What do you think of this chair?"

He stopped and studied on it a spell, walked around it, gave it a rub, picked it up to feel the weight. "I do declare that it's one of the best-built, prettiest chairs I've ever seed. Would be proud to have it in my home."

He walked to the door and out onto the porch, then said, "Just know this for a fact, Mr. Jones: If you see me following you, you got nothing to worry about. I'll do what I can to keep the other boys straight. They's some real good deputies, good people. But Twiddle's got most of 'em tied to the almighty paycheck. I'm one that just tries to stay connected to the Almighty. If you know what I mean."

I did and thanked him. "Anytime you're watching me, feel free to stop in and get coffee or a soda if I'm here. And, even if I'm not."

Shupe looked surprised.

"The only thing I ask is that you leave my beer alone." His eyes checked for a grin and got what they hoped for.

He put on his hat and gave me a two-finger salute. "Count on it, and thank you." He stopped and smiled: "Just something for you to think about: I said I followed the Lord, but I didn't say I was Baptist or Pentecostal. There's nothing in the Bible that I've found that said a man trying to walk the right path couldn't have a beer or two now and again."

He started to the car and stopped and said, "'Bout that chair. Thompson is my uncle. I grew up sitting on Thompson's lap in that there chair. Fine chair. Bet it'll grow on you in time."

I started laughing and kept it up as the car disappeared.

Tah-too early to bah-be laughing.

Laughing is always better than crying, Bob.

Tha-that's a rumor made up by some optimist that isn't about to gah-get his ah-ass whipped.

33

I hate showoffs. But then again some folks are just good at what they do.

Anonymous

After a bit I got tired of Bob thinking about Widder so I went in the house and picked up Betsy. Five minutes later I was standing in front of the Poem Board, taking pictures and reading.

Wasted time
Is time dead.
A corpse decayed,
Devoid of feelings.

Those who waste time
Are amateur morticians
Preparing their own body
For the grave.

Another example of a poem or statement that I don't know if I like or hate.
I-I lah-like the words, hah-hate the image.
Another good compromise.

Hum's was humming with six to eight early diners scattered around the room. I threw a wave at Glenn Alan, one of the two men I'd met at the Poem Board with Thompson a few days back, and saluted the rest.

"Well," the other man I had met at the Poem (*What was his name?, Oh, yeah, Hy!*) said, "Mr. Jones, can I have your autograph?"

"Please call me Adj, Hy. You want my autograph? What for?"

"Anybody that got hung at the end of a chain as gator bait by Jeb and lived to tell about it, I need that autograph." The entire group starting wahooing, slapping thighs, and pointing at one another.

Picking up a bunch of napkins, I got an advertising pen from near Hum's cash register—Jolly Funeral Home, Clarksville, Texas—and starting writing. A few minutes later, I started passing out napkins to the early morning crowd. The first man read the note and started laughing; it wasn't long until the entire café crowd joined in.

"Listen to this, Hum," a short, gaunt man with a full white beard said, reading from the napkin: "To my best friend in the world! Adnijio "Gator Bait" Jones."

"He can't be your best friend," another man said, waving a napkin, "'cause he's mine!"

The laughter picked up again and Hum pointed at a napkin. "Hmmmm."

"You want an autograph?"

"Hmmmm!"

I sat down on the nearest stool and wrote: "To Hum, the best cook and conversationalist in the entire metropolis of Uncertain, Texas. Adnijio "Gator Bait" Jones."

Hum took it, read it, and nodded. "Hmmmm." He almost grinned.

I heard the door slam behind me and from the look on Hum's face, I knew it was one of three people. My second guess was a whole platoon of Ku Klux Klaners in their Sunday Percales.

Right on the first one.

Swiveling around on the red leatherette stool, I came face to belly with Sheriff Twiddle. Since the door was a good fifteen feet away from my stool, I will say this: For a big, fat man, he moved light on his feet.

Even though it was the introduction side of morning, he had on a pair of knockoff, wraparound, mirrored eye-hiders. His face, the part that I could see at least, was florid and looked a little raw.

Sha-shaves with a meat gri-grinder.

"Howdy, boys," he said to everyone in the room but me. My head-on reflection in the sunglasses never wavered.

I will give him this, Bob was trying his level best to keep me calm. But Bob's rate of communication and my temper never seem to get in sync.

I lined up my reflection in Twiddle's sunglasses and started checking for errant eyebrow hairs, even licking my second finger of my right hand and using it to smooth down a couple.

Twiddle's lips, normally fleshy, thinned out like a pine thicket hit by a tornado. His mouth was now a gash.

"What's going on, Sheriff Twiddle, sir?" I said, continuing my facial check in the twin mirrors hiding his eyes. I added a second finger-salute on my other eyebrow. Looking into the sunglasses, I had a stray thought: I had never seen Twiddle's eyes. Beady, probably.

Bah-beady, assuredly.

And Bob liked to think he was the voice of reason.

Twiddle didn't say a thing while I completed my finger-and-facial calisthenics and since I can't stand a lull in any conversation. said, "I'll bet you've seen the movie 'Cool Hand Luke,' haven't you, Sheriff?"

No answer. I swear a little steam, or smoke, came from his right ear. I turtled my neck toward him and squinted. Nope, just a poofy tuft of hair.

He stood there, a pissed-off rock with a gut, staring at me from behind those golden mirrors. I reached in my facial ammo belt, trying to extract my special "sarcastic grin." Bob told me later I picked up the *know-it-all-educated-prick-smu-smirk*. Both were good. Either would fit the occasion.

"Hmmmm."

My breakfast call. I heard Hum put down a plate behind me, making a bit more clatter that the situation called for. I swiveled back around and with my back now exposed, I said, "Sit down, Sheriff, and have some breakfast. My treat."

The next thing I heard was the screen door slamming.

The collective sigh from the café crowd stirred up a nice breeze.

"Is he gone?"

"Hmmm-mmm."

He *was* one light-footed law enforcement officer.

"You got a deaf wish, Mr. Jones," one of the old-timers sitting in a side booth asked.

Deaf wish?

Dah-death wah-....

Oh, got it.

"No sir, just a registered smart-ass, I guess."

The room exploded into laughter. More from relief than humor.

I was just finishing up my last bite of eggs and contemplating whether to get Hum to hand me a couple strips of floppy bacon that were warming on the back side of the grill when the front door screen squeaked and then slammed shut again.

The instant change in the room atmosphere was palatable.

I hung my head, closed my eyes and tried to get my brain ready for Round 2, when...."

"Hello, boys."

Jesus! I thought without turning around. It's worse that I thought. Rayon Finnigan.

I heard the old man heading toward the back of the café, scooting a chair out of his way as he went. I could forget about the extra bacon. Hum was gone.

"I got me a good'un to tell you fellers this morning," Rayon said, apparently finding a good seat with maximum view of the assembled audience.

"Just a second, Rayon," Hy said. "Mr. Jones was just starting a story. Weren't you, Mr. Jones?"

I swiveled around on the stool and looked at the men, most of whom were seated behind Rayon. Their heads were nodding like hens snapping at a salamander

I nodded and took a sip of coffee. A long sip of coffee. I started running stories through my head and finally settled on one that was the gospel truth...with certain embellishments to make it *flow*.

"When I was a young reporter up in the Arkansas Ozarks, I went down to Yellville to cover this murder trial. The case was pretty clear cut as I recall: One man dead; one man on trial for shooting him. The story on the street was that there was an argument over a card game and one man had shot another one right in the backside as he dove out a window. Bullet went clean through him, stopping in his throat after hitting his heart dead-on."

I chanced a look at Rayon. He was staring at me with Harmony-eyes.

"In a small town like Yellville where 'big news' could be some mad teenage setting fire to his Bible in protest about having to play a part in the Christmas play at the local Pentecostal church, a murder trial was something special."

"Like in Uncertain," somebody offered up.

I acknowledged the contribution with a raised cup. "As I recall, it was the first day of the trial and the courtroom was packed. Every seat was taken up and people were lined up around the wall. Several people who claimed to have bum knees and the like had even brought in lawn chairs. The state was represented by a young prosecutor trying to earn his stripes, if you know what I mean. He had all his questions lined up on this note pad and he was primed to win his first big case in a big way.

"Back in those days, murder was a serious offense and Arkansas then, like Texas now, had no problem with cooking up a couple of inmates on weekends in what was known in the law enforcement community as 'Southern fried convict.'"

A took a sip of coffee and noticed Hum was back behind the counter.

Nah-not a bad sta-start.

Don't mess up my rhythm, Bob.

"One of the first eye witnesses to take the stand was a man name of T-9-C Evans—Letter 'T,' number '9.' letter 'C.' T-9-C. He was a little bitty man, smaller than Jeb Huckaby..."

"Now, that's small!" one of the men said in a stage whisper.

"...and it was clear he had never been in a courtroom before, much less been asked to speak in front of a roomful of people. As my grandmother said, he was 'nervousing' pretty bad."

A couple of chuckles bounced around.

"This young prosecutor started grilling T-9-C good from the get-go.

This how the conversation went," I said, going into the story using a variety of voices for effect:

"Tell the court your name."
"T-9-C Evans."
"The court needs your real name, please."
"T-9-C Evans."
Court reporter: "How do you spell that?"
"T-9-C, T-9-C, Evans, E-V-A-N-S."
"That's your real name?"
"Yep."
"T-9-C?" the court reporter asked.
"Yep."
Judge: "How'd you come by that name, Mr. Evans?"
"My mama named me that 'cause I's so small when I was birthed. Three pounds, some folks say."
Prosecutor: "Hmmmm. Okay. Now, Mr. Evans, were you playing cards down at the Rickmore residence on the night of September 23, 1971?"
"Yessir, I was."
"And were there other people playing cards that night?"
"Kinda hard to play cards just by yourself."
"Judge, please ask the witness to be responsive to the questions."
Judge: "T-9-C. Do what the man says."

"T-9-C just nodded, then the prosecutor started up again."

"Mr. Evans, in your own words, please describe for the jury what events occurred on the night in question in the residence in Snowball."
"Well, there was five us playing five-card draw and they was a couple more fellers sitting in the corner drinking Jack and water. Or maybe it was just straight Jack, I don't rightly rec-collect."
"Please continue, Mr. Evans."
"Well, everybody had done thrown down they hand 'cepting Rafe. He's the feller that got shot, and Marlon, he's the feller what done the shooting."

"Well," I said, "at that the defense attorney jumped to his feet like he had a cattle prod applied to his privates and objected seven ways to Sunday. The judge told him to sit himself down and then told T-9-C to just answer the questions. The prosecutor then resumed his questioning."

"*Now, Mr. Evans,*" he said in his best professional, lawyer-type voice, "*what happened then?*"

"*They was quite a big pot in the middle, thirty or forty dollars, as I recall. They raised back and forth for a time, then Marlon called Rafe and Rafe threw down a good hand…three aces, diamond, spade and hearts, a ten and an eight. Marlon threw in his cards, then picked 'em up and turned 'em over. They was two pairs, fours and nines, with a high-card ace. The ace was the puppy's foot.*"

"*Puppy's foot?*"

"*Yep. Spades.*"

Pause. "The prosecutor did a little circular hand motion to get the testimony started again," I said, doing a good demonstration of Widder's hand jive.

"*Then what happened?*"

"*Well, I re-checked my hand and turned over one card. The ace of diamonds.*"

"*Did you say anything?*"

"*Nope. Didn't have to.*"

"*Then what happened?*"

"*Marlon started counting aces on his fingers and when he got to the thumb, he pulled out his old Army issue .45.*"

"*What happened then? Did anybody leave?*"

"Well, T-9-C fixed that prosecutor with a quizzical look and said:

"*It's obvious you ain't never been in a card game with five aces and a cocked .45. Leave? Hell, everybody left!*"

The café, like that courtroom so many years ago, erupted in laughter. Hum pounded the counter and hmmmm-ed a couple of times in a different octave. All the men whooped and hollered.

All except Rayon. If looks were cannibals, he'd be serving me up as jerked joker.

Rayon just pissed me off. So, adult that I am, I got up, bowed almost to the floor and did a little shuffle-off-to-Baltimore dance move. Just to piss him off back.

Throwing a wad of ones on the counter, I waved gaily to all and hit the screen door with a purpose.

Tha-that ending flourish was cha-childish.

Yep. Felt good, too.

Fah-first you piss off the Lah-ledbetters, then the sha-sheriff. Now Rah-rayon.

He'll get over it.

"*Wha-which one?*"

I threw him an inner look that would have busted a rock.

Ah-oh, Rah-rayon. Kah-keep that dramatic crap up ah-and folks will think you're gah-gay. Nah-not that there's anything wrong with tha-that.

Political correctness is lost when coming from a stuttering conscience.

Deputy Shupe was in the parking lot and I wandered over as a time-killer to recover from my victory over Evil Storyteller Rayon.

"Morning," he offered up before I had a chance to engage my tongue. "Sounds like Hum's showing Dep-e-ty Dawg cartoons in there."

"Deputy Dawg? Is that an insider law enforcement joke?" I said.

He grinned. "Sorry, I can't axe you to get in and sit down. You understand."

"No, problem. What's the agenda today?"

"Just follow you around, mostly. Any big hidey-sneaky plans I need to know 'bout?"

"Hidey-sneaky plans? Nope, going to check on my boat. I need to go find something else to shoot since Buddy's blind was burned down. Guess I could go to the sheriff's office and file a report."

"Your motor's already back on the boat. Checked it out this morning. New cowling and I heard that Tim fixed the motor up nice. As far as going to the sheriff's office, guess you could," Shupe said. He picked up a piece of paper and handed it to me out the window. "Or you could just fill this out and give it back to me sometime or other. At least, you'd know it did get filed proper."

I took the form and thanked him.

I told him I was going on home and told him to stop by for a cup of coffee. He nodded.

After parking in the driveway, I walked over to Widder's. Stepping on the porch, I could feel her gone. I went home, started a fresh pot of coffee. I sat in the horny chair just to prove I could and listened to that electric coffee pot bubble. That sound has always been a comfort to me, reminding me of the old metal coffeepot at my grandparents' house. Nannie was always the first one up, and when I heard her slide-clump gait, I was usually right beside her as he put on the coffee and started puttering around in the kitchen, getting ready for the morning breakfast rush.

She always got the first cup of coffee, black. Even from an early age, I got what she called "sugar milk," a touch of coffee in a small cup, with heaping helpings of sugar and milk still teat-fresh. For just a few minutes we'd sit at the table and talk. It was *my* time with my grandmother, not easy to come by in a family of thirty or more grandkids. The whole mess was a needy bunch, as I recall. None more than me.

Checking out the window to see if Shupe was around, I saw his car across the road, opened the door and waved him over. Then I went inside and fixed two travel mugs of black coffee.

Shupe was sitting in one of the porch rockers. I handed him a cup with the logo of the National Forest Service on it. I sat down and we commenced to rock. After looking at the logo on his cup, he looked over at the mug in my hand.

**World Cup
Qualifying Round
Trinidad-Tobago
vs.
Costa Rica
2001**

"What's that 'world cup' thing? you don't mind me axing."

"Soccer. Futbol," I said, spelling it. "It's the most popular game in the world."

"Soccer is?"

"Yep. That's a fact. More people watch and play soccer worldwide than all the games played in the U.S. combined."

"Naw!"

"True. The World Cup happens every four years, like the Olympics, and teams from all over the world compete and then the best teams get together and play until a winner is crowned."

"Like baseball or football or basketball?"

"Like that."

"So, where is these countries Trin-e-dad and Toe-bag-o and Coastal Ricka?"

"Trinidad and Tobago are two neighboring islands in the West Indies. Costa Rica is a country in Central America, south of Mexico."

"And you saw them play soccer?"

"Yeah, I happened to be on a shoot in Costa Rica and heard that the teams were playing. It was interesting, that's for sure. The field was surrounded by an eight-foot-high barbed wire fence and there were policemen in full riot gear stationed about every fifteen feet around the entire stadium. Some cops were riding horses that had body armor."

Shupe looked at me intently. "You're joshing me."

"Nope. It was a big deal. Kinda like an East Texas high school football homecoming game."

We both took a sip of coffee, then I said, "I love sports of all kinds. I love crowds even more. I'm a people-watcher, Deputy Shupe. Watching people, sometimes, is more fun than what they are watching."

I took a sip of coffee and could see him thinking about that. "I know what you mean. I like to go to the county fair and just watch people."

"I do the same thing, only I get to do it all over the world."

We sipped our coffee in silence until I noticed his cup was empty. "Refill?"

"Nope, thanks. Better get back in the car and park it somewhere else. I know Sheriff Twiddle was down this morning, but he went back to the office. Boys up there said he was madder than a miser with a hole in his pocketbook. You have anything to do with that?"

Thinking about the confrontation at Hum's, I hung my head and grinned.

Shupe got up and said, "Thought so."

Walking to his car, he said, "Have a nice day now, you here. If you decide to do some hidey-sneaky stuff, give me a head's-up so I don't appear too stupid to The Good Sheriff Twiddle."

I threw him a wave and told him I would fill out the form and put it in the mailbox. He could pick it up at his convenience. He gave a thumb's up.

I went back in the house. After rinsing out the cup, I unplugged the coffeepot and filled out the incident form. I then started gathering my equipment. I put the loaded Glock in one of the two waterproof boxes and used a black Magic Marker to put a "G" on the lid.

Jah-G for gun. That's oh-original.

Bob, didn't your mother-voice ever tell you that if you can't think something nice, don't think anything at all?

He didn't come back with a snappy reply. Sore loser. I got all primed for a good pout.

Fifteen minutes later I was at the dock, loading the boat. The sound of footsteps on the dock caused me to turn around quickly. It was Harlan. I'd been in Uncertain for about a month or so and I could not remember ever seeing Harlan out from behind his store counter.

"Going out?" he said.

"Yeah, just looking today," I said, putting the small ice chest in the front of the boat. "Nothing really planned." I stood up and shook his hand. "I figured if I was on the lake I'd be less likely to run into Sheriff Twiddle."

"But maybe more likely to run into Harmony and Bother."

"Maybe. But I can't let them keep me from my appointed rounds."

"That's a joke, right?"

Sah-sometimes it's hard to tah-tell.

I thought you were pouting.

"Yes, it's a joke." I figured he didn't come out to the dock to ask if I was going out on the lake, so I just waited.

"If I was you, I'd steer clear of Carter's Chute for a couple of days. Talk is some folks expect you to go back to the blind. Might be good to wait a few days."

"Thank you. Under the circumstances, it sounds like good advice.".

"When you get back, you can tie up your boat to the back of the store. It'll be safe there. I sleep on the second floor over the dock. Most folks know not to mess with what's mine."

"I really appreciate the offer, Harlan. If you're serious, I'll take you up on it. It sure can mess up a person's day when mysterious things keep happening to your modes of transportation."

He nodded, shook my hand again, turned and started walking back to the store. Without turning around, he said, "You're welcome to leave your car in my parking lot if you've a mind to."

"Another good suggestion and thank you!"

I moved the car and before starting the short walk back to the dock, I went into Harlan's and had him fix up three bologna sandwiches from his meat and picked up two bags of chips and two ?Dr Peppers.

The boat was still there when I got back to the dock and looked to be undamaged. I checked the double gas tanks and was surprised to find both of them full. An envelope was stuck under one of them; I opened it and there was a bill from Trapp's for $36. I made a mental note to go there later. And I threw a couple pleasant thoughts about nice town, nice people, but Bob didn't bite.

Five minutes later I was heading to a stretch of Caddo called Turner's Bend. It was a good fishing spot, according to Buddy, but being it was Thursday, I didn't expect too many fishermen to be out and about. It was already too late to get the early-morning-golden-glow shots I thought I was so famous for, so I marked today off as a scouting trip.

One of the regular fishing guides in the area told me over a cold beer one night down at the dock about an accessible beaver's lodge. Checking it out today seemed like a good move. Heading across open water at about twenty-two mph....

Nah-knots. You're on wah-water.

Wouldn't know a knot if I was to see one, Bob.

What about a nuh-nut? With a mirror, that's a pah-possibility.

We ought to work up a stand-up act and hit the comedy circuit.

Wah-we'd kill 'em!

Our only hope, Bob, would be to play to a full house of professional mind-reading deaf mutes with abstract senses of humor.

Going by a crudely drawn map that I had stuck in one of the waterproof ammo cans, I found the small channel marked on the map. It was directly across from the big logjam I'd heard was caused by a tornado about ten years back. Entering the channel I eased along at minimum speed. The cypress trees were very close together here, but not like at The Cathedral. I still kept a close watch on the channel. If I sheared off a prop, it's be a long row home.

The channel opened up into one of those mysterious round holes set in the middle of the cypress forests. It was like giant had bounced around the woods on a pogo stick. A thin layer of cirrus clouds mixed with puffy cumuli had replaced the spotty cloud-drifts of early morning. One group reminded me of camels eating dolphins. Another looked like two twin, fat sheriffs sucking on a single licorice stick.

Kuh-cumuli? Cah-camels eating....

You don't gain points by repeating what I think, Bob.

Jah-jesus! Tha-then think something more eh-intelligent.

I looked up at the clouds. There was a little hole in the right front quadrant that looked just like a kangaroo giving birth to...Demi Moore! She's bald-headed, just like in *G.I. Jane!* And, look, over there, low, the way the clouds are starting to bunch up. They're forming into...yes! It is. It's John Wayne in 'True Grit,' riding into battle, with guns in both hands and his reins in his teeth. He's riding a five-legged mongoose. Can you see it, Bob?

Jesus!

No stutter. Pissed off. Big time.

The beaver lodge was on the opposite side away from the channel to the open water. It was a "working" lodge; tree limbs with white markings were visible on the top and sides of the lodge. I figured from past experience and research that the opening to the lodge was facing the small clearing. There didn't seem to be any place to put the boat where I would not disturb the beavers. To build a blind here was not a very good option. Beavers like seclusion; start hauling in lumber and hammering and they more than likely would pack up the kiddies and move. Usually beaver pair up and have babies in the spring. It was spring. Maybe...just maybe.

A friend of mine from National Geographic had shot a famous shot inside a beaver lodge and I made a mental note to call him and ask about particulars. The only thing I could think of right now to get beaver-working shots was to get somebody to come out with me, hitch a climbing tree stand to one of the cypress trees, have them take my boat home and hang out in a tree for a couple of days.

"I'm getting too old for this crap," I said aloud. I knew I was just griping for effect. I also knew I would do whatever it took to get a good beaver shot for the book.

I located a tree with a perfect open view of the lodge. Using my hand spread as a guide, I figured it was about 25 inches in diameter. I didn't think I could locate all the equipment I needed by tonight, but maybe by the weekend, early next week at the latest.

I heard a single, distinct slapping sound off to my right. Beaver letting me know he or she knew I was here? Tree limb hitting the water?

Bob? Nothing. Double P time in the old mental ward. Pissed and pouting.

Turning the boat around, I eased back out in the small channel and slowly headed toward open water. I was still well back in the woods when I heard the roar of a boat powering fast across the lake.

For some reason I stopped and waited. The boat flashed by quickly. But not too quickly that I couldn't make out the occupants: Harmony and Bother. They had been skirting the edge of the trees. Just before the channel opening the boat had turned at a ninety-degree away from the woods. All I could see were their backs. Still got shivers.

I'd seen the Ledbetters on the lake before, but always in an old, slope-sided, aluminum fishing boat with an middle-sized Johnson motor. This boat was new. The motor was a monster. The last time it had been running it was probably on a big Boeing.

The boat headed straight for the big logjam. I thought "trotline." The boat settled just short of the big pile of trees that looked like a discarded canister of Pick Up Stix. I grabbed Betsy and the big lens out of the metal suitcase and focused in on the pair. Harmony was swiveling his head, looking up and down the lake. He was driving, as always. Bother was turned backwards, apparently listening to what Harmony was saying.

Harmony sidled the boat up to the stacked logs. Bother reached over the side and grabbed a good-sized limb. He nodded and Harmony put the boat in reverse. The limb started moving. The limb had to be attached to a floater log, one not really attached to anything. Bother turned loose of the limb, and Harmony maneuvered the boat around until it was facing the opening left by the moved log. He eased the boat forward, stopping where a medium-sized log looked wedged into the pile about head-high. He moved up with Bother and together, they lifted the log up and to the left slightly, then swung it around and settled the end on a second floater log.

Harmony eased the boat into the opening, and the two brothers repeated the process in reverse, effectively closing—and disguising—the opening.

If that don't beat all.

Bob was not responding to subtle thoughtversation. So I gigged him.

Bob, I need your help.

Sah-something bad.

We'd be fools to try and find out what it is.

Nah-no argument hah-here.

Man's gotta do what a man's gotta do.

I-I-I vote we head back home and spend the rah-rest of the day studying those cla-clouds.

34

It's not 'snooping' if you have a good reason for doing it.

Anonymous

I waited for a good four or five minutes before I moved the boat, then idled out into the edge of the main lake. Turning directly west, I hung close to the shoreline, running the motor on bare-minimum. Today was not the right time to go scouting. I also wanted a good overall look at the area, and I knew a couple of places to go to get that.

My problem, and a problem that's hounded me all my life, is that I'm an instantaneous-gratification person. I do something good, I want a cookie. I see something intriguing, I want to know what it is. Not tomorrow. Now.

Bob started on a long speech, for him, about *pah-patience is a vah-virtual*. It was so long I fuzzed out in the middle and started a side helping of brain dump about how to see what was inside that logjam.

By the time we hit the dock, I didn't have a germ of an idea of what to do. I had the entire battle plan.

In sight of the dock Bob reminded me to take the *bah-boat* to Harlan's. I started it up again and motored the 200 yards or so down the shoreline, ran it to the protruding underlip dock at the back of the store and tied both ends of the boat up snug.

By the time I had finished, Thompson showed up and helped me carry my equipment and cooler, saving me a trip.

I told him the photos should be back by Monday and he said he'd be "obliged to see 'im."

I went in the store to thank Harlan again for his hospitality, but he shooed off my thanks, saying again the boat would be safe. "Make sure you're safe, now, you hear?" he said.

Back at the house, I stowed away gear, pulled out a beer, picked up the envelope Widder left, shook out the key and walked over to her house.

After just a few hours, the house had an empty smell. I went to her bedroom, which she said was where the computer was located. I wanted to check if she had sent any emails, knowing that was the second dumbest thing I would do today. Flapping the finger-ship S.S. F&*^ You at Sheriff Twiddle topped the list. It was only mid-afternoon but I didn't see any way in hell I was going to better that one before bedtime.

I went to the computer between the two bay windows on the far wall, I took stock of the room. It was decidedly feminine. A white iron bed with blue trim took up the center part of the left wall. White carpet, white and light blue, frilly coverlet with matching dust ruffle; a watercolor of water hyacinths (original, no signature; I checked), a white-on-white ceiling fan, a dark antique end table with a small lamp with a colorful stained glass lamp shade. There was a pale yellow robe (see-through, I checked) hanging on a hook behind the door. Sticking out from under the bed, half-hidden by the dust ruffle, were the frog house shoes that had made such a vivid first impression.

The right-hand wall was completed covered, floor to ceiling with a three-section, built-in white bookcase. The only break in the bookcase was a door, which I bet was a closet. I checked. I won the bet. I was on a roll.

The bookcase was filled, top to bottom, end to end with books. Big books, little books, new paperbacks, antique editions of obscure novels.

I checked out the titles, starting at the left and working to the right.

The first section was almost entirely taken up with self-help books and case after case of audio tapes with titles like *Action Strategies for Personal Achievement* by somebody named Brian Tracy; *The Psychology of Human Motivation*; Bergen Evans' *Vocabulary Program*; Earl Nightingale's *Lead the Field* and *The Successful Communicator* series; plus taped series by Kenneth Blanchard and Eli Bay.

I thought about the tapes and books and what they meant to somebody like Widder. At some time in her life, she needed validation for her feelings. Maybe, even, for her *being*. She sought out experts in the fields of communication, personal power brokering, motivation, success in management, and human relations to show her *the path* to wisdom and success. I sat down on the edge of the bed and thought about the tapes, about her listening to them over and over again, trying to memorize the words and put the messages into practice.

My heart ached for her, for her feelings. But it embraced her desire to improve the image she had of herself. It is one of the heartaches of my work to have seen so many people in so many parts of the world simply give up on life and accept whatever is offered.

Obviously Widder didn't do that, is not going to ever accept doing that. She's living. Or trying to. Trying is the first step of succeeding. Nightingale, I think.

I got up and walked back to the bookshelves. The middle section, the one over the door and down the right side of it, contained "tonners," as a couple of my literary friends referred to them. Widder must have had thirty or more hefty books that weighted a "ton." T. Harry Williams' *Huey Long*. Norton's *World Poetry*. McMurtry's *Lonesome Dove*. Three or four volumes on Abraham Lincoln. Lewis and Clark. Autobiography of William Randolph Hearst. Theodore Roosevelt. Franklin. Eleanor. Mother Teresa. Gandhi. Clinton. Ike. Patton. Mao. Truman. Thatcher. Che. On and on and on.

Eclectic. To the *nth* power.

I picked up the biographies of Che and Margaret Thatcher, two ends of the bio spectrum, and thumbed through the pages. Both had definitely been read. Turned down corners and off-color edges caused by thumbing.

I moved on down the shelves, scanning titles, paying particular attention to the antique books. I have a few first editions of which I am proud. I coveted some of the ones in Widder's collection. A 1903 Author's National Edition of *Huckleberry Finn*. Nine early 20th Century editions of the Tarzan novels by Edgar Rice Burroughs, including *Lord of the Jungle, Tarzan the Terrible*, and *Tarzan and the Ant Men*. With original dust jackets. The 1926 Modern Library edition of *Moby Dick*. A 1924 New Library edition of Dumas' *The Three Musketeers*. Taking up almost an entire shelf were an almost-complete first edition collection of novels by Zane Gray, most with the distinct incredibly artistic dust jackets intact.

I took down one of Gray's novels—*The Last Trail*—and read the first sentence aloud:

> *Twilight of a certain summer day, many years ago, shaded softly down over the wild Ohio valley, bringing keen anxiety to a traveler on the lonely river trail.*

It was about fifty years ago that I first read those lines. The simple, descriptive style of Gray fueled a love for reading that still burned brightly.

Yuh-you love Gray.

Bob knew I had a similar collection at home in Atlanta. I walked over and studied the titles again. If my memory wasn't failing me, the only Gray books I had that weren't on Widder's shelves were *The Young Forester* and the little-known *The Red Headed Outfielder and Other Baseball Stories*.

This is spooky.

Wah-weird, too.

I put up *The Last Trail* then made sure all the edges of the books were even.

I started to turn to the computer, when a title of a paperback in the last section caught my eye: *Texas Hellion*.

"Must be about John Wesley Hardin," I said aloud.

Nah-not likely.

It wasn't. The front cover showed a raven-haired beauty in a dress that covered only the middle and bottom of her prominent, protruding, and perfect breasts. A brawny cowboy dressed all in black was pleasantly manhandling her. The cowboy looked smug; the woman turned-on. The way all men wished it were in real life.

The back page summary set the literary stage perfectly:

> *The daughter of a law-abiding judge in a lawless land, Molly Hardman is a school teacher by day, an outlaw by night and a sexual hellion when it suits her fancy. And it's no secret she has a very active fancy! Into her life rides Lance Stoddard, former outlaw, present sexual predator, and current U.S. Marshal for West Texas. When the two met, one will die. But two lives will live forever in the lore of the lawless land.*

Haysus Christo! Do people really read this claptrap? Hardman? Sexual hellion? Suits her fancy? Lance? Sexual predator? Hello? Can it get any more phallic, vaginalistic, and lame?

Vah-vaginalistic?

If it's not a word, it damn sure should be, Bob. The fine line between pornography and just plain bad taste is way too broad.

I put down *Hellion* and picked up the one next to it: *Georgia Hellion*. Next to it was *Louisiana Hellion*. Then *South Pacific Hellion*. I counted sixteen different paperbacks with *Hellion* in the title. Not one of them was named *Trailer Park Hellion*. Probably just an oversight.

Ten or so the other books had *Hellcat* in the title and five included *She-Devil*. Surely, Widder isn't that desperate, I thought, flicking through some of the books. None appeared to have ever been opened, much less read or used for personal pleasuring.

I looked at the remainder of the books in that section. There were more than a hundred paperbacks total, all in the romance genre. Some of the author's names I knew—Ann Rule and Danielle Steel. Some of the titles stuck in my mind's eye: *Barefoot Bride; Dancing with the Devil; Dueling in the Dark; Herotica, Vols. 1-4*.

Several of the books had a particular how-to bent: *The Art of the Romance Novel, Writing Romance: Creating a Best Seller, Bringing Life to Your Romance Novel*, and *How to Write and Sell Romance Novels*.

I bet Widder wants to write about us!

Stah-steamy stuff. Wah-wow!
I'm such a romantic, I bet I could write a romance novel.
Yah-you could write under the name Dah-dumb Juan.
I turned my attention to the computer and was surprised to see she had an iMac. The computer was set up higher than I was used to. It sat on a fat book, probably to relieve neck strain. I powered the computer up and saw she had the OS 10 software. From the icons that popped up one by one in five rows across the bottom, it was apparent the iMac was loaded for computer bear.

When the buzzing and whirring stopped, the folders indicated she had access to three Internet links: Internet Explorer: Mac and Netscape. On a lark, I clicked on the Explorer icon and when it popped up with an MSN opening page, I clicked on "Favorites."

Not much there, only eight or nine items. But what was there caused Bob to do his Scooby-Doo impression: "UrrrrhhHHHHeeh!"

I ran my fingers down the list slowly:

Bartlett's Familiar Quotations
Dictionary.com
Ask.com
Flowgo.com
Amazon.com
BarnesandNobles.com
Wal-Mart

With the exception of a couple of clothing outlets and *cooking.com* listed, that was it. I noticed an "untitled" folder and started to click on it, when Bob *ah-advised* me against it. I knew he was right so I "accidentally" clicked on it rather than doing it on purpose.

That folder had some hidden "favorites," including direct connections to Drudge Report, Cajun Grocer, Italian Chef, a slew of recipe sites and one named *PRWA.com*.

Nothing caught my fancy, so I clicked into email, hoping that would be one from Widder with the subject title: "Missing you so damn much I can't stand it!"

There were three messages, the subject closest to what I wanted to see was from *homedepot.com*. The subject line read: "Get rid of bugs fast with PestyCide Bug Killer."

The second message looked like a chain letter asking people to pray for the kids at Pastor Simon's Kancer Korral for Kids and the third was from a David Rothell. The subject: "Deal almost done!"

Bob knew I wanted to click on that one and thought me to do so would be *tah-tacky*. For once, I yielded to reason over self-indulgence.

I got out of all the programs, powered down, locked up and went home.

But not before borrowing *Texas Hellion* from Widder's collection of huff-and-puffers.

I wanted to find out what happened with Molly and Lance.

It was after five but I took a chance that at least one of the businesses would still be open, and hit it lucky on the first call. After talking for several minutes I had a meeting scheduled for eight the following morning.

I debated about heating up a can of Campbell's Bean with Bacon Soup or going to Hum's and having the Thursday Night Special—chicken and dumplings, corn on the cob, turnip greens, black-eye peas and corn bread.

In my mind I opted for the soup.

Bob then proved that two positives can, by God, make a negative.

Yeh-yeah, right!

35

Asking a friend for a favor isn't scary. Asking an acquaintance for one is.

Anonymous

Hum's was jumping. I parked at the very edge of the parking lot, squeezed in between a Dodge 250 dually and a tie-dyed Volkswagen camper van. I used to own one just like it in 1970. Back then, me and common sense were only nodding acquaintances.

Nah-not like now.

I could smell the chicken and dumplings from the parking lot and I took that as positive sign Hum had some left. Just about every table was full, so I sidled up toward the counter and saw an empty seat next to Jeb Huckaby. I slapped him on the back and we grinned and shook hands.

"Chicken and dumplings good?"

"Not many people are eating anything else."

Hum looked in my direction and I pointed at Jeb's plate and held up a finger.

"Hmmmm."

While I was waiting for the Blue Plate Special, I talked over my plan to find out what was going on behind the logjam. Jeb only asked a few questions and then agree to help me. On one condition.

"Name it. If I've got it or can get it, it's yours."

"Thompson said you took his pitcher. I'd be obliged to have you take one of me."

Cah-can of worms.

"Done. And done," I said, shaking his hand, "I got something to do tomorrow morning, but if you want to come by after lunch, I've just the place in my backyard."

"By that big, lightning-struck tree. Thompson told me."

Hum came up and slid a plate toward me that was so full of food, it was leaking off the sides.

Damned if the Blue Plate Special didn't come in a blue plate.

Why is it that sometimes big funny things can't even make a person smile, but little funny things can make them laugh out loud?

Jeb left before I was halfway through with the meal. "See you about noon tomorrow," he said. "Got to get home and get my beauty rest for my pitcher."

A couple of people stopped by to just say hi and the warm feeling running around the room was comforting.

Sah-safety in numbers.

That cliché is mostly true, Bob. Except for those on the outside of the herd.

And when it came to Uncertain, or at least parts of it, I was about as far outside the herd as one could get.

I asked Hum for a check, which he waved off with a "Hmmmm." I peeled off two fives and slid them under the plate, waved and joined a line of folks heading to the door.

The line moved slowly and when I got to the door, I could see why. A big-butted deputy sheriff had Jeb spread-eagled over the hood of the cop car and was pawing at his ass with one big hand, while holding Jeb flat against the hood with the other. The scene was bathed in surreal colors created by the flashing cop car lights.

Nobody moved. No one said a word.

Always my cue.

Ah-enter Fool No. 1, through cab-center curtain.

Edging through the crowd, I went down the steps and walked over to the two men.

"Evening,...."

The deputy jumped, slamming Jeb's head against the hood. I grimaced.

Ah, ouch! I bet tha-that hurt.

Although I didn't realize it at the time, Bob later told me I said, "Ouch!" real loud.

The deputy released Jeb on the upward leap and was pointing a gun at me when he came back down. He was the same deputy that was laughing with Twiddle about my motor problem.

Without a single command from my brain, my hands jumped to head high, palms flat. "Whoa! Hoss! I was just in the middle of saying, 'Evening, Jeb. Evening, Deputy. Nice night.'"

Nah-not middle. Bah-beginning, actually.

Not now, Bob. Jesus!

The deputy's gun was shaking more than a little. It was mostly shaking up and down. If it went off, I figured he'd hit me somewhere between my forehead and crotch. I couldn't think of a place in that range where I'd want to take one for the Gipper. Or Jeb.

"Don't move!" he screamed in a falsetto.

I willed my body into stone mode. I couldn't help thinking though that with that voice, I bet he's in tenor in a gospel quartet. Probably the Church of the Flaming Gay Cross.

"Police!" he screamed. "Face down on the ground! Now!"

Too many episodes of "Cops" was my guess.

While this Barney Fife wanna-be didn't necessarily make me want to follow orders, Mr. Smith and Mr. Wesson added some heft to the argument. I looked around for a nice, clean place to "face down" and couldn't find any. I took a step to my right and the deputy said: "Don't move! Face down on the ground! Do it! Now!"

Putting my hands on my hips, I faced the deputy square up. "You've got to be more specific with your instructions. First you said, 'Don't move!' Then you said, 'Face down on the ground!' It's a physical impossibility to do both. Do you want me to not move or to get on the ground?"

The deputy's face muscles began rigor-ing. The muscles were so tight you could see the outline of his skull.

"I told you to get on the ground first!" He said in a voice that I swear to God sounded like Gomer Pyle. If he said, 'Gaaaaaaooooooolllllly!' I was going to bust a gut.

"Have you looked at this ground? There's rocks and stickers and tin can lids and.... What the hell is this?"

Somebody had emptied an ashtray in the lot and there were three used condoms in the mixture of chat and dirt. I stood there staring at what looked like three tiny, crushed Goodyear blimps.

"Deputy! Look at this! There are three rubbers in the dirt! You don't expect me to get facedown on the ground in that, now, do you? Can't I just lean over the car hood like Jeb or something?"

I turned my head around to the crowd and said, loudly, "Hum, you've got to clean up this parking lot. I can't 'face down' out here without taking a chance on getting lockjaw."

The deputy's eyes went to the rubbers and back to me—four or five times. I could almost see his brain trying to process the information. I could also see he was almost ready to make a decision about making a decision, when the whoop of a siren broke his concentration.

The siren was on the main road, coming this way, moving fast.

Within fifteen seconds, lights flashing and siren on full volume, a second cop car came around the corner near the dock. It did a reasonable bat-turn into Hum's parking lot. The car stopped inches from the rear of the deputy's car. With the reflection of the lights from the café hitting the slanted windshield, it was impossible to tell who was in the car. When the car door opened, the interior light outlined Sheriff Twiddle. Even though it was dead-night, he was still wearing the mirrored glasses.

After opening the door, he sat in the car for a couple of heartbeats, his head filling half the windshield. Grabbing that small water tower-sized Mountie hat, he exited the car, settled his hat and surveyed the scene. And smiled. A shark-in-a-school-of-tuna smile.

Before speaking, he took in the porch crowd. I glanced over my shoulder and from the gathered crowd, couldn't imagine there was anyone left inside. Clearly a third of the population of Uncertain was standing on that porch.

"Well, well, well," Twiddle said, his fireplug thumbs hooked into his shiny Sam Browne, "if it ain't my two favorite lawbreakers, Mr. Jeb By Gawd Huckaby and Mr. Big City Smart Mouth. Good job, Deputy Ledbetter. Good job!"

Lah-ledbetter?

Bob, incest can't be all bad if everybody's doing it.

Twiddle stood there, posturing for theatrical effect, then said, "Deputy Ledbetter, what's the situation?"

Deputy Ledbetter was still holding the gun on me but the shaking had lessened considerably. "I was patrolling the area, Sheriff, and saw the subject Huckaby exit the eating 'stablishment. From his mannerisms and the way he was walking I had reason to believe the subject was intoxicated."

Definitely too much "Cops."

"I caught my boot heel on the bottom step," Jeb said.

"Shut up, Jeb! Not another word," Twiddle shouted. He motioned for the deputy to continue.

"I e-ffected the stop and the subject became right surly and non-responsive, so I placed him under arrest. I was searching him for our mutual protection when Subject No. 2 approached me in a hostile and threatening manner."

"Whatcha got to say for yourself, Jeb?" Twiddle said.

"Had supper. Going to my truck to go home. Caught my boot heel on the bottom step. Stumbled. End of story."

"Have you been drinking?"

"You know better than that, Sheriff. I been on the wagon for years."

"Some people fall off now and again, Jeb. I remember a time when you fell off mighty hard. And I remember who helped you up, too."

"Fuck you, Johnnie!" Jeb's voice was as hard as a three-week-old biscuit. "That was ten years ago and I paid that debt a hundred times over."

"Now we can just add cussing in public to the charges. Got anything else to say, Jeb?" The only noise came from the corps of tree frogs behind Hum's. "Didn't think so. Deputy Ledbetter says you was drunk, you was drunk. Them's the rules. Them's the laws."

The deputy's gun was still pointing at me but I slowly lowered my hands, believing that he wouldn't shoot with a hundred witnesses standing behind me.

"Excuse me, Sheriff. I'll bet that Jeb will agree to a field sobriety test to show he's not drunk."

Twiddle was about three feet from me. Without moving he shoved me so hard I fell backwards, hitting hard on my right side where thirteen pointy rocks had taken up residence. My right hand landed right on top of two of the three used condoms.

Don't say it, Bob. The set-up's too easy.

Sitting on the ground, legs hitched up and ankles crossed, I tried to control my temper. Everybody knew I was going to fail. Especially the three that counted. Me, Bob and God.

"You don't tell the law what to do, Boy," Twiddle said, leaning over toward me and screaming. "The law tells you what to do."

I shook my head slowly, my eyes never leaving his sunglasses. Bob and I joined in on a non-harmonious, alternating chant: Dumbass! *Duh-dumb*ass! Dumbass! *Duh-dumbass!*

I must have been smiling or smirking or something because Twiddle took half-a-step toward me and slapped me open-handed with his right hand. My head snapped around until I could see the faces on the people on Hum's porch. A collective gasp oozed off the porch and slid across the parking lot.

Now that hurt!

"Not another fucking word, Mr. Big City Smart Mouth." Spittle flew from his mouth like grass from a Weed Whacker.

Stretching my neck to see if the ligaments still connected my head to my shoulders, I turned back to the sheriff, put my hands on the ground and levered upright.

Twiddle, as expected, pulled his gun, but kept it pointing to the ground.

"This shit stops now, Twiddle. Jeb is not drunk and everybody at Hum's knows it. I ate dinner with him and will testify he was sober as a judge. Not knowing the local judges around here, that is a figure of speech. A figure of speech is…never mind! I did nothing wrong but tell your shaky-assed deputy 'good evening' which, as far as I can tell, is not breaking any laws here or anywhere else in the country."

I took a deep breath and continued on down the verbal path to Sheriff Hell.

"Your deputy over-reacted, probably on your orders, because Jeb took me for a boat ride. He pulled his gun on me because you and your men are looking for an excuse, any excuse, to get my butt in your jail or beat me up, or both.

"Look around you, Twiddle! There are witnesses all over the place. They all know me and Jeb have done nothing wrong. This is the second time today you have harassed me and the second time today you are going to leave me alone. Why?…."

Twiddle started to open his mouth, but he shut it when I did the talk-to-the-hand thing that elementary teachers do to shush unruly students.

"That was rhetorical, Twiddle. R-h-e-t-o-r-i-c-a-l. In case you don't know, Twiddle, a rhetorical question is usually defined as any question asked for a purpose other than to obtain the information the question asks. For example, if someone were to say to you, and I'm not, you understand, 'Why are you so damn dumb?' that would be a statement regarding opinion of the person addressed rather than a genuine request to know. You following me so far?"

The deputy had lowered his gun until it was pointing in the general direction of his left foot. Jeb had stood up and turned around. He had a front-row seat for a unique event and was enjoying the hell out of it. I couldn't see Twiddle's eyes but from his facial expression, I surmised he hadn't fallen asleep standing up.

There was a murmur behind me that seemed to be growing. I forged on.

Jah-Jesus! You're on a rah-roll.

"If we break down this situation, Twiddle, here's what we have: One, your deputy tries to make a false arrest. Two, your deputy pulls a gun on an unarmed citizen and threatens to terminate his life for no reason whatsoever. Three, you publicly compliment the deputy for his illegal actions. Four, you assault my person. Five, you slap the green-frog-slipper gollywads out of me while I was sitting in a totally submissive position on three used rubbers. And you did it in front of witnesses!"

Even in the dull lighting from the indirect reflection of Hum's porch lights, I could see Twiddle was close to an aneurysm. I decided to push him over the edge.

I turned my back on Twiddle, facing the porch gathering. "All those in favor of Sheriff Twiddle and Deputy Shakygun Ledbetter turning Jeb and me loose, and the two of them getting back in their cars and getting back to the business of administering justice in the county...raise your hands!"

I figured it would take a while for the hoped-for psychological pack mentality to kick in. I was wrong. Dead wrong.

Starting with Harlan and Hum, hands shot up and stayed up. Nearly all the hands. Some folks put two in the air, as if someone was actually going to count them. Only two middle-aged men on the edge of the crowd to the right kept their hands down. In fact, both had both hands stuck so far down in the pockets of their jeans they could have been scratching their knees.

Pra-probably Ledbetter kin.

Motioning in front of my body with my hands to indicate the hands should stay up, I whirled around and spoke softly to Twiddle but loud enough for Jeb to hear me. The Uncertain grapevine being what it was, I figured everybody else in town would know what I said by lights-out.

"The ayes have it, Sheriff," I said. "Looking foolish in front of a bunch of people twice in one day probably is a record for you. If I were you—and I thank God every single day I'm not because if I was as dumb as you, I'd walk out in front of a red-balling chicken truck and kiss the grill—I'd rein in Deputy Do-Wrong and go back to whatever it is you do when you're not harassing citizens and generally making a fool out of yourself."

Twiddle looked at the folks on the porch and I followed his sunglasses-hidden glare. Every hand, with the two noted exceptions, was still raised.

I felt prouder than a sixteen-year-old male ex-virgin.

Twiddle didn't say a word. Just like earlier, he turned and went back to his car, threw that turkey platter of a hat in the back seat and backed out of the parking lot. His deputy, who had moved the gun upward to point somewhat in my direction, watched him leave. Finally, he moved his gun in what looked like an attempt to cover the whole dadgum porch and backed—backed!—to his car, got in and drove away.

As the deputy's car hit the main road and turned left toward town, the porch onlookers broke into spontaneous applause. I turned and did the best job I could at copying Will Rogers' patented oh-shucks routine.

Jeb sidled over to me and patted me on the back. "Mr. Jones," he said, "I really appreciate what you done. But, if the truth be known, I think you just turned that single grave you been digging into a double."

With the applause still going, punctuated now by a few hoots, rebel yells, and Cajun ai-eeeees, I smiled, shook his hand and said: "Crossing a line that can't be uncrossed always feels better if you have someone to cross it with."

He turned to walk to the porch but stopped and turned back to face me. "Green-frog-slipper gollywads?"

"Sometimes my mouth gets ahead of my brain and my tongue covers up my eyeteeth so I can't see what I'm saying."

He shook his head.

"If you're still living on August 22, I'd be honored to have you as a guest at my birthday."

August 22. A long, long way off.

36

Saying something is "simple" is a sure way to make it complex.

Anonymous

I headed for my Jeep, but a chorus of a variation of the theme "Come on back here" rained down on me from the porch.

"Pie and coffee is on the house!" somebody in the back of the friendly mob hollered.

"Hmmmm?"

I went up to Hum and threw my arm over his shoulders. "How about we split it?"

"Hmmmm!"

For the next hour, the story of the quadrangle slice of life involving Jeb, the deputy, me, and Twiddle was told and retold. As the story gathered bluster, there were so many intricate details added that if I hadn't been a part of it, I would have sworn it happened to someone else.

By the time Hum ran out of pie and switched to ice cream, the deputy had been holding *two* shotguns, one on Jeb and one on me, and I had kicked Twiddle in his privates. I also made him lick my shoes while he was on the ground, after he apologized for being born illegitimate and horseshoe-stake dumb.

It was all in good fun. But if there's one thing I've learned in my travels is that people with inflated egos can't abide being made fun of. For Sheriff Johnnie Twiddle, today had been a double-dipper.

It was getting late and I tried to beg my way out of the impromptu homecoming-type celebration several times. The crowd was not in a mind to relinquish a visiting hero of my stature so easily.

"What was going through your mind when you were sitting on them rubbers in the driveway?" one elderly man I didn't recall ever seeing before asked.

"Just that I was dead-set certain that whoever used them earlier had a better time that I was having at the moment."

The crowd erupted in applause.

Harlan ventured, "Gosh, Mr. Jones, when you asked folks to raise their hands, I thought I was going to be the only one to raise it up."

"At the time I asked it, I was hoping to get just one," I said.

This set the group off again

After a bit, the mood sobered and I got up to settle the bill with Hum. Hum indicated there would be no charge by saying "Hmmmm" and making a slashing motion with the edge of his hand.

"A deal's a deal, Hum. I said we'd split it."

Glenn Alan came over and said loud enough for everyone in the room to hear: "We already took care of the bill, Mr. Jones. We took us up a collection to pay for everything. We owe you that much."

"Owe me? Nobody owes me a thing."

Glenn Alan said, "Oh, yessir we do. You done provided us with the best goldurn show ever seen in these parts. And it was free! The least we can do is pay for the refreshments."

Thompson cracked up the group with one last comment: "If you schedule another round with Twiddle next Thursday, I'm betting they'd be a whole bunch more folks down here to see it."

After one more round of 'good nights', I jumped in the Jeep and headed home, Three men got in their vehicles at the same time and followed me. As I pulled in the driveway, they pulled in behind me, one by one, turned around, honked and headed back toward town. The last one, Glenn Alan, said, "Just making sure you made it home okay. Be safe, now, you hear?"

UNCERTAIN TIMES

I'd only been in Uncertain for a little over a month. Tonight was the first time it felt a little like home.

For only the second time since I came to town—the first being the first night at the lodge—I locked both doors. I also dug the Glock out of the dry box, took out the clip, ejected the bullet in the chamber, and practiced a few dry snaps, shoved the clip back in, put a shiny new bullet in the chamber and put it on safety. I placed it on the floor next to my bed.

I got ready for bed, turned out the overhead light, leaving just the lamp on the nightstand on. I went in the living room, picked up *Texas Hellion*, got a glass of iced water and got in bed.

You can judge a lot about a book from the first few paragraphs. *Texas Hellion* was no exception.

> *Molly Hardman's day at school had been a bad one. First the Bayard twins had gotten into a fight and busted the school's only chalkboard. Then a mysterious fire broke out in the wastebasket during recess.*
>
> *Molly needed to relieve some stress in the worst way.*
>
> *That's why she was going to rob the Overland Stage from Tulsa.*
>
> *She was almost hoping the driver or shotgun rider would give her trouble.*

Well, Bob, what say we skip a few pages.

Gah-go directly to tha-the end.

I thumbed over about thirty pages and scanned a paragraph in the middle of the left-hand page.

> *Lance didn't have time for foreplay; his posse would be here within five minutes. They were going after the Texas Hellion.*
>
> *He jerked Betsy's red satin gown off her shoulders and down to her waist. It was obviously a practiced move; not a single button was broken with the maneuver. He reached for the thin chenille covering that hid her breasts from his prying eyes and hand but she put up a dainty hand to*

stop his brazen assault. "I'll do it." She did, button by button. Slowly. Oh, so slowly.

The moonlight streaming in the window caressed her bulbous breasts like a warm light-wind. The nipples hardened in the light breeze, then hardened much, much more under pressure from Lance's calloused fingertips.

Jesus! This is so bad, it's good.

Cah-can we get some sla-sleep.

In a minute, Bob.

Actually, it was just a few minutes longer than that and then sleep hit me like a springy screen door slaps a slow cat.

The plan was in place. Aunt Melba was going *down*.

Two days before, Avery's home economics teacher and study hall monitor, Melba Brewster, gave me and Dedron Denton a week of detention for playing poker during study hall. It's not like we were playing for money; we were playing for matchsticks. The matchsticks would be exchanged for money *after* school.

She was called Aunt Melba because she acted and looked like everybody's busybody aunt. Tiny woman. Five-foot even. Square face split by a button nose and squinty eyes covered with cat-eye glasses with faux diamonds. She always wore her hair in ultra-Mennonite style, swirled bun sitting high, squared up to her neck and top of her head. Her hands were short and stubby. Fingers the size of Vienna sausages. She always wore printed, loose house dresses, short-sleeved. Arm fat fluttered between her elbows and armpit like holey Viking sails.

Detention meant arriving at school thirty minutes early and sitting in the study hall, and staying late for another thirty minutes. The early session didn't bother us; the afternoon session cut into basketball practice.

We tried to reason with Aunt Melba, but she wasn't in a reasonable mood. We even had the coach talk to her. But being an old maid, she knew how to ignore men. I appealed to my mom and dad for help. Mom decided the experience would be a "character builder." She actually used those words. Dad said, "Whatever your mom says." If his beliefs and words are what a man is remembered by, those four words would have been chiseled on daddy's tombstone.

Dedron and I came up with the revenge plan talking on the phone the night before our first early-morning detention session. We divvied up the "supplies list" and agreed to meet at the school the next morning at 6:30, an hour before detention was scheduled to begin.

The plan was surprisingly simple: Drive Aunt Melba crazy.

Working like squirrels gathering nuts before the first hard freeze, we divided the workload up into manageable chunks. Using a brace and bit and the smallest drill we could find at the Future Farmers of America workshop, Dedron drilled about thirty tiny holes in the back of the bookshelves connecting the study hall/library to the history room. I tied a long strand of monofilament line to the left-side cord on the Venetian blind closest to Aunt Melba's desk. I had Dedron go into the history room, raise the window and lean out to catch the end of the line that I threw him, which was weighted with a flat washer. Leaving the line very loose, the other end was tied to a small nail driven into the outside wooden window frame next to my seat in the front of the class.

The final step was placing several very thin, foot-long pieces of sturdy wire in the chalk board tray in the history room.

After running a few tests, we congratulated ourselves. We were certified geniuses.

7:30. We were both at a study table when Aunt Melba came into the room.

At 8:15, first bell sounded and as we went to class.

Leon Tucker, the basketball coach, taught history. Someone asking a simple question about a certain defense or an upcoming game could easily distract him. The Spanish Inquisition would quickly be forgotten for an explanation of the box-and-one defense.

At the first opportunity, I stuck my hand out the open window, coiled the clear fishing line around my hand, pulled it taut, and gave it a big jerk.

The scream from the library was to my ears like a cold Pabst is to a thirsty high school dropout. Coach went running from the room and the whole class followed. Aunt Melba was running out of the study hall screaming, "Gah-ghost!" Her arms were flapping like she was trying to get some serious lift. She headed across the hall, darted into the principal's office, and slammed the door.

Coach questioned the study hall kids and all said that the blind, as Peanut Ghormley described it, "started flapping around like a broken-wing bat."

Coach went over to the window and raised the blind, lowered the blind and raised it again. Nothing. Principal Murphy came in and repeated the exercise. Nothing.

Everybody was ordered back to class and Aunt Melba was told to go back to study hall.

It was only a couple of minutes before Dedron went up to sharpen his pencil. He picked up a wire out of the chalk tray, poked it in an almost invisible hole and pushed. An audible thud could be heard through the wall connecting the two rooms. Coach was studying some plays at his desk, so I went to the blackboard to write down a few history dates. With Dedron still at the other end of the wall, we coordinated a double-wire push and two books were pushed off the shelves in the library.

Thunk!

Thud!

"Aaaaaaggghhhhhhhh!" Decapitated banshee noise followed by stuttering wail.

We found out later that Dedron's first wire exercise kicked *I Married Adventure* by Osa Johnson off the shelf. Aunt Melba looked askance, but went over, picked it up and replaced in the vacant hole.

But when *Black Beauty* and *Oliver Twist* came flying off the shelves simultaneous, she lost it, again running from the room in sheer terror. There was a side benefit to the hijinks, combined with Aunt Melba's reaction to them. We scared the pee-tiddlewads out of just about all the girls in study hall and half the boys. Several students had to phone their mamas to bring them some dry underwear.

Aunt Melba took the rest of the semester off after the haunted Venetian blind went into ghostly spasms twice and *Rebecca of Sunnybrook Farm* and *Billy Budd* went flying off the shelves at two-second intervals.

UNCERTAIN TIMES

Dedron and I were young. We were brilliant. We should have been school legends.

If we ever could have told the story.

I woke up about midnight and remembered the dream. I don't think it's normal to feel badly about childhood acts of intra-school terrorism and smile about it at the same time. Which I was doing.

Pah-point taken. Yah-you're not normal.

My throat was a little sore so I took a sip of water from the glass by the bed and tried to get back to sleep with the intention of going back to Avery High. There was one high school episode that I enjoyed more than most. Resurrected it every chance I had.

I listened to the frog lullaby for a time....

It was mid-October, 1962. This was the day. THE day. Tonight, the Avery basketball Bulldogs were hosting the Annona Lions. The game of the year for both teams. Actually, THE game of any year. Avery and Annona were separated by seven miles of Highway 67. An immeasurable distance in regard to school accomplishments, student character and intelligence, demographic culture and degree of collective youthful couth separated the two schools.

Avery residents had more culture and couth in their little thumbs than Annona residents could ever learn at a finishing school. The whole damn town of Annona was a finishing school: You were born there, you were finished.

Avery, population 332, had a bank, café, a barber shop, one giant general mercantile store, two mom-and-pop grocery stores, a movie theater, hardware store, and a drug store. Annona, population 413, had a combination gas station and café, a business that whittled out inscriptions on tombstones, and a small building that sold horse feed and tack. Residents had to drive eight miles west to Clarksville to do their banking, fill prescriptions, get something good to eat, get a store-bought haircut, see a movie, buy dry goods, or purchase ten-penny nails or a plumber's helper. They could have driven to Avery since it was closer, but they wouldn't.

Annona residents wouldn't really need a plumber's helper; most of the residents in that piece of Redneck Hell still used outhouses. In Avery, Annona was known as "Turd City."

To say Avery and Annona had an intense rivalry is like saying Lincoln and Douglas were debate competitors. The rivalry between the two towns was not based on intense athletic competition; it was based on rural logic. They hated us; we hated them back.

The hatred factor racheted up a notch when school started that year.

The first day of classes, students were greeted by an act of rural terrorism. Along the entire side of the gym facing the highway, in bold, red letters were the words: Annona Seniors '63. Knowing what we did about Annona, the message was surprising. Everything was spelled correctly.

The first reaction from the students was one of calm restraint: We were going to round up every kid in town, convoy to Annona, and burn down the town. We planned to do our level best not to kill a single resident.

The superintendent announced that a full-school assembly would be held second period in the gym. When the time came and we were all seated, Superintendent Alex Slaughter got up and introduced the assembly speaker, James Monroe, Annona superintendent. The boos came down like flash flood waters in a New Mexico arroyo. The Annona superintendent patiently waited for the rowdiness to subside, then calmly told us that the damage would be repaired, starting that very day. "The entire side of the Avery gym will be repainted," he assured us, "by the entire senior class of Annona High School."

The roar of approval was the loudest in the history of the gym, rivaling the last-second jump shot by Randall Mayhew two years earlier that defeated Annona for the district title.

He also told the assembled group that if "Annona Seniors '63" were seen painted on another structure anywhere, the seniors would forego their senior trip—New Orleans—as punishment. More applause, cheers, and jeers.

On the day of the all-important District 3-B basketball match-up between the two schools, our coach urged us to remember the desecration of our gym. As a rule, the boys watched the first half of the girl's game and then went to the boy's locker room to get dressed. Room. Singular for teams. One. The girls had one; the boys had one. Visiting teams had to dress on the stage, set at one end of the gym. A heavy, maroon curtain served as a dressing room curtain.

It was in the first minute of the game that I took an outlet pass from Charles Mickey David and went down court on a lone duck fast break. As I hit midcourt, Anne Jewison, a shapely senior forward for Annona, fell through the curtain, off the stage and onto the court.

Covered only by a coat of sweat.

About the free throw line, the fact that a naked seventeen-year-old female was standing in front of me hit me like a brick from a giant slingshot.

I stepped *on* the basketball, skidded on my back and crashed into the stage, headfirst. I ended up with my head next to Anne's left foot. I noticed there was a corn on the outside of her big toe and that the foot was connected to a nicely turned ankle, which, no pun intended, in turn was connected to an extremely lickable calf. The calf did not have trace of hair stubble on it, I was so close I started to count her pores. The calf was joined by a knee to a thigh that still had a residue of a tan line, which was joined by another thigh....

She had the look of a trapped and strangling ferret. She tried to cover three parts of her anatomy with two hands. In some things, failure is not only accepted, but appreciated.

I smiled up at her and, just before some damn do-gooder Church of Christ-er threw a coat over her, said: "Would you like to go out sometime?"

When I got home after the easy victory, as always, Mom and Pop were sitting at the kitchen table, drinking coffee and talking.

They both looked at me as I entered. I stopped midway in the kitchen and looked at their faces.

"What?" I said.

Pop shook his head and said: "You stepped *on* a basketball you were dribbling! How is that possible?"

I went to sleep that night, as I would on many other nights, with my mind dwelling on things that bounced other than basketballs.

Six months later, three weeks before the Annona seniors took off to New Orleans on their senior trip, me, Cowboy, and Turnip Melbrook drove to the other side of Annona and parked the car on a deserted dirt road near a railroad track. We followed the tracks back to Annona, slipping into the woods about a quarter mile from town. From there we carefully walked into town, did what we came to do, returned to the car without being seen, and drove home.

The next morning the residents of Annona were greeted by the blazoned words "ANNONA SENIORS '63" painted in Annona's school colors on the town's water tower.

Despite protests from students and parents, the superintendent cancelled the senior trip as per his promise the previous fall.

I consoled my girlfriend at the time—Annona's Anne Jewison—on her loss and for the next week was kind, gentle, and endearing. I sent her cards of sympathy, wildflower bouquets, and small gifts. On the day Annona seniors were supposed to leave for New Orleans, Ann was as despondent as she was ever going to get in her entire life. Looking out for both of our interests, I persuaded her that it was the perfect time for both of us to surrender our official virgin status.

"It'll make you feel better," I said. I thought that was a fair statement. I *knew* it would make me feel better.

The official love nest was the back seat of my 1956, black and white Ford Fairlane with red-white-and-black tucked-and-rolled seat covers.

It's the honest-to-God's truth that I have always felt guilty about those events of my senior year.

I felt guilty because I did not send those responsible for writing "Annona Seniors '63" on the Avery gym thank you cards.

Bob woke me up early the next morning.
Yah-you like that stah-story.
With memories like that, Bob, you can stay young forever.
Buh-but Anne didn't gah-get....
I know she didn't get to go to New Orleans, Bob. And I've always felt a little sad about that. But, on the other hand, she got to go someplace much better than New Orleans.

UNCERTAIN TIMES

Wha-where?
Adj Heaven.
Jah-jesus!

After spending some quality time with two cups of coffee, I ran over to Widder's to check to see if there was any email messages. There was two new ones: *Cooking.com* had a special on Cephalon; David Rothell was wondering if she got his first message. I forwarded both Rothell messages to the email address she had left stuck to the computer screen and tucked the original in a file dubbed "Personal" without even peeking.

I got to Hum's by seven, had the usual while getting happy nods and humorous asides by the regulars. I was headed toward Marshall by eight.

A stop by the vet's to check on Moosie in order. Doc had taken to brining her to work with him and, for the most part, she stayed in his office, content to roll up on an old Army blanket in a corner.

That changed when she heard my voice. She barged into the outer office, barking in that full-throated Dane bark that defies description. But if a description should be attempted, it is like a snipped lion's roar. In a long tunnel.

When Moosie rounded the corner into the office area, she scared the crap—literally—out of a snuffling, smashed-nosed Pomeranian in for its shots. I grabbed Moosie by her ears before she could bowl me over and we play-wrestled for a few minutes before the receptionist handed me a leash and said firmly: "Take her for a walk."

On a leash, Moose thinks she's a Lepazaner stallion. She walks in an exaggerated gait, picking up her feet very high, and folding her front paws backward until they almost touch her foreleg. Her head is held high, chest thrust forward. Why walking Moose, at this moment, reminded me of Ann Jewison standing in the moonlight beside Rhoden's Pond almost forty years ago, I don't have a clue.

Gah-give me a brah-break.

Squaring off a couple of short blocks ended us up back at Doc's and he was out from his session with a bunny with a sliced ear and an elderly cat "off its feed."

"How's my Moosie baby," he said, and she nearly jerked my arm out of its socket lunging on the leash trying to get to him.

I eased Moosie closer and she gave him a tongue bath and, I swear, he kissed her on both ears and the end of her nose!

"I love Great Danes," Doc said.

"I hope she's not too much of a bother, Doc."

"Moosie? A bother? No way. She's a dear, a big, itty bitty Moosie bear, oh yeth she is."

What went on between them at night at Doc's house I really didn't want to know.

It was only a short drive to the airport and I ended up at a hanger at the end. The words "White Aviation" were in bold letters over the office door. Underneath in a slightly frilly font were the words: "Flying Is Not For Fools."

I tried to figure out the public relations message that motto was sending, but came up short.

With my sense of humor and the condition of the human condition, I half-expected to see a black aviator named White running the place but I was disappointed. The "White" in "White Aviation" was Timothy White and his name fit him. He was, well, white. Porcelain, actually. If he had been any whiter he would have been the inside of a new refrigerator.

"You must be Mr. Jones," he said, getting up from the desk and coming out from behind the counter. We shook hands and he said, "You said you want to fly over Caddo Lake and take some aerial photos, right? What areas are you interested in?"

There was a big map of the area on his wall, so I went over and studied it a bit to get my bearings. After I found Uncertain, it was a cinch to go northeast until I came to the area where I thought the logjam was located. I indicated that I wanted a fly over of that area, as well as Carter's Chute.

As he was with me on the phone, he was completely cooperative and helpful. Customer service workshop graduate.

He had an over-wing Cessna that he said he had used for aerial photography before. I was familiar with the plane, having shot from several similar models over the years. I asked if we could remove the door and maybe hitch up a safety harness in addition to the seat belt. No problem. He had already anticipated that, pointing to a plane door leaning against the far wall of the office.

The trip to Caddo took less than ten minutes and I immediately recognized Hum's and Harlan's,.

It took less than two minutes to get up to the logjam and I recognized it even from several thousand feet. It really was a massive mess of logs.

Over the sound of the wind rushing into the cabin, I hollered at White to go back over the logjam as low as possible. "One thousand feet" was what he hollered back.

Making sure my extra safety line was secured around both seats and a metal hoop behind the seats used to secure cargo, I leaned slightly out of the plan and focused in Betsy. I really wasn't planning on taking pictures, just using the lens as a telescope. The first pass clearly showed a tiny channel leading from the backside of the logjam. Where it went I couldn't see from that angle; cypress trees obscured its path.

I indicated for him to fly over again—lower—and from a little bit to the west. This time, I could see a little bit more of the channel; it looked like it went into the cypress grove. Then stopped.

I indicated with hand signals to come from the north. He headed toward Uncertain and then swung in a wide loop, lining up perfectly on a course that would X the first two runs. From this angle, the channel behind the logjam wasn't visible, but a small clearing in the middle of the watery forest was. It was there and then gone in a second. I indicated I wanted him to do a U-ey and go back on that line again. When I gave him the high sign, he was to tilt the plane.

White was a good pilot. He made the U-turn-back like a seasoned square dancer and hit the line I had indicated perfectly. Just before the logjam, I indicated by flipping my hand to sidewinder the plane. A half-second later all I could see was trees rushing by and they seemed way too close. I counted to two and started Betsy's shutter firing. I ran through the entire roll.

As the blood starting redistributing itself to the entire body from my right shoulder area, I saw White had started to head toward Carter's Chute but I told him that wasn't necessary, that I thought I had gotten what I came to get. We had agreed up front on a package price, so he was happy. His profit margin for the trip just rose appreciably.

A couple of hours later, after doing some quick shopping at Wal-Mart, I was back in Uncertain, ready for an early lunch at Hum's.

There was a good crowd in the parking lot, bigger than usual for a Friday. Common sense said people were gathering at the site of the last night's incident to get eyewitness information.

I knew they'd have to get it from somebody other than Hum.

Tell us what happened yesterday between Twiddle and Mr. Jones.

Hm-mmMM? Eh hmmm-mmm-mmm-mm?

The one last night.

Hmmm? Hmn, Hm hmmmm hmmmmmmmm hmmm hmmmmm hm hmm hmm hmm!

Haaaaahhaaaaaaahhaaaaahhhaaaaaaaa! That's that best story I've ever heard!

Yep, that's probably the way it would go.

Yah-you're an eh-idiot.

Yeah, Bob. Keeps me sane.

I ordered the Friday Lunch Special without even looking at what it was. Having been around the world and eaten food in about thirty or more countries, I knew the secret to Hum's cooking: Lard. Not Crisco. Not extra virgin olive oil. Not oil squeezed from peanuts or little furry canolas. Pure-dee lard chunks melted in a skillet or broiler (or rubbed directly on some meats and other items like baked potatoes).

Lard was heart-stopper food if you believe most scientific accounts. What those scientists don't say is that lard is manna from...heavy. It is a fact that a chicken leg fried in pure lard would put weight on quicker than a horse syringe full of uncut andro. But for country cooks and those lucky enough to get to eat what they serve up, old-fashioned brick lard was, is, and always will be the caviar of country fare.

Bob keeps reminding me not to eat heavy foods. I am overweight according to the government-issue weight charts. But those charts are researched, produced, and distributed by fat white guys who get their jollies from researching, producing, and distributing information that will piss people off. The government puts out those charts just to make people think they are fat. If the entire country would lose an average of thirty pounds per person, two things would happen: The government would produce new charts showing that, according to the revised data, everyone is still overweight; and the earth would fly out of orbit because of the lack of proper weight holding it in place.

I am probably twenty pounds overweight, but they are comfortable pounds, not portly, gut-sagging, belt-busters. About a year ago I lost thirty pounds in a relatively short period of times by eating nothing but fruit, fresh vegetables and lots and lots of fresh black-eyed peas. The regimen these days is when I gain a few pounds, I eat fruit and black-eyed peas for a few days to shed weight and stay in the two-hundred-ten-pound range.

The secret to a good diet and maintenance plan is to go out and buy whatever celebrated diet book is on the New York Times' best seller list this month…and eat it. For every meal, eat a page, warmed up in the microwave and flavored with a smidgen of soy sauce and pepper. Supplement the pages with fresh fruit and a heaping bowl of black-eyed peas. It is my experience that an average person can lose about a half-pound to a pound for every twenty pages eaten.

I actually started writing a diet book about eating diet books. When I wrote everything I thought I knew about the subject, the entire book came to just under a weight loss of a pound per average person.

My agent said he didn't think many people would buy a twenty-page book.

I told him that maybe we could add more pages by just using bigger type.

The lunch special was fried chicken, corn on the cob, crowder peas, and fried green tomatoes. I was hungry. It was good. Culinary love. Wham! Bam! Thank you, Hum.

After paying the check I was on my way home to meet Jeb for the picture-taking session when a group of men on the cafe porch, led by Hy and Glenn Alan, stopped me.

Glenn Alan said the "rumor on the street" was that Sheriff Twiddle was talking big about "taking that Jones feller down a peg." I like expressions like "rumor on the street" and always take them to their logical conclusion. In Uncertain, there is only *one* street.

"Gentlemen," I said, "don't fret. The sheriff is a bully; he's used to getting his way. He knows that sooner than later I'll be moving on. He also knows that I will stand up to him and if he tries to hurt me, he will pay. He knows I have put Lawyer Mitchell on retainer. He also knows how Mitchell dearly loves to make him look silly in court. Twiddle's between a rock and hard place right now. And his gut instincts, pun intended, tell him that I will be leaving and taking my attitude with me. And then his worries will be over."

Hy spoke up: "But will Jeb's troubles be over?"

I thought of a bunch of replies, including "Jeb's a grown man; he can take care of himself," and "Twiddle knows Jeb has a lot of friends."

In the end I didn't say anything. There was nothing I could say that was going to make a bit of difference in something that hadn't happened yet.

Jeb was waiting at the house. He was dressed simply in fairly new jeans, a nice, if slightly elaborate cowboy shirt, and black cowboy boots with red trim. His main accessory was a belt buckle the size of Twiddle's hat. The buckle had a miniature cowboy on a miniature horse chasing a miniature calf with the intent to throw a miniature rope and catch it. There was no writing on the buckle that I could see so I figured it for store-bought, not won.

Jeb helped me move the equipment to the backyard and this time both of us carried the horny chair to the tree.

"You need all this here to take a pitcher?"

"Only when the subject is mean and ornery."

"You want me to sit in the chair?"

"Nope. I want you to hold it over your head and dance on one leg."

He looked at me and grinned: "Do you ever answer a simple question with a simple answer?"

"It's against my religion."

"What religion are you?"

"Orthodox Druid."

"Is that anything like a Mormon?"

"Exactly the same, except Druids can have fun."

I was still worrying with the way things were left at Hum's. I told Jeb about the conversation as I was setting the lights and loading film in the camera.

"Jeb, I've stirred up a hornet's nest and you may be the one who gets stung."

Jeb slumped down in the chair. His face took on the saddest expression. Talking low and slow, he said, "About ten years ago, after my accident, my back got to hurting so bad that I had to get relief. I got myself hooked on crystal meth. It didn't help the pain that much, but it made me forget it. Twiddle picked me up in a raid and told me I was going to prison for life."

He stopped and took several deep breaths.

"To stay outta prison, I served as Twiddle's personal snitch. I gave up some people I knowed, but mostly real bad drug dealers. There came a time when he wanted me to snitch on a couple friends, but I couldn't do it. He's been on my ass ever since."

I started to say something—Lord knows what—and he raised a hand to stop me just in time. "It don't matter what you do or don't do. Twiddle is gonna be on my ass one way or another. From now on. And that's a fact."

I went in the house and pulled us a couple of beers out of the fridge and went back outside. Neither of us said much for a while; we just sat there. Thinking. Sipping.

About halfway through the beers, I picked up Betsy and took a few test shots. Jeb had a nice face. It was regular, not off-center like so many people. He skin was leathery from the sun. He had lived a hard life, and, through the lens, I could see the hurt behind his eyes.

After the roll started automatically rewinding, I told him I was done.

"That's it?" he said.

"Well, yes, unless you want something specific."

"What I wanted was for you to tell me that Widder was sunbathing nekkid. That's the only reason I came over here."

We finished the beers, got a couple more, and sat in the backyard for hours, talking, laughing, and telling stories.

He asked me once if I had ever seen Widder "nekkid, in the flesh."

If I had know Widder better, I might have taken offense, but said, "Only in my mind."

"Hell's bell's, Mr. Jones, then you ain't no better than any the rest of us."

It was dark when Jeb "eased on toward the house." As he drove away I got the key to Widder's and went over to check the email.

Only one new message since this morning. The subject line read: "Adj. Wish you were here."

I expected any text message from her to be short. It was and I didn't mind a bit.

> *Adj:*
>
> *Everything is going well with my visit to New York. The paintings arrived okay and I was there this afternoon when they started hanging them for the show. I'm going to see "Lion King" tonight at the Amsterdam Theater. It is supposed to be the best show on right now. Or, maybe, since, ever.*
>
> *I am probably boring you, but I've avoiding saying what I want to say. I'm here. You're there. It just doesn't seem right somehow.*
>
> *If that scares you…it's okay.*
> *It scares me to death.*
> *C.C.*

I hit the reply icon and typed:

> *C.C.:*
> *I'm here. You're there. I Miss you.*
> *I'm not scared.*
> *That's a lie.*
> *Come home.*
> *Adj.*

I sent it off and ran off a copy of the letter and the reply on Widder's HP printer, folded it neatly, and slipped it in my back pocket.

I clicked onto the Internet and called up *landvoyage.com*, a firm specializing in aerial and satellite photography, as well as topographic maps. Before I came to Caddo Lake, I had ordered up some photos, but none of the particular area involving the logjam.

I had an account with the company and it took just a couple of minutes to locate an aerial shot I wanted, order a eleven-by-fourteen print, plus one zoomed-in version from a satellite. I paid extra for overnight delivery. Which meant I would get it in two or three days.

Later, in bed, I thought about Widder's note and my reply. It made me think of that time back in Avery and my first sexual experience with Ann. I really liked Ann. But I also readily played on her emotions to get what I wanted at a time when I needed it.

Was I doing the same thing with Widder? There was an attraction there, for sure. But how deep is the attraction? Am I still sufficiently shallow to work and play with a person's emotions to get what I want?

When Bob started in, I started to tell him to piss off. But curiosity kept my thoughts silenced and focused.

Wha-what if Widder is dah-doing the sah-same thing?

What are you thinking about?

Sha-she may be playing with your eh-emotions.

So, do you think I'm shallow?

O-o-o, you're shah-shallow all right. But maybe you're not by yah-yourself.

I sat there in the dark, my hands interlocked behind my head. Thoughts kicked through my mind like a herd of stampeding wildebeest.

It was right before I went to sleep that the best thought of the day hit me: Wonder what I could get for Bob on eBay?

37

Time flies when you're having fun. And if you're not having fun, time can seem like a lighted cigarette dropped in your crotch on a busy freeway with no place to pull over.

Anonymous

The next three days went by as slow as days could go. There was no zoom or fly. Just crawl. The days were not like the light speed illusion in *Star Wars* or *Star Trek*. Expanded, loose reality turned into perception. They were a mixture of Deep South Alabama twang mixed with dripping Vermont syrup. On a cold day.

There were no more e-mails from Widder even though I checked twice a day. I wanted to send her a note, but male ego kept the fingers from pecking out the words. Or, maybe I didn't know what to peck out.

Saturday morning, about seven, there was a rapping on the door that pulled me from a dream about a girl in college named Nekkid Nell McGruder. I didn't know if her first name was Nekkid, but that's all anybody knew her by. Somebody fixed me up with her one time for a fraternity mixer. Being a photographer for the school newspaper and yearbook opened lots of doors and lots of opportunities. As far as I can remember, there was never a door I didn't walk through or an opportunity I didn't embrace. Nekkid Nell was an opportunity and a photographer's perk and at the time I was twenty and constantly percolating.

I eased out of bed, awake enough to take the Glock as I walked toward the front of the lodge. Hiding the gun behind my leg, I went to the entryway door and peeked around the jam. The top half of Jeb was framed in the big window in the door. He was grinning and waving like Floyd the barber down in Mayberry when Andy would drive by.

Wha-wha-wha....

It takes Bob a while to get it all together sometimes.

Laying the gun on the table by the door, I opened the door and Jeb's word gushed out like bottled milk dropped on a concrete floor.

"Get dressed, Mr. Jones. I done seen something you gots to see. Get dressed quick-like!"

Despite numerous questions, Jeb just stuck to the central theme: Come on. It's urgent. You'll like it. It's something special

Throwing on clothes and grabbing my cameras and both ammo boxes, I jumped in Jeb's truck, still spitting mouthwash out the window as he backed out of the driveway and headed toward the dock.

Ten minutes later we were scooting across open water in the general direction toward the Carter's Chute channel.

Jeb hollered over the roar of the motor: "You ever take the Carter's Chute channel fast-like?"

Fast-like? I had an idea I knew what he meant and shook my head. Then I crammed both cameras in the empty dry box, tied them to the boat with a snap-end bungee cord and grabbed the gunwales with both hands just as he pointed the boat in the channel's entrance. He sounded an air horn and opened up the throttle. The waterway to Carter's Chute has about ten to twelve sharp turns, starting with a hard left. Add to that the fact that the channel is only about twenty feet wide at its widest point and you have little room for error if you are scatting. Which we were. Scatting-squared. If his motor had of had overdrive, we would have been in it.

Jeb hit the first turn wide open and the boat keeled over hard left and my left fingertips were *in* the water. I looked back at him over my shoulder and he had a grimace on his face like Dr. Frankenstein when he screamed: "It's alive!"

I was still looking at Jeb when he reined the boat back straight, then immediately whipped the wheel into a right-hand turn. He found his rhythm quickly and the boat was zigging and zagging and cutting a perfect swath through the center of the channel. If we weren't in the middle, we were dead. But when you are grabbing adventure and giving that sucker a tonsil-deep French kiss, it's not nice to sweat the small stuff. Like, maybe, dying.

It was like riding the Judge Roy Bean Roller Coaster for the first time. Exhilarating. Exciting. Wondrous. But about the ninth time Jeb laid that boat over until there was nothing above me but sky and nothing below me but water I swore to God that if I made it to Carter's Chute alive I would never, ever do this shit again.

The last curve before entering Carter's Chute was a right hand turn and in the middle of the short straightaway immediately following, Jeb shut her down, coasting to a nice, easy glide.

I swallowed. Then swallowed again.

I didn't have any idea what the expression on my face was, so I just gave Jeb a right-handed thumb's up over my shoulder. My left hand had cramped holding onto the gunwale. The fingers didn't want to turn loose.

I was levering at my fingers one by one, when the boat stopped. Puzzlement blanked my face. Followed by disbelief.

Where Buddy Parlay's duck blind used to be was a new structue. It looked taller, definitely bigger. I looked back at Jeb and he was just sitting there, smiling.

"Wha-where…wha…how…." I hate it when I sound like Bob.

"We all did it," Jeb said. "Everybody nearly that could, pitched in."

"Everybody? Who?"

"Them," he said, his hands sweeping over the water. I turned around and I saw movement in the trees to the left and right of the blind. Boats of all descriptions, colors and shapes eased out of cypress groves and started puttering toward the blind. Two or three people were in each boat and many of them were waving, some with both hands.

Jeb eased the boat forward and the majority of the boats arrived at the blind about the same time. From this angle I couldn't see any heads of the mama or baby birds in any of the three nests. I couldn't believe they were still around, what with all the banging and noise building the blind must have made.

"Don't worry none about your birds, Mr. Jones," Hy said. He was in a boat with Glenn Alan, Thompson and another man I had seen around town. "We put most of the blind together in town, moved the pieces out here and put them together with screws. No noise much, excepting for driving the pilings. We done that when both mama and papa birds were gone."

My eyes swept the faces of the men—and one woman, Miss Baxter, who I offered an earnest nod. I silently thanked them before I said: "It has been my pleasure to enjoy the hospitality of many different people in many different countries. In all my travels, in all the acts of kindness I have been privileged to be the recipient of, your gift is the greatest of them all."

Silence. Then Jeb said, "Do it mean you like it?"

"It do."

Harlan told me to "go on up and check her out," and helping hands pushed Jeb's boat up to the ladder. I took Betsy and my wide-angle zoom and went up the ladder slowly, enjoying the feel and smell of the newly cut cypress lumber. When my head evened up with the floor of the blind, the first thing I noticed was a chair sitting in the middle of the floor. It was the horny chair from my living room.

I looked down at the gathering and said, "How did you…."

Thompson spoke up: "It ain't the same chair, Mr. Jones. I built you a new one, seeing as how you liked the other one so much."

The fast-moving fog of laughter spread over the lake. I sat in the chair and laughed and cried until my eyes were dry and my stomach hurt from the effort.

This blind was certainly bigger than the one it replaced. The side screens were of a dark green, camouflage material and could be rolled up by using a double-cord system. The gun/camera flaps were evenly placed and stitched to keep the edges from fraying.

A little six-inch shelf ran all the way around the inside, about six inches from the top of the opening; cup holders had been cut out at regular intervals. A new addition allowed the back panel to be raised or lowered; it could be latched to the ceiling with an eyehook.

"Boys," I said, going to the entrance and looking down, "What did Buddy have to say about his new duck blind?"

Jeb said, "We didn't tell him. Now when he comes out here to build a new one, that's another little surprise party we all are planning to attend."

Making a big show of studying the interior, I said in a serious voice, "I know you meant well and everything, but this just won't do."

They all waited for the punch line.

"There's no refrigerator or sleeper-sofa."

The obligatory chuckles came and a man I didn't recall ever seeing before said, "Maybe we will just have to have your drinks and eats catered." Hum opened a big ice chest and started passing around biscuits and sausage sandwiches. Jeb opened up his ice chest and tossed me up a cold can of Minute Maid Orange Juice and said, "You may not want to drink regular orange juice being used to, as you are, drinking that Mexican beer."

I smiled and flipped the lid on the orange juice. "As a not-so-famous poet once said,

Drinking beer has naught to do with thirst,
But everything to do with…drinking beer"!

Hy: "I'll drink to that" and he raised his can in a silent toast. Then he decided to give a real toast. "Here's to Mr. Jones, who has more guts or less sense then most anybody I know."

The laughter picked up again and toasts to my ignorance, naiveté, or abject stupidity sprinkled down like raindrops from a sunny spring thunderhead.

I took the opportunity to take a picture of the gathering, and said "Hey!" loudly so that they all looked up more or less at the same time. "Gonna frame that one for the house," I said, spreading my arms wide. "Gonna put it over the fireplace."

Thermoses of coffee appeared from bottoms of boats and live bait wells and with Hum supplying Styrofoam cups, we eagerly switched from unleaded to caffeinated premium blend. Jeb climbed up the ladder balancing a three-quarter-full cup of coffee and this time I proposed a toast. I had been sitting on the edge of the blind but stood up, raised my glass and said:

"Here's to the men and women of Uncertain. I raise my glass in earnest to the beauty of their spirit, their neighborly attitude, and their acceptance of a stranger into their midst."

I took a sip of coffee, but got strangled and sprayed those in the boats nearest the ladder when a voice said: "Who's Ernest?"

Everybody took time with the coffee, relishing the feel-good moment. I checked on the nests and I could see fuzzy heads on two nests. Another shoot was called for.

Putting down the back flap was relatively easy, and I did my best imitation of scampering down the ladder because I knew that virtually every eye was glued on my backside. In one respect, falling in the lake would have just added another dimension to the story. It was a story that didn't need an addendum.

Jeb was the last to pull away from the blind and I had turned on the seat to face him.

"Thank you!" I said.

He didn't say anything, just nodded.

"Feel like another rolly-coaster ride?" Jeb said as we eased up to the entrance to the channel.

I grabbed the gunwales with both hands, put my head back and shouted: "Why the hell not?"

Yah-YEEEEE-HAW!

38

Ask most people how many friends they've got and they'll be stretching it to name six or seven. Those that think they have more are either real nice, rich, or lying.

Anonymous

Back in town, I asked Jeb if he had seen the Poem Board this morning and he said he had driven by it "slow-like" coming to my house but it "didn't make no sense." I asked if he would mind driving by it on the way by to my place, knowing he wouldn't.

This entry was a headscratcher.

There are things on this earth
That are absolute proof
That God exists,
That He reaches down His hand
And blesses things that give human beings pleasure.

Like Krispy Kreme.

What the hell is this?
Tha-that's right, you na-know.

I'm not arguing with the logic, Bob, just thinking what's the reason someone felt compelled to publicize the fact?

"What? Jeb said.

"What?"

"Naw, I thought you said something. You had this funny-looking look on your face."

"No, I was just thinking."

"You understand this one?" he said, pointing to the board.

"Jeb, I thought I was understanding most of them, but what I don't understand is *why* and *who*. Why are they being written and who's doing it?"

We stood there, while I took a couple of shots and wrote down the lines on a piece of paper I found in my pocket.

"That's the difference in you and folks hereabouts," Jeb said. "You wonder about stuff like this; we just accept it and go on. We could find out, I reckon, who's doing it. But some folks like the mystery. Gives us something to do. Something to think about. Something to enjoy."

Maybe that was my problem; I've never been one to "accept it and go on," I thought to myself.

Tha-that's part of yah-your charm.

Yeah. That and pissing off fat-gutted sheriffs.

Jeb didn't talk much on the way home but as he pulled into my driveway, he said, "What's Krispy Kreme?"

"A donut."

"Who writes about God making donuts? Huh. I know who we be looking for then, who's writing on the board."

"Who?"

"Some fucking nut."

Hah-hard to argue with lah-logic.

Back at the house, I checked the mail and, in addition to a couple of flyers and a letter from my agent, there were two big reinforced photo mailers, both from Pro Printing in Atlanta. I had been a customer of Pro Printing for more than fifteen years, mainly working with the office manager, Nick ("Call me Nicholas") Finch. There was a standing order that for any film I sent in—Nick handled it personally. I didn't question it, but Bob thought it was because *Nah-Nick wanted to see bah-bare-breasted natives.*

Nick knew my style, knew what I liked. I could send in five rolls of film and leave a sticky note for Nick to send me a proof sheet and an eight-by-ten of the "best one in the series," and invariably, he knew which one I would have personally selected.

On Thompson's roll, I had written a note that said: "Print two eight-by-ten of the three best ones. Soft focus/cheese." On the shots of Jeb, I specified only, "eight-by-ten, six best." On the roll taken from the airplane, "one ea. Eight-by-ten, all. Crop to center."

After getting settled at the kitchen table and getting a beer, I discovered the results were as ordered.

Thompson's photos could not have been any better. The "three best" were those taken in the middle of the roll and were shot after he had time to relax and without him smiling. I easily picked out the one where he was looking for Widder sunbathing; his eyes were wider and a touch of a grin pulled at the corners of his mouth. I didn't know if he would like that particular one, but it was going in my portfolio. His face was soft due to defusing through a special soft-focus filter; in the days when I was printing my own stuff, I resorted to thin cheesecloth for softening up "hard" photos. Nick forgives my archaic instructions.

Jeb's were different, but, in their own way, just as good. I wanted Jeb's face to show everything, the hardness of his life, the innate intelligence, the pain and haunting look in his eyes.

I put a picture of both men side by side, intending to pick the best one. Couldn't do it. Different. Both excellent.

Eh-it's no big dah-deal. Just push a little buh-button.

Jesus, Bob! Why couldn't you be an inner voice of few words? Don't think back. That's rhetorical.

The photos of the fly-over were pretty much what I expected, what I thought I saw. There were several from different angles of the logjam. Two clearly showed a narrow clear channel running east to west, then disappearing at the beginning of what looked like a bend back to the north. None of the others showed any sign of the channel.

I flipped through the bunch quickly. Nothing. Wait a minute. What's that? On one frame, shot directly from overhead on the final pass, there was a small open space. The clearing looked to be a flat piece of...could that be a small island back there in those trees?

I went in the bedroom and pulled an old suitcase from under the bed. After rummaging around for a bit, I came up with a jeweler's loupe that my dad had used to study stamps and coins. I dropped it on the photo. There was a distinct flat rectangle slightly off center of the photo, in the upper left corner of the clearing. Some branches were lying on the—was that a roof?—whatever the heck it was. Limbs? Camouflage, maybe? With the loupe, I moved bit by bit from one end of the clearing to the other. What is that? Directly opposite the rectangle was a—something. A slight shadow made me think it looked like something stuck in the ground. What was that?

Guess I'd just have to go in there and find out.

Ah-and are we sub-surprised?

Leaving the photos on the table, I went next door to Widder's and picked up a stack of mail from the box. Three boxes sat behind one of the rockers. UPS. I opened the door, dropped the mail and went back outside and retrieved the boxes, all marked "Amazon.com." Lots of reading, Widder. Don't know why you'd need all this, since you have Molly and Rance and the rest of the cowgirls and cowpokes. Get it, Bob? Cow-girls? Cow-pokes?

Yah-you're ha-hopeless.

Oh, by the way, Bob, what was that secret you and Widder had about....

Dah-don't ah-ask.

But I just....

Teh-ticklelock!

Since I wanted to make sure everything was safe and since I did not want to leave a letter bomb in Widder's house, I flipped through the envelopes. A return address from California. Mr. And Mrs. Mitch Collins. A relative, perhaps? A couple of bills. More bills. The last envelope I started to throw away; at first glance I took it for a phony check from a clearinghouse. Even the addressee was wrong. But something about the address caught my attention: C. McLaughlin, Rural Route 7, Box 241, Uncertain, Texas. The return address was Rotenone Publishers, Phillips Towers, Suite 210, 13478 Benson Road, Chicago, Illinois.

Rotenone Publishers? Chicago? Never heard of it. McLaughlin. Why does that ring a bell. McLaughlin. Have I met any McLaughlins in Uncertain? Charles, the guy down at Hum's all the time? What's his last name?

Lah-lots of questions.

You are absolutely no help, Bob.

I-I-I know something ya-you don't know.

Not by God likely.

I swear Bob started whistling *Bridge Over the River Kwai*.

I hate you when you think you're being clever.

Wah-one of us has tah-to be.

What am I missing here?

Eh-eh-everything.

What? A letter from somebody named McLaughlin from some publishing house in Chicago. What am I missing? McLaughlin. Where have I heard that name?

It wasn't a bolt of lightning that torched my brain into recognition mode. It was more like a blinking light at a mental four-way stop.

I hustled back to Widder's bedroom, turned on the light and stared at the bookshelves. Walking directly to the section holding the romance novels, I studied the books:

Georgia Hellion, C.C. McLaughlin, Rotenone Publishers.

South Pacific Hellion, C.C. McLaughlin, Rotenone Publishers.

The Art of Writing Romance Novels, C.C. McLaughlin, Rotenone Publishers.

I counted thirty-seven romance novelettes, plus three how-to books listing C.C. McLaughlin as the author.

Widder is C.C.? That can't be right?

Yah-you are such an eh-idiot.

That's an old line, Bob, and getting a bit worn.

Bah-but no less trah-true.

This has been my day to butt heads with logic. And Bob.

The loses were adding up fast.

I turned on Widder's computer, accessed Google and typed in *C.C. McLaughlin*. Access to 1,317 site links popped up. Most of the ones I clicked on were for specific books and were simply links to book outlets, *wal-mart.com* to *barnesandnoble.com* to eBay. In none of the ten or twelve sites I went was there a single picture of the noted—and as several sites made note of—award-winning romance novel writer.

A search for Rotenone Publishers was what I expected: It was second-tier publishing house, mainly set up to turn out paperbacks of specific genre—romance, stories of valor and glory set in medieval or Old West times and mass-produced short science-fiction pieces.

After sitting there for a time staring alternatively at the screen and the book shelves, I closed out the Internet program and had just clicked on the File name to power down when I noticed a icon header right under the icon named "hard drive."

It was named simply "ideas."

Bob was working up to a good stutter when I clicked on it and a page of type popped up. No header. Just copy.

The first few lines snapped me like a wet towel in the boys' locker room.

"First Draft—Rance and Kat"

"That's a tickle tongue tree," Rance said, pointing to a short, barrel-topped tree at the edge of the forest.

"You're pulling my leg," Kat said, still staring at the tree.

"No, not now. Maybe later. It's called different things, toothache tree for one, but the common name is tickle tongue."

"I've lived in this area my whole life. I've never heard of a tickle tongue tree."

"I don't doubt it," Rance said, taking off his hat and wiping the inside band to get rid of the sweat. "There used to be a lot of them in this

area before the settlers came. Folks don't like them because of the short, sharp thorns all over the tree. Instead of just getting pricked occasionally and dealing with it, they just cut 'im down."

The euphemism didn't slide by Kat and she felt a growing heat running up her ribcage and chest. She could feel her neck flush and she prayed it would not go up into her face.

"Why tickle tongue?" she said, surprised that her voice seemed strong and clear.

Rance got down off his horse and went around Kat's horse. His arms reached up to her. "Here, I'll show you."

Instinctively, she reached down and put her arms around his neck, before unhooking her left knee from the big curved horn of the sidesaddle. The horn scraped against her thigh and she momentarily felt a tingle…as she sometimes did when dismounting.

Rance put his arms around her waist and she slid to the ground. Almost to the ground. Rance held her tightly to his chest, so tight that she had trouble breathing. Her feet dangled about a foot above the short prairie grass; her breasts were smashed against his hard chest. She felt herself getting aroused, willed the feelings to stop, and failed in the attempt.

Slowly, ever so slowly, Rance let her slide down his body to the ground, dropped his hands from around her waist and walked away toward the tree.

She took a step and stumbled, quickly regaining her balance, but not quickly enough for Rance to miss the misstep as he watched her over his shoulder. He smiled and kept walking.

Bastard! Kat thought, picking up the hem of her long dress and following along behind him. How she wished she had on jeans, work shirt and cowboy boots, her regular garb instead of the store-bought clothes her mother made her wear. As it was, she didn't wear half of the undergarments that came with the dress. Kat couldn't imagine how women survived in the Arizona heat wearing three layers of undergarments plus a dress that had to weight as much as a saddle.

By the time she had gotten to the tree, slightly twisting her ankle in *the process when one of the fancy high-heel boots got caught in a clump of sage grass, Rance had already broken off a short, wide-based thorn.*

"Stick out your tongue," he said.

She did, but jerked it right back in.

"'If you don't stick out your tongue, I'll have to give you a spankin'," Rance said, grinning.

While that idea intrigued her, she stuck out her tongue and this time she kept it out. Rance touched the broken side of the thorn to her tongue and rubbed it back and forth then tossed the short, sharp spiny thorn aside.

A few seconds later she said: "It's tingling!"

"Told you. Tickle tongue."

Rance explained that all parts of the tree are poisonous if ingested but merely rubbing a thorn's backside against her tongue did not contain enough poison to matter.

"Indian women would take a bunch of thorns and grind them up and make a poultice, to use on wounds and even on large bruises. It's especially useful for toothaches."

I stopped reading and sat staring at the screen.

A cloud-thought passed behind my eyes and I went to the "Favorites" icon and scrolled down the list until I saw: PRWA. I moused it and a very professional Web page popped up: "Professional Romance Writers of America, Inc." It didn't take much imagination to type in *C.C. McLaughlin* in the space provided and hit "go." The screen filled with a short bio of the organization's treasurer—and a professional portrait of Widder. I couldn't help thinking that the right spotlight was too high, casting a slight shadow on the right side of her nose.

The realization hit me like a bowling ball in the pocket: Widder is C.C. McLaughlin, writer of romance novels, pastoral artist and breaker of hearts. A creative, deceitful hermit, she isolates herself in a backwater town at the end of a paved road and lives her fantasies through fictional characters in romance novels.

Mah-maybe you're reading too much into eh-it.

No, Bob. I don't think so.

Hah-how do you fah-feel about....?

Sad, Bob. I feel sad. And you know something else, I don't want to be Rance.

Nah-now I know yah-you're reading too much into eh-it.

It was getting late and I was hungry but I wasn't up to another night of entertainment at Hum's. After looking in the refrigerator at all the goodies to choose from, I headed to Hum's.

At Hum's, a group of men were serving as sit-down doormen and they waved and hi-ed me as soon as I stepped foot from the Jeep.

One man said, "I don't thank we've met, but I'm Jim Williams. Everybody calls me King. 'Everybody' includes you."

"Thank you, King. I'll bet there's a story behind the name, right?"

"Son, they's a story behind everything. Mine's short-like. Back in the 'fiftys, I was on the rassling circuit for a spell. Went by the name The Kountry King, with a 'K' where the 'C' should be in Kountry," he said.

Thompson piped in, "He was a good one. I went all the way to Natchitoches to watch him rassle once. He woulda won too, if that referee had of been honest."

King stood up and shook my hand and said, "Folks said you tell a pretty mean story. If you got a minute, can you spin a yarn?"

I looked around the porch and saw only men folks; no cars pulling up in the parking lot either.

"How about a poem instead?"

"A poem?" King said. "You mean like on the board?"

"Not exactly. I don't think this poem would do for the board, if you know what I mean. Ready?"

Hatsful of nods urged me on.

It was very dark, the moon was high.
We were all alone, just she and I.
Her hair was soft, her eyes were brown,
I touched her leg, she made a soft, soft sound.
Her skin so soft, her legs so fine,
I ran my hand along her spine.

UNCERTAIN TIMES

I didn't know how but I tried my best.
I started by placing fingers upon her breast.

Pausing to look around and seeing no women within earshot, I continued:

I remember my fear, my fast-beating heart,
Slowly she spread her legs apart.
I started quickly and felt no shame
When all at once the white stuff came.

I paused again, letting the tension build.
Yah-you're having way tah-too much fun.

At last it's over, it's finished now,
My first time ever,

Long pause.

Of milking a cow.

Stone cold silence. Then Thompson guffawed and what followed sounded like a mass dust mote attack at the Allergy Testing Institute.

Five or six diners inside the café got up and came to the door to see what was going on. I was standing against a post and shrugged my shoulders with raised palms up. Without another word, I opened the door, walked to the counter, sat down and ordered the Friday Night Special—catfish, jalapeno hushpuppies, French fries and cold slaw. Plus ice tea served in a Mason jar.

After cleaning the platter and talking to half the people at Hum's I made it home by 8:30.

There was a half-full bottle of Alice White in the fridge, so I dolloped some in a peanut butter jar wine glass and walked outside toward the lake.

I leaned against the tree and thought about Widder and C.C. and Rance and Lance and Molly and Kat and tingle tongue trees and writing and painting and hermiting and teasing and the sheriff and Harmony and Bother. I was trying to figure out what went where and what to do about all of it.

All I was figure out that drinking Australian shiraz and thinking crazy-quilt thoughts would give you a headache just one sharp pain short of a light-flashing migraine.

An hour later I was in bed, asleep and dreaming about a time when the hardest thing I had to do was try and lie my way out of a good idea gone bad.

It was a summer Saturday morning in East Texas. 1957. Early. About nine. The temperature was already scrapping the bottom side of ninety and there was high humidity to boot.

I was at Turnip Melbrook's, which is usually where I was on most Saturdays during nine months and just every day in the summer. Turnip, his mama and his sister lived in a big yellow-brick house on Highway 67. It was one of the fanciest houses in town; it had a circular driveway and was one of only three houses in town with a separate garage with an apartment over the garage.

I liked going there because I could get away from my sister, who was six years younger and loved me so much she made me sick. Her idea of having fun was following me around and asking questions like:

"Why's the sky blue?"

"Do eggs really come out of chicken's butts?"

"Wanna see me do an imitation of a dog with its foot caught in a skunk trap?"

This particular Saturday was already heading toward boring. We thought about going down to the tomato sheds and fighting wasps and hornets but we had done that twice already this week and we both had gotten stung and Joe had gotten in trouble. Turnip was allergic to wasp and hornet stings and earlier in the summer he had gotten stung right between the eyes by a big hornet and his face swelled up so much he couldn't see. It looked like to me he was trying to explode. His mama Beulah Mather Mae told me not to laugh when I went to check on him after the hornet attack. "Yes ma'am," I said and walked into the room where he was convalescing. I laughed so hard I nearly busted a gut. She politely asked me to go home and don't come back until I quit making fun of her son.

I thought that meant never. We made fun of each other all the time.

"Whatta you wanna do?" I said.

"I don't know. Whatta you wanna do?"

"Let's go up on your garage apartment roof and hold four ends of a sheet and jump off," I said.

"Let's don't. You may feel like a whipping but I don't."

I looked at that roof and said, "Let's make a parachute and throw stuff off and watch it float to the ground."

Now we had a plan. Turnip went in the house to find an old sheet but his mama stopped in as he was digging in a hall closet and, upon hearing our plan, she said she would help us make a parachute. That woman could sure sew. In five minutes, she had taken four old handkerchiefs and sewed them together to make a nice-sized square. Then she took some heavy darning thread and made four connecting lines from the four corners; to that she sewed on a lightweight fabric belt cut way down until it was about five inches in diameter, when fastened.

"Think that'll work?" she said, handing Turnip the contraption.

"Oh, my gosh, yes!" I said. "It's perfect!"

"Be careful and don't fall off the roof!" she said, in the weird form of mother-speak universally used.

After getting out a ladder hanging on the garage wall and putting it on the landing to the entrance of the garage apartment, we took a softball, a football and a school book Turnip had forgotten to turn in at the end of school, and carted them to the garage roof.

We both climbed up on the roof, latched in the softball and, since it was his roof, Turnip tossed it off the apex of the roof.

The feeling we had was like NASA officials on the first space shot: Euphoria.

Then it dawned on us that both of us were on the roof and the parachute was on the ground. Plan B was that one of us would be on the ground at all times, catching the objects and seeing that they would get back to the roof. Each launcher would get five drops and then switch positions with the ground crew.

For the next two hours we tossed everything off that roof from his sister Slyverne's Betsy Wetsy doll to twenty Army men all scrunched together in the belt harness to a stuffed squirrel that belonged to his grandfather.

The mistake was coming to a group decision to launch the family cat.

Turnip's mama had gone to town and, when confronted later, he said parachuting the cat was my idea to keep from getting the holy tar beaten out of him. I said it was his idea to keep from getting the holy tar beaten out of me. In the end, we both lost a considerable amount of holy tar.

The family's white cat was called Snowy. She was white. The Melbrooks were short on creativity. We quickly fitted her in the little harness. An argument ensued about who was going to throw her off the roof first. It was his cat but it was my turn. We compromised: Both would go on the roof and toss the cat off.

Snowy went up to the roof willingly and didn't even shy away when we were on the roof. She got a mite miffed when we held her over the edge and got a dew claw into Turnip's hand just as we chunked her up in the air a bit. The parachute opened and the cat literally floated to the ground. She hit softly. Then took off lickety-split under the house, dragging our parachute with her.

It took us forty-five minutes to catch the stupid cat. We finally had to corral her in one corner of the pier-and-beam house and Turnip had to hold her close to keep her from scratching. Once outside, she calmed down and we proceed to map out Launch Two. This time I was to go to the roof and toss Snowy into the air. Since we did not want to spend the rest of the day crawling under the house chasing a parachute-dragging cat, Turnip would catch it before it hit the ground running.

Snowy again went up on the roof willingly but started to fight and spit more than a little when I got her over the edge of the roof. After getting a couple of minor scrapes, I tossed her into the hot, humid East Texas air.

Somewhere between the launching station and the landing zone, Snowy came up with four tiny, operational chain saws. When she hit Turnip's hands, she started at his fingertips, sawed her way up his arms, up his face, over his head and down his back…and ran under the house with the parachute.

From my vantage point on the roof, I could see Joe standing in the same spot, arms outstretched, silent. "Turnip, are you okay?"

He turned his face toward me and my first thought was, "We going to get the holy tar beat out of us!"

His face was a thin red mask of blood. There was blood running down his arms, neck, and his back.

As I ran to get off the roof, Turnip started to bawl. Not cry. Not whimper. Bawl. When I got to his side, I didn't have a clue what to do. I ran over to the outside water faucet and turned on the hose, put my thumb in the end and sprayed him down. Twice. I could then see the cuts, which were too many to count—stalks in a cornfield.

"What're we gonna do?" I asked him. "What're we gonna do?" he asked me. We finally agreed to go to his bathroom where I used an entire box of G.I. Joe Band-Aids in an attempt to stop the bleeding.

I heard his mama's car in the driveway. I ducked out the backdoor, saying, "See you tomorrow. I had fun. Bye!"

By the time I had gone the mile across town to my house, Turnip's mama had already talked to my mama. After careful consideration and discussion, we scheduled my whipping for about 6:15 when Dad got home for supper.

That night, just before Dad gave me the first lick with the belt, I said, "Why am I getting a whipping? It was Turnip's garage, Turnip's cat, and Turnip's mama sewed the durn handkerchiefs to make the parachute. What did I do to deserve a whipping? I'm the one who saved his life by spraying him down and doctoring him!"

I can still remember that first lick. I can still remember thinking on-the-jump, as it were, that somebody should be whipping Turnip's mama for being such a helpful woman.

39

When a scary illusion becomes reality, it's time to run like a bunny...or just sit back and enjoy the show.

Anonymous

Sunday I was out in the blind by 6:20, had some yowee! pictures by 7:10 and was heading back to town by 7:45. I hadn't gone by the Poem Board that morning; the appointment with fuzzyheaded baby snakebirds with the sun highlighting them in a golden glow was the day's priority. The sun, birds and camera cooperated, which is a clear recipe to making for a happy nature photographer.

Hum's was closed on Sunday, so I went by the Photo Board, snapped a couple of pictures, wrote down the words, which were, I thought at first read, a rather pedestrian effort.

If life were depicted in colors alone
I would want my life to be:
Pennants at a used car lot
Golf pants
A ferris wheel bedecked in neon
A jigsaw puzzle of a yellow submarine
An explosion at Sherwin Williams

Tammy Faye Bakker's eye shadow
Kilts at a gathering of the clan
Sam Peckinpaugh's rendition of a bloody fight
A New Mexico license plate
A Christmas bag of M&Ms
A child's smile after finishing a candied apple

I-I like tha-this one.

I liked the part about Tammy Faye and the child's smile. Deep but simplistic verbiage.

Back at the house, I had a bowl of Cheerios with some milk just on the okay side of "blinked," and called Doc's house to check on Moose, but had to leave a message. I couldn't force myself to say "Geetchie, geetchie, goo" or whatever the vet-to-dog translation was, so I just said, "Doc, Adj. Just calling to check on Moosie. No need to call back. Will come in early next week and replenish dog treats." I was missing Moosie. I wonder if she was missing me.

I went over to Widder's to take back *Texas Hellion* and check the email, No new messages.

After putting *Texas* back in its place, I picked up *Alaskan Hellion*, read a half-page near the middle, put it back and went home. With time to kill and wishing some of it would simply die, I pulled out the big fireproof trunk under the bed and picked up all the proof sheets of previous shoots on Caddo. I had already marked more than a hundred in red grease pencil, but it was always a good exercise to go back and look at the rejects from the first cut to make sure I didn't miss something special in my excitement about another shot.

This time it proved to be a rewarding two hours. I found two photos that had been essentially culled that now, after a second review, seemed not only worth of consideration for the book, but with just a little tweaking of light-and-shadows in PhotoShop, would be outstanding pictures.

I'm not one of those liberal-lens purists that scream about the vile aspects of darkroom or computer-generated enhancements to make photos better. Any ethical photographer would never subtract or add crucial elements to a photo and claim the finished product was authentic. But photographers for generations have been using various techniques to "create" better photos, more acceptable photos, including using less light or more light in the darkroom to add character to background or accentuate a certain portion of the photograph.

In every book I've ever published, there is a disclaimer—not in small type—that not only acknowledges enhancement of photographs via lighting techniques, but celebrates it.

One of the photos I missed on the first day was a picture of a bald eagle landing on a top-of-the-tree perch. A closer look with the loupe disclosed a small fish hanging in the bird's left talon. It would replace a picture of the same eagle, wings spread, simply standing on the edge of the nest.

The other was of a nutria. In the original scan of the proofs, I didn't even see the giant water rodent. I was shooting a relative close-up of a blooming water hyacinth, and just as I released the shutter, the nutria bobbed to the surface on the other side of the plant. I now saw that just his eyes, nose and whiskers were visible. Blown up over a centerfold in a tabletop book, it would be an awesome shot.

Sometime after noon, I started to head out and just drive around with my windows down and see what I could see. I had the envelopes with Jeb's and Thompson's photos just in case I ran into them. Just I opened the front door, Thompson drove up in his old pickup and I went out and handed him the envelope containing his pictures.

He didn't say a word, just nodded and opened the envelope and slipped out the photos. He went through them slowly, then went through me again.

"Much obliged," he said, not looking me in the eye. "Didn't know I could look that good." He said, "much obliged" twice more, then backed out of the driveway and headed toward down.

Hah-he liked tha-them.

I think so, Bob. I definitely think so.

With absolutely nothing else to do and without the desire to do it if I had something to do, I drove the entire circuit of the lake, stopped on the east side in Louisiana. I took some photos of some kids jumping out of a huge cypress tree on a rope and flying through hanging tendrils of Spanish moss before letting go of the rope and hitting the water. I crossed a one-lane bridge on a back road short cut and caught a deer drinking at the edge of the lake. With the 500 mm. lens it was if I stood right next to the smallish, four-point buck and cracked off a nice shot as he raised his head quickly, water dripping from his face. The buck was in subdued light, and even with the brackish water, the mirror reflection was rippled in an interesting way.

I was back home in three hours. There was a note on the door from Joe B.B. wanting to know if "me and the Missus and the kids" can get "a pitcher took" like Thompson.

I spent the rest of the afternoon acting like a dog with worms, dragging its butt around on a shag carpet. I was tired, depressed, and sad, not necessarily in that order.

I went to bed early, popping a couple of Tylenol PM's just in case sleep was planning on being elusive.

When I woke up on Monday morning, I didn't remember dreaming and Bob *thought tha-that was uh-unusual*.

I was fine with that. With the way I felt, I figured if I dreamed it would be about Jason or Chuckie or even a maniacal alter ego that stuttered while chopping up my psyche with a miniature broad axe.

Bob didn't see the humor in the imagery.

I was standing on the front porch when Jeb pulled up in his truck. I was traveling light this morning, just two cameras, a single dry box and a small waterproof—water-resistant, according to the label—backpack. In the backpack was enough food and water for two days.

We did the expected man-thing—"Yo, Hoss!," "Yo, Man!"—and I put everything but the cameras in the back of the truck, next to what looked like a brand-new climbing deer stand. I put the envelope with his photos on the dash and told him to look at them when he got back to town. He looked at the envelope, then at me, and nodded.

"That bad, huh?" Jeb said.

"Nope, that good. I don't want you hugging me and crying and slobbering all over the place."

"That wouldn't happen even if them was nekkid pitchers of Annette Funicello."

Annette Funicello?

Mah-mickey Mah-mouse Club.

I know who she is, Bob. I didn't know anyone else still had a crush on her. Jesus!

Within thirty minutes Jeb had pulled the boat into the clearing with the beaver lodge and picked out a likely tree for the stand. I had used a variety of tree stands over the years and if there was a part of the job I hated worse than being beaten with a creosoted cross-tie, this was it. Sitting in a tree stand for a day or two is not my idea of having a good time.

Jeb secured the stand to the tree, and even though I knew how they worked, I let him instruct me on how to "walk" it up the trunk, without comment. The stand was positioned on the side of the tree away from the lodge; I hoped the tree would hide me from the beavers but still allow me to lean and shoot from around the sides.

Of all the stands I had ever used, this one was by far the best. A simple lift-stand maneuver was all that was required to ratchet the stand up the tree, about twelve to eighteen inches at a time. When I was up about fifteen feet, I had a perfect, unobstructed view of the entire clearing. The dry box and backpack were secured to the bottom of the stand by ropes; to get them, all I had to do was lean slightly left or right and pull them up with the ropes.

"What time you want me back, Mr. Jones?"

"I'll probably be here for a couple of days. How about five o'clock tomorrow afternoon?"

"Why don't I stop by this afternoon just in case?"

I knew from past experience that beavers spook easily when their working or living areas were disturbed. But when things settle back down, they are usually back at work in short order.

"Five o'clock today, then."

"I'll be here." Jeb turned the boat around and was gone.

I scrunched around, trying to get comfortable and brought up the backpack and got a half-liter bottle of water out and took a drink. Jeb hadn't been gone five minutes when I heard a slight noise and stuck my head around the right side of the tree. A beaver had surfaced near the lodge and was obviously checking out the surroundings. I unlimbered Betsy from where she was hanging from my left shoulder and the fifty mm. pulled me in close. The beaver's head almost filled the camera's entire frame. Just as I was ready to shoot two smaller beaver heads popped up, both to the right of the adult. I cranked off two shots that I knew were going to vie for prime positioning in the photo story of Caddo.

Even though the noise from the camera shutter was not loud, all three beavers nose-dived and I shot one more shot as their rear-ends were submerging.

I blew out a breath, having forgotten to breathe for a while. That third shot, if I got it, would vie for the cover with the photos of Maude and Harold and the baby cormorants and the close-up of the alligator's head.

Dah-don't count your bah-beavers....

It's too early, Bob. Let me live in my own perfect-picture fantasy world for a while.

It wasn't ten minutes before the beavers reappeared. Four this time, two adults and two babies and they went about their business like nothing had ever disturbed them. Within the next three hours I got three great shots: One of the two babies sitting on the side of the lodge, facing each other and gnawing the bark off some fresh limbs; another of what I took to be the daddy beaver putting a new limb in the lodge; and, an extreme close-up of mama-beaver gnawing down a small tree, her long, brownish teeth glistening as she chiseled away. In that last photo, I could count her whiskers and see splashes of tartar on the huge front cutting teeth.

It wasn't even ten and I already had some of the best photos shot the entire time in Uncertain. Seven hours until pickup time. For the next several hours, I just burned film, as a mentor once called it, shooting everything that moved and some things that didn't.

After a while I got tired of shooting close-ups of leaves and common wrens, flycatchers, and jaybirds. I knew I had a return trip to look forward to in the fall to get the onslaught of wood ducks, mallards, snow geese and coots that fell out of the sky in November and December, using the lake as a rest stop on their way further south. Caddo Lake became a hunters' hot bed during that time and shotgun toters from four states tried to get the variety of ducks to fall out of the sky on purpose.

I had been avoiding thinking about Widder and Harmony and Bother and Sheriff Whittle. But an excess of time has always tended to flood my mind with bothersome things; that's why I always try and stay busy. This particular tree stand was designed so it was possible for the occupant to actually stand and stretch, and I had to do that occasionally because the seat edge tended to cut off circulation to my legs. There was a safety chain that went around the sides and front. In addition, the tree served as a nice backstop to a possible header with two half-twists out of the stand.

It has been my pleasure and my pain to be stuck in awkward surroundings for days at a time and I have invented ploys, solutions, and games for being different aspects of a lengthy stalk in a hide. Old Crown Royal bags can be used to keep metal items for banging together; gray tape works just as well. Some long-term photogs have perfected the art of urinating in a plastic bottle carried expressly for that purpose. I've done that many times, but, depending on the surroundings, I have found that peeing *down* a tree truck is quiet and is a way to guarantee your penis does not get *appendagacus claustrophobicus* by having its little head and neck stuck in a small bottle opening.

Having nothing else to do since the beavers were into heavily repetition mode—go here, go there, see a limb, chew it, go here, go there—I stood up, stretched and peed down the tree trunk.

I had no more than gotten seated when the beaver I had tabbed as the male stopped what he was doing, which was chewing a small limb in preparation to *go there*, and stared in my general direction.

He swam over to the tree and stopped directly under my perch. He sniffed, wrinkled his nose and sniffed again, this time wrinkling his nose until his front teeth were bared. He then dove into the water at the base of the tree, resurfaced, dove again and then came up and settled on a large trunk flange growing out of the side of the tree. I grabbed Gertie with the 300 mm., focused and waited. The beaver stood stock still for about 15 seconds. Not a muscle moved. Not a twitch.

Then the beaver rolled over onto its back and started wallowing around in the general vicinity of where my urine entered the water. And then it started slapping its tail. I snapped eight quick shots and knew in that bunch I had some keepers. The beaver's front paws were curled up like a baby's hands, its eyes closed, its back paws were stuck straight out behind it. Water splashed up the tail would come across as still droplets in the air; the tail would be partially below the water level but still totally visible.

Yah-you nailed that wah-one.

Yes, Bob, I did. And I know what the cutline will say: The Power of Pee.

I ate a can of Vienna sausages with some fairly fresh crackers and washed it down with a slug of water from a plastic squeeze bottle. I've never been particularly fond of Vienna sausages. They remind me of the tiny red dicks on little, snuffling, lap-sitting dogs. But I was in a foul mood, so I punished myself by eating a second can.

It was still more than four hours until Jeb was due back so I slid down in the tree stand seat, crossed my arms and let the warming early afternoon sun do its magic.

I was peddling my red-and-white Schwinn hard down Texas Farm-to-Market-Road 2198. I was about half-way to Lydia, Texas, a small crossroads eight miles south of my house. I was in a hurry. I was thirteen and in love.

Lydia was the home of the Slocum sisters, four of the prettiest girls ever to set foot in East Texas. There was Beatrice June, Wayvonne Jewel, Selma Jimmie and Merle Jean. Merle Jean was thirteen, the youngest, and has just graduated into courting-size. We were in seventh grade together and with the Slocum sisters it never hurt to get in the courting line early. The competition in rural East Texas was fierce. Four knock-down-gorgeous sisters were hot commodities in a small population county.

The eight-mile bike ride was a breeze. When you're in love, distance doesn't matter. Lust is fuel and power for any journey.

Ty Cobb Slocum was sitting in a swing on the porch of a dog-run, shotgun-style house, swinging and watching me approach. Ty Cobb was a local legend back in the '60s. There was a rumor he had tried professional baseball for a while, but got kidded out because of his name. He was mostly known as a professional "noodler." He jumped in the Red River that separated the north part of Red River County and Oklahoma and "noodled" for catfish. I've since learned that in other parts of the South, this weird practice is called "hogging" or "grappling." It is an activity that requires a human being to go underwater and grope around in submerged logs or holes in river or lake banks until they encounter a catfish and then stick a hand and arm so far back in the fish's mouth they can grab them by the gills and haul them out.

Dad called it "shit-crazy hand-fishing."

Ty Cobb also went frog-gigging down on Sulphur River and it was rumored he sold frog legs to fancy restaurants in Texarkana and Marshall. All both of them.

"Good morning, Mr. Ty Cobb," I said in my best be-nice-to-the-parent voice.

He didn't say a word, just rocked.

"Is Merle Jean at home?"

"And what if she is?"

"Well, I'd like to see her."

"How old a boy are you?"

"Thirteen, sir."

"Same age as Merle Jean," he said.

"Yes sir, we're in the same grade at school."

"Come back when you're sixteen."

"Sir?"

"Come back when you're sixteen. Don't allow no hairlegs around my daughters till they sixteen."

Hairlegs?

"Sir," I said, "I rode my bike out here. Eight miles from town. I'd sure like to see Merle Jean."

"How long did it take you?"

"Less than an hour."

"Take you the same time to get home. Now get!"

I got.

Three years later, I drove up to the Slocum house in my 'fifty-six

Ford and Ty Cobb walked out the door just as my foot hit the bottom step.

"Mr. Slocum," I said, "I'm Adnijio Benjamin Franklin Jones and I'm here to ask your permission to take Merle Jean to the movies in Clarksville. I was here three years ago on my bicycle and you told me to come back in three years. It's been three years. I'm back."

He glared mean at me, then his eyes softened. "She and her mama done talked to me about it. It seems like a nice thing to be doing on a nice night like this. What time do you plan on getting her home?"

"What time do you want her home, sir?"

"Good question. I like that. Ten o'clock. Not a minute later."

"Yes, sir. No problem." Actually there was a major problem. The movie wouldn't let out until about nine and Clarksville was a good thirty-five minutes away and that estimate included taking Ninety-Mile-an-Hour Corner at about ninety-five. That timetable would cut heavily into PP time—parking and petting.

"Come with me," he said, and walked around the corner of the house.

He led me around the house and through a latched gate to a tree about thirty yards from the back of the house. Under the tree, there was a hole that contained more big bullfrogs than I had ever seen in one place.

"You mistreat Merle Jean, you try and fool around, you touch her anywhere but her elbow helping her in and out of your card, you get her home one minute past ten, and I will by God head-daub you in that mess of frogs."

I dropped Barbara at her house on our one and only date at 9:40. Didn't touch her elbow neither, thinking I might miss the mark by accident.

All I could think about during the showing of *"Sink the Bismarck"* was what I would look like with a faceful of frog-piss warts.

The sound of a motorboat snapped me out of my nap and I looked up just in time to see Jeb turn down the small channel.

It took more time to get down from the tree stand than it did to get up. My legs had just fallen asleep. My butt had died.

Twenty minutes later all the gear was stowed and while we worked, I described the beaver photos to Jeb. He didn't say much. As we started to pull out, he said, "Widder's home."

For just a split second I felt like I was falling in a pit full of frogs.

Jeb dropped me by the house and I carried my cameras, ammo box, and backpack to the porch. I pulled up opening the screen door when I saw Widder come out on her porch. I waved and she motioned me over.

I could tell something was up. Her arms were crossed, her left hip was jutted out and she was tapping her right foot. The international signals for a pissed-off member of the feminine gender.

"Hi! Welcome home! Did you have a good time?" I said as I walked up her path.

"Why did you tell Thompson you had seen me sunbathing nude?"

Any psychologist worth his or her salt will tell you that starting off a conversation with a "why" question is guaranteed put the other person on the defensive. I started to relate that fact to Widder but the look on her face automatically closed off that avenue of conversation.

"I didn't tell Thompson I had seen you sunbathing nude. I was taking Thompson's picture by the tree in my backyard and every time I'd get ready to shoot a frame, he would get this weird grin on his face and I was trying to throw him a mental curve ball. No pun, or puns, intended."

"You told him you had seen me naked." A statement.

"Not true. Someone else in town asked me if I had ever seen you nude...."

"Jeb."

"Yeah, him." (Damn! This *is* a small town.) "And I said, 'only in my mind.'"

Silence. But the arms uncrossed, the hip unjutted and the foot stopped tapping.

"You told him that?" Widder said.

"If you don't believe me, ask Bob," I said.

That got a smile out of her. My brain gave my ass permission to move from "attention" to "at ease."

She invited me in for a cup of coffee and she spent the next hour talking about New York and the gallery, the showing, blah, blah, blah.

I was trying to concentrate but I was as fidgety as a front row member of the audience at a flea circus where half the performers decided to go on the lam.

"What's the matter with you?" Widder said.

"Nothing, C.C. It's just that, well, why didn't you tell me you were C.C. McLaughlin, famous romance writer."

"Hah-how...? Wha-what...? How...."

"You're starting to sound like Bob," I said. "I was using your computer and saw your books on the shelf and then did some research and figured it out."

Yah-you looked at her mah-mail!

Research! Gawddammit! It falls under the category of research!

"What did Bob just say?" Widder asked.

"He said he's glad you're home. C.C., you didn't have to lie about having a show of your paintings. If you are a romance writer, that's great. You could have told me that."

She got up from the table, walked to the coffee pot and warmed up her cup. She didn't offer to warm up my dregs.

"Why do you think I lied to you?"

"Why" again? Somebody needs to talk to her about that.

Yah-you're doing such a gah-good job.

"I think you were embarrassed," I said.

"Embarrassed? About what?" she said.

"Lance and Rance and Molly and Kat and all the other characters with manly-man and slutty-slut names. The only people who read that stuff are...." Her roadrunner eyes told me that I was on the edge of the cliff with one foot in midair.

"Are what?" The look intensified. I was Wile E. Coyote and I was *going down*.

Tah-tell her what yah-you used her bah-book for.

She said, "What did Bob just say?"

I ignored the question and opted for pure panic mode. "I'm sorry, Widder. I was talking without thinking. I'm sure there are some intelligent people who do enjoy the escapism of a well-written romance novel."

"Some intelligent people?" she said. "Is that what you think? That I write grabbie-feelie drivel for fat housewives and truck drivers with holes in their shirts who sit around in their trailers and get busy with their own personal version of the Mother-Thumb-and-her-four-daughters hand jive from reading my books in between watching Jerry Springer and Judge Judy? Is that what you think I do?"

She was no longer mad. She had just graduated to royally pissed.

Mother Thumb and her four daughters?

Then, she said, "I think you better leave."

I didn't budge until she walked by me, went to the front door, opened it and pointed to the outside.

On the short walk home I wondered how did this hole get so deep and who dug it?

Wah-one-man job. Gah-guess who?

Stuck in my door were two envelopes, one from Harlan, the other from Hy. Both wanted to know if I would shoot pictures of them and their families.

Jesus!

Trying to cheer me up, Bob did his best Stan Laurel impression: *Ah-another fine mess yah-you've gotten us eh-into.*

Grabbing a couple of beers, I headed to the lightning-scarred tree, knowing for the first time how the damn tree felt. And wishing lightning would strike in the same place twice.

Sitting there, sucking on a Mexican-brewed longneck, I knew I should be happy. The photo book was going well; I only had a couple of more shots I really wanted to shoot to complete this cycle. I would be leaving and heading back to Atlanta. Going home. Then after a few, long weeks of editing photos, writing copy and working with various editors to get the entire thing together, I was going to take a month off to sit on a beach somewhere and do nothing. But, then, I had to come back in the fall and gets some seasonal shots.

I should be happy? Right?

Sitting under that tree, for no apparent reason, I started missing Moosie. When she was a baby puppy, not the lumbering steroid dog she is now, I used to hold her close and sing her a song. Still did, on occasion. Without giving it too much thought, I started to sing in a low, medium, quavering baritone:

You are so beautiful
To me.
Can't you see?
You're everything I ever hoped for,
You're everything I ever need.
You are so beautiful
To me.

If I wasn't such a manly man, I swear I could have cried.

"That was nice."

Widder's voice, coming from right next to the tree, scared the gollywads out of me.

"Jesus! Don't sneak up on a fella when he's morosing."

"Do you make up words just because you can? 'Morosing.' Is that a word?" she said.

"It is now." Scooting over to make room for her to use the scar for a backrest. "Care for a beer?"

"Thank you, kind sir. I thought you'd never ask," Widder said.

She eased herself down, settling in, shoulder to shoulder, and took the beer from my hand. We didn't say a word until the beers were simple memories.

"I owe you an apology," she said.

"No, no, you...."

"Please," Widder said, flopping one hand in a gesture that grade school kids all over the world understands means "shut the hell up." "For a long time I have locked myself away in this house, this town, and not allowed myself to…well, live. I was just existing."

She stopped and was silent.

ADHDers hate silence. I felt like a silence was something that needed to be filled by the sound of my voice. "Would you like another beer or glass of wine?" She nodded.

As I jogged to the back door, I thought: "God, I hope I have some wine." I did and less than two minutes later—with half the time used up to wash out two glasses—I was resettled on the ground next to Widder.

"I found myself not doing much, living off insurance money and waiting around for it to run out," she picked up without missing a beat. "I started reading romance novels, mainly Harlequin-type stuff. It was something to do, something to take my mind off my problems and my self-imposed isolation."

I wanted to ask if she ever got excited writing about what Lance did to Molly—every chance he got!—but in this case I gave Mr. Discretion a warm, fuzzy hug and gave Mr. Curiosity a kick in the ass.

She took a sip of wine: "One day I was reading a novel called *Her Name Was Trouble* and realized that I had never read anything that dreadful in my life. 'I can do better than this,' I thought and started writing that day." She took another sip. "Eight days later, I finished the first *Hellion* book and without knowing how anything worked, just mailed it to an editor at Rotenone whose name I had seen in credits for another book. I didn't know that was against protocol and that most books sent in that manner are trashed. Or worse, ignored."

She stopped, glanced and me and wriggled closer, reaching down and holding my hand.

"Long story short: Something in the naïve approach I used in sending the book to the publisher enticed the editor to read it, mark it up, and mail it back with a simple note: "Fix it. Send it back in."

She said the rewrite took a couple of weeks.

"A couple of months later, I signed a contract for five more books. I felt relieved, happy, even. Someone had validated that I was important, that I was worth something. Even if it was writing romance novels."

I started to speak.

"Let me finish," she said. "For a while I was…if not happy, then content. I cranked out the romancers and enjoyed living on the lake. But there was something missing. I knew it but couldn't identify it and worried that if I ever did find out what it was, there was nothing I could do about it."

Another sip of wine and a longer silence. "One day, on a lark, after watching a how-to show on the Public Broadcasting Network on painting, I bought some basic painting supplies and started slapping paint on canvas. I swear it was like God had reached down and touched me and told me this was my gift."

Lah-like Kah-Krispie Kreme.

Jesus! Bob, there's a time and a place for everything and this ain't it.

Widder was looking at me. "Bob?"

"He was comparing your comment about God and painting to Krispie Kreme donuts," I said.

The smile was immediate. Laughter rolled off her lips.

"I really, really like Bob," she said, wiping her eyes. "Oh, where was I? Oh, yeah. So I started weaning my financial dependence from romance novels to paintings. The writing I felt I had to do; the painting I love to do."

Silence. But this time I felt she wanted me to say something.

"You're good. You know that, right?"

"Everything is coming together, actually. The show in New York—and there was a show, by the way—went well. I sold eleven paintings in two days, a record for the gallery. And the owners have commissioned more painting as soon as I can get them up there."

"That's great! Eleven paintings! Not being nosy, but curious, how much do your paintings go for? I've got some collector friends all over the place that would love to have one of your paintings."

"Usually three to six, some higher."

"Whoa, Widder! That seems way too cheap. You are very, very talented and selling your paints for three to six hundred apiece, well, that's...."

"Thousand."

"You have a thousand paintings! That is unbelievable! How...? Where...?"

"Dollars. My paintings are selling from three to six thousand."

"Each?"

She smiled, took a sip of wine, and squeezed my hand.

I did the quick math and whistled softly. Hell, my books only sold from forty to eighty dollars and I only got a small percentage of that. I told Bob to remind me to take up painting.

Bob's stuttering laughter, I thought, was totally inappropriate and certainly nonsupportive.

Widder hopped up and brushed off the seat of her jeans, and held her hand out. "Come on," she said, "I want to show you something."

I grabbed her hand and she helped me off the ground and led me through the back gate to her garage.

I thought to Bob: Six thousand for a painting of a duck, water rat, deer, a couple of trees, stagnant water, and a small chunk of sky? Damn!

The garage was secured with a combination lock and she quickly dialed in a number and stepped inside. She reached around the jam and an inside light popped on.

"Come on it," she said.

I stepped into the room and looked around. The small, single car garage was almost completed filled with homemade shelves and virtually every bit of space in the shelves was filled with competed paintings.

Widder reached up and closed my mouth. "Painting is a mental escape for me. Sometime I need to 'escape' more than at other times."

I gave a "do you mind?" sign and she gave me a "go ahead" nod.

I picked up a painting nearest to me and held it up to allow the most light from the double hanging fluorescent bulbs to hit it. It captured a lone fisherman, sitting in a small, metal boat under a gigantic cypress tree. The water was like a flawless mirror, except in a small circle around the fisherman's cork. He had a nibble! From his relaxed position, I assumed he was asleep; his hat was pulled down over his eyes. The detail in the tree—bark and Spanish moss—was unbelievable. A slight darkening on the base of the tree showed where water had lapped up above the water line when the boat had approached. On the first scan I had not seen the cormorant sitting on a high limb; it was smallish but I could almost count the feathers on its chest.

Without saying a word, I moved from painting to painting, from shelf to shelf, marveling at the technique, the artistry, the unbelievable realism Widder had captured.

"I've said before they are like photographs," I said, turning to her, my eyes filled with admiration. "They are better than that. They are better than photographs because you've captured something alive inside the scenery that photographs can't capture."

She was leaning against a row of shelves, arms crossed and right ankle flopped over her left foot. She was smiling. "I was hoping you'd say that, you silver-tongued devil."

I did my best aw-shucks routine. "Thank ya, ma'am. Please, just call me Rance."

I could tell Widder was tired, so I told her I was really glad she was back and for her to get some sleep.

"I've got an idea for a project that, if I decide to do it, I will need your help," I said.

"What project?"

"Let me think on it tonight and we'll discuss it tomorrow. I've got a few details to work out."

I turned to leave and she said, "Come through the house. I want to give you something."

I followed her through the house to the entryway. She gave me the finger-pointing command to "stay," and I followed the command to the letter. I didn't want any more hip-jutting and foot-tapping from Widder.

A few minutes later she brought out a paperback book and handed it to me. *Stormy Passions*. "A gift, from me to you," she said.

I looked at the back cover and read out loud:

> *Beau is just out of prison and he has no where to go.*
> *Except home and hell, which are both one in the same.*
> *He's got five years of pent-up paybacks and the first on his list is Val, the daughter of the richest man in Randolph County…and the reason he was sent to prison.*
> *Some paybacks are hell. For Beau, this payback is going to be fun and he meant to put Val through Hell.*

I opened the book to see if she had signed it, but she shut the cover and pushed me to the door.

After she finger-waggled a good-bye and shut the door, I stood on her porch and read the writing on the fly cover: "To my own, sweet Beau. Turn to Page 134 and think of me. Val."

As I stepped off the porch I turned to Page 134 and started reading. I read four lines and said aloud, "Frog's a-goshen!"

And I could hear Teasing Tina laughing from inside her locked and secured house.

She was well on the way to giving me a good case of premature exasperation.

40

When somebody hits you in the head and then brags about it later, why do they say they "whipped your ass?

Anonymous

I went down to Hum's to ingest some calories. The usual gaggle of men—Joe B.B., Thompson, Hy and the rest—was sitting on the porch.

"Before you go in, Mr. Jones," Hy said. "Give us just a short story. We just got done listening to one of Rayon's and my ears need cleaning out something terrible."

"Boys," I said, "you don't want to hear a story from me. Heck, all my stories are true and true stories don't hold a candle to a good, well-thought-out lie."

Well, that got them to going and before they started begging too hard, I pulled up an overturned red coke crate and sat down.

"Up in Nevada County, Arkansas, where I grew up there was this man that was a fixture in the community name of Ol' Hugh. Well, Ol' Hugh was a 'mite tetched' as they said back then, and he really was pretty much of a mess. One of his legs was all gimpy-like and he kind of swung it around when he walked. He didn't have any teeth; most of them were knocked out in a logging accident when he was young. The story was that a holding chain snapped and the end link deprived Ol' Hugh of twenty-three of his twenty-eight teeth. He just had the others pulled because he those remaining were 'eating up' his gums, as he told it."

The group was listening intently, pulled in tight. "Ol' Hugh had some rubberized teeth but he only wore them when he ate goober wheels, so it was a big joke for one of the boys to cough up a nickel ever so often and buy a goober wheel and give it to him. He'd say 'Thankee' and reach in his back right hip pocket and haul out those teeth, slap 'em in and start to chipping away at the candy.

"Ol' Hugh was also a story teller, but he really wasn't a very good story teller because he was tongue-tied. His favorite story was about being on the Titanic when it sunk. The fact he had never been out of Nevada County did not deter his enthusiasm for telling the tale. As Ol' Hugh told the story:

"'Dare wah wough ona da beh shippa. Anna da ban wah playyen moothic an da ni wah so cleerer. Den all awf a thudden da wa this louwa nawise and da shippa thopped.'"

"It was always about there," I said, "that one of the men would stop him and say, 'Da shippa thopped?'

"'Itta thopped deadda!' Ol' Hugh would say and the men would laugh and cut up. Then Hugh would continue with the story:

"'I wah on da fron a da shippa and heppa da weemen and kitchs inta da smaa bows. Da ruh outta bows do I jumth in da col wader. Tree das gaw bah fo I wah peeked up by nudder bows. An that's de hoe stowee.'"

"Ol' Hugh also had stories above visiting 'hedhuntoes in da jaggle.' To tell the truth, it was fun listening to Hugh, but you couldn't watch him when he was geared up in story mode. His eyes flitted around like a monarch butterfly having a spasm and, without any teeth, he tended to drool quite a bit," I said.

"Well, there was this one Saturday one of the boys decided to play a joke on Hugh. When he arrived, the man asked him, 'Hugh, which hand do you wipe with after you go to the outhouse?' Hugh just looked at the man, then down at his hands, raised his right hand and said, 'da white wah.' The man laughed and said, 'Dadgummit, Hugh, I use toilet paper.' And the group of men just cackled.

"Well, that was such a good joke that the next week, thinking Ol' Hugh wouldn't remember what happened the previous week, the man asked Hugh again, 'Which hand to you wipe with after you go to the outhouse?' Hugh looked at the man, then down at his hands and said, 'Needah one you damn bool, I uth a torn tob."

That broke up the front porch meeting and while they were still laughing, I went in Hum's and settled at my usual seat at the counter.

"Hmmmm," Hum said in greeting.

"Same back to ya, Hum. Whatever's good, that's what I'm going to have."

A couple of people stopped by and asked if it would be too much trouble for me to shoot a picture of their family and I told them I would be happy to do just that. "We'll get together and work out a time," I told them.

Yah-you got a plah-plan.

You know I've got a plan, Bob. A good one. I'm letting it percolate until it's perfect.

Mah-may not hah-have that long.

I heard a commotion on the front porch and a couple of people inside the café got up and went to the door and looked out. I got up and joined them.

Sheriff Twiddle's car, plus two other county cars were in the lot. There were three deputies standing around; standing at the back of Twiddle's car were Harmony and Bother. Twiddle had Widder backed up against the back right door of his car and his belly was rubbing against her. He had his hands plastered above the rear window, on both sides of Widder; I could see him sliding his fat elbows up and down her arms.

"Excuse me, boys," I said. "Duty calls."

Thompson grabbed me by the arm. "Don't, Mr. Jones. This here is what he wants."

"I know. Excuse me, Thompson. I shouldn't keep the good sheriff waiting."

Bah-bad plan. Wah-worse execution.

I had a plan germinating when I went down the steps, but it started going to seed when I saw Twiddle bend his head like he was going to whisper in Widder's ear. I elbowed my way between the two, facing Widder and said, "C.C., my dear. I'm sure glad you could join...."

I heard a scuffling noise. Then there was a loud noise, a rushing sound, a piercing pain, a bright light, followed by suffocating darkness. After the noise, the sound, the pain and the light, I welcomed the darkness with open arms.

In between the pain and the light, I thought I heard Widder shout something but whatever it was didn't register.

The light! Turn off the light!

There was this light boring through my eyelids that seemed to intensify and focus on the piercing pain at the back of my head. Another bout of darkness descended. I remember being truly thankful.

Later, I heard a voice and tried to open my eyes. I must have cracked one open because I was sure that I saw Doc. What was I doing at Doc's? He's a vet! I must have closed that eye because when I opened it again, I saw Jeb, Harlan, and Thompson. Jeb was moving his mouth but no sound reached me.

I remembered hearing someone saying my name softly and far, far away. I tried to open my eyes. That's the last thing I remember. Trying.

I dreamed that I was the old black man in the famous part animation/part real movie "Song of the South." I was singing "Zippedy Doo-Dah" and had this little cartoon bluebird on my shoulder.

I dreamed about Ann from Annona and Nekkid Nell and Widder and Harmony and Bother and....

"Adj. Adj. Can you hear me?"

I opened my right eye slowly, then opened the left. Too much. Of everything. I shut them both and started over. This time I got them both open and at least one of them stayed that way. Widder was leaning over me and I swear I have never seen anything prettier or smelled anything that good in my entire life.

"Adj, you're in the hospital. You're going to be okay. Harmony slapped you with this big leather thing and...."

"Sah-sap." Jesus, I get hit in the head and start talking like Bob thinks. *Rah-rest, dah-dummy.*

"No, you're not a sap. You tried to protect me and...."

"Nah-no, not me. Tha-the leather thing. A sap."

"Ohhhh. I didn't know that. Sap? Hmmm. Anyway, he sapped you twice before all the men came off the porch. Twiddle and his deputies tossed you unconscious in the back of his car and they drove off."

I tried to raise my head but it was a lost cause. "Did you say Harmony hit me?" I know I was saying the words. But they sounded disjointed and rumbly.

"When you got between Twiddle and me, Harmony ran from the back of the car, carrying the sapping thing and hit you twice, once on the back of your head and then above your ear as you were going down. Twiddle and his men threw you in the back of his car and a couple of deputies made it appear that they were fighting with Harmony to get him in the back of one of the other cars."

She paused for breath and I noticed she was a great breather. When she took deep breaths, she smoothed all the wrinkles out of her blouse.

Yah-you're getting better.

I realized she was holding my hand and I think I squeezed it. "Why...why am I still alive?"

"The men at Hum's all jumped in their trucks and cars and followed the sheriff back in town. He tried to get the other cars to stop them, but they just drove around the cars and followed you all the way to the jail. Someone used a cell hone to call Mitchell at home and he was standing in the jail parking lot when Twiddle pulled up."

She paused to brush a hand across my forehead. "You need to rest."

My eyes were closed, but I gave her the "keep going" hand thing.

She said, "Talk about mad! Mitchell made Twiddle take you to the hospital right then and swore if he didn't he'd call the State Police in to take you. Then he said that charges better be filed against Harmony or there'd be hell to pay. Twiddle was fit to be...."

I instinctively knew I was going to slip away again and be out for a while. I tried to get out "poem board" before the lights went out again and set the stage for a happy, funny....

It was late Sunday afternoon in rural Nevada County and since there were no organized Sunday night church meetings for whites, most folks were content to visit around the community. It wasn't hard to find a good game of Rook—no stakes, no betting—or join a front-porch gabfest to discuss the weather, work, or the business of other neighbors not present at that particular moment.

The more energetic folk, mostly youngsters, teenagers and older men not welcome at just any house, traipsed down the rutted road toward Laneburg and cut through the woods to the backside of the Church of God in Christ church (the COGIC Church, as it was called). The men and boys didn't attend churches services in the traditional way, did not sit in the hand-hewn pews inside the church. The church was segregated...blacks only. The whites watched the goings-on from the outside, standing in the stand of pines and catching the action through the windows.

The whites-only spectators mostly stood just outside the light patterns that blasted through the bottom half of the eighteen-pane windows and arrived about an hour later than the majority of black church-goers. The blacks arrived before dark. They gathered in bunches outside the church to discuss who was seeing whose wife while "whose" was on a chicken haul to Memphis and, who was on a owl-dookey-slick slide to hell for doing whatever particular folks thought was against biblical teachings.

The conversations continued on into the church until the Rev. Leroy Alexander jumped up to the pulpit and asked for silence and opened the service with a rousing prayer. Bro. Leroy's weekday job was at McKittchen's Slaughterhouse in Emmit; he was the head guts bucketer. The work was steady and Bro. Leroy was a respected member of the community, a sentiment shared by blacks and whites alike. As Homer Glenn Whiteman, a pasty-white white man, said, "Ya gotta respect somebody do a job like that."

The main differences in black and white church services in the fifty's were the method of preaching by the preacher and the reaction to it by the women folk. Black women shouted for no apparent reason at all and several would gang up and perform a "group faint" ever so often. Some of the closest menfolk tried to catch the fainters before they banged something vital against a pew or the floor. Others, citing the "Lord's will," let them fall.

As a rule, black preachers did more guttural hollering, more shouting and stomping and used a wide variety of theatrics to whip up emotions and wring participation from the congregation.

Some rural white preachers thought they were the reincarnation of Billy Sunday, sliding down the main aisle screaming they were "safe with the Lord." They were in the minority, so to speak.

Males attending rural churches, black and white, reacted similarly, shouting "Amen!" frequently, and "Oh, yes, Lord!" to a particularly poignant statement by the preacher. Both groups sent staccatos of "Hallelujahs!" during the sermon from official Amen Corners, usually set to the right of the preacher.

In hot weather, in any church, there was constant movement. Cardboard fans, decorated with the smiling faces of white politicians or advertisements for the local funeral home, flittered and flicked. White handkerchiefs, hand-embroidered with colorful designs, fluttered like flags of surrender at a religious battlefest.

Bro. Leroy always took himself some time to rev up his sermon. He started out talking low and quiet-like. Before long the women folk would start a low, eerie, communal moan. The moan increased in volume, riding the rhythm of the sermon like a cork on a choppy lake. It wouldn't take much to set the women off once the preacher got going. A single word emphasized in a phrase—"*JAYsus wants YOU to follow him-ah! Gawd wants YOU to listen to his word-ah!*"—could set off high shrieks and some women would snatch at their breasts as if trying to bare their hearts to the Savior.

On one particular Sunday night, the COGIC church was packed with blacks and the pine thicket was packed with whites. Bro. Leroy was wound up tighter than Dick's hat band, as the saying went. He was giving the devil the dickens. He was talking about sinning and that God didn't like sinners and that sinners ought to get right with God and that God will punish sinners if they don't....

That's when Boy Wilson shook loose from the arm of his wife Blanche, stood up, and called Bro. Leroy a "lyin', sumbitchin' hypocrite."

In half a heartbeat, the moaning of the women stopped, the "amens" dwindled to nothing. Bro. Leroy froze and tried to stare down Boy.

"I ain't gonna call you Brother Leroy," Boy said in a loud voice. "I'm gonna call you Fornicatin' Man 'cause you been diddlin' Blanche and I know what I'm gonna do 'bout it." Blanche let out a wail just as Boy pulled a pistol out of his pocket and aimed it at the preacher.

Bro. Leroy was clutching his Bible to his chest when the first bullet hit the podium. "Oh, Gawd," the preacher said.

The second bullet hit the wall just to the preacher's right. "Gawd save me!" was his plea, as he spread out his arms in the sign of complete surrender.

The next shot hit the Bible, jerking it from Bro. Leroy's right hand.

"Gawddamn!" the preacher said as he dove out an open back window of the church.

All the white men and boys had been watching the tableau as if it was a dream. They weren't a part of it; it was simply something offered up for observation. They suddenly became a part of it when Bro. Leroy ran right into their midst, saw them and screamed. He screamed just like any black man in the 'fiftys would if he ran upon a group of white men standing in the dark just outside an all-black church.

Just then Boy let loose another shot through an open window, the bullet hitting a nearby tree. That caused a general disorganized retreat from the thicket of everyone there…with Bro. Leroy leading the charge-away-from-the-action.

Boy Wilson and Blanche left the county the next day. Bro. Leroy left the night of the shooting; he even left his car at the church and never returned to get it.

After three or four Sundays, a church deacon hotwired it and converted it into a church vehicle. It was used to pick up the elderly parishioners and get them to church, and occasionally to make a deacon-run to a Texarkana all-nudie review.

Miss Lize Murtaugh, an ageless black woman who benefited from the ride to church each week, told the congregation in a general talk-around one Sunday that "Some good can come from bad. Take diddling, for example. By diddling Blanche and going off and leaving his car, Bro. Leroy helped this congregation more than his preaching ever did."

The next time I woke up the room was empty. The sharp pain in my head had settled into a dull, distant ache. After I focused my eyes a bit, I

UNCERTAIN TIMES

punched the call button and a nurse and two Candy Stripers swarmed into the room like locusts in a wheat field.

"Oh, you're awake!"

"It's so good to have you back."

"What can we do for you?"

I managed to croak out, "Water, please."

Before the Candy Striper closest to the water could move, a voice behind them said, "I'll get it, Ladies."

The helpful hospital helpers parted like tangled hair hit with conditioner and a comb. Widder was at the door, dressed demurely in an ankle-length pale pink dress with a white scarf used as a belt. It looked like she was braless because two parts of her were cold. Now I know and appreciate why hospitals are kept chilly. Doctors need diversions, too.

She came over and put her left hand on my head and took my left hand in her right and squeezed.

"Water, please," I croaked again.

She poured some water in a Tommy Tippy-type adult glass and stuck the straw in my mouth. The first sip was too big and I got strangled. Choking and bucking and coughing is not conducive to keeping one's head inert. Some brain matter definitely ran out my right ear onto the pillow.

Widder got a wet wash cloth and wiped my face, leaving it folded over on my forehead. The cloth felt good; her hand on my face felt better.

"How long...."

"Three days. You've been drifting in and out most of the time. Dr. Bledsoe said you had two concussions, but that you're going to be okay."

Three days? How could I have been out three days? I know I thought the words but I don't think I ever got them out before I slipped under that comforting dark blanket and was gone.

Widder was still there—or had come back—when I opened my eyes again. She had on a different outfit—the top had green and white vertical stripes and was at least a size too small—but I couldn't see what she was wearing below the waist. I remember reading that fantasies often aided the recuperative process.

"Welcome back," she said, smiling. "How do you feel?"

"Water, please. Not from the official patient sippy cup but from your lovely hand."

Her laughter was musical. "Oh, you're feeling better all right."

I had closed my eyes just for a short rest when I heard her say, "Water, sir," and I opened my dry lips. I first felt the edge of her hand, then a small trickle of ice-cold water went partially in my mouth, with the rest going off the side of my face to my neck. "Jesus! That's really cold!"

She laughed again and I tried to smile as she dried me off with a soft paper towel.

I rolled my eyes at her and said, "I think that the water went a lot further down than you think. You need to finish the job."

"You *are* definitely feeling better." She said Moosie was fine and the house was still standing and as far as she could tell, all my equipment was still in place. She had checked the mail for me; nothing important that she could see except some bills, which she paid. She said nothing about repayment but I asked Bob to remind me of the debt.

Nah-no problem.

She also taken my cell phone and menu-ed up the number of my agent and advised him of the situation. "Mr. Goodlaw is quite excitable. He was talking about hiring a squad of private bodyguards and filing federal charges against everybody in the county. I think I convinced him to hold off until you can talk to him. He also sent the biggest bouquet of flowers in the history of this part of the country, but they were so pretty I took them home."

"Knowing Mark like I do," I said, "the flowers were probably imported from Thailand or someplace." I strained to set up a little higher in the bed and Widder hooked an arm under mine to help me. The effort set off an intense pounding in my left temple, but it was manageable. She saw the look on my face.

"Are you okay?" she said.

"Getting there," I said between clinched teeth. "Don't worry about Mark. He gets excited about the color of toilet paper. Have you talked to him since?"

"He calls about eight times a day on your cell phone," Widder said, "and I answer it exactly once a day. I made a wise decision not to give him my phone number."

I grunted in agreement. And went back to sleep.

The next day I was feeling better and Widder brought me hand-written notes from the Poem Board. I was mentally lamenting the fact that I didn't have any photos of them to continue the series, when she said, "Hope you don't mind. I used your camera—Betsy, is it?—to shoot photos of the board.".

She handed me four sheets of paper and I scanned the lines.

Life if one fast-moving train.
You must make a choice when it comes by.
You can watch it roar past…and wave
As it disappears around the bend.
Or you can jump aboard and hold on to your hat
And relish the sweep
Of the wind as it rushes by.

"What do you think about that one? Widder said.
"I like it. I like the sentiment a lot."
"It's my favorite."
The second one was vastly different.

There was this girl I saw once,
She was sunbathing topless and she had perfect breasts.
I looked,
Stared, actually, and thought:
Those are perfect!
I invented a name for her—Hannah—
And made pretend that if I had muscles
And looked good at the beach
She would like me.

But I will never have muscles
And will never look good at the beach.
But she did have perfect breasts.
And her name was probably
Lajuana or Scrotetia or Marvadean.

"Scrotetia? That's just weird," I said, and then realized I had said it aloud.

"I now believe that somebody is just having a good time," Widder said.

"They've certainly piqued my interest."

Pah-piqued?

She's a writer. She knows what it means.

Flipping the top page over to the bottom, I read the third offering:

Why do fools fall in love?
I don't know.
Why don't you knock on their door and ask them?

I went over them all one more time before setting them aside. I turned my head slowly toward Widder and said, "Anyone knock on your door lately and ask that question?"

She reached over and grasped my hand, doing that little knuckle-rubbing thing with her thumb. "If they do, what do you want me to say?

The next day, at my request, Widder brought my cell phone and I retrieved a number from the internal phone book. I tracked down Shirley Bellamy, a friend of mine who does shoots for several nature-oriented publications. She had heard about my misadventure—"Everybody in the industry has heard the news," she said. "Mark has been working overtime." After a brief first-hand rundown of the incident and my recovery, I gave her a list of things I needed.

"No problem. Got it all right here," she said. She said she'd overnight the package. Then said, "You owe me. Everglades. November. You and me," and hung up. I decided to wait until after I got the package to tell her

UNCERTAIN TIMES

I probably was not going to meet her in the Everglades this fall. Too conflicted for me. Too much history for us.

Two days later I was discharged. Every day in the hospital Widder spent a couple of hours with me, always bringing the freshest poem from the board.

The two newest offerings were, as most of them had been, puzzling.

Conflict.
Minds crashing
With inner strengths
At odds with
Reality.
Perceptions give
Sway to reason
And logic.
A Rolodex of reasons
Will not damper
The enthusiasm for
Conflict.

I read that one three times before moving to the next.

Who says God doesn't make mistakes?
He's never said why good people have to die!
When the question is asked,
No answer is ever good enough.

The day I was released, except for a here-and-gone killer headache over my right eye, I felt fairly perky. For about twenty minutes at a time. When I got home, Shirley's package was sitting on the floor by the front door and a stack of unopened mail was neatly stacked on top of it. There were seven get well cards from Mark and the gang. The postmarks showed he actually sent three in one day.

Between Widder and all the women in Uncertain, I didn't have to do much for the next several days. I did call Mark the first day and tell him

I was probably not going to die but it was still iffy and that doctor said that electronic transmissions from cell phones were bad for my recovery. The last thing he said to me was, "When can you get out and shoot some killer pictures, Sparky?"

I quickly found myself holding court in the deer horn chair as people came in by the small town bunches All hoped I would get well soon. All bearing foodstuffs. Neither Harmony and Bother not Emile and Mofo bothered to come by or send anything. Neither did Sheriff Twiddle. Good beatings make bad neighbors.

There was enough homemade chicken soup and chicken and dumplings and roast and fresh bread and desserts of all kinds to feed the entire town. There were so many green bean casseroles lined up on the kitchen counter that I seriously considered UPSing a couple of them to Mark and the gang.

In the South, if whatever ails you doesn't kill you, you can almost count on a bout of obesity by the end of the convalescence period. My dad was from Missouri, which is as close to being in the South as one can get without actually claiming Southship, and he absolutely abhorred the southern practice of folks showing up with food when people were sick or dead. He made mom promise that when he died, she would spread the word, "No food."

"When I'm dead, I don't want no damn picnic."

Mama said he felt that way because he wouldn't be able to get a second helping.

Deputy Shupe came by and said there was a warrant out for Harmony's arrest but no one was allowed to follow up on it. No surprise, really. Didn't expect the warrant. Certainly didn't expect him to be arrested.

In the end, Widder put all the leftover food in a couple of black plastic bags. After dark she and Jeb toted them to the county sanitation station outside of town. I hoped county crews picked that stuff up fairly often. Green bean casseroles turn toxic in three to four days.

Bob was being extra good, not bothering me with stuttering drivel unless it had a purpose, so I had plenty of time for uninterrupted thought. By the time I got home, I had mapped out three plans, one that were guaranteed winner, one that could be more than a little dangerous, and a third that I had to do to be assured of retaining my sanity.

I discussed one of the plans with Widder and one with Jeb when Widder was occupied on the porch with some neighbor woman bearing more food. The third I kept to myself.

Widder was totally enthusiastic about the first project saying "It'll be the biggest thing ever in Uncertain since the earthquake." She took a handwritten list of things I needed her to do, looked it over and said, "No problem."

Bob agreed the idea was *sub-super*. These days Bob agreed with her on everything.

Jeb wasn't too keen on helping me with the next project, but it wasn't too hard to talk him into it. Due to my condition, we put off initiating that particular action plans for a week.

For my first two days home, Widder had slept in the living room on a camping cot she hauled in from someplace, checking on me frequently. The second night I raised the covers, inviting a snugglethon, but she gently pushed the covers down and kissed me on the cheek. On the third night, after noticing dark circles under her eyes, I insisted she sleep in her own bed. She didn't argue much and my thoughtfulness got me another cheek kiss.

That night about ten, I eased out of the house, carrying Betsy, a wide-angle lens, and Shirley's box, which I loaded in the back seat of the Jeep. As quietly as possible, I started the car and drove down to the dock. Uncertain at nine is dead. At ten, it's buried. Not a soul around, no lights on except safety lights at barns and at a couple of houses.

Using just the car dome light, I opened the box and took out a small, solid black camera and a thirty-six exposure roll of film. I removed a small black box with a cable release with a camera connection, and two special C-clamps and a couple of other doohickeys. Sticking a mini-Maglite in my shirt pocket, I headed back to the road. It took less than two minutes to get to the Poem Board and, as I had expected, this morning's poem was still on it. Just to the right of the board, there was a smaller tree with a fork about seven feet up the trunk. I attached one C-clamp to the right fork and one to the left but didn't tighten them. I connected the little black box's male plug to the loaner camera's female docking port, then screwed the camera into the right-hand C-clamp, locking it down tight on the limb. I used the left-hand C-clamp to connect to the first clamp, further stabilizing the camera.

There was no way I could determine exactly if the camera lens was set up to precisely frame the board. But I was confident the camera would capture the entire board and extra space around it.

I walked over to the board and looked back in the direction of the camera and even though I knew where it was, I couldn't see even the faintest outline of it. It took just a few seconds to walk back to the tree, reach up and turn the camera on and walk away from *behind* the tree so as not to activate the motion detector.

Five minutes later, I was in bed and a minute after that I was sound asleep. I didn't need any memories to keep me in that mode until Widder woke me up at nine with the sounds of her piddling around in the kitchen mixed with percolating coffee. The noise and the smell of good coffee and clean, perfumed woman overwhelming my aural senses.

Auh-aural senses?

We've got to expand our literary horizons, Bob.

Lah-leave me out!

Hard to do, Bob, when we're joined at the psyche.

Psy-psycho, maybe?

At what point did Bob start getting so logical?

Widder heard me rustling around and asked what I wanted for breakfast. "Anything will be fine," I said, throwing on an old pair of jeans and a t-shirt advertising a feminine hygiene product—The Keeper—some friends had given me as a joke one birthday. The catch line said, "I Tried the Keeper!" and under that was a picture of what looked like a dark red rubber funnel. In smaller type underneath the illustration were these words: "Wear this **natural gum rubber cup** internally and feel clean all day. Environmental friendly! Holds up to **one ounce of menstrual flow.**"

"I'll be right back," I said, sliding outside. I drove directly to the Poem Board and the early morning gawkers had already made their run; not a soul in sight. First, I checked the camera. Still there. Quickly, loosening the C-clamps, I eased the camera from the tree fork and looked at the counter. Every shot taken. Physically, I didn't feel like doing a jig-jump and clicking my heels together. I did three in my head.

Bob likes it when I do a mental dance.

I was walking back to the car when Jeb drove up next to the dock. "How you doing?" he said.

"Better, Jeb. Every day a little better."

"Want to think about not doing what it is you thinking about doing?" he said.

"It's got to be done, Jeb."

He nodded and started to leave the parking lot, then stopped and said, solemnly: "Nice shirt."

I chuckled, stowed the gear, made sure Betsy was loaded, grabbed a notebook, and went back to the board. I read the poem through twice before writing it down.

The old man,
Sweating profusely
Under the midday sun,
Watched in amazement as his hands
Moving mainly through muscle memory,
Quickly plucked the field peas
From the long, narrow rows.
"Good harvest," he thought.

I like this one already.
Dah-ditto.

The youngster at this elbow
Watched and mimicked every movement.
"You're a natural born peapicker,"
the old man almost shouted.
The old man and his shadow
Filled the small gunny sack in short order,

Straightened in union and quit for the house.
The row of magnolias fronting the yard
Shielded the old man and the boy
As they looked beneath the branches.
The wraparound porch
Was filled with relatives,
Sons and daughters
And their sons and daughters.
The old man smiled.
"Good harvest!"

Jah-jesus! Tha-that's good.
Couldn't have said it better myself. Even without a stutter.

Back at the house, I read the newest poem to Widder over bacon, pancakes, and coffee. She echoed earlier sentiments about the poem's worth.

"Why the different styles, though?" I said.

"I've been thinking about that," she said, "and I think it's kind of like writer's block. I can go days at a time and not write a single word; then I get cranking and the thoughts just pour out of me so fast, it's hard to stop. Some days the writer is inspired; other times he is just filling up space."

"You sure it's a he?"

"The writer's a man. There's a male theme running through many of the writings. Here," she said, pointing at the latest offering, "there are two males as central characters. In another poem, the word 'Rolodex' was used. That's a word most women would avoid using, especially in a poem. Several days ago the poem was about a bare-breasted woman and women with odd or funny names. Definitely a male is writing the poems or sayings or whatever the heck they are."

While we were eating, we went over our dual project in detail. She was excited about it and suggested we set it up a week from Saturday, and even offered to make posters.

"Posters?" I said, in my best "Treasure of Sierra Madre" bandito voice.

"Youah donne need no stinkin' postahs! Just tell one person in this town and get the hell out of the way."

She took a sip of coffee and deadpanned: "Nice shirt."

41

When a good idea starts to go bad, it's usually too damn late to do anything about it.

Anonymous

After breakfast I sent the film off overnight delivery with a sticky note to the lab: "Eight-by-ten—all. Overnight, *por favor.*" Then I spend the next half-hour getting some supplies and equipment together for my project with Jeb.

Widder puttered around for a while, then came in and asked if I needed anything. With my no-but-thanks, she went off to paint. I didn't tell her about my little venture, knowing she would try and talk me out of it. The way I felt, she might have succeeded.

Jeb had kept his antenna raised the last several days and said that Harmony and Bother had not been seen since last Friday. One of the relatives had mentioned the boys were supposed to get in late last night. From past experience, and from talking to Jeb, Thompson and Harlan, I knew their pattern was to head out into the lake about noon or later. Jeb was picking me up at 10:30.

Jeb showed up on time and forty minutes later we were at the logjam and Jeb was levering the floater log out of the way. I had to help him on the head-high limb. The effort started up a killer headache. With the small channel was open, Jeb used a battery-powered compressor to blow up a tiny, one-man rubber boat. While he did that, I put on a pair of Jeb's waders and tied an ammo can containing Betsy, film and the two big lens, around my waist.

"She's ready," Jeb announced. He held the small, six-footer raft steady while I got in, handed me a kayak paddle and pushed me off in the channel. "I'll be back after I see Harmony and Bother come back to town. If they don't come out here by four or five, I'll come give you a holler. You take care now, you here?"

I waved at him over my shoulder and watched as he struggled to close up the channel opening.

From the aerial photos, I knew it was not over 100 yards or so to the small island. What I didn't know was there were several crooks and bends in the channel, making the distance feel a lot further.

After about five minutes—in which I stopped and listened 10 to 15 times just in case—I came to the edge of the island, which was not an *island*, per se. It was a floating raft of heavy vegetation and logs, totally overgrown with various grasses, deposited there via bird droppings and high winds. About thirty yards away, I could see the roofed structure, which was actually just four posts supporting a fiberglass roof and four, rolled-up fabric or plastic panels. It dawned on me that with the panels down—Rain? Cold?—the light green roof would let in sufficient light so someone could have at least minimal visibility inside.

To the right of the shed and further back on the "island" was the vertical object I had seen in the photo shot from the plane. It was rectangle and looked to be about four-feet high by three-feet wide. There were markings on it, but I couldn't make it out from this distance.

Still sitting in the raft, I got out Betsy and the 300 mm. lens and focused in on the object.

It was a wooden grave marker. Made from several pieces of 2x12 lumber and then stuck in the ground, the marker had four lines of lettering, each letter obviously hand-carved.

MAMA
Althea Marianne Murphy Ledbetter
June 1958 - 1994
One things certain. She in heaven.

I realized I had not been breathing, the fact punctuated by a return of the pounding headache. I swept the camera lens over to the shelter and could see a several boxes wrapped up tight in an opaque sheet of heavy plastic.

Then I stopped breathing again. A motor could be heard scatting across the lake. I looked around wildly for a place to hide just in case. The "just in case" quickly became a reality. The boat, which could not have been more than fifty yards away, approached the logjam. Harmony and Bother were early!

I had been so caught up in trying to decipher the findings on the artificial island that I had not even thought about where I was going to hide. I knew where the best angle to take photos was…directly behind me, on the other side of the channel entrance. But there didn't seem to be any cover in that direction. As my ears picked up sounds I took to be the floater log being moved, my eyes scanned the thick, flooded timber.

There! A couple of fallen trees had clumped up about thirty degrees north of the channel entrance. Trying to hurry and make as little noise as possible, I paddled between the trees and cypress knees, heading toward the fall.

It was easier than I thought it was going to be or either I was more pumped than I thought possible. I was behind the trees with time to spare. I eased out of the boat and slipped quietly into the water, which came up about a foot above my crotch. I wedged the boat between two limbs and put the ammo can, a bottle of water, two bananas and a Ziplock bag of iced oatmeal raisin cookies on the bottom tree trunk. Betsy was cinched up tight and held to my chest with an Xed configuration of wide elastic manufactured expressly for that purpose.

I willed myself to be as still as possible so the ripples would dissipate. Since I was on the backside of the fall, any ripples I made would expand away from the island. Good thinking on my part.

Blah-blind ah-ass luck.

Not now, Bob. Please, not now.

I could hear voices as Harmony and Bother approached the island from the channel.

The voices were indistinct. The first voice I could easily understand was Bother.

"...always say mean things to me, Harmony. You never nice to me."

"Nobody got to be nice to idiots, Bother. Hell, boy, you the king of the idiots," Harmony said.

By looking though a six-inch opening between the two logs, I could see Harmony run the boat up to the log nest. Bother hopped out and tied the front line to a limb and started to walk down a big log to the island when Harmony shouted: "Dammit to hell, Bother! Get your lazy ass back here and get some of this gear."

Rolling his eyes as he turned, Bother went back down the log and took two five-gallon steel drums with wooded bucket handles from his brother. I focused Betsy on the label on one drum: Acetone. I zoomed back to get both brothers in the shot and hit the shutter release.

The sound seemed louder than a fart in confession. I flinched but did not take my eye off the scene. Harmony was busy untying some boxes in the boat well, but at the sound, he stopped and looked up. His eyes started to my left, then swept over the tree fall and back toward the channel. He gave a mouth-and-head shrug and then went back to work.

Bob asked me to *plah-please* not to take any more photos until Harmony and Bother were on the other side of the island.

It was a reasonable request and I acquiesced.

Within a couple of minutes, all the supplies were unloaded and Harmony had a fire going in a butane stand I had seen used to heat up kettles of oil for cooking fish or turkey. Bother went over to the headstone and knelt down for a minute or so, then sat cross-legged at a right-angle to the front of the tombstone. From somewhere in the boxes he helped carry, he had extracted a regular-size spiral-bound notebook; a short pencil appeared from his shirt pocket and he started writing in the book. Or making marks. Or pretending to.

Harmony put a pot over the flame on the one-burner heater and added some ingredients, stirred them together and then added other ingredients. Using the camera, I focused in and panned over the supplies he had brought. At least two unopened boxes of lye. A box with "24-Drano" on the side. Red Chief kitchen matches. Epsom salts. Three cartons of "3-N-1 24-Hour Cold Tablets. He was cooking, but it wasn't a test batch of chili for the FireAnt Festival Chili Cook-off. Harmony was cooking up a batch of methamphetamines. Crystal Meth. Crank. Speed. Ice. Batu. Chalk. Zip.

Known as "The Devil's Drug" by sanctimonious cops and televangelists, meth is inexpensive to make, cheap to purchase and more addictive than a teenager's first successful attempt at masturbation.

The rumors about Harmony and Bother were true. They were cooking and selling meth. If I knew anything about local law enforcement, Twiddle knew about it and while he may not be an active participant, he was certainly not following up on the rumors.

For the first hour or so, I took an occasional picture, the sound swallowed up by Harmony's puttering. He had put on a surgical-type mask that covered his nose and mouth as he worked and stirred and poured. Every once in a while he would holler at Bother to fetch him something. Bother would hop up and fetch whatever it was, then return to his spot near the headstone.

Even this far away from the cooking operation, I could smell the ingredients, which came across as a mixture of industrial ammonia and cat piss.

My legs had started to go numb from standing in one spot about an hour after the brothers arrived. A couple of hours later, they were all-the-way numb. And quivering. In addition to that, my ADD symptoms were kicking in, and I got bored looking at the island through my little hide-slit. Bob tried to help, going through his who's-on-first routine, but I was not in the mood. I started checking out the scenery, but quickly saw that my movements were kicking up tiny ripples, which radiated out in three directions from behind the fallen trees. While the trees kept them from going forward, the ripples, nonetheless, could be seen going out from the sides of the fall if anyone happened to look.

I checked the island scene: No change. Bother was sitting, writing; Harmony was pouring, stirring, and cussing.

Willing myself to stand still, I ate two bananas and the oatmeal cookies and drank some water. I had my photos; I wanted them to leave so I could at least walk around in the lake muck and get some feeling back in my legs.

A movement to my left at the waterline caught my eye and I glanced down. My first reaction was to scream and water-walk to Uncertain. A large water moccasin had apparently emerged from under the tree fall and was floating motionless about five feet from me. I could only see the very top of a couple of curves in his back, but I could see the head real well. It was big. Twiddle hat-huge. It was aimed directly at me.

Some people have an irrational fear of snakes. I was not one of those people. My fear of snakes is completely rational. Having been bitten on my left calf by a moccasin while in college, I know as a first-hand fact that moccasins are evil, cunning, and single-minded in their purpose to bite humans in soft places. They were put on this earth to instill fear in the entire human race. I respect their purpose and have worked very hard to avoid them at every opportunity.

Reaching up on the log, I gently grabbed the handle of the ammo box, quietly closed the lid and held the box just above the water line as sort of a shield. The snake thought that move was interesting. It came forward to investigate. I pushed at it with the box. It tried to go around the box.

Jah-Jesus!

Not now, Bob. If you can't help me, don't think. Besides by the time you—

The snake stopped my Bob-talk by trying to climb *over* the box. I bopped its nose several times before it quit trying to crawl in my waders, finally wriggling back in a small space where the two big logs touched.

Checking around behind me, I saw a medium-sized cypress tree about ten feet away, and it appeared that the base of the tree would be concealed from the island by the log fall. I had enough pictures, so I put the ammo box back on the tree trunk, then backed carefully up to the smaller tree and rested my back against it. Only a small slice of the artificial island and the tail end of the Ledbetters' boat were visible from my new position.

At this point, anything was better than bellying up to a snake's den.

Leaning against the tree took a little pressure off my legs, just enough to stop the quivering and the imminent feeling I was going to fall face-down in the lake, impel myself on a sharp cypress knee and die.

As always, in times of inactivity, my mind took over and swept me away.

Every member of the Bartlett clan went to church, at least on the Sundays when the circuit preacher was in the community. The only exception was Uncle Earnest. He didn't like church and made no bones about it. He said he didn't like going to church "and hearing the same stories you done heard before told in the same way you heard them the other 100 times. Once you've heard about the parting of the Red Sea, then, by damn, you have heard about the parting of the Red Sea. I've heard that tale and there's no reason to hear it again."

Uncle Earnest did go to church. Once.

Every time the family made the trek up the hill and down the main road to the asbestos-sided non-denominational church, my grandmother asked her brother-in-law to go. He always politely declined. One day, for no apparent reason, he agreed to go, surprising Nannie to no end. He put on a clean pair of overalls, a clean blue work shirt and even took a swipe at shining up his brogans with a wet rag.

The word passed quickly in the shotgun house: "Unc's going to church. Unc's going to church."

The whole family hied up the lane for the half-mile walk to the church. The story went that Unc even whistled an off-tune rendition of "Onward Christian Soldiers."

The Sunday School lesson was about Samson and Delilah, not the parting of the Red Sea, which, most family members later agreed, was a positive thing.

The circuit preacher had been hounding Unc to come to church for some time and the preacher was both surprised and pleased that he was in attendance. He welcomed the entire family, of course, as preachers who are short on parishioners and shorter on capital, do. He spend extra time pumping Unc's hand, making sure he felt welcome.

At the end of the sermon—which Unc later described as "being about sin. The preacher was dead-set against it."—the preacher asked Unc to "lead us in a season of prayer." Unc did and prayed something fierce. He asked the Lord not to bring a drought and not to bring a flood and to bring the "fires of hell" down on a visiting redbone coon dog that was a chicken-killer, and to please not let the well go dry. Unc ended it by blessing Mary and Joseph and Baby Jesus and everybody in the church and, most of all, Sampson.

Everybody generally agreed it was a fine prayer.

The preacher then asked another sinner to pray. Unc, beads of religious fervor-sweat running down his face, looked up, apparently shocked. He shook his head and closed his eyes. Then another person started to pray. When the fourth person stood and started to pray, Unc bolted from the pew, stomped to the door, and was gone.

Daddy George took out after him and caught him at the end of the church driveway. "What's the matter with you, Earnest? You have durn near embarrassed the whole family? Why caused you to stomp out of the church like that?"

Uncle Earnest fixed him with a slit-eyed stare: "If that self-righteous sumbitch don't like my prayer, he can kiss my ass!"

A noise snapped me back to attention and I re-focused on my surroundings, I could see Harmony in the back of the boat, arranging a box. Whoa! If I could see him....!

I inched to my left, and almost stumbled. My back was tight; my legs were numb. I was light-headed. This whole episode was, as Bob and Jeb had said over and over again, a dumb idea. Widder would have said it too if she had known about it.

I quickly put the trees between myself and the boat, effectively blocking Harmony from view.

"Come on, dammit," Harmony hollered at Bother. I watched the brothers loading up the boat, waited until Bother stepped into the boat to shoot a couple of pictures, figuring the noise of the shuffling round would camouflage the noise of the camera's shutter.

Five minutes later, they were gone and I had never been more happy to see anyone leave in my life. Except for the time in college when I was jilted by this cheerleader and ended up with a fat friend of her's and....

Jah-jesus! Nah-nobody but me here and I-I know the story.

I waited until I heard Harmony's boat motor cut loose and fade in the distance before I gathered up my equipment, put it in the boat and walked carefully over to the island., I wanted to inspect the site up-close. Harmony had re-covered all the supplies with the tarp. It took just a minute to uncover it and check out the contents. I had recorded most of the ingredients, but took pictures of other boxes that were not visible from my hide. Most of the boxes looked like they came from Sam's Club or some other place where people could buy discounted items in large quantities. I had just started to recover the pile when I noticed a mailing label on a box of "Red Phosphorus."

It had been shipped to "County Sheriff's Department, Attn. Sheriff Johnnie Twiddle, County Courthouse, Marshall, Texas." Capitalized and underlined were the words: "FOR ANTI-DRUG DEMONSTRATION PURPOSES ONLY."

I don't remember much about the next few minutes but Bob later said I *lah-laughed out loud*. I also don't remember doing an Irish jig before taking photographs of the label, the box and the surroundings either. But I certainly wouldn't doubt it.

Thirty minutes later I was sitting in my little raft, inside the logjam entrance, when Jeb came tooling up. Together we eased the logs aside and, after I got in his boat with my equipment, we deflated the raft and headed home.

"Get what you needed?" Jeb said.

"Jeb, if I told you, you wouldn't believe it. You're going to have to wait to see the pictures."

He looked at me with a small grin itching at his face. "I reckon it'll be worth the wait."

"Oh, yeah. Of that, you can be certain."

When got back to town, I took a film mailer out of the ammo can, filled it out and put a note inside similar to the one I sent off this morning. Jeb said he'd make sure it went out today. When he dropped me off at home, we shook hands and he backed out of the driveway. As I entered the house and shut the door, I happened to glance back and saw him start down the road and then stop. Widder entered my angle of vision, walked up to the truck and leaned on the window, either talking or listening, I couldn't tell which. Twice she glanced at the house; the second time, she shook her head.

Probably asking advice on how to get me in bed.

Ah-of all the guesses eh-in the world, that's certainly wah-one.

I went to the kitchen, pulled out two beers, drank about half of one in three quick gulps, then sat down at the table and started unpacking and cleaning gear. I heard Widder knock three times, followed immediately by the sound of the door opening.

"Back here," I said, about the time she appeared in the kitchen door. I held up the beer, which she took and came and sat down.

"You're an idiot." I waited. That was all.

I said, "That seems to be the consensus. First Bob, then Jeb, and now you. I think if we took a vote of everyone in Uncertain, the final outcome would probably be unanimous."

Uh-less there were a cah-couple of votes for stah-stupid.

"What did Bob just say?" Widder asked.

"He said there could be a couple of votes for 'stupid.'"

"Hmmm. He has a point." She sipped her beer, looking at me as I cleaned the camera and lens. "So, what did you find out? Jeb said you got some pictures but wouldn't say what you had."

I didn't say a word, but I did stop cleaning and just stared at Widder's face.

"Damn it, Adj!" she said. "You don't have a lick of sense. You almost got killed last week and then this week you go looking to get killed all over again. What is wrong with you?"

I thought about the question and acknowledged it was valid. "Remember the conversation about 'pricks' and 'prickettes?'" I said. "With everything that has happened, it's gotten personal. The ball is rolling and I can't stop it." I stopped talking and picked up her left hand and started gently rubbing the knuckles with my thumb. "If I could stop it, I wouldn't."

"This is crazy," she said, shaking her head. "In a few weeks, you'll be leaving. One way or the other."

She got up, leaving her unfinished beer on the table, turned without another word and stomped out of the house. She slammed the door for effect.

I drank the rest of her beer, knowing her assessment of the situation was right on target. Right down to the stomping and slamming.

After the conversation, I took a quick shower and went to bed.

Sometime later, there was a weight on the edge of the bed and I felt Widder slip under the cover and snuggle tightly against my back.

I was sleeping, as always, on my right side and started to turn over, but a hand stopped the rotation of my shoulder. "No," she said, softly. "Go back to sleep. I just need to hold you. Go back to sleep."

It's easy to follow orders when they sound so damn sincere and pleasant.

I woke up sometime after dark and Widder was gone. It hadn't been a dream; I could smell her in the pillow, the sheets.

I was starving so I got up, clicked on enough lights to keep me from getting injured on the way to the kitchen and…was surprised to find Widder sitting at the kitchen table, wearing nothing but a short, cotton nightgown that almost covered her lap.

She had been crying. Her face was red and her eyes glistened from left-over tears.

She got up, met me at the door and hugged me tight, then lifted her face to be kissed. I started kissing her, but then she took over. In my fifty-eight years I thought I knew a thing or two about kissing. I was wrong. She moved me from kissing kindergarten to kissing college in about fifteen seconds.

As abruptly as the kiss started, she stopped. Tears were flowing. She looked at my face and kissed my bottom lip, sucking it just a little before letting it go.

"This is just too hard, Adj," she said. "Too damn hard."

Then she turned and left. For once, I didn't make a joke about what she meant about "hard."

I didn't watch her walk away either. It would have been too damn hard.

42

Plotting is easy. Proper execution isn't.

Anonymous

After Widder left, I rummaged around in the kitchen pantry and found a lonely can of sardines in mustard sauce. I opened it and ate the slimy, yellow fish with a dirty fork. It was a good enough supper for someone stupid.

Jah-jesus!

Bob hates sardines.

Good. I didn't want to suffer alone.

I didn't have a single dream that night. Or, I didn't remember it if I did.

I woke up especially tired, with a headache bad enough to drive a duck to give up swimming. I didn't make it down to the Poem Board until about nine, and a group of five or six men, including Jeb and Hy, were standing around the board. They saw me coming but didn't holler or wave. Not a good sign.

As I got up close, the men parted and I saw what was written on the board:

Re-elect
Sheriff Twiddle!

_____

**Proven leadership
A man of the people**

"What the hell is this?"

"Your guess is as good as ours, Mr. Jones." Hy said. "This ain't okay. It ain't even right."

Jeb spoke up, "Take a pitcher, would ya, Mr. Jones. This ain't right."

I took a couple of pictures and then wiped the board clean with my shirt tail. Then I went to Hum's with a couple of the boys and ate a breakfast I didn't want but felt obligated to order. The talk in the café was the Poem Board's latest missive.

There was no talk of organizing a lynching. There was, however, talk of buying rope.

I went back home and debated stopping by Widder's but decided against it; my male ego told me it was her move. Bob said I was a *cha-chicken sha-shit*. I wasn't in a mood to argue with a stuttering psyche or even be mind-rending sarcastic. I let the statement stand as undisputed fact.

Pulling my iBook from its case, I plugged it in and started comparing photos to notes taken on various shoots. I started cranking out pithy, descriptive paragraphs that I hoped—with an editor's help—would create the perfect symbiotic relationship between photos and words.

Sometime after noon, Widder came over and brought me a ham sandwich, some chips and a draft copy of the flyer she had been working on relating to our project. As usual, I was amazed by her artistic ability and didn't offer a single change. She said she'd have them up by the end of the day.

As she started to leave, I grabbed her hand. She gave mine a little squeeze, and threw a sweet smile my way as she left.

I worked on the cutlines until my eyes would no longer focus. I took a break, took a beer to the lightning tree and took a short nap. When I woke up, I went back to work until the words I was pounding in the laptop were no longer making sense. I went took two Tylenol P.M., chug-a-lugged a small glass of red wine, and went to bed.

I willed myself not to dream.

Gah-good. I nah-need the rest.

I got up extra early the next morning with a stiff neck and loose mind. While drinking a cup of coffee to clear the two-inch layer of phlegm from my throat, I skimmed over my cutline efforts from the day before. The first twenty or so efforts were acceptable; the others needed major rethinks. The differences occurred after Widder had visited.

Jeb was at the Poem Board when I got there. Today's effort was simple…and complex.

It's not enough to be.
It's not enough to want.
One must surpass be
And go directly to
Be with a purpose.
One must surpass want
And go directly to
Get with a purpose.

"You want to explain this one to me?" Jeb said.

"Jeb. I don't know what it means," I said. "I would guess it means that people should do things for a reason, not just to be doing them."

"Is that what you be doing with the Ledbetters and Twiddle??

"Ohhhhh, yeah!"

He smiled.

And agreed to let me buy his breakfast.

On the way to Hum's, Jeb said: "That's a nice thing you be doing for the folks hereabouts?"

"Nice thing?"

"Yeah, that thing you be having at your house next Saturday."

"Oh, that. It's going to be fun."

At Hum's I saw Widder's poster in the window and I had to admit it made me feel good. I stopped to read it because posters like this just looked and read differently when they were displayed out in the public eye.

Attention Uncertain Residents
First Ever Uncertain
**Family Photo Day
SATURDAY, MAY 2
10-2**
Free Photos
By Famed Nature Photographer Adj Jones
Free soft drinks; bring food to share; plan to spend the day

As Jeb and I entered Hum's every person in the room acknowledged our presence. Hy said, "Hey, Mr. Jones. Or you really gonna take pitchers of everybody what shows up?"

"Boys, I don't know a thing about that flyer. It sounds like a big ol' late April Fool's joke. Fact is, I'm going to be out of town that Saturday."

There was silence, then Hum said, "Hmmmmm?"

I thought Hy was gonna cry. "You are funning us, right?"

"Yes, Hy, I'm funning. Tell everybody you see, we're going to have a real good time. We want everybody in town to come on out."

"Shoot, Mr. Jones, I'm glad it's not a joke. Widder put up those flyers last night. Everybody knows by now," Hy said, getting a positive response from the crowd.

Hum had already started on orders for me and Jeb and he looked over his shoulder as he flipped an egg. "Hmmm?"

"If you don't come for a free picture of you and the Missus, Hum, I'll be mighty disappointed."

"Hmmmmm!"

After eating and visiting with folks I went back home and re-attacked the chore of rewriting cutlines. I was trying to stay focused using lukewarm coffee as a crutch when I heard the crunch of the mailman's tires. Actually the rural route carrier was a woman named Mattie, but "mailwoman" or "mailperson" was just too awkward. If they had a mandatory course in political correctness, I would have flunked. On purpose.

I went outside, got the mail, which included two large photo envelopes with extra padding and took it to the kitchen.

I opened the skinnier of the two envelopes first, knowing those were the pictures of the Ledbetters on the island. I only shot eighteen photos from my hide. Everything was as I remembered it; every photo showed what I wanted it to show; every one was in crystal-clear focus. There was a note from one of the lab technicians—a friendly sort named Ralph—that said: "I'm sure there's a story behind these and I want to hear it. Beers are on me the next time you're in town."

I opened the other photos and a cover sheet was on top of the first photo. A second note from Ralph read: "What the hell are you doing? Where are the animals? You know, the East Texas snugwarts and the diving flitternhogs? Ha!"

Sliding the note to the side, I looked at the greenish tint created by the infrared film. The camera had obviously moved a little in its position in the fork of the tree, the lens aimed higher than I would have liked. But the poetry board was as clear as infrared film can produce. In the first photo, there was nothing in the picture but the board and several trees. I quickly flipped through the pictures and it was the sixth picture before anything was added to the frame. In the lower left edge of the photo was a triangle, a sort of a flying wedge hovering in midair. I looked at the next picture and realized it was a part of a short-sleeved shirt. In each progressive shot, the shirt got bigger until an ear, then half a head joined it. The shape of the head was vaguely familiar. No recognition-tumblers fell into place to open the mental lock.

The person looked as if he—Widder had been right—reached in his pocket and withdrew something (chalk?) and began writing. I had gone through more than thirty pictures when a stray thought jumped up and hit me between the eyes: The film is going to run out before the guy turns around!

It was almost as if the one-dimensional image heard me and in the next photo, I could see a little bit of a profile. I imagined he had heard something and was turning to see what it was. He kept turning until the last frame when he was not quite face-front to the camera but his face was clearly visible.

Well, fub-fuck me!
Me too.
The face in the last frame was Bother.

I took the photo over to Widder's but she was gone. Her car wasn't behind her house so I decided to drive around and see if I could find her. For some reason, I took the entire packet of photos of Harmony and Bother with me, throwing them on the front seat. I stuck the single picture of Bother over the sun visor. I checked to see if the Glock was in the glove box where I had put it last. It was there. It was loaded.

As I was driving by Harlan's, I spied Jeb's truck, pulled in, jumped out and almost ran into him at the door.

"If you don't have anything else better to do," I said, "why don't you come with me?"

"Where we going?"

"On an adventure, my good man, on an adventure."

"Well, hell, what we doing standing around here?"

As I swung the Jeep around to get out of the driveway, I handed Jeb the island photos and headed on the road out of town. Without even consciously thinking about it, I started looking for Harmony's truck.

"You take a mean pitcher," Jeb said, rustling through the prints.

"I'll take that as a compliment."

"Take it that way, because it is one."

I was passing by Logan Brothers Feed and Seed when Jeb grabbed my arm: "If you be looking for the Ledbetters, there they be." Harmony's truck was parked on the south side of the slightly canted wooden structure. Without Jeb, I probably would have missed it. I turned around in the next driveway, backtracked, and pulled up in front of the store.

"What you got in mind?" Jeb said.

"Don't have a clue, Jeb. I'm just feeling ornery."

"Sounds like fun. Let's went."

We entered the wide roll-up door of the feed store and stood there for a minute letting our eyes adjust to the darkened interior. Jeb sidled off to my left, touching the back of my arm as he did so just to let me know where he would be. Thompson was leaning against a rack of garden seeds and he touched the brim of his straw hat.

One of the Logan brothers—they were twins and I couldn't tell which was which—tossed me a "good morning" as did a couple of other men whose features I could not yet make out. I flitted my eyes around the cavernous room, marking location of men, shelves, stacks of feed and anything else that I might need to know in case of…whatever.

Harmony was sitting on a stack of feed sacks, facing the door; Bother was sitting with his back to the door, playing with a tallish baby chick. The chicken was bright purple, a left-over from an Easter batch.

"Well, well, well," Harmony said, not making any move to get up. "If it ain't Mr. Smart Mouth. How you feeling, Mr. Smart Mouth?" Bother turned to look at me, hoisted the baby chick and offered a sickly grimace.

I smiled and nodded. "Never felt better, Disharmony. I think you finally knocked some sense into me. I just stopped by to say thank you and to give you a present."

He stiffened. "Give me a present? You crazy!"

"Assuredly, but it's the least I can do for all you've done for me and the good people of Uncertain." With that, I handed him the envelope of pictures I shot at the island.

He looked puzzled when I handed him the envelope. When he opened it and flipped through the first two or three photos, the puzzlement turned to an expression that could only be described as panicky. That look was replaced by some semblance of anger. When he looked at the last photo, he carefully stuck them back in the heavy mailer and set them down on the feed sack next to him.

He looked at me, his eyes lid-heavy and then he snake-smiled.

"You know this means I gots to kill you daid, don't you?"

"No, not necessarily," I said as I picked up a huge grain shovel and hit him in the face. It was a good lick, lots of backswing and a solid connection. Lots of positive-drive hip action. Harmony went over backwards like a high diver doing a reverse somersault with a half-gainer, and hit the hard concrete floor. Hard. Except for a little shudder-twitch when his body settled on the concrete, he didn't move.

Bother made a low moaning noise. I gave him a fast glance but he hadn't budged. He was just sitting there, petting that chick—harder, faster.

Two fingers on Harmony's jugular told me his heartbeat was strong, if just a little thready. Thinking about what would happen when he woke up, I used my shoe to push his foot out flat to the side and drove the edge of the shovel straight down on the ankle. Twice. I felt—and heard—several bones pop in the process.

I looked around the room; no one had moved.

"Gentlemen," I said, "I personally abhor violence, but when Harmony threatened to kill me, I took the opportunity to defend myself. The little ankle thingee was to give him time to think about what he said he was going to do to me. And also to make sure it would be quite a while before he was able to do what he wanted to do to me in the first place. Are there any questions?"

Not a word from anyone.

"Thank you all," I said, bending down to pick up the manila envelope from the feed sack. I took out the pictures and tossed them on the counter. "I'll bet you'll enjoy the photos I showed Harmony. I hope to see you all Saturday."

I started to leave and heard Jeb stirring behind me. I held up my hand, motioning him to stay where he was.

I went over to Bother, grabbed his left ear between my thumb and forefinger, pinched and twisted. He yelped, and as I pulled up, he stood up. I led him outside with little resistance, walked him to the Jeep and deposited him against the back door. He never quit petting that purple chicken.

I handed him the green-tinted photo shot two days ago and he looked at it like it was a Warhol painting of a fire hydrant.

"Bother, I don't know how and I don't know why, but I know you are writing the things on the Poem Board. I am telling you that some of them are as good as anything I have ever read. Do you understand me?"

Glancing up from the picture, he nodded.

"I want you to promise me something, Bother. I want you to promise me you'll keep writing on the Poem Board. The people in Uncertain like them and it gives them something to look forward to every day. You have a gift. Use it. You got me?"

He nodded and I got in the car, honked for Jeb.

"What was that all about?" Jeb said.

"You said one time there was something you didn't want to know, Jeb. So, if it's all the same to you, I'm not going to tell you."

43

Truth is...subjective. But then again, so are lies.

B. Ledbetter

I hadn't been home five minutes before I heard Widder's knock. The next thing I knew she was standing in the kitchen, arms crossed over her chest, hip jutted out, right foot a-tapping.

"What?" I said, trying to sound irritated.

"What's the hell's wrong with you! You picked a fight with Harmony?"

"C.C., I didn't pick a fight. Wasn't any fight," I said.

"But I just heard...."

"The cypress telegraph is a little sloppy today. I said it wasn't a fight. I didn't say Harmony won't be hurting for a while. Harmony is thirty-five years younger than I am. You really thought I would fight him? What kind of fight would that be?" I said.

Shut up, Bob. Don't think it.

"He threatened to kill me and then his face happened to run into a grain shovel. Then his ankle ran into the same damn shovel, so he will be walking with a major limp for quite a while. That boy ought to be more careful."

Widder looked at me carefully to see if I was lying. A look of relief slid across her features. She then looked around to see if there was any fresh coffee. When she discovered there wasn't, she started a pot.

She turned around and leaned against the sink. There were tears in her eyes. "When are you leaving? When? And don't lie to me."

"I don't know yet. Probably in a couple of weeks," I said.

She nodded like that had been her guess.

"Wid... C.C., I...."

"NO, Adj. Don't say anything," she said. "I need to talk right now and I'd appreciate it if you would just listen. I know it's hard for you, but just suck it up!"

She paused. Took a deep breath. "When you came to town, you brought a breeze of excitement with you. To folks hereabouts, at first, you were a nice, if weird, distraction. You were the main topic of just about *every* conversation in Uncertain for the first several weeks."

The coffee stopped bubbling and she stopped, got down two cups, checked them out, rinsed out one of them, scrubbing it with her fingertips under the running faucet. She filled them up and gave one to me, returning to stand by the counter. I noticed she gave me the fresh-scrubbed cup.

We both took a couple of quick, nervous sips.

"In my little world, everything is simple," Widder said. "I get up, piddle around and start to work, either writing or painting. I do what I want to do, when I want to do it. No complications. Limited responsibilities. If I want to dress up, I do—although I certainly don't do that very often."

Another sip of coffee.

"But I could have if I wanted to. When you moved in, you were a one-dimensional diversion, a splash of newness to the old routine." Sip of coffee. "I found myself watching for you out the windows, chronicling your comings and goings. Usually, I avoid participating in the gossip channels here, even though I am on several 'phone trees.'"

She put down her coffee and double-curled the first two fingers of both hands to illustrate the quote marks, then picked the cup back up and took a sip.

"Without realizing it, I got caught up in this mysterious-stranger episode in the usually boring soap opera *Days of Uncertain,*" Widder said. She refilled her cup. She arched her eyebrows toward me; I got up and poured out the cold coffee and she refilled it without looking up.

I didn't move back toward the table. "C.C., all I ever..."

She took my elbow and led me back to the table, then returned to the cabinet.

Kah-keeping her distance.

Fairly obvious, Bob. She's got something to say and she's gonna say it. All the way through. Without major interruptions.

"What did Bob say?" Widder said.

"Just noted you were making sure to maintain a safe distance."

Her eyes moistened.

Clearing her throat, "Yes, well, as I was saying, I found myself intrigued by this mysterious stranger. Infatuated might be a better word. I wanted to get to know him better, you know. I had all these romantic notions about him and...us. Then one day, as my feelings were starting to escalate, I realized I was just living out parts of my romantic fantasy world. *Texas Hellion*, Chapter 22. *South Pacific Hellion*, Chapter 16. *A Price for Love*, Chapters 9, 18 and 32." She took another sip of coffee.

A Price for Love. I don't think I saw that one. Remember those chapters, Bob.

When Bob was disappointed in me, he didn't think. I waited. He was disappointed in me.

"What?" Widder said.

"I'm sorry."

"What did Bob say?"

"Nothing, actually. He doesn't think when he's mad."

"He's mad at me," she said. Statement, not a question.

"No, me. He's mad at me."

She looked down and her mouth turned up in a sort of half-sad grin.

"Don't be mad at him, Bob. You of all little voices ought to know he just can't do any better. Where was I? Oh, yeah. I was getting you all mixed up with my fantasy world. The trip to New York was an eye-opener for me. I have been to big cities, lived in one in California, so I knew what to expect, know what goes on there and usually when I visit I just try and have fun. This time was different. This time I was actually thinking about how it would feel to travel all over the world and be in different places all the time. To...leave Uncertain."

She stopped and waited.

"Yah-you thought about how it would be to be with me? All the time?" I said.

She nodded. "And I found out I couldn't do it. I know you never asked, and never would, but...."

This time I held up the "freeze" sign. And got up and walked over to her. "C.C., I don't know what the future holds, but what I do know is...." Her "freeze" sign was back up. I ran right through it. "BUT, what I do know is that there is a feeling deep inside me that I haven't felt in a long, long time. I think it would be a mistake, a BIG mistake, if we don't allow that feeling to take root and grow."

She looked up and laughed.

I must have looked stunned because she quickly said, "No, no, it was not the sentiment, it was the words. 'Take root and grow.' I swear I've used that phrase twenty times in my books. You just struck my funny nerve, that's all."

Funny nerve?

Yah-yeah. It's cah-connected to....

Jesus, Bob! Not now!

"Bob?"

"Yes, he's trying to be a comedian. He's not helping. In fact, neither are you. C.C. Dammit, what I'm trying to say is...."

Her fingertips went to my lips. At any other time, I would have welcomed the gesture. This time, it was a guillotine blade falling.

She leaned up, pressed her lips to the back of her hand and put extra pressure on my lips.

"I can't, Adj. Can't you see?" Tears rolled out of her eyes and down her cheeks. "I can't change! I won't change!"

I didn't look up when she left the kitchen. I didn't hear the front door close. I don't remember much about the rest of the day. I know I went to bed early and don't remember waking up the entire night. I also remember when I awoke the next morning I was so tired and achy that I just rolled back over and stared out the window and watched a single dandelion head swaying in the morning breeze.

44

Tears of laughter and tears from heartache are both tears, but they're never the same thing.

B. Ledbetter

The next week was fast-paced enough to keep my mind halfway occupied. Widder had organized the Uncertain photo-a-thon to the point where I didn't have to do anything but talk to folks and click the camera shutter. I had a couple of small digital cameras with me, but I ordered a Nikon digital with a couple of lenses, had it delivered overnight and spent a couple of days on the lake getting familiar with it. My editors had advised me that, sooner or later, I should think about moving to digital for my work. "It's the coming thing," they had said.

Coming thing, my ass. I've still got three boxes of eight-tracks in my garage in Atlanta. One of these days I'm going to listen to them.

With the camera order were twenty 256 Mb memory cards; at the maximum setting, each would hold about twenty images.

The Nikon worked great, actually. I spent half-a-day in Buddy's blind, and shot a good picture of Tiffany sticking a small fish so far down one of her babies throats I expected to see her bill come out of the bottom of the nest.

The two Hewlitt-Packard high-speed photo printers that I had requisitioned from my publisher had arrived by FedEx and were set up at Widder's. Extra memory to handle the load was added to Widder's computer.

Jeb and a couple of the boys were delegated to get folding tables and chairs from several local churches and have them set up by eight o'clock Miss Baxter was recruited to check everyone in, get names and other pertinent information, as well as match up the photos taken with the cards on which the images were taken.

At a small organizational meeting at Widder's, I suggested numbering the memory cards A, B, C, and so on. Miss Baxter told us they would be numbered 1, 2, 3, etc.

Mah-math teacher.

Assuredly.

During the week word leaked back that Sheriff Twiddle was planning to arrest me for the assault on Harmony. The boys at the feed store had gone to the county prosecuting attorney's office and signed a statement that Harmony had threatened to kill me and I had acted in self defense. Jeb told me that the prosecutor had even interviewed Bother. Even he made a statement that Harmony had threatened to kill me.

Lawyer Mitchell also made it clear that if charges were filed against me, there was more than a distinct possibility that a lawsuit would be filed.

Deputy Shupe came by the house on Wednesday and said the surveillance had been pulled off because all the deputies were supposed to working fulltime on Twiddle's re-election campaign.

"Truth be known," Shupe said, "I don't think Sheriff Twiddle's got a chance in hell getting re-elected. The folks hereabouts got you to thank for that."

He went on to say somehow there was a batch of pictures floating around the county that showed Harmony making meth somewhere on Caddo Lake and that one picture in particular tied Twiddle to the operation.

"Why, Deputy Shupe. I declare! I don't have a single inkling what you are talking about?" I said.

I asked if the political message on the Poem Board would harm his chances?

"That didn't set well with a whole bunch of folks. Did you know politicking signs for the sheriff have been painted all over the county, some on barns, some on empty buildings and even one on the brick square in Marshall. The sheriff's denying he had anything to do with it, but folks are claiming it's the work of some not-too-bright supporters."

We sat there a minute, thinking, then I said, "Would the law be interested in where that meth-making operation is located?"

"The county sheriff's department wouldn't be, I can tell you that," Shupe said. "But I know some state boys and federal boys that would be mighty interested. Somebody—I'm not gonna say who—done sent them pictures you took up the law enforcement ladder."

I told him about the log jam and about how to get in it and he followed me over to Widder's while I typed up a statement about what I had seen and done in the process of producing the pictures. I added in there the fact that Bother was not directly involved, but seemed to be forced to carry supplies by Harmony. I met him down at Harlan's, and Harlan's wife notarized the statement.

"I guess you'd agree to come back here and testify if need be?"

"Deputy Shupe, I would love to come back to Uncertain at some time in the future."

He took a minute to think about something. Then he asked, "Would it be all right if I came to the pitcher-taking on Saturday and bring my family? I'll understand if you don't want me there."

"Show up early and plan on staying all day."

Widder and I had been sugar-sweet cordial over the past several days, but I knew my attempts were poor excuse of acting. When I was helping set up the printers, she had taken my hand and rubbed it against her cheek and then got up to go make coffee. There was a definite pattern emerging here. I hate patterns.

I had dog-eared Page 134 in *Stormy Passions* and in every single reading, it was not Beau and Val getting it on, but Adj and Widder. I couldn't help but think what might have been if we had met thirty years ago. Bob *rah-reminded* me for the thirtieth time that thirty years ago, Widder would have been ten.

UNCERTAIN TIMES

Fuh-fuck you, Bob.
Bob laughed, a rare occurrence for either of us these days.

Even in my depressed state I had been going to the Poem Board, and there were new writings on the board every day. I took photos and wrote down the words, but I could tell something was different in the construction of the lines and even the rhythm. It was as if Bother was not just playing or experimenting, but trying to make them better.
I was glad someone was trying to make something better.
My days seemed listless and unending. Nights were filled with tossing and turning with no good memory-dreams that I could remember.

On Friday, the day before Uncertain's photo festival, I woke up refreshed and for the first time since the discussion with Widder my head didn't feel like it was lower than my scrotum.
That was about to change.
My first stop of the day was the Poem Board where I recorded the most recent offering.

Spider dancing on slender strings·
Looking for a few simple things
To consume.
Sun stripes shoots through distant limbs,
Bonding to air like a woman's whim
At the mall.
Whitewater racing through a mountain brook,
Twisting, turning in an Ozark nook,
Free and flowing.

Mixing imagery more than a little, but the thought was appreciated.
I had a light breakfast at Hum's—oatmeal with butter, sugar and cream, and toast—and it was over the second piece of toast that I decided to run an errand that I had been putting off.
Jeb had given me directions the day I had "shoveled" Harmony and I

tried to compose what I was going to say on the ride out to the Ledbetter place.

It was early and most folks would have arranged to visit later. But knowing country folk were usually up early and this not being a social call, I figured 7:30 was a good time to be calling.

I ticked off the landmarks that Jeb had talked about—the overgrown foundation of an old school house, a "crookedy" limb hanging over the road, a small, one-lane bridge over a wet weather creek—then took what I hoped was the appropriate side road just before getting to a crossroads.

At the end of a winding, one-lane dirt road, there was an old barn board-sided house that looked like it had last seen paint when Truman was battling Dewey. The roof sagged, the porch sagged worse, and one side of the barn looked like a giant had sat on it.

Three or four dogs that looked like they could be squirrel or coon dogs started barking their heads off at the first sound of the Jeep. Two long-eared hounds that had some treeing Walker and blue tick in them raised their heads to look at me. Other than that, they didn't budge.

I had the gun in the glove box but didn't even consider pulling it out. I figured if I really needed it, I was in trouble anyway.

Before I could get to the door, it opened. Bother stood in the subdued light filtered by surrounding trees and the porch roof. Parts of him were swallowed up by the darker-than-dark interior of the house. He looked surprised. Maybe he didn't. It was hard to tell with Bother.

He started to shut the door. I said, "Bother! Don't!"

He stopped and disappeared in the darkness, leaving the door ajar. Trying not to appear hesitant to anybody that might be watching, I went inside and found myself standing in a room that could not have been more dark if it were in a windowless coal bin. The outside light from the door was absorbed by what seemed like black flooring and walls. Standing there, waiting for my eyes to adjust, I could hear a rustling sound to my right—Bother moving?—and a watery, rasping sound, also to the right. Turning that way, I willed my pupils to dilate, to see.

I caught a glimpse of a light object—Bother's face—as it turned to look in my direction. I focused on that area, and slowly began to pick up shapes and objects. Light reflecting dimly off a piece of shiny…wood?

Two fabric-covered straight objects next to each other starting at the floor...legs? I blinked several times in rapid succession. Then I could see Bother, at least, the top half of him, standing behind what appeared to be a chair. Wheelchair? In the chair was what looked like a pile of clothes. The smell coming from that part of the room was overwhelming. I imagined what caused the stench and felt my throat constrict and eyes tear up. I took an involuntary step backwards.

I had smelled that distinct odor once before, in a hospital in Africa while on assignment to cover poverty, hunger, disease, and death for a national publication.

The pile of clothes moved and I said, "Mr. Ledbetter?"

"You tha man what whupped Harmony." Not a question. The voice was weak and strong at the same time. Suppressed, yet defiant.

"Yes sir. He threatened to kill me and I did what I had to do."

"That's always been his problem. Don't listen. I told him to kill you. He was stupid to give you a warning. I taught these young'uns to give more then they get. You gave Harmony more then you got. Harmony's smarter then Bother, but both are just plain stupid."

"Kill me? For what?" I said.

A full-throated cackle rose from the chair. "For what? For disgracing the Ledbetter name, that's what? Nobody stomps on our name. Nobody."

I was silent for a long time.

Then, "Is that what Althea did? Disgrace the Ledbetter name?"

Bother looked at me for the first time, his eyes open wide.

"Don't you mention that whore's name in this here house," Ledbetter screamed. Or tried to. "She's gone and that's the end of it."

"That's not the end of it. I've seen her grave."

The cackle started up again but this time it was cut short by a chest-wracking cough that started as a clearing of the throat and ended with a full-fledged deep-chest coughing fit. A skeleton-like hand came out of the pile of clothes. It was holding an off-white handkerchief and the wad went back in the pile higher up. When the coughing had subsided, the handkerchief came back into view. This time it had a spattering of what I took to be fresh blood on top of old stains.

"You ain't seen shit!" the old man roared. "What you seen was a stupid wooden board Bother carved and stuck out there on that island. That's all you seen. All!"

For some reason, I believed him, mainly because I couldn't see him burying his wife anywhere when Caddo Lake was just outside his back door.

I walked over to the chair and threw off the top layer of clothes. The face that stared up at me looked like a squirrel's head that had been spitted over an open fire. Despite the poor light or maybe because of it, I couldn't see a single place on his face that was not covered with open sores or scabs.

Without another word, I went to my Jeep truck and drove to town. I stopped at Harlan's and bought some industrial strength disinfectant and a plastic kitchen scrubber. Using the fish-cleaning hydrant down at the dock, I scrubbed my hands until they were red and hurting.

I sat there on the ground, looking out over the lake, wishing to hell I could wash the part of my brain that stored certain memories with the same stuff.

When I got home I decided to cheer myself up and started singing the old '60s song, "Blue Moon," doing all of the parts, including the bass chorus line and falsetto lead.

Wha-what're yah-you doing?

Gettin' on with life, Bob.

Suh-such as it is.

Maybe, Bob, I need a diversion. What do you think?

Tha-that sounds like a plah-plan.

Wonder what Nekkid Nell McGruder is doing right now?

Gah-guarantee she's not tha-thinking about you. Jah-jesus!

I truly love it when Bob makes me laugh.

45

Chaos is aversive. Controlled chaos can be an aphrodisiac.

B. Ledbetter

By seven o'clock Saturday morning, the church tables had been set up all over the back yard, leaving a huge space under the lightning tree for "pitcher-taking," as Jeb called it. Miss Baxter's registration table was set up under a twenty-by-twenty-foot maroon tent emblazoned with "Cummins Funeral Home" on two, short side flaps in pristine white.

Jeb had rounded up some folks to help us get set up, promising them, I found out that morning, they'd be first in line to get their pictures taken. Didn't matter to me, but I warned him he might be messing up Miss Baxter's structure and plans. That worried him more than slightly.

Widder had arranged for a couple of Harlan's granddaughters to be runners between my backyard and her computer. But since the day was supposed to be clear, relatively cool, and the humidity not supposed to be a factor, I suggested we run extension cords out her window and set up the computer in a shady spot as an extra added attraction. Widder, who had resigned herself to being cooped up in her house all day, endorsed the idea with a hug, a quick, impersonal cheek peck, dry squeeze of my hand, and a single up-and-back knuckle rub with her thumb.

I tried to think of another idea that she would like even better. She was gone before my brain could conjure one up.

As the first carload of folks drove up at 7:30, I asked Jeb to help me move the deer horn chair under the tree. Widder raised an eyebrow, but I just winked and said, "I just had a seed of an idea. I'm going to water it and see what pops up."

Bob liked the idea and sent me a positive thought.

I told Widder Bob liked the idea. Widder stuck out her tongue at me, and Jeb said, "Bob who?"

Of the two responses, Widder's tongue was the most memorable.

By the time I had the new Nikon digital set up on the tripod, the production lights in place and the chair placed exactly where I wanted it—lining up the lone horn sticking out just a bit on the top right back with a unique part of the lightning scar—thirty or more people had arrived. They were standing around talking, and checking out the tables that seemed to be sprouting food.

Widder threw me that little get-going hand circle and I said in a loud voice: "Ladies and gentlemen, young adults and kids. First I want to thank you for being here for the First Ever Uncertain Picture Taking Extravaganza. I do believe you are all going to be a part of history today. I have checked with some photography experts and this is, as far as we know, the first attempt, ever, to take photos of residents of an entire community."

General applause and a few hoots and whistles greeted the news. I went on to thank all the people who helped set up the event and ended by saying, "I was a stranger here and you accepted me. You took me in. I will never, ever forget this place, you people, or this experience as long as I live."

I tried to keep the catch I felt in my heart out of my voice.

Bob said, *ah-as usual*, I failed.

I asked Miss Baxter to call out the first group for a picture and she said in a school marm voice: "The Harlan Harlingen family, Harlan, Zoe Aben, their son Joe Jimmy, wife Alistene, and twin sons, Beryl and Squirrel."

Squirrel? I looked at Widder and she mouthed in a stage whisper, "Nickname. His real name is Genesis Exodus."

Even God would bless "Squirrel" over his given name.

"Excuse me, Miss Baxter," I said, as Harlan and his family were making their way to the front. "Harlan and Mrs. Harlan and their family are not the first to get their picture taken."

"Yes, they are! They are first on my list."

"Well," I said, in a voice as haughty as I could make it. "It's my camera and I say they are not the first." Pause. "The first is…you, Miss Baxter."

She played the part of the good sport, got up and sat in the chair in a pose that reminded me of royalty. I turned on the lights, focused the camera in medium tight, told her I was counting to three, and shot the first frame on "two." I panned out, taking in the entire chair, part of the big tree limbs that made a canopy and about two or three yards on each side of the chair and, after asking her to put her hands on the chair arms, clicked that one off when she relaxed.

After Miss Baxter, I shot Harlan's family, the Doolittle brothers, a couple of spinster sisters named Tuttle, and Hy's family, seventeen members in all. I put some of the smaller kids in the grandparents' lap and one rambunctious two-year-old on his daddy's shoulders. I swapped out memory cards while the Brewsters—dad, mom, six children, including two sets of twins—were getting into place. Widder took the card from my hand, our fingers touching. She didn't seem to notice. I noticed way too much.

As the Brewsters started getting into place, Dad Brewster automatically sat down in the chair, but I knew it was going to be a long day and I need to stay sharp, so I eased him out of the chair and stacked the two sets of twins in the chair and on the arms, putting the older children to the sides and the parents at the back. It was, as they would say down at Olin Mills', a "real cute picture."

By the time I had moved out the Brewsters and stuck Glenn Alan, his wife, a son, a daughter and their spouses and six grandchildren in and around the chair, Widder had two photos out and a third on the screen. A large part of the crowd was now behind her, crowding in, peering over her shoulder. The comments about the photos, the way they were set up, the finished prints were almost totally positive.

The only negative comments were in fun. Jeb said, "Hy, I swear, you've got the biggest nose in the county!"

About every three or four groups, I would take a short break, get some coffee from a forty-eight-cup percolator, borrowed, like the tables and chairs, from a nearby church. I tried to time my breaks with Widder's but most times she just waved off my efforts.

About eleven, when I was shooting a family with the last name of Tibodeaux, I heard a conversation tone change behind me. Four middle-aged men and a boy of about sixteen had arrived. It was not hard to see they were musicians looking for a gig. They were toting guitar cases, fiddle and bass fiddle cases and three or four drum cases.

Jeb came over and asked if I minded if the "Uncertain Stump Jumpers" were to set up and play a few sets. In a voice I hoped was loud enough for most folks there to hear, I said, "Mind? Heck no. I insist!"

In less than fifteen minutes, the band was set up, with enough electrical cords running out of my back door and windows to power a small city. The young man was apparently the lead singer because he introduced the group and from the names, it was obviously a family band. He introduced his dad, and his three uncles—his name was Dwayne (pronounced Doo-wayne). His dad got the crowd clapping by hitting the first note of "Orange Blossom Special" on his fiddle and sawing on it for six or seven seconds.

I took a break while the crowd's attention was on the Stump Jumpers, waited until Widder was between printing photos and nodded my head toward my house. She nodded and held up her index finger. I went inside, making sure to close the door, pulled two beers from the fridge and sat down at the table. I was already tired and estimated we still about forty or so more families to go.

Hah-happy tired.

Right on, Bob, I thought just as Widder walked in the door.

"How's Bob?" she asked.

"Fine," I said, handing her an open beer. "I just thought I was tired already and still had a long way to go and he said it was a happy tired. Happy tired. I like that."

Widder took a sip of her beer and sat back and closed her eyes. "Happy tired. I like that, too. Seems most of my life I've just been plain tired." It was not a self-serving statement designed to generate pity. It came across as a stated fact.

"Jeb said you might go up to talk to Hiram Ledbetter."

"Did. Yesterday. You didn't hear? The Uncertain rumorphone must be busted."

She looked surprised, then did the hand thing. There was a time I thought it was cute. Then it was annoying. She had worked her way back to cute.

"An experience I never want to repeat," I said, drinking down half the beer in four swallows. "There is absolutely no wonder those boys are screwed up. He probably killed his wife, you know, and dumped her in the lake. It's sad, but it won't matter much longer; he's dying and it won't be pretty and he will suffer greatly."

Pause for another swallow. "And, for whatever it says about me, I'm glad he's going to suffer."

I caught Widder's grimace out of the corner of my eye. Then she said, "Does he know he's dying?"

"Oh, yeah. There's no way he could not know. And he's determined to go out just as mean as he can, cussing everybody and everything and blaming everybody but himself for the misery of his life. If I was going around killing people, he would be at the top of my list."

She asked if Harmony and Bother were destined for jail time because of my photos. I hadn't shown the photos to her but didn't question where she had seen them. Uncertain just kept getting smaller and smaller.

"Harmony, assuredly," I said. "Bother is a different story. All he did that I could see was tote supplies. Sheriff Twiddle? Now that's a different story. A good investigator can follow the evidence to put him away for a long time."

"I don't know," she said.

"Don't know what?"

"Twiddle has not remained in office and walked the crooked and crookeder path for so long by not protecting his rear end."

"To remain in office, he has to get elected," I said. "I think his little campaign slogan on the Poem Board and other painted advertisements around the county was a bad mistake."

She nodded and took a sip of beer. She leaned her head back, closed her eyes…and snapped them back open.

"You didn't?" she said.

In my best Tweetie Bird imitation, I said, "I cannot tell ah wie…."

I then told her the whole story, one part that she had just guessed, other parts that she would never have imagined.

As we walked out of the back door, the band stopped in mid-chorus of "Rocky Top" and swung into "Here Comes the Bride." Widder's face flushed faster than an industrial toilet. But being a man, it took mine longer to turn the color of a baboon's ass. Everybody in the yard applauded and yelled.

We buckled down and got back to work. I can't remember having a better time since that dark moonless night on the second green at Buena Vista Golf Course in Las Cruces, New Mexico. That's when these two Mexican beauties were figuring up innovative ways to thank me for including them in a photo spread on old Hispanic churches. I still remember the way….

"Mr. Jones," Miss Baxter said, "are you ready for the Shupe family?"

I glanced up from putting in a new memory card in the camera—and carefully stowing away an old memory card from my brain—and shook hands with the deputy. He was wearing a starched and pressed uniform, regulation boots, and was holding his hat in his hand. "Mr. Jones, this is my wife Baby Ann, and our kids, Harold, Maude. and Little Baby."

"Baby?" I said to his wife. "Your name is Baby?"

The whole family laughed. "Mr. Jones, my name is Mary Ann, but everybody has called me Baby since I was one. Little Baby is also named Mary."

I looked at the two older children and said, "Harold and Maude are two of my favorite names."

It was fun shooting the Shupes and I purposely created an antique-y looking photo set-up with the deputy sitting upright and stiff in the chair with the family gathered around him. I asked for one shot with no smiles.

I then encouraged them to open up and be free. One of the best ones was with Little Baby wearing her dad's Mountie hat and Shupe replacing it with a Dallas Cowboys baseball cap that Harold was wearing in the other photos.

Rayon Finnigan showed up and I slipped him in as quickly as possible. To get him settled and loose, I asked him to tell a short story. The groans from the onlookers were good natured. Mostly. He started a story about how his great-uncle Chester lost an arm at a pie-eating contest in Mobile, Alabama, and when I had a shot of him with his mouth open, I said "Next!" in a directorial bellow.

The line did not get a standing ovation. It did receive considerable applause.

The last group was shot about 3:30. Thompson's daughter and her family had flown in from California just for the event and there was not a prouder papa at the gathering.

In every other photo, someone, usually the head of the household or, in the case of some couples, two people sat in the chair. With the Thompson clan I asked them to leave the chair vacant, with Thompson dead center standing in back and daughter, her husband and two teenagers, a boy and a girl, cupping him, two to a side.

Somebody in the crowd said, "Why ain't somebody sitting in the chair?"

I winked at Thompson. He acknowledged it with a nod.

After the Thompson clan, I started to unscrew the camera from the tripod, when Jeb came over. "Sorry, Mr. Jones. you ain't done just yet. You done forgot two folks."

I looked around the yard and could not see anyone I hadn't seen through the lense. Jeb took my elbow and gestured me to get up, marched me over to the chair and pushed me down. Then he walked over to Widder and did the same number on her. Widder tried to stand by the side of the chair, but Jeb just shook his head, took her hand and led her in front of the chair. He pushed her down in my lap.

He went behind the camera, and said, "Now, howdya work this thang?"

I walked him through the simple steps and he shot three photos. The best was one with me laughing out loud and Widder lazing back with her right hand behind her head in a beauty pose, her left leg sticking straight out, trying to look vampish.

I checked it out on the digital image and again on the computer.

I told Jeb it was one of the best photos I had ever seen.

And meant it.

The first to leave were families with small children or people with Saturday night obligations, Masonic Lodge dance, bingo, bowling league and the like.

The band had played every song the boys knew and some that I told Widder were almost certainly made up on the spot. After the Stump Jumpers had played a couple of hours, somebody put the cardboard box that one of the printers had come in on the ground in front of the band and by about eight o'clock, I estimated there was several hundred dollars in ones, fives, and tens in the box.

Some folks had started dancing on the grass in front of the band by mid-afternoon. But most wore out quickly and by six o'clock, people were sitting at the tables and in lawn chairs, listening to the music and getting thirds or fourths on the remaining food.

Widder had joined me at the end at one table and we both were pretty happy with the day's events. I got up to check on what desserts were left and she asked if there were any more of the "Turnbull's apricot turnovers" to bring her one. There was exactly two left and after I had rescued them from the plain paper plate, I darted in the house and got a couple of glasses of cold milk.

Widder looked happy when I sat down the turnover and milk. We just sat there, fattening up and listening to the band do a country swing version of what I swore sounded like "Tiny Bubbles."

When that song wore down, I saw Jeb sidle up to the band and then do back to his place by the punch bowl. The band struck up a recognizable rendition of a song I knew, but couldn't put a name to. "What is that song?" I asked Widder. "I know it, but can't place it."

She looked at me with sad eyes: *"Tears on My Pillow."*

I looked at Jeb. He grinned, winked and raised his plastic punch cup in a mock salute. I turned and checked out the lake for a bit.

When we were through with dessert, the band looked like it was starting to break down the gear so I hurried over and asked the lead singer to play a waltz.

I hurried back to Widder, bowed and said, "May I have this dance?"

She rose smoothly, curtsied. She let me lead her to the impromptu dance grass.

The leader did his "one-and-a-two" start-up routine and the band launched into a song too fast for a waltz. Just as I started to take the first step, Widder started laughing, fell against me and then everybody left joined in.

"What?" I asked, holding out my hands. "What?"

By now, Widder was sitting on the ground, holding her sides. "The song," she said. "The song." She was laughing so hard she couldn't get out another word.

"What?" I asked again.

The sah-song. It's Sha-Shania Twain's 'You're So Stupid.'"

46

There's a time to stay and a time to leave. Unfortunately, some folks often get the two mixed up.

B. Ledbetter

Five days later, I drove out of Uncertain, my Jeep packed to the window tops with equipment, clothes, and gifts from the townspeople. I was planning to ship a lot of stuff to Atlanta, but Jeb said the people wanted to do something for me and offered to rent a small trailer to drag behind the Jeep. It was a nice gesture and one that was not overly expensive, so I accepted.

The day before I was to leave, I got up early and went into Marshall and went by Doc's house before he had time to get to work. I asked him if he would consider keeping Moosie. Bob and I had discussed it and came to the conclusion that with my lifestyle, with all the traveling, keeping a Great Dane was impossible.

Doc's eyes teared up and he said, "I just love Moosie."

I gave Moosie one last hug and stroked her ears. Her eyes were on Doc the entire time.

That afternoon Jeb pulled a rented U-Haul trailer over and hooked it to the Jeep, and he, Hum, and Hy carried boxes and sacks out and loaded them as I packed up. Widder brought us some lemonade and pimento cheese sandwiches. She didn't stay.

I had tried to talk to Widder. I thought she had tried to talk to me. But there was a basic truism that interfered with any meaningful conversation: She was staying put and I was leaving.

Sunday, after the photo shoot, she asked me to come over for coffee.

She had a present for me. It was a painting. Of me. Laughing over a camera lens with Caddo Lake in the background. You could count my laugh lines, see the large pores in my nose, and see the Jones' gene circles under my eyes and even a light dusting of fine hair on the edge of my ears. I looked at the painting, then at her.

I began cry and couldn't stop.

She held me in her kitchen for a long time, rubbing my head and back. No words, just me quietly crying and her…caring about me, loving me.

A couple of days later she asked me to come over again, this time to autograph one of my books—*Thailand's AngkorWat*. I was flattered and wrote:

To C.C.
The most amazing woman I've ever met. Sometimes life's paths cross but are not destined to join. In another life, I want our paths to meet and continue on as one path.
Adj B. F. Jones

I didn't want her to read it until I was gone, but she insisted. She read it, touched the words with her fingertips and showed me to the door. Just before she pushed me out the door, she went up on her tiptoes and kissed my lips. As I walked down the brick pathway I could hear her sobs. They sounded like thunder tearing up jack at the edge of a cold front.

As I pulled out on the main road, I wanted to stop and say goodbye. Widder was on her porch. She waved, blew me a kiss, put her arms tight around her chest and went into the house.

I sat there for a moment, looking at the door, willing her to come out.

Her will was stronger than mine.

I got out of the Jeep, grabbed a big paper sack from the back seat, walked up to her porch and put it in a rocker. I wanted to knock and hand it to her personally. I finally turned, walked away, got back in the Jeep, and made a beeline for the Poem Board.

The bunch of people gathered around the board parted as I walked up.

I focused on the words. Halfway down, I knew it was going to be one of those damn crying days.

Strangers,
Simply by the nature of being
Strangers
Can come into a place
And make people
See things they see
But don't "see,"
Act differently
In different ways
And believe in things
They never thought possible.

I insisted that everybody crowd around the board for one last picture. When I looked at the photo later, there was not a smile on a single face.

Thompson and Jeb insisted I go to Hum's for breakfast. I stayed longer than I meant to. As I started to leave, I gave Jeb one of my small digitals, several memory cards and an instruction booklet. He said he would take photos of the board every day and mail me the full cards.

It was somewhere around Vicksburg that I decided to have a talk with Bob.

Yah-you don't have to tha-think a thing.

Yes I do, Bob. I owe you that. You've been my best friend for a long time. It's time I fucking grow up and quit relying on a crutch—even a great crutch. I've used you to see me through the tough times. Now I need to rely on myself. I'll miss you as much as anything I've ever missed in my life.

I know. When you see Widder, tell her I said hey.

No stutter. I guessed it was to get my attention and keep the conversation going. What I was doing was hard enough without prolonging it.

Or maybe it was because he wanted to go away quickly. It was hard enough without prolonging it.

I decided not to drive straight through to Atlanta, and ended up staying in a cheap motel just off the interstate. I reached for the phone fifteen times to call Widder. I convinced myself I couldn't remember her number and that I really wanted to watch the "Gunsmoke" rerun. It was the one where Kitty is saved by the wild girl raised by wolves or buffaloes or something.

I was home before noon the next day and the Jeep was cleaned out an hour later. I went to Whataburger for a greasy onion burger and a milk shake. I wanted to clean out the trailer and return it before end of business.

When I arrived back at the house, I opened the trailer…and stopped dead in my tracks. My eyes flopped open like a crazed Venetian blind.

The deer horn chair from the Carter's Chute blind was sitting right next to the door, secured on both sides by straps.

I got up in the trailer and sat in the chair and started laughing. I could almost see the whole Uncertain gang thinking about me opening the back of that trailer and laughing until they cried.

Then I thought about the sack I left at Widder's. The photo album was filled with the absolutely best photos I had ever taken in my life, from photos of my grandparents when I was a kid to the one of Harold and Maude and the chicks. The inscription on the inside cover—in gold ink—said it all: "Live life to the fullest every day. With love, Adj."

Also in the sack was a copy of Zane Gray's *The Young Forester* I had picked up on eBay to add to her collection.

But the best leave-behind was the embroidered pillow that had the close-up of a boy's and girl's face and they were kissing, sort of chaste-like, lips all pooched out and leaning in to one another. There was a big yellow moon just over the girl's shoulder and below the couple were these words:

Man was, is and always will be
looking for a cheap date good enough
to take home to Mama.

And I prayed she laughed when she saw it.

47

Some things are meant to be. Some things are not. Be is relative.

B. Ledbetter

Betsy was cooperating nicely. She was focusing properly. I liked to think she liked the new ultra-wide-angle zoom; more field of vision, more in-focus detail.

When she was happy, I was happy with Betsy. I was also happy with the model. She was smiling a Mona Lisa smile, head down, eyes upturned. Her boy-short, highlighted hair caught three casual sunrays that had danced around leaves from a nearby tree. I had decided to use a bright-green, leafy bush with even brighter red berries hanging in clumps as a background. The model's nice tan and boat-necked brighter-than-pastel yellow top contrasted much better than "acceptable."

Pushing the button halfway down to focus, I held it there and eased the face-image from the center of the viewfinder to near the far corner of the frame.

Making sure the sign was visible and in focus at the left of the frame, I cracked off six or seven shots.

Straightening up, I stretched my back and said, "I think you'll like that one for the dust jacket."

"What if I don't," the model said.

"Well, too bad. Yo' done had your pitcher took by the best they is. Yo' cain't do no better than that there."

She laughed. Her mouth opened so wide I could see her uvula. It was at times like this I missed Bob. That line was a natural opener for one of his comments.

"So, are we done?" she asked.

"Not by half. Not by a full measure."

"More photos?"

"Nope. More living, loving and laughing."

I set up Betsy on a tripod, tripped the timer and took one shot of us together, making sure to get the sign in the background: *Café Tres Generaciones, Allejula, Costa Rica.*

Several weeks later, she was trying to select a photo for the back of the dust jacket. She rejected the ones in Costa Rica and settled for one taken closer to home. It was of me sitting in a chair made of deer horns, with her sitting in my lap. In the photo, I was laughing out loud and she was lazing back with her right hand behind her head in a beauty pose, her left leg sticking straight out, trying to look vampish.

We had already selected the cover picture—a family of cormorants having breakfast—and the typographical design that went along with it.

Caddo Lake
In pictures and paintings
Photography by Adnijio B.F. Jones
Paintings by C.C. Jones

"I like it," I said with feeling. "Let's rodeo!"

"Yes, let's," she said softly, as she took my hand and began rubbing my knuckles with her thumb.

Yah-YEEE-HAW!

Epilogue

I made it three days in Atlanta without Widder. The morning of the fourth day, after the third consecutive dream about the day spent with her in the blind, I got up at four a.m. and drove straight through to Uncertain. It was late afternoon when I pulled into town and I was heading directly to her house but caught sight of her car at Hum's.

Widder was sitting at a table about halfway to the rear of the café with her back to me. I put my finger to my lips as other people became aware of my presence. I walked directly to her table, spun her around, grabbed her by the ears and kissed her, as my grandfather once said, "slap-dab on the mouth."

I said eleven words: "Will you marry me? Everything will be all right. I promise."

Three days later we were married behind the little hunting lodge, standing next to the lightning-struck tree. An after-the-wedding photo showed more than two hundred people at the wedding, including Bother, who stood over at the side. The original deer horn chair was the centerpiece for the photo, which was taken by Jeremiah Hix. His name and the words "Eqine Photographer" were stenciled on his truck. Jeb and Thompson cracked up at the look on my face when I saw the advertisement. Jeb served as my best man and Thompson walked Widder down what served as an aisle.

Widder's two sons, Roy and Robert, came to the wedding. They were not too happy about it. When they got into town and had visited with their mama for a while, we went down to the lightning-struck tree and talked. Roy said that I was too old for their mama. Robert nodded. I got the impression that Robert nodded a lot at what Roy said.

"Nothing I can do about my age, boys," I said. "Some things I can change. Age isn't one of them."

"It doesn't bother us now," Roy said, "but what happens when you're 65?"

"I retire and your mama will be in her peak earning years."

They went back in the house and told Widder I was a keeper.

Widder was a hard negotiator but we finally agreed to spend a minimum of forty-five days in Uncertain in the spring, fall, and winter. With the heat, humidity, and mosquitoes, she gave up the summer without much of a fight. I agreed to arrange my photo assignments around that schedule and no matter where I was headed, Widder would go with me and paint, or write.

She also said the marriage was off if Bob wasn't part of the family. It took more than three months to coax him back. That's not true. It took that amount of time for me to figure how to apologize to, well, myself. When Bob did pop back near the end of the Costa Rica trip, he was magnanimous and only called me *sta-stupid* once before doing his stuttering man-in-black routine: *Hah-hello. I'm Jah-Johnny Cash.*

When he started singing *Wah-we got mah-married in a fah-fever...* I laughed till I cried. And Bob gave me a big, ol' mental hug.

The Caddo Lake book sold more copies than any project with which I had ever been associated. It opened up an untapped genre for tabletop books. The idea of combining art and photographs as companion pieces to tell a story, and not using one or the other as filler material, caught the public's attention.

Three months after the wedding, Harmony was arrested, tried and sentenced to forty years in prison for the manufacturing and sale of crystal meth. Bother received five years probation in the same case. The Texas governor granted him clemency shortly afterwards.

Two days after Harmony went off to the Huntsville Penitentiary, his father died. Law enforcement officers had gone out to Harmony's floating island way earlier, but, as suspected, there was no grave. Just the wooden marker. Someone pulled the marker up and gave it to Bother, who placed it to the side of his house, facing the lake.

Sheriff Twiddle was defeated for re-election, winning less than twenty percent of the vote. The feds tried to make a case against him for supplying Harmony with ingredients for meth, but couldn't make it stick. Dated paperwork surfaced that indicated the materials had been stolen from the sheriff's office. Four years later Deputy Andrew Shupe was elected sheriff.

The photos of the first ever Uncertain photo day were published the next year in a small, horizontal tabletop format. It won several national and international publishing prizes as the first recorded attempt to photograph the population of an entire community.

"The People of Uncertain" was a minor financial success; the profits from that book and one called simply "Poem Board," 365 pictures of the verses written on that old blackboard, with shared credits were used to establish and promote an annual event—the Uncertain Poetry Festival. More than 15,000 attended the first festival, which consisted of 100 blackboards set up in the Rich Pasture. People came from all over the country to construct original poetry in a natural setting.

Sometime the next year, the county planned to widen the road into Uncertain and the original plan called for the removal of the little stand of trees where the Poem Board was located. A citizen's rally convinced the county quorum court to widen the road using the land on the other side of the road. Two more blackboards mysteriously appeared at the site, one to the left of the original board and one to the right. The one on the left was marked "For Kids"; the one of the right, "For everybody else." Bother kept writing on the original board, always at night, alone with his thoughts.

Somehow or other, folks in Uncertain found out it was Bother who was writing the daily offerings. He became a local folk hero amid much tongue-clucking, tsk-tsking, and exclamations of "No shit!"

An English professor at a small college in Marshall chronicled the daily poetry offerings for several years, then published: "The Poems of Uncertain." It was a huge success in academic circles. It went largely unnoticed in the commercial world for several years but one day it was touted on a syndicated talk show and become a New York Times' bestseller. The professor made a healthy contribution to Uncertain and several sizable anonymous donations were added. A town meeting was held to decide on how to spend the money and it was decided to build a combination art gallery, library, and community center.

Widder and I attended the opening of the "Jones Center."

The professor also talked his college into setting aside a scholarship for Bother. With special assistance from students and faculty, he graduated with a degree in English and eventually had several volumes of his poetry and thoughts published. The first volume was dedicated to "Mama and Mr. Jones." The second volume to the "People of Uncertain, Texas."

The townsfolk gathered at the lightning-struck tree every spring for free photographs. Every year, to open the activities, those who had their photos taken last year but who are no longer among us were remembered, publicly and privately.

Between the third and fourth year, Thompson died.

I shot the photos the following spring as usual. One of the photos shot was of an empty deer-horn chair with an old slouch hat prominently placed front and center.

also available from publishamerica

HEARTS ON THE MEND
by Floriana Hall

It is a known fact that heart disease is the number one killer of women. Understanding that, Floriana Hall feels that she is fortunate to be alive today since she had no apparent symptoms. A chance remark to her family physician led to four different tests before it was found out her main artery was 100 percent blocked, two others ninety-five percent, and one ninety percent. She knew about her genetic factor, but was told that her heart was fine at every doctor's visit.

Floriana experienced a quadruple heart bypass on September 4, 2003. She felt compelled to write her bizarre story to help mankind.

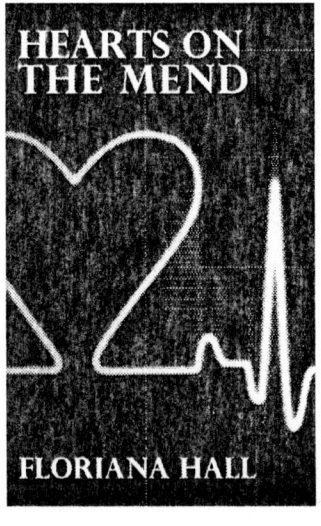

Paperback, 78 pages
6" x 9"
ISBN 1-4241-2038-1

About the author:

Floriana Hall, born in Pittsburgh, Pa., on October 2, 1927, is a Distinguished Alumna of Cuyahoga Falls High School, class of 1945. She attended Akron University. She and her husband have been married 60 years, have five children, nine grandchildren and two great-grandchildren. She is a member of St. Martha's church in Akron, Ohio. Floriana has written twelve books, nonfiction and poetry. She is the founder and coordinator of *The Poet's Nook*, a group of local poets who meet monthly at Cuyahoga Falls Library.

available to all bookstores nationwide.
www.publishamerica.com

also available from publishamerica

INSIDE PASSAGE
by Eunice Loecher

Michelle Lawson wins the trip of a lifetime on an Alaskan inside passage cruise. Disaster strikes in Skagway when a tour bus breaks down, leaving Michelle stranded. While struggling with the decision of how to rejoin her ship, Michelle learns Todd Harper has been released from prison. He is a violent stalker who terrorized Michelle the previous year. Returning home to Erie, Pennsylvania, is no longer a safe option.

After finding a job and a place to live for the summer, Michelle believes she's safe. When a newspaper story reveals her location, Todd Harper comes to finish what he started in Erie.

God teaches Michelle to trust and depend on others. Through it all she discovers acceptance, community and the future God has planned for her.

Paperback, 171 pages
5.5" x 8.5"
ISBN 1-60563-732-7

About the author:

Eunice Loecher is an award-winning author of numerous devotionals, essays, and poems. Her novel, *Living Water*, is available through PublishAmerica. You may contact Eunice at crafty2@newnorth.net or visit her website: www.euniceloecher.com.

available to all bookstores nationwide.
www.publishamerica.com

also available from publishamerica

UNICORNS DON'T WEAR SHOES
by Helen M. Hogan

When Wes Wilson discovers a body in the barn where he boards his Quarter horse, he faces unexpected accusation from the chief deputy. Wes postpones his dreams—of competing with his stallion in cutting horse shows and of dating Cathy McLeod. He helps rescue Mrs. Magers' lost pony from the slaughterhouse. Young Susan screams in horror as foreman Sutherland kills the stable cat's kittens, so Wilson wades in. As principal, he hopes to expand his high school's programs against opposition from his vin-dictive superintendent. With his teacher accused of kid-napping, Wes figures out the hiding place. Meanwhile, he learns the murder victim is not Mexican but Syrian and in the U.S. with two others on the Homeland Security watch list. The terrorists move in for an explosive ending.

Paperback, 413 pages
6" x 9"
ISBN 1-60441-107-4

About the author:

Retired from teaching college English, Helen judges several horse breeds. She loves traveling with her husband of thirty-eight years, Berry Hogan. The couple enjoy sitting in the backyard swing with a glass of wine and playing with their dogs. Helen M. Hogan's published mysteries include Warning Shot and Driven to Win.

available to all bookstores nationwide.
www.publishamerica.com

also available from publishamerica

DRAWING CONSTELLATIONS
by Jim Hunter

Galen McNeil always considered himself immune to superstitions...except for this Friday the 13th. One year ago exactly, his girlfriend broke up with him because she claimed God told her to, and Galen can't help but reminisce. His reflections are compounded when an evangelist reads Galen the same passage from the Bible that his ex quoted a year ago that day! The coincidences are almost too much for him when the conversation is interrupted by a beautiful woman who vies for Galen's attention. Stunned by the conflation of past and present, Galen is unable to act and the woman leaves without giving her name or number. For the next week Galen puts up signs in the middle of the park, entreating the woman's return as he tries desperately to regain what was lost and answer tough questions about his life and his place in the world.

Paperback, 151 pages
5.5" x 8.5"
ISBN 1-4241-7380-9

Filled with fully fleshed characters, staccato, realistic dialogue, an off-beat wit, and a philosophical subtext as poignant as it is heartfelt, *Drawing Constellations* presents a gripping cross-section of our culture and our changing time.

About the author:

Jim Hunter was educated at Miami University, Ohio. He currently lives with his family in Oberlin, Ohio. *Drawing Constellations* is his first novel.

available to all bookstores nationwide.
www.publishamerica.com